Praise for *Whisperwood*

'[An] eerie, folklore-steeped debut [...]
Fans of the grimmest works of the brothers
Grimm will want to check this out.'
Publishers Weekly

'Modern horror done right, with gorgeous
writing, moody overtones and a pace that keeps you
turning pages well past your bedtime…a new face of
horror has arrived.'
Mike James, author of the *Hotel at the End of Time* series

'Dark, but also achingly heartfelt, clever, and funny.'
Lauren Bolger, author of *Kill Radio*

'*Whisperwood* by Alex Woodroe is a phenomenal mix of
folklore and fantasy grounded with an authenticity that
makes the story leap off the page.'
Brennan LaFaro, author of *Slattery Falls*

ALEX WOODROE

WHISPERWOOD

This is a **FLAME TREE PRESS** book

Text copyright © 2023 Alex Woodroe

FLAME TREE PRESS
6 Melbray Mews, London, SW6 3NS, UK
flametreepress.com

US sales, distribution and warehouse:
Simon & Schuster
simonandschuster.biz

UK distribution and warehouse:
Hachette UK Distribution
hukdcustomerservice@hachette.co.uk

Publisher's Note: This is a work of fiction. Names, characters, places, and
incidents are a product of the author's imagination. Locales and public names
are sometimes used for atmospheric purposes. Any resemblance to actual
people, living or dead, or to businesses, companies, events, institutions, or
locales is completely coincidental.

Thanks to the Flame Tree Press team.

The cover is made by Flame Tree Studio, working with the fine
and wonderful artist Broci who created the illustration
especially for this book. The art is © Broci 2023.
The font families used are Avenir and Bembo.

Flame Tree Press is an imprint of Flame Tree Publishing Ltd
flametreepublishing.com

A copy of the CIP data for this book is available from the British Library
and the Library of Congress.

1 3 5 7 9 8 6 4 2

HB ISBN: 978-1-78758-843-1
PB ISBN: 978-1-78758-842-4
ebook ISBN: 978-1-78758-844-8

Printed and bound in Great Britain by Clays Ltd, Elcograf S.p.A.

Woodroe, Alex, author.
Whisperwood

2023
33305256893037
sa   07/26/23

ALEX WOODROE

WHISPERWOOD

FLAME TREE PRESS
London & New York

Dedicated to all the seekers looking for escape.
May you always find it, and may it always
be more than you'd ever hoped for.

There was a devil there the day I died. He looked like a respectable man wearing his Sunday best and his hand weighed the world on the back of my neck when he pushed my head underwater.

There was something else there too. A tall figure of shadow and horns that only appeared when I was near enough to dead as to make no difference.

The shadow devil got in the way of the human devil's plans, saved what was left of my life.

Now they'd both gone back to the hell they came from, and I was left with only questions. What deal had I unknowingly made? How much greater would the price be? Why me?

Whatever the answers, they would have to work very hard if they ever wanted to find me. That much, I'd make sure of.

PART ONE

WELCOME TO THE WOODS

CHAPTER ONE

Tracks on the Borderlands

The strangest thing about the stuffed bear skin was that it wasn't even the largest one I'd ever seen. Granted, this one was posed mid-menacing roar, balanced atop a pockmarked border stone engraved with the local dialect equivalent of 'Don't ye come in here, or else.' Whoever set it up had taken some creative liberties too; red ribbons trailed from its hollow eyes and pin-sharp claws, suggesting the bear had, perhaps, seen too much inside the pine forest that surrounded it.

"And you're sure this is where you wanna go?"

In the excitement of finding a free cart ride into the village that nobody went to, I'd forgotten to get the elderly merchant's name, and was too embarrassed to ask now.

"Sure as a bear at the fishmonger's."

He harrumphed, flogged the horses back into a trot, and adjusted his pipe from the left side of his mouth to the right. "What would you possibly want with the arse-end of the arse-end of anywhere civilized?"

I couldn't well tell him the truth, no matter how many times he asked or how easy I felt in his presence. What people really wanted were stories loosely based on the truth, but closer to their experience than to the teller's, and he'd definitely never experienced anything like mine. I couldn't tell him the man I'd once foolishly trusted tried to drown me, and I wanted to get as far away from anyone who'd ever said his name as one could without falling off the face of the earth.

Although that one-way trip had crossed my mind too.

Instead, I told him the other half of the truth. "I'm looking for folk tales. Mysteries, unexplained things."

"Why'd you want a thing like that?"

How much closer could I skirt by the real story without bumping into that wasp's nest?

"A little while ago, when I almost drowned –" and never you mind by which hands and why, "– I saw something otherworldly. I've been looking for answers ever since. Looking for proof that there's anything more to this world than the eye can see."

My story suggested friendly water spirits more than it did the visions of horror that traveled with me everywhere I went, but why burden him with something like that?

He grumbled low in his throat and nodded. The gray hairs at the back of his head swayed like birches. "That there is. That there is for sure. You be careful, you're likely to get what you asked for o'er here."

Everyone said that about their favorite out-of-reach places. Everyone thought there was something out of the ordinary just a step beyond their usual world. It almost never amounted to anything, and I knew firsthand how easily rumors spread. Still, Whisperwood was barely spoken of in more than three hushed words by inn firesides where stern matrons shushed people away from too much telling. Whisperwood allowed nobody but this merchant in or out. Whisperwood devoured stray nomads whole. It held such promise.

"You think there's something to the rumors? Something in the woods here?"

He nodded again, slow enough to make it look like he was swaying with the cart. "Would you help me with the market?"

His abrupt change of topic took me off guard, and by reflex I replied, "Of course!" in my sweetest voice before I could catch myself. I squeezed my eyes shut and took a deep breath, shaking my head at my own foolish willingness to please anyone who so much as glanced at me kindly. *Damn, that'll be a delay.*

"If you help me with the market, I might be like to tell you a tale or two. There's no time now, we're nearly there."

We neared a stream beyond which the ground gently rose and left its marshy airs behind. Our horses shook their manes about and made concerned noises, but they felt the crack of the whip and carried on. Halfway across the bridge, where the water was loudest, and the wood had a hollow, rotten sound to it, they tried to stop again. Again, they were thwarted.

What a promising sign. What did they know? What did they suspect? Could horses even be superstitious? Was that why horseshoes were lucky?

The woods gave up no answers yet.

The merchant's voice sounded like crackling autumn leaves among the silent trees. "We're here now."

He pulled to a stop in a pine clearing a little way outside of town, clearly as far as he was allowed to go. There were hitching hoops and troughs for the horses, benches and tables for the merchant, and a few scattered children dancing in a wide circle around an old water-filled pot, chanting and tossing coals into it at seemingly meaningful intervals. Their hands were black with soot, and as we creaked to a halt, one line stood out: "The old crone from the branches sings: Come here and sit awhile with me."

Giddy with the anticipation of what they could tell me, when the merchant's pointed cough reminded me of my promise, I nearly leaped off the cart.

"Can I help you unpack?" I stood on the back of his cart, hanging from a shelf full of rattly boxes with a smile as broad as the day was long, trying to look like I'd meant to offer all along.

"There's an idea. Careful now, if you break anything, you have to pay for it."

I glanced at the heavy cast-iron and copper cookware tied to various bits of the cart. A bison trampling across them wasn't likely to break anything.

Spry as a cat, he hopped off the driver's seat and offered me a hand down. "What's your name, then, phantom hunter?"

"I'm Anna. You?"

He mumbled, "Enache," over his shoulder, barely pausing from unpacking parcels and displaying his wares on the wooden tables and benches quickly and efficiently.

Beautifully decorated combs and brushes went at the back, out of the reach of thieves, their plain wood versions forming the frontline. Closest to him, he saved intriguing knickknacks, which, by that logic, must have been of the highest value in that curious marketplace: bags of salt, chunks of old silver, bundles of herbs, and vials of liquids I could scarcely identify.

As I got to untying little leather straps, I kept a longing gaze on the bunch of children at play. There was so much to be learned from childhood games – in one town I'd wandered through, the song that they used to determine who would go first in a game of catch was secretly instructions on how to avoid a vicious, infectious illness.

Catching wind of my overly interested looks, one of them signaled to the others, and before I could blink twice, they'd scattered among the trees and toward town.

"Are they scared of us? Is that why they're running back to town?"

Enache's eyebrows met neatly in the middle of his forehead, making a deep, dark groove that seemed cut with a straight razor. "Dove, we're the least scary thing for miles. Get on with it, the ladies will be here soon."

He might as well have said the end of the world would be there soon, for all the gravity in his voice.

I set to work. When all the packages were unpacked and all the wares sorted, we were both surprised at how quickly it had gone. He took off his shawl and spread it out under the nearest walnut tree, handing me half of his lunch packet in the process. A good thick slice of sour bread and a rasher of bacon set my stomach rumbling.

"It's only fair. You did ease the burden, both on the journey and the unpacking."

I sat by his side, content as a cat to have a little respite, while the townsfolk arrived. Wielding his bread like a wand, he pointed to the slow stream of bundle-carrying women emerging from the lively town.

"That's Miss Crosman. I hear she runs the common house, the mail, and acts as moral police. Terrible combination. It's a good thing they don't get visitors, or she'd put the fear of God in them. Stay on her good side if you're stayin' at all."

"Why do they have no visitors?"

He smiled, flashing a golden tooth. "Because nobody comes here."

I chortled crumbs all over his blanket, and he smiled too. We sat in silence waiting for the womenfolk to make their slow and sinuous way down to the trading post, and every now and then he'd point one out and tell me what little he knew about her. A pair of sisters, a freckled red-haired orphan, a very pregnant smith's wife. It was only a beginning in getting to know my – hopefully – future neighbors, but it was better than nothing. While they were still out of earshot, he seemed to make up his mind about something and turned to me again.

"Look, I'm not one to mind other people's business. But have you ever considered you might just get what you came for here? Are you ready to call yourself a fool?"

"I try to make a daily habit of it. Calling oneself a fool keeps the spirit humble. Do you really believe there's danger here?"

With an exaggerated shrug, he nodded toward the first of the women to reach our clearing. "I don't know. They seem fine."

Stern, unsmiling, silent figures approached us. There was no cheerful market chatter, no gossip and elbow nudging. They sniffed at the air like wild creatures, too unfamiliar with strangers to accept them but not knowledgeable enough to stay away. Every single one of them paused at the very edge of the clearing, looked around it, then moved inside, as though the safe passage of the woman before her was no guarantee of anything. One by one they stopped in the center, pulled on the collar of their respective dresses, and made as if to spit in their bosoms in what I imagined was a gesture of good luck.

Yeah. Entirely fine.

That fearful nature should have been mine too, perhaps, after what I'd suffered in my own end-of-the-road village. I had no explanation why it wasn't, and why I still hopelessly and helplessly trusted everyone even as I had trusted Alec. On the other hand, their open and consistent use of ritual was fascinating. Back where I was born, even just singing too loud or knowing the Latin name of a plant while simultaneously being a woman put us at risk of a noose, and here they were, practicing their folk magic. I didn't know whether to be envious, or terrified of whatever dangers they faced that taught them counterreactions.

Enache took his place behind the main table and spackled a large smile across his face. A well-rehearsed mask, it fit him like a second skin. I rubbed the chill out of my hands and shook the knots between my shoulders loose. There was work to be done, and I promised I'd do it.

It took me just about as long as I expected to get my first disapproving scowl, and in a way that felt comforting and familiar. At least I knew where I stood. It came from Miss Crosman herself, the other women waiting deferentially for her to examine the crockery first.

"Hmph."

Miss Crosman obviously expected me to introduce myself. She stood before me, looking down her nose at a spoon, stealing glances at my muddy apron. I desperately wanted to smile but forced myself not to, so my face took revenge by doing a funny little half twitch instead.

"Mmph-hmpf!"

I could resist no longer. "Cough drop?"

I couldn't stop the corners of my mouth from creasing that time, and beside me, a silver mustache twitched violently.

"Well. Master Byrne, I hope this isn't going to be a regular occurrence?"

I wasn't even sure who she was talking to until Enache responded. "The lady helping me? No, certainly not."

Miss Crosman seemed pleased, but I already knew very well

where the sly merchant was going, and my lips tensed to prevent the laughter.

"Good. I'm glad to hear it."

"She'll be staying with you."

There must have been a bitter chill in the air or something. A lot of things froze all at once and didn't thaw again for a good few seconds: Miss Crosman, the other women, the leaves, the sun, the hairs on the back of my neck. Some of the women spat in their bosoms again, and that time I recognized the gesture for what it clearly was: a way to ward off evil.

"I am not amused." She looked ready to vomit.

Even the merchant seemed taken aback. "Ask her yourself."

I busied myself untying and tying my apron string for no reason whatsoever. Suddenly, it didn't seem funny anymore.

She looked at me like one does at dirt on one's shoe. The little strings that wrapped around her hat and head dug deeply into the sides of her jaw, and for a moment I wondered if she was even breathing at all or just propelled herself forward using pure scorn.

"Fine. If she's done with life, it's no business of mine."

She moved on to the combs as if I had less importance or presence upon her day than they did, and I wondered whether she had meant that threat, or only intended to frighten me away from their private little community.

Swallowing my nerves, I looked to Enache for comfort, but found only a calculating gaze. I drew close enough to whisper to him without being heard by any of the women now milling about the tables as though released from a spell.

"I'm going to sit right here and do a good job. And later, you're going to pay me in answers." I wasn't as confident as I sounded, but hoped he wouldn't notice.

He didn't make any sign that he agreed or disagreed, but didn't send me away either, so I got to work. For the first time in a long time, a current of chilly fear blew past the ankles of my previously sunny excitement.

CHAPTER TWO

A Shadow Darkly

The light was fading, but not in any hurry. We'd finished the day's work and all the customers were gone, some more satisfied than others. A lithe woman with a slight harelip got quite upset that Enache hadn't brought her any lye powder for her face. Her name was Ancuṭa, and she threatened to return next month with a pitchfork. I liked her.

Sweat clung in a layer between my body and my shift. Orange clay powder rose easily with every footstep, and I wouldn't have been surprised to find it under my dress and in my drawers. We put away some leftover merchandise and a lot of trade goods from the town, and Enache seemed pleased.

They had brought him beautifully painted wooden toys, intricately woven baskets, and incredibly detailed lace. There were jars of ale and barm, hardy tooled leather pouches, and hundreds of curious trinkets I'd never seen before. Every item he traded for was obviously of great value, and he looked every bit like the cat that got the cream, so I took advantage of that moment to press him for more answers about the unusual town.

"Look, missy. I won't lie to you. This place unsettles me. But have I ever seen or heard anything that proves anything? No. It could all very well be a case of the heebie-jeebies, combined with too many cousins marrying cousins. Actually, for sure, that last part is true."

"Then tell me the stories, at least."

"I don't know much. Strangers go in and never come out, people supposedly vanish in the woods. They say you either leave by sundown or not at all. The merchants that came before me never went farther than this post, and they never stayed overnight, and so I don't, either. Townsfolk never leave. Some folks say they're a cult. Children go missing, most of the animals are dead. In a place like this, that's often just called winter."

"But you think there's some truth to it."

"Some, but who knows how much? There are a hundred different tales of what's out there. The Devil, a witch, a giant man-eating elk, the ghosts of dead children. It's also possible that all of those are nothing more than rumors."

I knew firsthand how unfounded rumors began from fear and shadows and phenomena people couldn't quite explain. I'd dedicated my time to studying nature, and people, and medicine, so I could help dispel those shadows – and folklore when all else failed, to better understand them. There was almost never anything to fear aside from people themselves. And yet, a chill went down my spine. I stood in silence for a moment, watching him fiddle with the bridle on one of his horses, fumbling about to tighten it with great haste.

"Is that why you're in such a hurry to leave?"

He caught himself and reddened a little. "If you're told that a particular patch of forest may or may not have ornery black bears, and you have no business going into that forest, wouldn't you make every effort to never find out the truth?"

"I like the truth."

He harrumphed and perched on his little driving seat, the sky turning pink behind him. With one hand, he reached into a coin purse tied to his belt, counted off without looking, and pulled out some coppers for me; more than I would have guessed.

"For a day's work."

"A bit much for a day's work, Enache."

"My day's work in a town that only sees one merchant a month is worth quite a bit more than standard. Besides, you look like you urgently need a meal and a good night of sleep."

I chose to ignore that jab. "Thank you."

He squeezed my hand and set off with some haste, his final warning to me tossed over one shoulder. "If you change your mind, you can still get out before the sun is down!"

Shadows gathered at the edges of the horizon and clung under tall pines. They chased his cart as he sped off, but I knew he'd feel better and slow down as soon as he was over the bridge again. Shame I was left with only the shadows for company.

The coppers clinked nicely when they joined the few others I had in their secret pocket in my satchel. I kept a silver coin in my boot, one in my apron, one in my corset. Grandmother taught me to do it for good luck. I figured out when I grew up that the good luck was not losing all your money in one go when you got robbed.

The other coins I had were gold, and those weighed heavy on my conscience. They didn't truly belong to me; I only stole them before running away that spring as a sort of safety net against the world. I hadn't touched them, hadn't even counted them, didn't want to look at them. I wanted nothing to do with them, or the man they truly belonged to, but I couldn't just leave them at the side of the road. Could I?

By the time I stood in the town square, the sun was already halfway below the earth. Crimson water stared up at me from inside a neat stone fountain, and I reached into my pocket for a copper. It somersaulted and joined others on the bottom with a splash as I made my usual wishes – safety and answers, in that order – and I felt eyes watching me watch it. Would the townsfolk like that I paid a little tribute, or judge me for mimicking their customs? Only time would tell.

Across the dusty road sat a massive slab of building with a large wooden door set in a dark gray granite wall. The colors of the woven tapestry above the lintel were faded, but patterns still clearly evoked their meaning: a blue owl with starry yellow eyes perched over a bed, a spoon and fork on either side of a wooden platter, parchment and quill, a set of scales. The doorjamb was completely covered in symmetrical angular carvings that made up intricate patterns, and dried herbs hung above it. I smelled basil and other earthy things I couldn't identify.

It was certainly the reasonable first stop for any weary traveler.

And it would certainly be the guesthouse run by my dear acquaintance, Miss Crosman, but I was far too tired to bear the thought of her. What I needed was a place to spend the night that was out of the way, maybe even a little distance into the woods. Then, in the morning, I could figure out where to go.

Down the main road, houses huddled in comfortable intimacy. There were so many more rows of them than I'd have guessed, and many narrow side streets branching off them. I wouldn't have been surprised to learn that this little town in fact held four hundred families or more. In the gathering gloom, oil lamps flickered to life and the smell of food wafted out of the houses. Suppertime.

A soft scraping to my left drew my attention, but there was nothing there.

I stepped a little more quietly, just in case, and slowed my breathing. It looked like Whisperwood had all of the markings of a bustling community, dark stores and workshops lining the main street that stretched between the town square and a mill in the distance. The streets were empty, but I could hear healthy, happy noises from inside houses. Laughter and cutlery and crackling fires reassured me that this was, in fact, a living, breathing town. Only the curious bundles of herbs and carved doll-like trinkets hung with red-and-white string from the jambs suggested stranger dealings.

That noise again. I froze for a moment and held my breath. Still nothing there. It had sounded like big footsteps crunching pebbles underfoot. There couldn't have been anything. The road was only a few steps wide, I would have seen—

A crunch again. Something behind me. I didn't break into a run. I didn't want to make that much noise, nor turn my back to whatever it was. I faced the area where the sound came from and crabbed my way sideways back toward the guesthouse. Quietly, gently, my heart racing a thousand beats per minute.

Another. Closer this time. I thought I saw the little pebbles shift a few steps back, near a wall. I couldn't help but wonder if it knew I was aware of it, whatever it was.

I sped up, gathered my skirt in one hand, turned a little more. The guesthouse wasn't far now, but there was a large patch of darkness between me and that massive wooden door. There were no lit windows there.

My body fought me every step of the way, begging to break into a run I refused to concede. I needed to be quiet enough to hear it. No way I'd let it get—

Closer.

I ran. My head turned almost involuntarily to check behind me, and I had a glimpse of a shadow I couldn't begin to describe. It was larger than I, and there were definitely eyes. It reached for me. It might have had horns.

A few more steps landed me on the guesthouse threshold, but the next crunch was so close behind me I couldn't be sure it wasn't my own.

My hand reached out long before it made sense to do so. I dropped my skirt and almost tripped, but there was hard breathing behind me and no time. The door handle was cold, but the breath on the hairs on the back of my neck was colder and filled with malice. The door wouldn't open, and I wanted to cry. It scraped across the floor as I threw my whole weight on it, probably shouting. Whining, for sure. It was dark inside, but I didn't care.

Something grabbed at the back of my dress, picked at my apron strings. Something else grabbed at the front of my shoulders. I was pulled inside, and someone pushed the door shut behind me. I leaned back against it with my whole body, trembling, hoping it would be enough.

A light flickered on nearby.

A young girl with wispy charcoal hair stood before me holding a lit oil lamp. She seemed so frail, and her face was fraught with worry. I didn't know what to say to her. I wanted to comfort her somehow.

"I think we're safe now." My voice was a ragged whisper.

She looked at me, mouth open, her trembling hand giving the lamplight a dizzying, nauseating effect. She tried to spit in her collar, but missed, and hastily wiped her hand on her maid's apron.

From the top of the stairs came a loud, angry slam followed by great resounding footsteps.

"What devilry is this, Greta?" Miss Crosman glared down at the both of us.

A pertinent question. What had it been? And, more importantly, had I brought it there?

"I don't know, maestress. The young woman was wailing at our door. I let her in. She seems upset."

The ursine woman stomped down the stairs, gathering her shawl about her. She grabbed the lamp and held it steady in front of my face.

"It's you. Trouble. Well, that doesn't surprise me in the least. What do you want?"

"There was something outside."

She hushed me.

The young maid pulled the door open a finger's width and peered outside. "The herbs are still there, spitblood."

Miss Crosman pointed a fat finger at my face. "It was a wolf. Spitblood you escaped."

"A wolf?" I didn't believe it for a second, but didn't dare argue. It wasn't like I had any alternative explanation I'd have cared to share.

"If not a wolf, then your imagination. Be quiet." They exchanged a wary glance. She chewed on her plump bottom lip and considered me for a second. "Well, what'll it be? In, or out?"

I didn't think I'd ever in my life wanted to sleep in the woods any less than I did that night. "Miss Crosman, I believe I would like to rent a bed now, please."

Her clever black eyes shone in the steady light. "I see. Well then, my dear. I hope you won't mind a few easy rules."

"I'm not a foe to rules."

"No visitors, no pets. For as long as you're boarding in my care, you're bound to help and obey me. You'll sign a contract to that effect."

"A contract?"

"Nothing out of the ordinary, never you mind. Finally, this: you don't talk about anything you don't understand. Not under my roof. Are we clear?"

Behind her, the young maid's head bobbed up and down with greater energy than I thought her capable of.

I couldn't say that I understood much of anything in that place, so I nodded along. "That won't leave me with much to say."

"Good. Come along, then."

I followed her into her office.

CHAPTER THREE

Grayday

The last of the stars twinkled out into a cold gray morning. I slept like the dead, in my clothes, over the blankets, and woke up in the same position I'd collapsed in. After months of traveling, exhaustion and I were steadfast lovers. An odd dream nagged at the edge of my memory, dark and otherworldly like a raven pecking to be let in through the window, but it never came any nearer than that.

Probably a nightmare. Another familiar companion.

The little corner room had two windows. There was an empty chest at the foot of the bed, one rickety chair, and a sooty oil lamp on the desk. That was it. Not even curtains. I supposed nosy oglers weren't really a problem on the second floor, but it amused me to think that rising with the sun was simply expected.

Soft rustling from outside hinted at windy, rainy weather. I tightened my shawl around my neck and lifted my dress to a little over my ankles against the mud I knew would be everywhere. My boots could take the beating, I didn't mind. I loved rain. I wondered if Miss Crosman would have kittens over the raised hem. At least I'd get to start the day with a giggle, no matter how the rest of it went.

Out in the hall, everything was quiet and softly lit white. I passed the door to her office, the place where the maestress conducted town affairs. The night before, she'd taken me there to sign her 'nothing out of the ordinary' contract filled with vague favors and veiled threats.

Her door was heavily carved and hung with herbs. They were fresher, so I recognized more of them: basil, hemlock, wild dill. I wouldn't have minded being in charge of foraging for more. I'd asked her what sorts of favors she might need from me during my stay there, and she smiled and waved it away like it was the most normal contract clause in history. "Oh, this and that, my dear. Fetching things when you go about your businesses. Messages. Emergencies. That kind of thing."

The smile and lilt almost made my doubts feel unreasonable.

I shook the morning's shivers out my spine and knocked on the office door, ready to check in and ask if I was needed. The door swung open; the room stood empty. I was half-tempted to sneak in and snoop, but I wasn't half-stupid.

The large front door opened effortlessly too, this time. I blinked hard against the white light, speckled remnants of last night's dream finally fluttering away from the corners of my eye. I expected to be pelted by rain but there wasn't any, though judging by the rustling sound of the brisk wind, it wasn't far away. Taking advantage of daylight, I checked the door and surrounding area for signs of the previous night's encounter.

No tracks in the dust, no scratches on the door, nothing. Curiouser and curiouser.

The square itself seemed hastily abandoned, like there'd been a market day, but without any people. Little carts and stalls were set up all around the central fountain, but nobody tended them. I looked closely and saw that some were laden with food or produce. Pies, apples, sausages, and blocks of cheese all made my stomach grumble, but what could I do if there was no one there to buy them from?

They must have been scared off by the impending rain. The air was heavy and smelled like lightning, and not even food broke through that smell. It left me uneasy, not having seen a soul all morning. It made me feel like I was left out of some important gathering; not that they'd owe me inclusion after a grand total of one night in town.

I crossed the square to where a cheerful little bakery stood. The baker's door was unlocked, and clinking bells marked my entry. I was eager for food and a human voice.

"Hello!"

Nobody answered.

"Good morrow!"

Only the distant rustling wind.

I peeked into the kitchen, but everything was still. The large brick oven gaped, cold to the touch, sacrilegious in a bakery at that time of morning. My stomach gave a lurch, a nauseated heave like the ground was moving. I hadn't eaten since yesterday's lunch and my diet wasn't exactly steady.

Well, damn that place and all the trouble in it. If I couldn't buy the food, I'd just take something and make amends later.

I stormed outside, again expecting rain to pelt me, again startled when it wasn't there at all. One of the nearby carts had long links of smoked sausages poking out from under a red-and-white checkered cloth. I broke off a length and scarfed it down like a rabid animal, eager to get anything in my stomach at all. It tasted like absolutely nothing.

Taking a second length, I weaved around the carts to where some crisp-looking radishes huddled together in a basket. I looked forward to the familiar spicy sting of red moon radishes, but those tasted like water too. Maybe I was coming down with a cold. Maybe I was the problem.

I forced myself to keep chewing and leaned against one of the wooden carts. The same uniform white color covered everything, and nothing moved. No man, no bird, no leaf. I looked up, thinking to guess, from the speed and color of the impending storm clouds, how much longer before that unnerving rain would finally break. My eyes focused.

There were no clouds.

It wasn't a clear sky, not like any I'd ever seen before. A perfectly uniform paper-white surface covered the world. I swiveled in shock, looking for any natural formation or movement, but there was nothing. No swirls, no plumes, no flues. To the north, above the woods, a faint crimson sheen bled into the opaque dome. Aside from that, it was perfect, and perfectly unnatural.

The distant wind that had tricked me into expecting rain still blew, but nothing moved. I searched, scarcely breathing, for even one bird, one human sound, one moving leaf. Nothing.

That was a dead sky over a dead town.

★　　★　　★

Hours passed.

After rushing back to the guesthouse and confirming it was, indeed, abandoned, I wandered the streets like a fool in search of anybody, anything, to shake my fist at and ask a question. Nobody and nothing volunteered. The incessant droning of the wind never abated; the perfect white light never changed. I walked, I observed. I waited.

All the homes were empty and cold. Set tables and made beds seemed like pieces in an odd museum I could only enjoy through little windows. It would have been my greatest pleasure to observe those frozen moments of their lives, undisturbed, but I couldn't bring myself to invade their privacy. The shut doors remained shut, and instead I took the chance to run my hands over their beautiful angular carvings, intricate rope patterns that played with one another and wrapped around frames and pillars.

Most of the central buildings were granite and clay, put together carefully like puzzle pieces out of uneven and charming river stones. I walked down the main road all the way to the end of the houses where the path forked into a few directions. One went left and snaked around some fields. The way forward led to the mill. To the right stood the forest.

From that new angle I could see that there was a low stone wall right up against the back of the houses, separating them from the trees. It stretched all the way behind the guesthouse, and probably beyond. Where it met with the road leading into the woods, it formed a cheerful little arch above it, then cascaded back down to the ground on the other side and went off to separate the woods from the mill. I felt neither ready nor willing to cross it.

The mill, then.

The mill was still. Red shutters stood shut; neat doors sat neatly closed. The main entrance boomed when I knocked, but only silence answered. It felt good to release some frustration on something, so I knocked again anyway.

There was laughter behind me.

More shocked than pleased, I glued my back to the door and looked for the source. The high trill hadn't seemed malignant, but the circumstances were startling. In the distance, behind the wall, something moved. My body ran toward it before I'd ever made the decision to do so. Whatever it was, it bobbed along behind the low wall, occasionally brushing against it.

Too short to be a person, it disappeared entirely behind some of the taller sections. When I could see little hints, it seemed something of a blue-gray color. A wolf? No wolf would dance, relaxed, along the wall like that, as if to meet me where the stones ended. Perhaps some other odd animal of the area, something domesticated and lost.

Except, animals didn't laugh.

By the time I got close enough to the wall to see over it, there wasn't anything to see. Whatever it had been, it was gone. My breath caught up to me as I meandered my way to the arch, hoping to get a better look of the woods beyond the wall, listening for any more sounds, half expecting more crunching pebbles like I'd heard the night before.

The arch embraced me. Odd white crystals and delicate corn husk dolls strung on sturdy red-and-white braided yarn hung from it. I wavered for a moment and stepped under it. I could see clearly in both directions and all the way to the forest, and there was no creature.

As I stood perfectly still, the hairs on my arms rose. Quietly, I watched for motion. Blades of grass swayed a little, but that was it. Not even a butterfly disturbed my field of view.

Some instinct bade me stay within the shadow of the arch and step no farther. Beneath my toes, a thick line of white sand-like powder marked the edge of town. In the distance, majestic Zâmbru pine trees loomed dark blue and shadow-ridden.

My heart skipped a beat.

A pair of white eyes stared motionless from among the pines. Around them, in the shadows, I could just barely make out a shape that looked heavy. The distance and the sheer height of the trees made it hard to tell how large it might have been, but surely it looked far too tall to be a person.

It laughed again, then dashed from its half-hidden nook to a somewhat nearer tree. In the moment of light between one pine's shadow and the next, I thought I glimpsed a pair of curved ram's horns that chilled me to my very core. When it next stopped, they looked more like doe's horns, and I went from fear, to confusion, and back again. That was, quite possibly, the same creature I'd run from the night before, only more solid. More real.

My legs twitched, and I stepped forward, eager to investigate. I stopped myself. It wasn't the time to go looking for trouble. Trouble found me just fine on its own. Besides, I was utterly alone and completely clueless. What was that thing? Did it have something to do with the townsfolk vanishing? And, most importantly, was I safe?

I couldn't step any farther, I had been foolish to come that far.

More carefree laughter accompanied by rustles and crashes came from deeper in the woods. I took a step back as branches swayed and several more pairs of curious white eyes blinked open throughout the forest, like lively hanging fruit. Whatever they were, I did not want to trouble them. One more slow step back brought me firmly inside the confines of town.

Just then, another crystalline laugh broke through the pregnant air, this time from so close by my left elbow I could almost feel the vibration. I flung myself off the road and turned to find one of the massive, improbable creatures within arm's reach, towering over me. It looked like a nightmare made of muscles, rabbit ears, and doe horns, all covered in shimmering metallic gray fur. It exhaled, the wispy hairs under its chin waving, and sent a warm gust of barnyard animal and mushroom-scent rolling over me. It reached a clawed arm out to me. I wanted none of it.

Blubbering like a fool, I stumbled away, staring at it. In the absence of coherent thoughts, my body remembered to be careful about running from dangerous animals. It'd only make them give chase. Instead, I backed away, tripped over myself, backed away more. It never moved from its place, and I never broke eye contact, not until I was well out of sight of the arch and could finally run up to my room like a frightened child. There, I huddled under the blankets and kept my back to the wall, making promises to the heavens that I had no intention of keeping.

CHAPTER FOUR

The Fortune Never Stops

I woke up with a start and a pounding heart. I couldn't have dozed off for longer than a moment, but in that moment, I dreamt of a looming dark shape with ram's horns and fiery red eyes reaching out to me.

I was surprised sleep had found me at all in that agitated state. Exhaustion spoke louder than fear, perhaps. There were voices, footsteps, and other day-to-day noises coming from the street below me, and a second loud knock on the door. I leaped up at once, blood banging in my temples, feeling an urgency in that knock that I had no explanation for. Beads of sweat cooled against my forehead as I rushed to the entrance and opened it.

"My goodness." Miss Crosman gaped at my muddy and disheveled apparition.

I touched my hair and realized right away it wasn't in any state I could set right with a quick flick. My boots were barely visible beneath dirt and dust. She spoke slowly, gathering every word as best she could, probably as taken aback as I was.

"My dear. You are needed. Since you seem to have slept in…" she took a deep, tired breath, "…a bog, I'd rather you dressed before coming down."

"Yes, ma'am."

What else was there to say? I couldn't understand what was going on. Everything seemed so painfully, blatantly normal, and yet I entertained no delusions that the morning's events had been a dream.

In lieu of complaining about it, I went down the hall to the washroom and poured steaming water out of a pitcher into the washbasin. My hands shook. Getting myself under control would take some doing. Perhaps I wasn't naïve enough to question whether what I'd seen was real, but I certainly questioned whether I brought it there, or it'd been waiting for me all along. If it wasn't my doing, then the townsfolk knew – they must have. They knew and hid it from me, and perhaps it was best to hide how much I knew from them.

I sunk my hands in hot water up to the wrists and sat there, relishing the warmth, feeling shivers chase up my arms and out of my body.

When I finally came down, brushed and neat, with most of the dust beaten out of my dress, Miss Crosman was reigning at her desk surrounded by young boys all scrabbling about with bits of paper.

"That's for Miss Florentina, at the tannery. Hurry along unless you'd like to volunteer some hide. Good. What's this? Ah, a pay slip from the forge. Hold on, boy, where are you off to in a hurry! Your death is still waiting in the same place, no need to run about chasing after it. Let me write a reply."

I rocked back and forth on the balls of my feet. "Miss Crosman?"

"And this, for the smith's wife. Tell her I said to take this note to the good reverend. He can be trusted. She'll need the unsong. Off you get!"

I needlessly neatened my apron. "Miss Crosman."

"I see you can look like a decent enough human when you're not trying to blend into the shrubbery. Lovely. You will take this parcel to the brewery. It's fragile, and I don't trust the boys with it. And I don't want them anywhere near the booze, the greedy louts. Yes, I mean you, Thomas, don't you sulk at me. I'll rip those eyebrows right off your face."

I counted my fingers behind my back. "Miss Crosman, this morning—"

"We do not talk about things we don't understand." She made the sign of the cross, then yanked on her collar and spat in her bosom. I couldn't stop my eyebrows from twitching together at the violent collision of Christianity and pagan lore.

"Don't you frown at me, young lady. You're already getting into trouble and twice now have tracked mud into my halls. You could do with learning some blessings and unsongs yourself."

I opened my mouth.

"On your own time, if you please. This parcel needs taking. You'll take it if you want a bed tonight."

It didn't seem like she wanted an argument, so I took the little brown paper-wrapped parcel from the corner of her desk. It was heavy and clinked a little when I lifted it.

"Mind it. Glass is precious around here. You break it, you'll be here a year working off the debt. And don't think I won't find some use for you, even if it's just holding up the building."

I didn't waste any more time. Immediate danger always trumped hypothetical danger, and that woman was as immediate as nature made them.

The shock of being outside again had me reeling for a moment. The market square was just as it had been, carts laden and flagstones dusty, except now it was full of people milling about their daily business. The handful of buyers inspecting wares felt like a crowd to me, and the melodious chorus of their voices was pure bliss. It felt so normal.

Except for the sausage merchant who was quite upset at his neighbor, the vegetable merchant, both convinced the other had pilfered something. Was there any way on earth I could tell them it'd been me without sounding a lunatic? Any way I could tell anyone, for that matter?

Afraid to look at the sky, I tried to listen for the deceptive wind, but there was so much noise of life I wouldn't have heard it anyway. I caved and looked up. A white sky sat above us, but a natural one, full of the whirls and twirls of gray you'd expect right before rain.

"Wereslug?"

I wheeled toward the voice behind me, which was much too close for propriety. "I beg your pardon?"

A wiry man in brown work clothes hovered. "Wereslug, miss. For luck. Keeps away the Tides. The more people have one, the longer it'll take."

I hadn't the faintest clue what he was on about, but I trusted him about as far as I could throw him. He had the same pushy body language most snake oil salesmen had, leaning toward me with a handful of perfectly ordinary slugs.

"Those are perfectly ordinary slugs." Clearly, confusion brought out my best wit.

"Naw, miss. You'll see, they get all fuzzy when the moon's round and rush around devouring cabbages. Just keep 'em in a jar and you'll be fine. They's good luck to find. A copper each."

"If it's better for everyone to have one, why aren't you letting people have them for free?"

"Man's got to eat. Come on, a copper!"

I waved him off and turned away, irritated. I suspected he was taking advantage of the situation to turn a profit, but I just didn't know enough about the place to be sure. I hated not knowing enough.

A big wet drop plopped into the dust right in front of me. I put some space between myself and the vendor but realized I didn't know quite where I was going. One of Miss Crosman's boys rushed past me and I grabbed his vest to stop him.

"What you want, miss? If I don't hurry, old Crow-man will hide me."

"The brewery?"

He pointed to a spot in the distance where a tall stack stood halfway to the trading post, then rushed off. I went down one of the narrow alleys snaking vaguely in that direction and had to double back once or twice. By the time I was in front of the brewery entrance, it was bucketing down and any hint of dust I'd ever had in my clothes was well washed away and forgotten.

The building, and street around it, smelled like warm yeast and grains. That couldn't be a bad place. I made to knock on the door, but it swung open before I could reach it.

"Well, what are you standing out in the rain for? Come in!"

I hesitated for a moment, for fear she'd mistaken me for someone else.

"Come on, quickly!"

Clearly agitated, the young woman in the doorway grabbed my parcel with one hand and my sleeve with the other and dragged us both into the warm, yeasty building. A long plank table sat upon two wooden barrels in the center of the room. It was a little too dark and wet, but it was warm and oddly cozy, what with all the dirt and dust. It felt comfortable.

That was all I had a chance to see before I was forcefully sat down on one of the high stools around the table, a mug of ale before me and curious eyes staring at me.

"You have to tell us everything." The round-faced, dark-haired girl threw the parcel onto a nearby bar, making its contents rattle and clink.

A lad with her same jet hair, but lighter brown eyes, half rose from his barstool perch. "Mara, watch it."

"Oh, flog her stupid jars. She can drink her ale out of a piss pot for all I care. This is more important!"

The young man Mara snapped at didn't seem at all taken aback by her retort. On the contrary, there was a distinctly wet glint in his eye that suggested he'd be more than happy to take a tongue lashing in private. It also suggested he was well into his drink. All five of the men and women, none of them much older than myself, were well doused.

"Sorry, miss." He raised his mug at me. "Mara gets excited easily."

She kicked him under the table.

"Ow! Well, it's true. And sorry for the rest of us too, miss. We didn't know you were coming, or we'd have not drunk. As much. As quickly. Maybe."

They all laughed, but I didn't have any notion that they were laughing at me. I couldn't remember the last time I'd felt so at ease around a group of strangers, nor the last time I'd enjoyed an ale with one. As they giggled away, I took a deep drink of the ale they'd placed before me, and it tasted like a blessing.

"What Eugen means to say is…." Mara stood with her mouth open for a moment, searching for words.

Another young man, this one paler and looking a lot more sober and serious than the rest, began to explain things to me with endearing composure. "What Eugen and Mara mean to say is—"

"Shut up, Paul."

"Shut up, Paul!"

Mara and Eugen burst into laughter at their synchronicity, and I couldn't suppress a smile of my own. These here were rough-looking people, but they weren't bad people. I had a chance to glance at all of them in the half-light, as the laughter died down and I drained the rest of my drink.

Mara and Eugen were both dark-haired and tan and looked like a set pair. If it wasn't for the looks between them, I'd have guessed they were brother and sister. Paul was chestnut-haired and all sharp angles, his eyes dark but not as dark as the circles around them. There was a hunger to his face that immediately reached inside my body and made my stomach tingle, a look like he'd be capable of both terrible and wonderful things. Though I never understood what most people meant when they called someone attractive, nor why any set of features would be more beautiful than any other set, that look came close for me.

The red-haired girl was familiar, and I realized I recognized her from the trading post. Enache had pointed her out. She was the one who'd lost her parents and was living with the two recluses. She caught me looking and did her best to hide her freckled face. At the far end there was one more lad, passed out across the table but still holding a mug of ale.

"Sorry. Sorry. Don't mind us." Mara gave one last giggle and shook herself off. She beamed at me with intense interest, and the others seemed curious as well. Maybe country life didn't offer much by way of entertainment. "Like I said, you have to tell us everything."

"Everything about what?"

"About everything!" Paul jumped off the edge of his seat and the table wobbled from his intensity. "About out there. What's going on? What's it like?"

"Is it true that they're all loreless barbarians?" Eugen seemed genuine, but the others rolled their eyes at that question.

I suppressed a smile. "What do you mean by 'they'?"

"Well. People out there."

"People like me? From outside?"

He bit his lip and scratched at his dark stubble.

I put on my best 'I'm not a barbarian' grin for him. "Nonsense. We have plenty of our own lore we need to respect as we invade the dominant civilizations."

His precious face for that one second of disbelief had us all in another round of giggles. While they were subsiding, the red-haired freckled girl went to the bar and tinkered around for a bit. After a minute, she came back holding a large ibric of coffee and little cups for everyone. She sat mine down so gently and quietly I wasn't sure if she was a girl or a fox. I wanted to break her out of her quietness and show her I was a friend as best I could.

"Thank you, I was freezing. What's your name?"

"Perdy." Her voice was soft and cautious.

"Perdy."

"Actually, it's Pierduta. But call me Perdy."

"Of course. And our unconscious friend there?"

"Florin."

The boy was busy drooling on the table as she went and set a cup of coffee before him. Paul got up and, in one lithe motion, picked his head up by the hair, looked at his face for a second, then let it fall with a heavy *thunk* back to the table. Perdy jumped.

"Alive. He'll be fine."

A few seconds later Florin groaned a little, as though just realizing he'd been hurt, and tried lifting his head. Perdy sat next to him with a washcloth, washing his face and giving him sips of coffee. I could see a lot of love in her little hands, her wrists like the legs of a bird. It was touching. I recognized the way they moved – gentle, but steady – from my time as a field nurse. My sisters and I'd had to cure far worse than hangovers, but the best of them treated every injury with the same composure.

We sipped our drinks for a moment, but they couldn't contain their excitement for long.

"Is it true that you can move from place to place as you wish?"

"It's true. I've been doing that for a while now."

"Are all the places different from here?"

"Each place is different from the one before it."

"Is it true that there are cities under giant lakes?"

"Not ones that people still live in, no. But there are cities right next to water that looks like it never ends."

The questions kept going for a while, each one more innocent than the last. They didn't even seem to know exactly what they wanted to ask. They didn't really know what it was about their town that was so different – and neither did I. Yet.

"Now tell me about Whisperwood. Why have none of you ever left?"

They glanced at one another briefly, and a little of the warmth I'd built with them melted away. That was often the price of asking a hard question.

"Too much to do." Mara stared into her cup, reading who knows what in the coffee dregs, avoiding my eyes. "And it's not safe outside for the likes of us. Leaving is...not encouraged."

Paul nodded towards the unconscious lad. "He tries, often enough, and fails, and then drowns the desire to try again in potato brandy. Remembers how important what we do here is, maybe. For a while."

It felt like that wasn't the whole truth. "What is there to do that's so important?"

They shuffled a little and looked at Paul, who stared straight out the window, unflinching. It was Eugen who finally replied.

"We watch. We guard. The Wardens make defenses, the Praedictors scour history and mathematics and the stars to tell our future. The lucky ones, Walkers like Paul—"

He'd lost me completely, but Paul was ready to snap at him like he'd expected that turn of the conversation, the shine in his eyes like fires in the dead of night. "You think what we do is lucky? It's the most dangerous—"

"Paul. Let him be. You'll wake Florin." Perdy's sweet voice lulled him to sit, albeit grumbling.

Eugen went on with his explanation. "The lucky ones are chosen to go out into the Tides."

Tides? I was shocked at the thought that there might have been any truth to the wereslug merchant's tale and couldn't wait to hear more. "In the interest of fairness and out of respect for our newfound friendship, I ought to tell you I have no idea what any of those things mean. What Tides?"

Eugen nodded slowly. "So, it's true. I've read books about this. There are places that don't have Tides."

"I don't know what the Tides are, so I can't say for sure."

Paul glared at me from tired eyes that spoke of having lived too many centuries. "Yes, you do. Maybe you didn't, before, but you do now. I saw you." He stared, unblinking. "I saw you in the Tides this morning."

CHAPTER FIVE

Leaves of Glass

"You saw that too? The empty sky? Everyone gone?"

Paul shook his head. The gesture was tight and furious, like most of his body language. "They weren't gone. You were gone. And the sky wasn't empty, it was just a different sky."

I didn't understand, but joy overcame me, nonetheless. My focus narrowed on him, and I was rapt. Whatever the answers, I wasn't crazy, nor did it sound like I was to blame for what had happened. Most importantly, I wasn't alone. Determined, I started questioning him about Whisperwood, and did not stop for a long time.

Understanding any of it took over an hour. We talked, Mara made us a late lunch, we talked more. Often, they assumed I'd know things I had no way of knowing. They thought old books from the outside world referencing hearsay and fairy tales spoke about the same sort of thing that happened on a nearly daily basis in their little corner of the woods. That couldn't have been further from the truth.

I pieced together a curious puzzle I still wasn't sure I fully comprehended and, had I not seen plenty of strange occurrences with my own eyes, never would have believed.

The town was a frontier, acting as a lighthouse for the vast ocean of the unknown world beyond. They called that beyond-place Unspoken. It was populated by creatures the townsfolk called Whispers, because if they ever visited, they were only faint shadows and specters, like the one that greeted me on my first evening in town. They didn't belong in our world.

Every now and then, that ocean sent out a Tide. Only a small handful of people were sensitive to Tides, Paul, Perdy, and, apparently, I among them. When Tides came, the Unspoken covered Whisperwood like rising waters. Without moving, without leaving town, in that moment, I had been in a different place altogether, and the rest of the people of Whisperwood went on with their day quietly beneath the surface, hardly noticing I was gone.

"And that's why I was able to see them more clearly, the creatures from the woods?"

Paul nodded, his demeanor toward me warmer and more familiar by the minute. "I was watching from the chapel hill in case there was trouble, but those were only a harmless kind. I should have come to you, but it was so surprising to see a stranger at all, let alone a stranger who can walk the Tide like one of us trained Walkers."

Something irked me. "Miss Crosman must have known I was gone. I even tried to ask."

Before I could explain further, Mara burst into tutting and waved her hands in a broad dismissal. "The old crow, like most of the old'uns, they don't talk about any of it. They hang herbs and perform unsongs and say prayers and believe that if they speak of it, they draw its attention."

"And you don't?"

"I've a brewery to run and friends to keep sane. I don't have time to dance around in circles. Life is hard enough." They all nodded, and she sighed. "And there's no getting out."

Eugen smirked, elbowing a still-drowsy Florin in the ribs. "Not that the more adventurous of us haven't tried."

I perked up. "Now that you've told me this much, will you tell me the truth about why we can't leave town? Is it really impossible?"

Eugen was the one who answered with a solemn tone, and I could have easily pictured him lecturing a roomful of schoolchildren. "It's been that way for many generations. Sometimes stragglers wander in, but for the most part we have to keep this place safe. The woods that way are Warded to hell and back. Once you stay the night, you stay for good. And even we're not allowed to know exactly how they work."

Mara touched my elbow with a look of concern on her face. "Does that...frighten you?"

"I hadn't considered it, but I don't think so. Not yet. I think, in a way, this might be just what I needed. A safe and isolated place to recover—" I caught myself before divulging too much. "But why? What would happen if people came and went as they pleased?"

Again, Eugen took the lead. "The Unspoken isn't stable. It expands and shifts and changes every day. If word got out, people might come and put themselves in danger without knowing how to stay safe. Or worse, they might draw it out, and it would spread all over the world. It's a hard place, all it takes is a step chasing the wrong light or a wrong word to a woodland creature and snap! You're gone."

Mara scoffed. "At least, that's what the old'uns say. The 'speak not of the Unspoken' lot. Fat lot of help they are."

Paul slapped his hands against the table, causing Florin and me to jump. "Not for long, aye? We're going to change things. The old is on the way out, and we're going to end the reign of secrets and ignorance and fear. We'll push research and contact and turn this mess into well-oiled gears. You'll see. In five years' time we'll be unrecognizable." When he spoke, everyone listened. He was magnetic. "Scientific missions, diplomatic relations in every direction. And you know what else?"

I couldn't help myself. Enraptured, I played along without even thinking. "What?"

"We're going to need your help."

A dangerous joy and relief rose through my body. The moment hung in touchable tension until the tolling of a bell broke through it, sending the flutters of excitement and hope that had been building in my belly to the four winds.

Paul shot to his feet, flinging his stool back. "Shag it, the mass!" He then flew out into the street without another word, and we were all left staring at the door swinging shut behind him.

I closed my mouth with a snap, clutching my disappointment and sudden emptiness to my chest. "What's going on?"

Mara started to put our cups and plates away, and Perdy quickly rose to help. "He was supposed to say a few words at mass, talk about loving our neighbors and keeping peace with the Whispers. That bell means it started without him."

I could see they were about done with their break, and ready to get busy, and I didn't want to intrude on them more than I already had. Secretly, I hoped they'd welcome me again and again, and tell me more about their singular little town.

By the time we'd made our goodbyes, the rain had subsided, and I was able to take their note back to Miss Crosman without getting soaked. She wasn't in, so I left it on her desk and went out for another walk. The town beckoned me to understand its movements now that there were people moving in it, and I couldn't help but be curious about what role Paul thought I might play in their revolution, so I followed the sound of the evening bell toward the chapel.

The gloom meant everyone had lit their lamps early, and the yellow light from a window shone beautifully in one of the puddles across the street, a contrast to the deep dark blue of the wet flagstones. The main street felt almost familiar to me after only a day, the way it rose a little by the haberdashery and then dipped down to the entrance of the butcher's basement, the way tufts of grass sprung between the chunky, silver-blue stones.

I made a left onto a long, winding road between some fields of barley. Roots of ancient willow trees dipped their toes into deep irrigation trenches, while the trees themselves cavorted on either side, their canopies so thick as to nearly cover the sky.

I followed that road for a while, lost in thought and feeling almost relaxed for a moment, silence broken only by the heavy flow of water in the ditches. There was something to be said about the relief of being in a place that had its own problems, and the opportunity to leave mine at its impenetrable door.

Several hedgerows passed. A lonely sheep cried out in the distance. Soon, where I expected there to be another hedgerow, a low stone wall sat grumpily stuck in a low ridge. Beyond it, leaning crosses of painted blue wood sung their terminal songs. The stone chapel behind them was adorned with spectacular stained glass, the likes of which would have been at home in any cathedral. Astounded, I drew nearer.

A few final stragglers ambled away to murmurs of gratitude and reminders of 'peace and love to all God's creatures'. By the time I made it near the entrance, only two hushed voices remained beyond the wall. I took a step back to just where it ended and hunched down behind it, untying my boot. My goal wasn't to spy, but I couldn't bring myself to interrupt what was clearly an important conversation.

"Be steadfast, my son. This could be wonderful news. We'll need all the help we can get."

"You think the same as I, that we can trust her and enlist her?"

"Kindness is a virtue, as is vigilance. Assume the best, but be prepared for anything." The tone and words rang of priesthood, and I had no doubt that was the good reverend everyone mentioned.

"If the mayor brought her here, I swear—"

"Save the swearing for when you stub your toes. But no, I don't think he could have. I'll ask Master Artjom if they let anyone out over the last few weeks, but no. I want to believe God, the Spirits, or Luck itself sent her to us."

An awkward moment of silence followed. Shuffling noises on the gravel path.

"Let me come with you tonight."

"I'd rather not. Negotiations are delicate and they've been getting agitated. Last night, I was lucky I had food on hand to offer."

"But they are negotiating?"

"Of course. We'll make it. You'll see. With her help, perhaps."

"I have a bad feeling, Father."

"If anything goes wrong, it'll be your turn to make the hard decisions. Until then, be patient. Be kind. Be vigilant."

The stone was cool and damp as I pressed against it, making myself as invisible as possible, just in time to see Paul run off back toward town. He didn't notice me crouched in the shadows, and I felt the impulse to call out to him followed by a pang of guilt, but what was done was done.

I heard the crunch of boots move into the chapel and tied my lace back up as quick as I could. I counted to ten, then rose like nothing in the world was more natural. Nobody there. Good.

Inside, candles flickered, and a cold, oppressive gloom permeated everything. My first reaction was to recoil at the familiar damp mustiness I spent so much of my childhood being lectured in. After a second, all resemblance faded. This was no ordinary chapel.

A tall, grizzled man in plain gray robes loomed over the altar, a little book in his hands, murmuring to himself. He snuck it into his robe the moment he heard my voice, which was behavior unlike that of any other reverend I'd ever known.

"Excuse me?"

"Bless you, child." His arms opened in a welcome that his face was in no mood for. Clearly, he hadn't been expecting to welcome me just yet. In fairness, I'd be in no mood either if I had to subject my bones to that damp chill every day.

"Father—" Suddenly, my throat closed shut, and I couldn't think of anything to say.

"You can call me Andrei if the title doesn't feel right."

"Is it that obvious?"

He softened and smiled. "Yes. The spiritual leader before me was a stickler for clericalism and repetition. He didn't believe in reading from between the lines of the Good Book. Many of the townsfolk are still traumatized and shun the chapel. I have a much lighter hand."

"Pardon my ignorance, but what denomination is this?"

"Orthodox, at the root, but grown into its own tree, I think you'll find. A lot of our lore isn't in any books, but God sees us, and made room for us in his garden. We have our own songs and unsongs, stories and fables. Few visitors, no judgment, and no need to give ourselves names."

I wasn't entirely convinced he needed that many words to say 'cult' but who was I to judge? After what I'd seen, it would have been absurd to expect the locals to follow any religion that didn't include the Unspoken.

"I couldn't help but notice your beautiful stained glass."

At that, the smile deepened, and it seemed genuine, albeit tired. "You flatter us, my dear. It isn't really stained glass. Well, I suppose it is, in the sense that it is glass, stained."

He reached up to the nearest of the little windows, a magnificent study in greens and purples, and fiddled with a few latches. The entire window, wooden frame and all, came off in his hands and he brought it down for closer inspection. Left behind was only a hole in the stone wall, much like there would have been in any poorer parish.

"They are frames fitted with two panes of glass. I had them brought in by the merchant, one by one, over the years, as the town could afford it. The town supports several institutions, this chapel not highest among them."

He presented me with the glass, and I oohed in awe.

"I made the scenes myself, with God's guidance, and a little inspiration from friends." He winked. "I paint them onto one glass and cover it with the second, so that the paint will be protected in the center. For a while, at least. They will outlast me, for sure."

"It's magnificent. Crafty, for one, but the scene itself is breathtaking."

I was neither joking nor exaggerating. The one he had brought down was covered in detailed images of woodland, leaves picked out in hues of unearthly green and dreamlike purple, hints of creatures lurking in between the trees, and standing above them brightly backed by a yellow sun, the shadowy figure of a large herbivore with horns that branched out into a forest of their own. As he moved to replace the masterwork, I almost heard the leaves rustle.

Eleven other such windows surrounded the room, each more beautiful than the last. A blue-and-violet peacock, a woman in white seen through a dreamlike haze, and a flock of dark indigo sheep stood nearest to us. Perhaps those were the saints of that odd place.

"It is a small thing my tired old hands were permitted to do in order to bring a little brightness to this place, and teach my flock about their neighbors." His hands on the frame were neither tired nor old-looking.

"Neighbors?"

Turning back from the glass, his face shone purple and green, and his hand touched the pocket where his book was still hidden. "You will see. Soon enough."

He stepped into the corridor between the pews, pushing me back with his presence as he did so, a clearly strong and well-constructed country man with more than a hint of menace. I shuddered to think what this man would be like in his full fire and brimstone Sunday best.

"Speaking of our neighbors, I'm sorry to rush you away, but I've somewhere vital to be and can't spare another moment. Will I see you tomorrow, for the holiday sermon?"

I was sorry to leave, but so very pleased to have been invited back. It'd been a long time since I was welcome anywhere. "Forgive me, I've been on the road for such a long time. I'm not sure what we're celebrating?"

"A local tradition. You wouldn't have heard of it. It's the night Saint Prasila slew the Serpent. We offer tributes of milk and painted snakeskin so he will keep us safe."

By the end of his little speech, I had one boot out on the gravel and was struggling to keep the last one indoors. There was no winning against him, though.

"Bless you, friend. Hurry along to your room before it gets dark."

The chapel doors clanged shut between us.

CHAPTER SIX

Tenebrous Tendrils

Shadows deepened.

On a gloomy day like that, they never got longer, they only sprang into being out of nowhere and around everything. I felt the compulsion to rush home, like the good little hen I was raised to be, but I was old enough now that those feelings were fleeting and weak. Something made me linger.

Paul had said he wanted my help, but never explained in what way. My first instinct was to promise him anything and everything, pleased that somebody needed me. But what if, this time, I could learn a little more before committing to anything? What if I could avoid repeating past mistakes?

It stood to reason that the reverend was going to do something important, and by what I'd gathered from his conversation with Paul, it had to do with Whispers. What if I could just observe, unobtrusive, from a distance? Paul had watched me from the hill during the Tide; perhaps I could do the same. Maybe I could be of help.

Scuffling noises reached me from the back of the building. My feet fell softly on quiet mud and I circled around the chapel in moments, just in time to see a narrow wooden door open and pour blackness out into the evening. No lanterns back there, then. Fine.

Behind the chapel, a gentle slope rolled west and north toward the woods that seemed to surround the town on every side, and a shaded figure rushed down it. The light was such now that I could only distinguish the outline of trees and the general shape of the land, a doubtful final twilight before pure night sowed shadows in the corners of my eyes.

Careful not to stumble on any rocks and tumble down to my death – or great embarrassment – I let Father Andrei make it halfway down the hill before I matched his pace. More crosses surrounded us, reflecting starlight in white and turquoise glaze, painted with colorful figures and covered in writing I'd have loved to read, but I couldn't spare the time to approach one and risk losing sight of the reverend.

Years of finding my way through pitch-black rooms in complete silence in my father's house were proving useful now. I walked, arms extended, fingers probing the air, focused on movement rather than color, just like I learned in my own father's house.

Unfortunately, every step I took aggravated my sense of guilt and my confusion as to why I was following him at all, if not out of a misplaced and childish desire to be useful. I made the decision to turn back and recanted on it a dozen times. I was just about to finally follow through when he stopped right at the edge of the trees. The low stone wall didn't reach all the way here. Thick emerald pines stood like a fortress, instead, and cast a perfect line of impenetrable shadow that the priest's toes touched. The depth of that shadow made the rest of early night seem almost bright, pale mercurial light bouncing off the rising moon in gentle rays.

He stood still. I crouched behind a nearby bit of shrub, far enough away that nothing short of a sneeze would betray me. Tall, damp grass tickled my legs beneath my skirt and brushed against the back of my hands. The texture was rough and reminded me of cat tongues, and I briefly wondered why it was that the town had no pets. I hadn't seen a single dog or cat so far.

Suddenly, Father Andrei raised his arms. Someone had approached him from inside the woods. He spoke loudly, shouting what sounded like formal greetings, but I wasn't close enough to understand everything.

Cursing under my breath and immediately apologizing for it, I moved closer. At that moment, he was shoved back as though by a strong wind, and he stumbled against the side of the hill, falling to his arse and elbows. I slunk down and huddled into the shadows as best I could while still watching him, my eyes now better adjusted to the dark.

He seemed surprised, and that surprise was quickly turning into distress. Still steady of voice, however, he clearly said, "Wait," and "Talk about this."

I looked back toward town, trying to remember how long the walk was and how far I'd have to run if I needed to get help. Up a hill, in the dark, on the wet grass, it'd be a matter of twenty minutes at least before I came back with assistance. If Father Andrei's fate was to be ravaged by a bear – or Whispers? – at that time, I didn't think I was going to be able to stand in the way by myself. Curses.

He shouted, "Wait!" again, and for a moment, I thought he meant me. The line of dark shadow cast by the woods was again pressing right up against the soles of his boots. My brow furrowed but I couldn't for the life of me figure out whether the angle of the moon was even right to be casting that shadow at all.

I inched closer. Reverend Andrei's chest rose and fell in rapid bursts, but his wrists seemed pinned down into the ground. Eyes bulging, he frothed at the mouth as he spoke.

"We can make amends." He jerked. "We will absolutely release him. We will set him free by the next moon."

The forest was highly animated, much more than it could have been by any wind or birds. Creaking, the boughs and trunks knocked against one another as trees were taken up by an inexplicable fury. There was nothing in the darkness that I could identify, but the priest stared straight into the blackness like he knew something was there.

"You don't know what you're doing! There's no need for this. I came in peace, without the silver or any—"

A long tendril of darkness broke the straight line cast by the edge of the woods, erupting only a hand's width away from the priest's struggling body. I quickly searched for what might have cast that new shadow, but there was nothing to be found.

Chilled to my core, in my own puddle of shade next to a shrub, I watched, torn as to whether I should interfere. A foreigner, and not a very bright one. What could I do? What if I made it worse?

It was like the invisible bough of a pine tree extended over the priest and cast shadows upon him. Another came, and then another. They passed over pebbles and grass and stones and didn't shift or trouble a single one. Animated, his eyes followed their progress as best they could, but it looked like he was rapidly losing the ability to move. He was being held fast.

"Let me go." His voice was unreasonably calm. "I won't be able to tell them if you don't let me go. They'll come after you, instead. Please."

He yowled, then twitched like he was trying to get away from his own shadow but couldn't. Noninterference be damned, I had to help.

Rising to his aid, I almost fell flat on my face. I threw my arms out to shield from the fall and scraped my palms badly. My heel was held in a firm grip and the beginnings of punctures passed through my leather boots. Something was biting into my foot. I jerked to my side and looked for the thing that held me, but there was nothing there.

"No, please. Don't do this. We can't afford a war. Neither can you. Please—"

Father Andrei broke into screams as the shadows that surrounded him became agitated, circling around him and flicking to his body. Every time one connected, he flinched, baying and yelping, and I was reminded of a poor, lost animal being devoured by a school of flesh-eating fish. Frantic, I yanked at my foot to free myself, but the grip grew tighter, and a sharp pain shot up my calf.

Slapping at my foot, I only hit my own boot leather; and yet it was clear that some sort of living thing held me in an invisible mouth. One of the same shadows assaulting the reverend? Would the others turn on me once they were done with him? Panicked, I searched for their dark shapes.

Satiated, they sat across his body, only lazily pecking at him. His eyes rolled backward, and the corners of his mouth drooped. His moans were getting softer, but no less pained, and I scratched desperately at my boot, trying to unbind whatever bound me. Finally, with a frustrated groan, I untied my laces and slipped the whole thing off, yanking my leg out of the shadow before anything could grab it more securely.

Mud dug under my fingernails as I scrabbled for purchase. I dashed to the reverend as swiftly as my feet would go. Grass root clumps twisted my ankles and the impact from stepping into a deep hole jolted my hip, but he'd stopped moving and I had no time.

Some instinct beyond my rational mind made me step well clear of the pools of darkness beneath bushes and boulders. The moonlight dimmed a little. Hundreds of shadows flew across the sky, obscuring the light. I was halfway to Reverend Andrei when the last of the shadows across his body rose and joined the ones harrowing the moon. Only then did I notice that the grass beneath him was soaked in black blood.

The unknowable attackers retreated into the sky, feasting on moonlight now, and I feared for both our lives if we were still there when they finished that supper.

The priest lay on the grass as limp as a doll. Little strips of skin hung off him, reminding me of the fine strips of lettuce I'd sliced for the ducklings as a little girl in my grandmother's keep. An odd memory in that moment, but there it was. Slipping in slick blood, I knelt by his side in the pervasive smell of iron and grave dirt. ·

Touching my fingers to his wrist gave me no sign that he might be alive. To be sure, I licked the back of my hand, tasting mud and grass and blood, and placed it under his nose. Nothing.

There was no way I would be able to carry Father Andrei back gracefully or in a hurry, and no reason for me to waste time doing so. My next thought was to go back and pick up my boot from the bushes, as though I'd completely taken leave of what was left of my senses. Whatever those things were, they were still flying about, still hungry, and I knew nothing of them or how to keep myself safe.

Cursing myself for getting involved and being useless at it, I clambered up the hill on all fours in as straight a line as I could, eager to get as much distance as possible between myself and the woods. Brambles and thorns pulled at me as I ploughed through them.

Hurt, scared, and out of breath, I stopped at the top of the hill just by where the oldest of the gravestones lay. The spongy ground slushed when I sat, thousands of needles burning the entrance to my lungs, my ears filled with nothing but my breathing. Hugging one of the brightly painted crosses, I caught my breath. The moon was completely gone, the black border around the woods completely blurred, and the trees completely motionless.

Nothing moved, nothing betrayed any struggle. The only thing out of place was a dark lump lying still in the grass below.

CHAPTER SEVEN

And I Saw Him Standing There

I kept expecting something to happen – either people to come rushing down, or mysterious death to come rushing up – but nothing did.

Eventually, when my feet regained feeling, I got up and made for the guesthouse. It was a long and miserable trip. I was dirty and soaked, banged-up and scratched, bleeding from a hundred places. My bare foot was so cold my toes shot pain right up into my ankle with every step. Eventually I figured the wet stocking was making things worse, so I took it off. Then I put it back on again. Then took it off again. Then, defeated, I wept.

What should have been a ten-minute journey took me anywhere between an hour and an eternity in the dark. When, finally, the door of the guesthouse was in sight, rather than be braced by it, I was disheartened by the foreignness of it. The last fifty steps took another two eternities.

The guesthouse was silent. I crawled up the stairs to my room on all fours, took every soaked stitch of clothing I wore off my body, and rolled myself into a quivering ball under the pile of blankets.

★   ★   ★

Light bothered my dreams.

I was trapped in a dirty cellar, a pyramid of ram's heads staring at me from the corner. The distant sound of Alec's voice came to me from somewhere above. "Had to warn you about her. She's crazy. She'll come after you, next." Liquid shadows oozed out of the stacked skulls and surrounded me.

Light, again. A scraping noise in the room annoyed me.

A stabbing pain in my knee made me stretch my leg out from under the covers to relieve it. A loud cough from somewhere across the room woke me with a start, wide-eyed and clutching the covers to my chest.

"Ahem."

A man sat across the room on the only chair there was. His eyes were as bright as his wrinkles deep, and tufts of jet hair poked out of his colorful knit cap in all directions. He held himself in a stately pose and observed me.

"How may I help you?" I wasn't sure why I'd said that. Clearly, I wasn't in any position to help him, naked and barely conscious.

"You must be wondering what I'm doing here."

"Not at all. Please, make yourself at home."

I gestured toward the nothingness around us, my arm still underneath the blankets. He smiled, leaned back, and drew a tobacco case from the inside pocket of his tooled leather vest. It was a beautiful thing of carved black wood, and he treated it gently as he drew out a cigarette and a match.

The bright flare from the match made me ache behind my eyes, but the sulfurous smell was wonderfully refreshing. When I felt the first whiff of cigarette smoke, though, I withdrew back into the wall behind me.

"Do you smoke, miss?"

I shook my head. "Not for a while. I left it behind." Along with the memory of an ash-filled room where my broken and bleeding body spent so long a time, smoke and tar was all I could taste. The scars of cigarette burns I carried with me.

"Looks more like it left you behind. Need me to put it out?"

I steeled myself against my past and refused to let it corner me. "No. I would, however, be much obliged if you'd tell me what it is you're doing in my room."

"Don't you want to know who I am, first?"

"Sounds like you'd love to hear yourself tell me."

He blew thick curls of smoke out his nose. "Eduard Râmiş, third of my name. Lord Eduard will do. I'm the elected mayor of this town."

While he spoke, I scanned the room. Everything I'd had on my person the night before was gone. "Are you the one who stole my drawers?" Waking up properly, I found myself more than a little irritated by the sight of a strange, uninvited man in my room.

"That's very outspoken for a little miss who can't walk away without showing me her flanks."

"I might take that chance for the pleasure of evicting you from my chambers."

"Steady now. Your underthings, as well as the rest of your clothes, are downstairs being dried as we speak. Miss Crosman has taken care of them for you."

"Why on earth would she—"

"Because I obliged her to. They will be returned to you shortly, I assure you. I can make no use of them."

I must have blushed an unflattering shade of purple.

He smiled a little again. "I would like to apologize for these unusual circumstances. The situation was quite dire and there wasn't anyone else equipped to watch over you."

"Why did I need watching over?"

"To make sure you didn't die in your sleep from bleeding out or a knock to the head. You were in quite a state. Also, to make sure you didn't wake up changed into something less than your good self."

At that, he shifted, and I realized there had been a bright hunting knife tucked neatly under his right thigh the whole time, just in reach. He took it, swiped it across his trousers with a dramatic flourish, and snuck it in a holster beneath his jacket.

"Why exactly would I—"

"That's a question with a complicated answer, and there are easier ones first."

"Why are you here?"

"Because you witnessed Andrei Roman die."

I gasped, the memory falling over me like a bucket of rain. "You found him."

"We did. Him, your boot, the trail of mud you left behind you, the state your clothes were in. We pieced two and two and figured you'd been attacked together."

"Not together, per se."

"At the very least, you saw it happen."

"I did."

"Do you want to tell me what happened?"

And risk being locked away for lunacy? "Not really."

"I didn't expect you would. Let me win your trust a little further. While we know you had no part in his death, and we have some idea of what manner of thing it was that did, the things you saw are vitally important to myself, my office, and this entire town. I'm afraid you're going to help us whether you like it or not."

"By word of law?"

"By the desire not to upset your local community." It sure sounded like he weighed his own opinions quite heavily when it came to tipping the scales of the local community's mood. "Your local community you can't escape from."

I fidgeted under my covers. "You said you had some idea what it was?"

"Perhaps. This forest holds unique species. We coexist. Very few of them ever have contact with people. Our beloved –" he said that word with a grimace, "– spiritual leader took it upon himself to argue with them. It won't be a very long investigation, I think. Not very long, at all, no."

A sense of tension slipped away from me at once, and I realized I'd been holding on to the thought that maybe I had caused trouble to come to the reverend. It still hounded me in spite of what I'd learned at the brewery. The relief that it was unlikely to have been my fault was swiftly followed by a pang of guilt. A man had died, and I'd done nothing.

Eduard took a deep breath and shut one eye, looking at me like he was appraising an old battleship through a telescope. He stood, drew near, and gazed out the window behind me, pensive. I shuffled in my cocoon and looked too, and found the sharp pine peaks barely poking out of great white billows of mist, rising like steam into a crisp, cold turquoise sky. We waited in silence for a moment, then he turned away and paced the room.

"I'm going to need you to take us back to the scene and walk us through what happened. It may be vitally important to the safety of the town. The priest was engaged in some unpleasant dealings, I'm afraid, and there's no helping everyone from finding out. Ungodly. The sooner we put this matter to rest, and let the public know it's over, the sooner they can come back into the fold and support the cause of safety and spirituality again." He stopped himself. "We'll talk more during the formal interview. Just don't go anywhere." He smirked.

"Wouldn't dream of it."

"Before you turn that snide wit on me, young lady, consider this. Rumors are starting to spread about you bringing ill luck. Things were going rather well before you turned up." He shrugged in an exaggerated way that made me feel certain that wasn't true. "Some would say they're only tales over spun yarn, but some of the more faithful are wary. If you co-operate, there's no reason to worry."

"Wary of me?" I knew exactly how those kinds of rumors spread, and there was absolutely every reason to worry.

"Can't be helped. You can see how being seen co-operating thoroughly with the authorities is in both our best interests."

"How convenient."

"This is a great thing! You will be seen as a helpful and potentially welcome permanent addition to the town, and the town officials will get to put people's minds at ease about the priest's nocturnal dealings. Everyone will sleep better."

"So you steal my drawers, but worry about my reputation?"

"Someone has to. I hear you've made friends all over town. And enemies. There are several merchants with missing stock who seem to want to have words with you."

A flush of heat rose into my cheeks. So they knew it had been me, somehow.

He laughed. "I'm only teasing, I've settled that debt. But now, you owe it to me." He turned on his heels in proper military fashion and yanked the door open remorselessly. "And I will make sure you deliver. In my house, miss, everyone gets in line. Take the day to recuperate. I'm not unsympathetic. Then, tomorrow morning, we'll have our interview. Your belongings are with the maestress. Be vigilant."

I couldn't tell if he meant that last remark in general, or for my interaction with Miss Crosman. Soon, he was gone, and I still gawked as naked and confused as the moment I woke up.

CHAPTER EIGHT

A Pretty Path

My clothes were warm and dry, but would need mending soon.

My benefactors had even gone through the trouble of fetching my lost boot, now clean and dry, too. The maids brought up a comb, a pitcher of scalding water, and a basin. I took that as a firm suggestion and cleaned myself up, the sting of getting mud out of my scrapes and cuts better than any morning calisthenics.

I dressed myself gingerly and went downstairs, taking my satchel and bidding the cold little room goodbye. Miss Crosman was behind her desk, as usual, and I spotted the rest of my belongings spread out before her. She looked at me with no noticeable change of attitude from before, neither pity nor anger, and I found that comforting.

"This was in your boot."

She stuck my knife point down into her desk and the heavy bone handle made it wobble.

"And these strewn about various bits of clothing."

My silver coins slid across the surface toward me, followed by the pouch of gold. My chest tightened with guilt that she'd seen it, almost as though she'd immediately know it was stolen, and under what circumstances.

"You've a friend waiting outside. Been there for an hour. Said she needs your help. Go see her before people start to wonder what sort of trouble the two of you are bringing to my house."

"Yes, Miss Crosman. I'm sor—"

"Go on, we've nothing to discuss here. It sounds like you have plenty on your hands at the moment."

"Thank you, Miss Crosman. I'll be on my way, then."

"And none too soon. Take this as an opportunity to refresh your memory on how one is supposed to stay out of trouble when alone and friendless in foreign climes. We have enough trouble of our own."

I hesitated. "Any troubles I might be able to help with?"

"No."

She turned back to her letter, and for a moment I admired the large swooping motions of her blue-gray quill before humbly removing myself from her presence. Before Whisperwood, I thought I'd gotten used to living in unstable conditions, and adapted well to the strangeness of strangers.

No longer.

★   ★   ★

Outside, the air was crisp and smelled like fermenting apples. It was late morning, and the townsfolk milled about their business. I was pleased to recognize a friend sitting on the edge of the fountain, talking to one of the maestress's young maids.

Perdy saw me approach and smiled her shy, green-eyed smile at me.

The maid whirled around to face me. "Good morrow, miss."

"Good morrow, dear."

Perdy took a coin out of her pocket and extended it toward the girl. "I was just telling Greta that I would like to ask her a very big favor."

Greta took a deep breath and, grabbing hold of her apron with both hands, began to fuss over it and twist it every which way. Clearly, she was uncomfortable taking orders from anyone other than Miss Crosman, and given how the maestress terrified me, I could understand.

I nodded encouragement when she looked to me. "I'm sure it's all right, dear. You can trust Perdy."

Far from offended, Perdy only gazed at her softly, and the girl finally reached out and grabbed the silver coin.

"What am I to do, miss?"

"Please take that to the brewery. Ask Mara to give you one copper to keep for yourself, and use the rest to bring supplies. Food, ale, light. She'll know where."

The little girl nodded and disappeared like a fox behind a shrub, leaving no trace of ever having been there at all.

Perdy reached behind her and grabbed a satchel that had been lying on the warm stone lip of the fountain. "And this is for you, Anna. From all of us."

I opened the brown canvas bag and found that it contained a large loaf of crusty bread, chunks of dry meat, chopped-up hard cheese, and a heavy jar of something that looked deliciously like ale. My stomach grumbled and tightened itself into a hard little ball, then swelled with love for the thoughtful gesture. I almost burst into tears when I spoke.

"Thank you."

"I'm sorry for what you went through."

"Does everyone know?"

She nodded, her eyes perhaps a shade wetter and sadder even than before.

I shook myself off. Now was not the time to break down. "Is there something I can do to be helpful?"

She nodded again. "Walk with me? Please?"

I liked her thriftiness with words, not first but still high on the list of the many things that made me want to be close to her.

Perdy studied me closely too, as we made our way down the main road, side by side, quietly. She skipped and kicked stones like a child, and I couldn't help but smile. Eventually, as we neared the crossroads, she spoke.

"I need your help and thought maybe you'd not mind the distraction."

"Mmhm."

"You might understand. Most people in town cling to their families, but I found myself no longer able to tolerate my living conditions. My aunts are well intended, but...."

I doubted there was a soul in the world who could understand her better. "Say no more. You don't need to explain. If you need to live away from them, then that's that. Have you a place in mind?"

It took her a moment to answer, and I felt like the subject weighed on her.

"There's a house. I know where it is, and I have the key. My aunts are going to be livid, but it's mine by law."

"That's wonderful."

She leaned her head to one side for a moment and raised her shoulders. "But it's likely broken-down and a mess. I don't even know what to expect."

I smiled. "I can think of nothing I'd like more than to fix something and clean something. Make something better. You're doing me a real favor here."

She smiled back, and I could tell relief washed over her. Then, with a cheerful hop, she took the willow road I'd been on the night before.

That road.

A shudder started at the nape of my neck and traveled languidly down my spine. Looking at that road wasn't easy and walking down it felt impossible. I tried lifting my feet, but they were stuck to a ground made of molasses. Perdy saw, and offered me her elbow. That was it, no words, but I felt comforted. She had a gift, that girl.

I took it and we meandered like we had nowhere in the world to be. I vividly remembered going down that road yesterday, but nothing about coming back up it. Come to think of it, I wasn't even sure if I did come back through there, or by some circuitous route.

Perdy's gaze interrupted my train of thought.

I suddenly felt embarrassed. "I'm sorry."

"No, you're mourning. It's not a bad thing."

We walked along quietly for a while. The willows swayed above us, and with each step my fear faded, and I regained control. Little specks of sunlight played on our faces, dotting warmth on my skin through the brisk late autumn air and dancing bright sparks through Perdy's dark red hair.

Soon, where the road carried on vaguely rightward toward the chapel, we made a left into a small country lane I'd never noticed before. A grove of tall apple trees hid the main road from view and my shoulders drooped down, un-bunching from where they had been knotted behind my ears.

Perdy saw me loosen up and let go of my elbow. "I'm here whenever you need me."

"You're very good at this."

"I don't know. I just like people."

"I do know. I was trained as a healer when I was barely sixteen. Then war broke, and the need for field nurses was great, so there I was. You'd have been right at home with us."

She studied me with great interest. I thought for sure she'd ask me more about medicine and whether she'd be suited for that sort of job, but she surprised me. "So there are still wars? And warriors, like in stories?"

"Not at all like in stories, but yes. There are."

She walked on, quietly chewing her lip. I almost giggled at the thought of this small creature swinging a sword, but she was grave, and I felt like a shadow flitted across her gaze, so I tried another subject.

"What's this house like, then? How much work are we in for?"

"I've never actually seen it. It belonged to my parents."

"Oh! I had no idea."

"Only the older people in town remember it at all, and not even all of those. Nobody's lived there in over twenty years."

"You can't be much older than that yourself."

"I was a baby when it happened." Her tone was low and slow.

I pressed her no further. It would only make her shut down. Instead, we walked and breathed and admired the apple trees. I darted into the grove and filled my food sack the rest of the way with beautiful late-season apples. They were crisp, and the skin passed through every shade from bright red to violent green on one fruit, and I knew them to be good for cooking and keeping through the winter.

When I emerged again, Perdy seemed ready to tell me more.

"Do you know what my name means?" Her voice had a clever little lilt that blended right in with the chirping birds around us.

"It means 'lost'."

She smiled. "My parents and I were lost in the woods. I'd been born only a few days before, and there hadn't been time to baptize me. And if my mother told anyone what she intended to call me, they forgot by the time I came back out, years later. So, the townsfolk called me Pierduta, and my aunts took me in. Swore never to let me come back to this house, or go back to the woods, or do anything…of the things we can do."

I stared at the beautiful girl, taken aback by her revelation and what was surely the longest speech she'd given all year. I was still debating whether to press her further when we came within sight of a little shack. I wouldn't even have noticed it, as covered in ivy as it was, but Perdy stopped and looked mournfully at its green outline.

"I wish I felt more when looking at this place. A sense of belonging. Something."

"What do you feel?"

"Like somewhere there's another me, living this other life I never got to have. And I hate her for having all those options open to her that I don't have."

I didn't know what I could possibly say to comfort her, so I squeezed her hand.

"Anna, I hope you can forgive me."

"What for?"

"For using you like this."

"Using me?"

"It's not just about the cleaning. I'd hoped I might convince you to stay with me for a while. I don't think I have the stomach to do this alone, and Mara has so much…."

I didn't know what to say. Of course, I wanted to help her, and being away from Miss Crosman would do me good. But to impose on Perdy like that? I couldn't help but feel she only asked me for my own benefit.

I grinned as widely as I could. "Let's see what state the house is in, before we get too excited?"

Her smile was genuine and enchanting. We giggled like schoolgirls and broke into a run, racing one another the rest of the way to the front door. We arrived in a cloud of dust and merriment, but as it settled down to the ground, we both fell quiet.

CHAPTER NINE

A Dingy Dwelling

"It's...."

"Dusty." Perdy laughed, and it was a beautiful thing to hear.

I shut my mouth with a snap. "Dusty? Is that what we're going with?"

"Well, it's...."

We looked at it for another moment in awe. Layers upon layers of ivy covered the whole thing, so that only the corners showed any sign of what they were made of. There, the granite foundation, and the timber and daub above it, seemed intact. But who could say for the rest of it? The door was somewhere under that tangle of ivy, and hopefully windows too. It was hard to get a decent look from a distance because the whole place was surrounded by shrubs and trees, but it seemed like a stout little home.

At the far corner, an ancient walnut tree full of dark green leaves shaded most of the backyard and kept it protected from the encroaching thornbushes. A large branch had broken off and hung by the skin through a corner of the roof into the building itself.

"That's a problem." Perdy glared at the same hole I'd noticed.

"If that's the only problem, you can still be quite happy. Dare we try to find a way in?"

Smiling, we approached where the logical front of the building would be and thrust our hands under the ivy, looking for any sign of a door.

"You go left, I'll go right."

We made our way slowly across the face of the house, grateful that it was still small enough that the search wouldn't take long. I was even more grateful that I got to be there for her through it, and though she wasn't looking at me, I sent Perdy a warm smile.

She called out first. "I found someth— Oh, no, wait. It's a shuttered window. Never mind."

"Wait there where you are."

I went over to her and slipped my knife out of my boot.

"Cut off as many of the vines as you can with this, then see if you can wiggle the shutter open. Don't injure yourself, take it slowly."

I left her to her task and went back to my search. Eventually, my fingers touched what felt like a wooden edge of something. I followed it down and found that it extended all the way to the floor. The vines covering it were tough, but yanking them out by hand wasn't impossible. I took off my apron and wrapped it around my aching palms and was making good progress when I heard Perdy call out.

"It's clear, but I can't get it to open."

"Do you have a kerchief?"

"Yes, the one around my neck. Why?"

"Wrap the blade in it as well as you can so that you don't cut yourself, then smack the hinge with the handle a couple of times. Don't worry about being rough with it, it's better to have a broken shutter than walk into a dark room."

Silently, she did as I asked. Every time a clanging noise echoed off the rusty hinges, I flinched a little, even though I fully expected it. The hinge groaned and creaked as she wiggled it, but didn't release its hold. I let her keep trying, pretending to fuss over a stubborn vine while keeping an eye on her.

She studied the shutter for a moment. When she glanced at me, I appeared deeply engrossed in my work. She set to it again, this time tapping the end of the moving part lightly, rapidly. Rust fell off in flakes and her brow furrowed. When next she tried it, the shutter groaned but slipped out of its latch a little. A minute later, sweaty and covered in crimson specks, she let out a resounding, satisfied whoop.

"I've got it!"

"Good job! Can you see inside?"

I rushed to her, and we pulled the wooden storm shutters open, yanking free the last of the ivy. We both had the curiosity to press our noses to the glass, and we both withdrew just as quickly when we got a face full of cobwebs.

"Can't see a thing in there, anyway. The window is greasy. Help me free the door instead?"

We made short work of what was left. She returned my knife and pulled out a rusty key that seemed to molt an infinite quantity of earthy red flakes.

"Here goes nothing."

The door squeaked open into a large room, sparsely furnished with a table and some chairs, covered in cobwebs and dust but otherwise well-preserved. There were small animal bones in the corner and a few steps down to a sunken fireplace on the far end, which I dearly hoped would still work.

I noticed Perdy gaze into the fireplace, lost in thought.

"Well, there's not much that hard work can't set straight here."

"I don't remember any of this. It's silly, I don't know why I would. But still, some part of me thought that maybe it would mean something to me."

"Do you need a moment alone?"

She took a deep breath. "I need a cup of tea and some lunch. I have some things. Want to see if we can start a fire?"

"In there? You must be faint with hunger if you think that chimney will work without being thoroughly cleaned first. We'd need hours."

She pursed her lips and let out a little huff.

I had a sudden thought and asked her to follow me. We each grabbed a chair and went out to where the clear grassy area stood beneath the walnut tree. I showed her a nice spot of dirt not too near the house.

"I can set us up a firepit here in no time. Let's get the table out too. We'll need a place to rest when we take breaks from cleaning. And we can have tea and lunch out here. It's a bit cool, but a beautiful day." Realizing I was giving her instructions in her own house, I quickly adjusted. "That is, if you'd like."

She only grinned and nodded. "That sounds like the nicest thing I've heard all week. You're making it feel more like a home already."

I sent her out to gather twigs and sticks while I scooped out dirt and lined the pit with nearby rocks. When that was done, I set to building a fire and asked her to find any pot or kettle in the house. She came back with an iron teakettle and a copper cauldron.

Not long after, we were sitting at the table under the shade of the mighty walnut, well warmed by the fire. She had tea leaves in her pouch and there was a mint bush nearby, so we brewed a spicy and refreshing drink.

I read her future in my cards for her amusement, then told her about the myriad uses for the various parts of the walnut tree, the way my grandmother once told me. It was comforting to be near one again. We ate some of my bread and cheese, and some of her auntie's smoked pilchards, which tasted vile, and I had to hold my breath to eat.

When she finally broke our comfortable silence, it was with an offhand tone but piercing eyes.

"How much did you understand of what happened with Father Roman?"

"None of it. I can't even guess. Do you know what happened? Does anyone?"

She chewed on a bit of fish, not looking dreadfully eager to tell me. "This town has secrets that outsiders aren't supposed to know about. I think it has secrets that even insiders aren't."

"Don't we all?"

"What do you mean?" Much more curious and animated than before, she leaned forward over the table to better hear me.

I guessed listening came more naturally to her than talking, so I talked. "I have secrets too. I came here because I was running. I needed some place to hide. Nobody knows where I am, I think. I hope."

"What were you running from?"

"My family, my friends, my village. A terrible man who turned all that into poison for me."

"What happened?"

I didn't want to tell her everything. I didn't want to hide it all either. "I made a mistake. I was stupid and thought that as long as I had good intentions, I'd be fine. I felt needed, and my vanity made me throw all caution to the wind for the sake of that feeling. It cost me the love of my friends and family, my home, and almost my life."

She seemed saddened. "I want to believe intentions count for something. I can't imagine you being thoughtless."

"Everyone is wrong sooner or later, Perdy. You know that, by now. Even good people, and most of us aren't that."

"So they chased you away for a mistake?"

"Maybe I'm their mistake. If I get to have one, so does everyone else. Maybe even more so, because I'd caused the whole thing myself. They never asked to be involved."

She thought about it for a few seconds. "Do places get the same right as people to make mistakes?"

"I don't see why not. In the end, a place is more people. If anything, it should get more chances to."

"So you don't think there's such a thing as an evil place?"

"Well, now. I didn't say that."

The sun was high and bright as we put everything away and returned to work.

*   *   *

The fallen walnut branch poked a hole through the roof of the bedroom, which was ruined beyond all hope. We took the branch, shut the door on that bit of trouble, and promised to return another day. It would be much more comfortable to sleep in the main room, by the fire, anyway.

The final room was a small cupboard full of pots and pans, rusty tools, bags, and various knickknacks. The wood backing of the cupboard gave me pause. It was just the sort of place people would hide all sorts of things.

"Do you —" I almost asked her if she remembered a secret compartment but caught myself in time, "— mind helping me search this?"

She gave me a quizzical look.

"The room is shallower than the building, and this…" I knocked on the panel, "…sounds hollow."

After rolling up our sleeves, we pushed and prodded on the boards until one gave way. It wasn't even a door; the planks were simply jammed in place to create a fake back wall. Moving them revealed a far more spacious chamber than I'd anticipated.

Perdy shouldered her way in first. I heard her gasp, then cough violently. The boards clacked together as she stumbled out, chased by a cloud of charcoal dust. I let it settle for a moment and peeked inside to find a lonely white skeleton in a small dark chamber.

I stepped in and took a closer look. The skeleton sat in a perfect circle of white salt crystals about the size of coarse sand.

It was a curious thing; the tiny frame belonged to a child who couldn't have been older than ten, but the teeth seemed those of someone much older. Strange bumps rose at the crest of the skull too, almost like walnuts encased in bone. It was hard to count the crumbled ribs, but there seemed to be far too many. All in all, the effect was rather odd and otherworldly.

There was a cloth pouch on its sternum. I reached down, doing my very best not to disturb the bones in any way, and lifted it from the remains. Inside, a silver ring on a solid chain sparkled brightly.

"Perdy, do you know who it might have been?"

"No." She peered inside over my shoulder. "But whoever it is, it doesn't look like the salt protected them the way it should."

"Protected them?"

"From Whispers. They shouldn't be able to cross it."

"Maybe it did."

"What do you mean?"

"Maybe they stayed in there, safe, until they died." We stood in silence for a moment. "I'll not disturb it for now. We can ask around in town, someone has to know."

The pale skull stared off into nothingness.

"Do you want this ring?" I showed it to her, hoping to see some sort of recognition or reaction.

"Why would I?"

"It might have belonged to your family."

"It could also be someone who used the house after we were gone. No, I don't feel right taking it." She shook her head, then settled on an explanation with a nod. "Besides, if it's silver it should be put to good use. You should take it to the Wardens' Warren."

"All right, we can do that tomorrow." I wished I could do something more for her. "Just know I'm happy to give it to you if you change your mind."

We replaced the boards just as we found them. Perdy murmured a few words in singsong, something I guessed must have been a prayer for the dead in words foreign to me, and we went back to work.

Cleaning went easily between four hands. We used the branch to sweep most of the dust and dirt out, got rid of the stray animal bones and cobwebs and opened all the windows. Then I climbed up onto the roof using a rain collection barrel we found behind the house, lowered a rope down through the chimney, and had Perdy tie the bottom to our walnut branch. I then pulled the branch up through the chimney, brushing the sides and letting all the soot and grime fall back down.

Needless to say, more sweeping followed.

We sat together on the stone steps in front of the fireplace, working on sorting and cleaning the more useful tools and pots we'd found in the house, when she broke the silence again.

"I don't know if there's any place like this in the world. I can only hope there isn't."

"Because of the Tides?"

"The Tides are like sneezing when you catch a chill. They're awful, but not the root of the problem. Nor is the Unspoken, dangerous as it is. The problem is that the town isn't doing well, and the worse it does, the more it'll meddle and try to control the uncontrollable."

I didn't understand, but she was doing her best, so I let her speak on.

"Sometimes I worry that if the town makes more mistakes around the Unspoken, it'll be like children playing with matches near a gunpowder barrel. Neither is dangerous by itself, but the closeness of the two…."

"Is that what happened to Reverend Andrei?"

"I'm not sure." She bit on the edge of her thumbnail. "He didn't tell us what he was up to. We weren't supposed to know."

"Paul knew, though, didn't he?"

"Not everything, but I think Father Andrei was negotiating. Paul always talked about how he'd change things. Put them back the way they were."

"How were they?"

She shrugged. "I guess there used to be more co-operation between the two sides. More stability. I think they're delusional to believe it didn't come with costs." Her tone was almost petulant.

"The reverend seemed like a good person. Like he wanted peace and prosperity for everyone. Those beautiful paintings on the glass, they were Whisper landscapes?"

She nodded. "He just wanted everyone to be safe. It's true."

"It doesn't look like that's in the cards right now."

"There are all sorts of charms, wards, and rituals that help a little. Like the stone wall that we riddled with salt rocks. It'd be chaos without them. Hey, you know what? Let me teach you an unsong. Maybe it'll help, someday."

"I'd love that. I'd been wondering what they are."

"You're staying, right? I don't just mean for dinner, I mean here in the house with me? The unsong will work better if you do." She grabbed my hands, eyes filled with hope.

I couldn't put off deciding any longer. "I want to. Just for a little while. But are you sure?"

"That's settled, then."

She grinned and, without another word, rose and moved to the fireplace. I followed, and she positioned us on either side of it.

"We can start here, then unsing the rest of the house when we have time. Unsongs are like prayers, except they're of the natural world. I learned this one from Alina, the smith's wife. Repeat after me."

She took a deep breath, then started her rhythmic chant that wasn't quite sung and wasn't quite spoken, pausing after every line to give me time to repeat it.

"Little fire, roaring fire,
I'll lie down and fall asleep,
Don't you lie and don't you sleep.
Turn into a dragon with scales of gold,
With ninety-nine wings, with ninety-nine tongues,
With ninety-nine scraping claws.
Rise up like the day and burn evil away.
Rise up like the sun until evil is gone."

I couldn't tell whether it was only the effects of the lovely day, or something more than that, but I certainly felt more peaceful than I had in a while. We finished the unsong, and I sat on the steps to quickly scribble it in my journal while Perdy went on dusting the furniture, muttering here and there, singing to the chairs and stones and spoons.

CHAPTER TEN

I'm Never Gonna Drink Again

No further surprises troubled our work, though I did feel an odd sense of being watched whenever I was outside. I resolved to learn more about the strange ecosystem there, and maybe help protect the house as my contribution for living in it. For the moment, shadows got longer, and dinnertime drew near, so we brought back water from the nearby fountain and I set to making a stew.

The walnut branch served its final purpose in the fire, although it gave out far more smoke than I'd anticipated. I used up all my chunks of dried meat, the remainder of the bread, chopped apples, and a handful of rosemary from bushes that were just growing wild in the garden. We even sacrificed our one jar of ale in the stew to improve the flavor, knowing there would be more coming soon. In the end, for a poor stew, it came out as rich and delicious as any I'd ever had before, and it was ready just in time when we heard laughter coming down the lane.

"Come on, easy does it." Mara's strong, brash voice was hard to mistake. I knew beyond any doubt she'd come, and I knew she'd organize the others in spite of the terrible timing. "Steady on. One foot in front of the other."

Her voice and the clinking of jars preceded them by a good way, and we rushed to light a few candles out in front of the house to help them along. We only had one oil lamp inside, which we'd found with still a good amount of oil, but many candles.

By the noise and the laughter, I figured Florin was stone drunk again. Perdy had told me that he often resorted to drinking whenever the desire to leave town became so strong, he couldn't bear it, and I felt for the young man so full of passion and with nowhere to take it. To my surprise, he led the group with a lamp of his own raised high, polished and martial, silver sword at his side. It was Paul who was beyond all hope of salvation. Mara and Eugen half carried, half dragged him along between the two of them.

Florin reached us, all unruly dirty chestnut hair and boyish grin. "Hi, Perdy. You look well. Miss Anna, I guess I should introduce myself? I'm not sure I remember the last time we met."

Mara elbowed him as she passed. "Unfortunately, we do.".

"Saints, Mara, I said I was sorry. Let me be."

They dumped Paul into a chair unceremoniously and Mara hugged me, which was sweet and unexpected.

"I'm very sorry about what happened. We're here if there's anything you need. We brought a lot of ale and some fresh loaves. And I'm very sorry about him too." She thrust her head toward Paul, who was slumped across table and chair like a dirty dishrag. "We had to hold him down and force it into him, at first. But it had to be done, what with his father's funeral being tonight."

"His father's…."

They all stopped and stared at me, then at one another.

Eugen spoke first. "We're so unused to strangers, sometimes we don't know what you don't know."

Mara pitched in. "Paul is Reverend Andrei's son. We're all going to the funeral after this. You too."

I froze for a moment, thinking about how Paul had called him 'Father' and how I'd assumed it meant the same to him as it did to the rest of us. How many assumptions would I get wrong before I learned to stop making them?

"So you got him drunk because he's grieving?"

"Yeah. When someone dies, we drink. The closer you are to the deceased, the more you have to drink. It helps ease the soul into the afterlife if people who loved the departed aren't busy holding on to them here."

"That…" I thought for a moment and couldn't find anything comforting to say. "Makes sense."

"Is that not how you do it where you're from? Do people not drink for funerals?" Mara was already fussing with satchels, pulling out candles and tools and supplies for the house.

"Not professionally, no."

"Well. Whatever the case, you're in this too. So, bottoms up."

She had unpacked a seemingly never-ending series of leather-sealed jars while she spoke, and placed one in each of our hands. With all of us together and the light from their lamps, the house felt almost warm and friendly. I couldn't be more grateful to be among them that evening.

We ate and told lewd jokes and enjoyed the company. There was no talk of death or Whispers at the table, and even Paul got a little food and water down, to better 'prepare him for the next dunk', as Eugen put it. When we were finished, we cleaned up and made another pot of spicy tea.

Florin sat next to Perdy on the step right by the fire. He hovered over her and tried very hard not to sound like he was prying, but at the same time find out all he could about her day. He even got a little annoyed at the shutter situation, admonished her for not telling him what she was up to, and shot me a cutting look. Knowing very well what the feelings behind that look were, I couldn't help but forgive him. I wasn't far off from falling for her, myself.

Mara and Eugen sat with me at the table, nursing the half-sleeping Paul. Eugen lit a cigarette that smelled like winter cakes and tangy berries; the smoke rising from it was a steely shade of blue against the reds and oranges of our lamps and fire.

"Have the Whispers always been here?"

They didn't seem startled by my question.

"You've asked more questions today than we do in a year." Mara had her boots up on the table and sipped her tea out of a chipped china cup covered in elderberry patterns. "I think so. We don't know, for sure. Not really. But Eugen is the expert here."

"Expert, no less. Well, fancy that. Considering I can't even observe that which I'm studying, I suppose that's as true as it can be."

"You don't…" I tried to remember the expression Paul had used, "…walk the Tides, then?"

"No. But I'm a fan of history and decent at mathematics, so I'm training to join the Praedictors' Guild in a few years. Among other things, they study all the recounts of Tides, all the way back as far as anyone can remember, looking for patterns."

Lazy coils of blue wrapped around his fingers and hair. It was fascinating to watch his boyish demeanor fade and grow into that of a bard at the mere mention of the word 'history'. We waited, rapt, to hear more.

"It's said that when the first people settled here, many months, maybe years, would pass between Tides. At first, nobody even knew what they were, so we only know when they happened by journal entries mentioning spirits and hauntings. People guessed the phases of the moon brought them, which is obviously wrong. Then they started connecting them to the stars. It was all very unscientific. The few who saw them were tortured and burned as heretics."

My stomach clenched painfully and all the food in it turned to writhing snakes. Nobody noticed the sweat on my lip, and I stood, pretending to take more tea from the kettle to make sure they didn't. Eugen went on, content to be talking about his favorite topic, unaware of the echo his words found in my own past.

"And the Tides then were said to be much more delicate. They didn't reach as far or last as long. The town was well settled before they ever figured it out. Then, for a while, it seemed like they could be peaceful neighbors...until the whole town vanished. That was the first Whisperwood, about eight generations ago."

"They were all gone, truly?"

"Without a trace. People, horses, buildings. Everything. People came looking, and eventually settled again, discounting the whole thing as superstition and witchery. The whole cycle started again, only the Tides came faster and harder. Friendship only lasted maybe a generation. Then the Guild was set up to track them, the Wardens to contain them. We have evidence that Praedictors used to go into the woods to take measurements and try to discover how it works. Then, for some reason, they stopped."

"You don't know why?"

"It's a contentious topic that neither the mayor nor the Guild elders want to discuss. They seem convinced talking about it would bring harm. Whatever it is, they all seem to agree that we're to study from an 'agreeable distance', whatever that means."

Mara nodded. "It means 'not at all'. They want everyone to act like it's not there, but still sacrifice their lives, trapped in this town, never knowing the truth."

Florin rose, his voice burning with the fire he'd just warmed himself by. "And if you try to leave, they stop you. If you want to have a life outside, they curse you. If you want to be a warrior, they set you to smithing horseshoes instead."

The argument was clearly personal to him. It was obvious he held himself like a soldier, and his hand never strayed far from the light but sharp sword at his hip.

Paul raised his head from the table, pointing at the ceiling. "Foolsh, and—"

Suddenly, we felt a lurch.

Florin drew his weapon in an instant. He looked at me, then at Perdy, then mouthed, "No."

Another lurch. It was like being in deep water and feeling a current move. Not unpleasant, simply odd. Mara clutched Paul's shoulder so hard her knuckles went white.

Eugen stood too, and shouted as though he could argue with the unseen waves. "No! Not now!"

He started moving toward Paul, drawing a knife from his boot, but only made it a few steps. A third lurch, and they were all gone. Only Perdy and I remained, stock-still where we stood, and Paul, dreary-eyed and confused.

CHAPTER ELEVEN

Double Coated

Paul slurred and wobbled. "What the...bollocsh...."

"Be quiet!" Perdy rushed to him and ducked under his armpit, lifting him from the chair. "We have to get out of here, right now. This house isn't Warded at all. They might know we're—"

Something heavy thumped against the door, and we all jumped. Paul went a long way toward sobering up right quick. I saw a blurry outline of something pressing up against the door on this side, holding it shut. An afterimage of our friends, perhaps.

"This is bad. Tide?"

"You catch on quickly. There shouldn't have been one, but the Praedictors still get it wrong sometimes."

Again, I was frustrated by how little I knew. "Assuming whatever's out there means us harm—"

Another loud thump shook the dust from in between the door boards.

Perdy jumped. "Safe to assume."

"How do we defend against them?"

"Whatever we do, we better be very careful! We don't know what's going on here. Injuring any of theirs? Anna, we could start a war."

"I've no intention of hurting anyone, or any thing, but we need to do something!"

"I...."

She looked around, lost and confused. "We need a way out. We need to get to the safely Warded areas. The brewery, maybe? The chapel is closest. I don't know what's out there, so I can't be sure how we—"

The door almost jumped out of its hinges that time, and Paul straightened up for a moment.

"I think itsh trouble."

I started moving. "The bedroom. Come on."

We helped Paul along. Perdy opened the door, and he walked right into the frame, but he was getting better by the second. She shut the door behind us, hoping to buy another few moments, but I pulled it open again.

"What are you—"

"I have an idea!"

I was lucky it wasn't a heavy door, and luckier still we'd broken one of the hinges opening it earlier that day. I grabbed it from beneath and lifted, and the other hinge snapped right off. Then, with a wobble, I carried it to the corner where the roof was caved in. The three horizontal beams that held all the planks together would make it an excellent ladder.

Paul took the other side of it.

"Lemme help."

We propped it up, and I pushed Perdy up first. She made it to the roof just as the main door burst open and smacked against the wall with a crack. I shoved Paul up into Perdy's arms, and turned to the entrance, knife in hand.

A massive pale arm reached in and, before I could figure out what was happening, tossed a floppy white length of cloth into the room. Inches away from the ground, it suddenly became animated. It jerked and spasmed like a rag in the wind, searched for a moment, then finally found a center of balance that allowed it to flap both sides like wings and fly right at me. By some instinct, I grabbed my knife and put my hands up.

It looked off, like an upside-down mirror image of something seen through a fog. I half expected it to pass right through me, but the cold shock of it touching me cured me of those notions. I had my arms up right in time to stop it from completely wrapping around my head.

I got lucky. My hands felt numb almost instantly, but at least they were in the right place. I grabbed the top of the thing with my left and pulled down hard with my knife-wielding right, ripping it right down the middle. It fluttered down like an empty cloak, and as soon as it hit the floor I realized that's exactly what it was, collar and buttons and all.

Beady black eyes stared at me hungrily from only steps away. There stood what looked like a massive old woman, ropes of hair hanging down to the floor, almost too big to fit in the room without stooping. The crone had no face, everything under the eyes melting into a curved beak ending in a needle-sharp point that oozed and dripped, but the eyes alone spoke volumes of loathing. Her whole body had that same hazy quality that made my eyes water.

"Anna, come on!"

Paul's voice startled me into motion as the crone took another cape off her shoulders. She tossed it down as he dragged me up, in disbelief of my senses. He threw me into Perdy's arms so hard we almost tumbled off the roof, then reached down one more time and pulled the door up after us.

"She has things that...fly...." I didn't quite know how to express myself.

Perdy held me and stroked my hair. "The coats. They don't fly far. We're safe for a minute, until she figures out a way to climb up here."

"What is she?"

Paul let the door fall next to us and sat down hard, catching his breath. "Dochia. It's fine. We're fine. It could be worse. We're fine. It's fine."

Somehow, I didn't think we were fine.

"Paul's right, it could be worse. Her purpose isn't to kill. She's a trapper. I wonder which one of us she's been sent after?" She looked at me, concerned, and I felt exposed. "Either way. The coats numb you if they wrap around you, and that poison barb puts you to sleep. Stay away from that."

"I fully intend to!"

Paul laughed and showed every last one of his frayed nerves. "What now, ladies? 'Cause I'm not sure what we just did other than postpone the inevitable."

"You said there are safe areas near here. Do the Whispers know that?"

He nodded sluggishly. "Definitely."

"Which one would we be more likely to pick?"

He pointed off to the east. "Brewery."

Screeching and thumping sounds from beneath us made it clear that the Dochia was now back outside the house and deeply unhappy. I whispered, hoping it wasn't blessed with extraordinary hearing.

"Paul, take the door there, to that corner." I aimed him toward the brewery. "Balance it up so that you can drop it on this thing. Don't look at me like that, I don't know! It might slow it down for a moment. We only need a moment."

He frowned but did as I told him.

"Perdy, the other nearby safe house is the chapel, right?"

She nodded. "It's Warded to repel predatory Whispers, and the bell has powerful properties if it comes to that."

"Good. Go stand there, in that corner, quiet as a mouse. Get ready to jump off."

I moved over to Paul, stomping and clanging my way there.

He looked appalled. "Do you want to get us taken? Is that it? Because there are easier ways!"

"Hush. We're going to draw it to this side. The obvious one. Pretend like we're climbing down. I'll stay last and drop the door on it, then rush to the other side. You help Perdy jump off when I say, then be ready to catch me."

He nodded. It was a ridiculous plan, but he nodded. I almost laughed. None of us were ever going to like this plan, and I knew it, but it was all we had. I stomped and shouted.

Paul, half-amused, joined me. "Let's climb down now while we can!" Then, quietly, "You're banking a lot on it not being very smart, Anna."

"Odds are good. Most living things aren't."

Surely enough, the pale shape appeared around the corner. I signaled to Paul that it was time for him to go to Perdy, and together they huddled and waited.

My bluff so far was correct. I was right about the Dochia coming to where there was noise, and about it being slow. I hid myself behind the door, leaning it on the side, until the creature was nearly under me, desperately searching for us. It sent out another of its rags just before I pushed the door out right on top of it. As soon as I heard the crash, I sprinted for the other side, where Paul and Perdy had already disappeared over the edge. At the last moment, something wrapped itself around my ankle, and I rolled down the side of the roof in a heap, smacking my head on the tiles before landing atop my friends.

Arms lifted me right away and carried me off, and whatever had grabbed me was gone as if evaporated, leaving behind a terrible numbness.

We were already a good two hundred paces away when the Dochia peeked out from behind the house, and we were well on our way to being hidden by the grove of trees. Then, we just ran.

CHAPTER TWELVE

Corpseside Diatribe

"You dropped a door on the Dochia." Mayor Eduard sat firmly halfway between displeasure and incredulity.

We had almost reached the chapel when the first current hit us, this time reversing into the woods. By the time the Tides withdrew completely, we were already inside and had the pleasure of materializing in front of a solemn funeral congregation.

Candlelit and smelling of paraffin, the hall overflowed with people in dark clothing wielding neatly embroidered white handkerchiefs. A plain pine coffin sat before the pulpit, where a confused-looking man in violet robes was obviously in the middle of assisting the mayor in holding some sort of ceremony. The yellow light brought out every dark angle, both in the intricate carvings across each wooden beam and bench, and in the faces of the gathered crowd.

The casket was closed, but I assumed the deceased reverend was the only one in the room not giving us dirty looks, at least until Mara, Eugen, and Florin stormed through the open doors moments behind us.

"We were attacked." Florin stood in the middle of the aisle, legs apart, shoulders broad, unflinching. Sure of himself.

"Nonsense, boy."

"He's right, sir. We were. There's no doubt." Eugen lent his weight to the claim. "I can't speak on behalf of the Praedictors yet, as we have not consulted, but this was an unusual occurrence. I'm sure of it."

"Well, whatever it was, these three have sealed our fate, haven't they? Who knows what injury you've done, and what the repercussions will be!"

Paul looked tired and sore and not at all in the mood to be under any accusations. "Trust me, the ugly thing is fine. Probably not a scratch on it. Thanks for worrying. Meanwhile, this woman is bleeding. Are we going to wait for my dead father to get up and hand her a damned rag?"

I hadn't even realized that the sticky wetness down the side of my face was blood. I supposed I understood why everyone was staring at me.

One of the women near us stood and handed me her kerchief, a pristine white affair embroidered with squarish red roses. I recognized her from the trading post. She was the feisty one who nearly threatened the merchant when he didn't bring her white face powder. Now, she sat back down meekly, eyes wide, like most of the rest of them. I couldn't bear to ruin her handkerchief, so I just held it like I was daft and didn't understand what it was for.

Some murmurs rose from the pews, anxious, subdued. The mayor moved to a table off to one side and picked up an empty wooden flagon banded in iron. There was a small barrel nearby, and as he spoke, he drew a dark, rich ale from it. The smell of it was so strong it struck the back of my nose from ten steps away.

"Son, I know this is a rough evening for you. Make no mistake, we all appreciate the hardship of your situation. We will sort the politics out in due course, once the observances have been observed and the rites have been rited and all that." He swayed over to Paul with a honeyed smile on his lips. "You need to have another drink. You'll feel a lot better."

Paul took the flagon and looked for a moment at the mayor like a curious cat at a foolhardy bird. He then launched the flagon clear across the room, drenching the casket in ale and causing a great loud clang on the other side where he knocked a copper plate full of burning incense over.

Perdy jumped and called out to him, but he was beyond hearing. The mayor stared, fish-mouthed, and the whole room stood silent. Some of the men in the front row rose to their feet, sensing trouble, but they would never have made it in time.

Lightning-fast and belying his exhaustion, Paul reached out and grabbed the mayor by the neck, then threw him back, splaying him across Father Andrei's coffin. The mayor's legs grabbed for purchase in the air like those of an upended beetle.

"You stop that right now!" A large, red-bearded man in a leather apron approached the coffin, but Paul nailed him to the floor with one perfervid look.

"Keep moving if you'd like for me to crush his windpipe. I know some of you would and some wouldn't, and I can never keep track of who is on which side."

The man chewed on his whiskers for a moment but made no further progress. Gurgling sounds from the mayor were the only thing that broke the dead silence, but Paul wasn't nearly done with him. He pulled a little letter opener from behind his back, stuck it into the wood of the coffin above his head, and smiled.

"Now I'm going to talk, and you're going to listen. You and Father too."

His grin, even seen from the side, was terrifying. I wouldn't have wanted that rabid, end-of-the-rope look directed at me outside of the bedroom.

"You listen. I've had enough of this nonsense. Enough of your fearful and tearful ways. They are here, touching upon us every single day, your denial putting everyone I care about in danger, and whether or not you can see them is none of my goddamned concern."

He spat those last three words through his clenched teeth, leaning down into his captive with each word. He and the casket and the table it lay on wobbled with each shove, and the little dagger, precariously perched on its point, swayed, clocking the mayor on the head on every downswing.

"It's my turn to do something now, and you can be sure I'm going to do it. And if you thought you could come to my father's funeral and lobby, well."

He gave the neck between his fingers another squeeze. There was no doubting the seriousness of his threats, so nobody dared move. I got the feeling that many were also terribly curious about the outcome of that little political debate.

"We are going to use our resources. We are going to demand more of the Praedictors and the Wardens. We are going to send the Walkers –" at this, he thumped his chest once, hard, "– in. And we are going to behave like modern, civilized people. And if you think you codgers with inherited titles have a chance against those of us who have been training our whole lives to finally do something –" he lifted the mayor, blue-lipped, off the casket and into the air so that only his toes tapped codes on the ground, "– you are crazy, as well as old."

He must have been made of steel cables underneath those baggy clothes to be able to lift a much taller man like that. The onlookers began to stir and protest again, but he let the mayor down at once and turned to them.

"We only need a handful of you for the funeral rites, and my father is graciously donating some of his wake time for us to talk about the future. If you're in any way uncomfortable with this, see yourself out now."

Some shot straight for the door without a word. The short, violet-clad man with a greasy twirled beard and a red face grabbed Eduard and guided him out, pretending for all the world like he was behind the idea, even though the mayor, clutching at his throat and gargling softly, clearly couldn't wait to be out of there. Most of the people gathered came over to make apologies.

"I'm with you, Paul, of course, but my mother…you know how they are."

"We would stay, but I have to get the children home."

"We can't afford to make our landlords mad, otherwise we'd be with you."

To each he nodded and shook the hands of those who offered. It didn't seem like he was trying to make any more enemies. Finally, the last group left, and Eugen shut the door, enclosing the dozen of us left in silence and mournful, flickering candlelight.

CHAPTER THIRTEEN

Funeral Wrongs

"What now, brave leader?"

Still among us was the red-bearded man who had tried to stop Paul from killing the mayor. He poured ale for all of us and held the last one out for Paul, then drew it back just as he reached for it.

"If you throw this one at me, I'll castrate you."

"If you reach down there, you better count your fingers, Rareş."

"Stuffed a weasel in your breeches again, have you, boy?"

Paul laughed and finally took the ale, drinking it dry. "I'm glad you're still here. For a moment there, I thought you'd changed your mind. I had visions of you forging iron horseshoes for Eduard for the rest of your life."

Rareş spat at Paul's boot, but Paul jumped out of the way with a smile.

"Horseshoes are no work for a smith. Don't be daft. I just wanted to make sure you didn't get hanged as a murderer. Or get taken down by someone else less cautious than I."

"How thoughtful of you."

"Piss off." The hefty smith wiped beer out of his beard and belched like thunder. "You better have some right good plans for what we're going to do now that half the town hopes we walk into the woods and never walk back out again."

"I do. I've had them for years, if only big old bags of wind like you could shut up long enough to hear them."

My hand shook on my cup, and I lost track of their conversation. The white powder woman – Ancuţa, I remembered – was still with us too. She came over with a cup of water and cleaned the blood off my face while I sipped my ale. Florin held Perdy under his cloak and she was almost sleeping. Eugen and Mara, as well as most of the other townsfolk present, listened to Paul and Rareş speak. Some offered their advice. I was too tired to follow along.

"You'll be darn lucky if this doesn't leave you with a scar for your efforts."

"Thank you, Ancuţa."

"You know my name?"

"I saw you at the post. You were looking for white powder for your face."

"Ah, yes."

She kept wiping away at my cheek and chewed at her lip at the same time. Voices rose toward the front of the room, but while heated, there was no anger in them. Mostly, it was Paul talking about establishing the 'level of animosity' and Rareş calling him a dull axe.

Ancuţa sighed as though she'd reached a decision. "I suppose I might as well tell you it wasn't face powder I was after."

"It wasn't?"

"No. My face is quite perfectly spotless without it. Besides, lye powder is extremely dangerous. Only a fool uncultured in the ways of women would ever believe that it has any cosmetic uses."

I felt like a bit of a fool myself, but the idea that I was uncultured in the ways of most women was not new information to me.

"The lye powder serves in our warding rituals. I'm a Warden. It's my job."

"I've heard of your guild. You're in charge of putting up the Wards that protect the town."

"You've probably heard a great deal over the last few days. Frankly, if you're not doubting your sanity right now, I am."

"I've seen enough to force belief into me."

"So it's true, you really are a Walker. I'd heard rumors. Good! Town hasn't had a complement of three who can Walk the Tides in a long time. I'll have to teach you some tricks. How to stay safe. It can't make up for what should be years of training, and good luck remembering any of it, but it's better than nothing."

"I would love to learn more."

Her blond braids framed her sharp face, and the harelip made her look ever pouty and pensive. She nodded at me for a moment, perhaps agreeing that I might be able to learn something from her after all.

"Later. We have to mind the funeral first." She turned to where a small argument had already started and raised her voice. "Paul? Maybe now that the windbags have finally cleared the floor, it'd be appropriate that I take over and do the job?"

He considered something for a second, then nodded. Everyone returned to their seats and he took a place right next to me, filling me with a rush of gratitude for the support. Ancuţa went around the room, murmuring about what a useless sack of potatoes the mayor and his purple-clad priest had been, and blew out most of the candles. She lit a bunch of dry herbs that oozed indigo smoke in every direction. As she moved, she made sure to blow it toward every row of benches.

The smell made me queasy. "Paul?"

"Hmm?"

"What's happening?"

He came out of deep thoughts and his icy gaze mellowed a little as he focused on me. "Oh, she's – we're – skipping the Christian ceremony and moving forward to the more practical, usual customs. Nothing outlandish."

"Where I come from, we dress the dead in white and recite funny poetry about their lives. We pay women in black to cry and wail, because the louder the cries the more likely it is they'll be allowed into the afterlife."

His brow furrowed, but he smiled a little, and I was happy to have amused him. "Fair enough, I guess outlandish is a relative term. I'd love to hear what kind of poetry people would write about my father."

"What would you write?"

"I'm not sure. I didn't even know him all that well. I think he meant more to me as my moral leader than as my father."

Ancuța broke into a gentle song that most of the others followed along to, and after a measure Paul joined in too. It was unlike any other funeral song I'd ever heard, sweet but ending in cries that had the sound of war chants about them.

She flipped the casket lid open with a clack that made me jump. Chills passed down my arms. Everyone else watched calmly, almost bored. Across the aisle from us sat a little boy playing with a doll made out of corn husks and string. If he wasn't worried, I wouldn't be either.

Ancuța, fingers as light as those of a magician, produced a gold coin out of thin air and placed it on the left eye of the corpse. Another, silver this time, went on the right. I knew that ritual; we did it too – the coins were payment to be given to the ferryman that took us all across the river of death. What did the ferryman need them for, I wondered? Did he pay taxes? Need new trousers?

She then took a long, expensive-looking knife from the nearby table.

When she tore open his shirt across the chest, I couldn't help myself any longer. "Paul?"

He went on singing, and I realized I'd barely whispered his name. The boy across the aisle was half reclined on his mother and still limply animating his doll.

"Paul?"

"Hmm?" He turned to me, concerned, but not annoyed at the interruption. "What's wrong? You seem pale."

"What am I about to witness?"

"Oh—"

There was a wet crack when Ancuța stuck the knife up to the shaft right under the reverend's sternum, angled up toward his head. She'd had to put both hands on the handle and lean into it to do so. Judging by the length of the blade, the point of it must have been tickling the inside of his spine.

"You guys don't do this, I guess? We have…."

She shifted her grip so that she could push the knife forward toward his collarbone, sawing up and down, the flesh squelching as she did so.

"…and they inhabit the heart of the dead…."

The strain visible on her brow made it worse. A droplet of sweat fell into what was now a significant gash in his thorax.

"…cause all kinds of problems if you don't destroy…."

The body sprayed her with fine, pink-gray chunks that landed on her cheek and in her hair. She pressed her elbow down on his neck, and the sawing motions got smaller and faster. Bone dust rose into the air and she inhaled a pale loop of it.

"…under the eyes of witnesses, otherwise they take possession of…."

The little boy across the aisle dozed off.

"…the coins usually go after, but she likes to show off how she can perform the rite without shaking the head, which is said to be the mark of a…."

I shifted my body on the bench so that I could turn away and press my forehead to Paul's shoulder. He was startled, but didn't stop me. The coolness of his leather waistcoat on my face helped stave off the waves of dizziness somewhat as I tried to take stock of my chances of making it through without throwing up.

I'd never seen bodies treated so poorly outside of war, and the reverent context made it all the more jarring. I hadn't expected anything like it. My legs shook violently. I opened my eyes to check if maybe that would make the dizziness better and saw the boy had set his corn doll down and was staring at me. He poked his tongue out, and I pressed my face against Paul again. My heart pounded in my throat and I couldn't calm down, even though I was probably in the least amount of danger I'd been since arriving.

Paul put his arm around me, and I stayed there for what seemed like an endless vigil.

★   ★   ★

We stood watch all night. The bald, red-bearded smith nailed the coffin shut tightly when it was all done and passed large iron bands over both ends like those used to keep barrels tightly sealed. He'd brought them, red-hot, from outside where they'd been sitting in a fire all night. When he placed them onto the wood using huge metal tongs, the sap sizzled and released a not-unpleasant smell like that of burned sugar. Then he poured buckets of cool water over them. Steam filled the room and combined with the sappy smell to create an oddly hypnotic atmosphere. My head was full of warm cotton.

The iron bands tightened as they cooled and the wooden boards crackled, settling in together snugly. I doubted even worms would get through for a while, not until the wood rotted at the very least. Paul explained that the corpse would be rotted too, by that time, and the Whispers wouldn't care about it as much.

It felt like a lot of work to go through for what was now essentially a wooden box full of sausage stuffing.

We took turns standing watch in threes, as per custom. We slept on the benches and drank ale and ate dark wheat bread full of seeds and spicy herbs. They told me it served to confound the noses of those things that were looking for the deceased. Numbness took over me, and the ale helped. I slept on and off, but deeply. Not long enough for any dreams, at least. Small mercies.

By the time dawn came round, most of the gathering had gone to their own homes. Mara and Perdy left too, and came back a short time later with a large basket carried between the two of them in which they'd carefully arranged many small jars and two huge kettles full of steaming hot tea and coffee. I took a cupful of tea and it tasted like mint, pepper, and pine needles, the sharp vapors traveling up my nose and soothing the ache under my skull.

"Perdy and I have to go back and tend to the brewery." Mara picked up my empty cup and placed it in her basket with a clink. "But I'm really grateful to you for choosing to stay with her, Anna. With us. You didn't have to get involved, but I'm glad you did."

"I couldn't just leave you. I know you'd be fine without me, but I'm not sure I'd be fine without all of you. Not after what I've seen."

"I suppose all this must be very strange to you. If it's any comfort, we were all pretty terrified of you too, when you first walked in."

"Were you, really?"

"Yeah. Everything unknown is scary. Now it already feels like you've been with us for a very long time. I could see myself teaching you brewing someday. Maybe the more you learn about us, the easier it will be for you too."

"No other choice, is there?"

"None. You physically cannot abandon us right now." She grinned.

"Then, I volunteer."

She nodded and looked over to Eugen and Paul, caught in a heated debate over a notebook.

"They're making plans to take a trip inside later today. Eugen is going to check in with the Praedictors first. Florin's walking Perdy to the brewery, but I wouldn't be surprised if they were there later too."

"Won't you be?"

"Someone will have to keep Paul's ambitions well-funded. Luckily, someone inherited a highly profitable business from her parents."

She smiled again, and for a moment the only sign of tiredness on her face was the paleness of her thin lips.

I felt heartened by her. "Is there anything I can help with?"

"I'd love to take you with me, but the mayor wants you."

"The mayor? Isn't he...why would he...?"

"He's fine. Major bruising around the pride area, but he'll survive. He wants to meet you where Reverend Andrei died so he can ask you some questions."

I'd forgotten all about my interview, and wished the mayor had too. It couldn't possibly be a pleasant encounter, not after last night, and more likely it was his way of regaining control of the situation. Oh, how I loathed being regained control of.

Eugen stormed past us, stopping only briefly to kiss Mara's cheek and squeeze my shoulder.

Paul followed him shortly and crouched down next to the bench I was sat on. "Anna, I'm going to have to ask you a favor."

I would have been helpless to refuse had I wanted to. "Yes."

"You don't know what it is, yet. And you might not want to—"

"You need me to be with you when you cross over into the Whispers' lands."

"The Unspoken. Yes. Well, not to come with me, exactly. I doubt that you can even reach inside properly without a lot of hard training. Just to be on the outskirts. Seeing how you perceive the border, untrained as you are, could be interesting. Besides, I never hoped we'd have a Walker drop into our lap. It was only Perdy and me for a long time. I'd rather you started learning sooner, rather than later."

"Yes."

"Can I ask you one thing?"

I nodded.

"Why?"

"Why what?"

"Why are you so willing to do this for us?"

I thought about it for a moment, wondering which answer would please him most. I never wanted to be found again, it was true, but I could have stayed in Whisperwood and not gotten involved in any of this. Taken up baking. So why? I had nothing to lose. I had nobody to care for. I was curious. I liked them. I felt sorry for them. I hoped to gain knowledge of things I'd never even dreamed of before. I wanted to see if this was related to the inexplicable things I'd seen back home. I hoped to prevent more death. I wanted to justify my existence, assuage my guilt for being. I wanted, more than anything, to be useful.

"Because I want to be the kind of person who does the right thing. I haven't always been."

His eyes like frosty lakes held mine for a while, and whatever he saw in there seemed to satisfy him. "I don't want to waste any time. We'll be ready at noon."

"I'll be there."

We parted ways and, as I left the chapel, I noticed yet again how stunning the stained glass was now that early dawn sunlight was pouring in through the multicolored shapes. If nothing else remained behind me when I died but something as beautiful as that, I'd consider myself lucky indeed.

PART TWO

FEAR AND DELIGHT

CHAPTER FOURTEEN

Questions in a World of Gloom

Pine trees loomed in feral grace, no less fearsome during the day than they had been two nights ago, but stiller. I spent the walk down the hill distracting myself from the anxiety of revisiting that place by practicing what I'd say to the mayor in my head. It was a futile effort; I had no idea what he would ask me and even if I did, real life never went the way my mind predicted. It was the only comfort I had, so I did it anyway.

A cloud of cigar smoke and annoyance signaled his position.

At the edge of the woods a handful of people milled anxiously about, measuring things with lengths of yarn, and drawing strange shapes on the ground in lines of trickled sand by the laws of some arithmetic unknown to me. An older man in a pork-pie hat was placing wooden stakes equal distances apart, clearly marking out some sort of border. It seemed odd, however, that when he was done, he went about removing them, then placing them in the exact same positions, almost as though he was only pretending to be busy. But what did I know?

The mayor paced and puffed, his hat stuck haphazardly in his belt.

"Good morning, Lord Eduard." It struck me as I was speaking that the title couldn't possibly be real. They might have learned about it from books, but there was nobody who could grant it. He'd probably given it to himself.

The death glare he shot me could have melted a snowball in a witch's mouth.

"Look up 'good' in the dictionary." His voice was raspy and pained, and he'd wrapped a magenta silk scarf many times around his neck. It made him look like an angry mechanical turkey that ran on coal and trailed smoke. "Hurry up. I haven't got all day."

I sped up over the last ten paces and nearly tumbled when my foot slipped on a dew-slick clump of grass. The obedient man with the oily beard that had escorted Mayor Eduard from the chapel stood by, a ragged notebook and pencil in hand.

"We already know most of what happened. We're just missing some details that I sincerely hope you can confirm for us."

"I'd be glad to, sir."

He glared again, probably convinced I was mocking him. All I wanted was to end the interview and get a quick round of sleep before the afternoon's Unspoken visit.

"I'd take this seriously if I were you. At the very least, you should be eager to dispel the rumors that you had anything to do with this death, if not those of a more occult nature as well."

"You said you already knew—"

"I do, but the citizens…." He let the implication trail, banking on my being clever enough to chase it. "They say you're a bringer of ill luck. Not entirely unjustified either."

There were very clearly two kinds of whispers in Whisperwood. Wondering which was the more dangerous of the two was like wondering whether you'd rather die hanged or eaten by a bear.

"Are you superstitious, Mr. Mayor?" I wondered whether he'd notice the change in how I addressed him.

His eyes flicked to the woods for the briefest of moments. "Superstition implies irrationality. I am afraid."

"Of the Whispers?"

"Spitblood, be quiet about what you don't understand!"

All around us, mutters died down and people stilled, quickly crossing themselves and spitting in their bosom before glancing back to the mayor. He yanked at the collar of his shirt and spat in it, confirming my suspicions that he was just as tied to the traditions here as Miss Crosman. I made a note to ask Mara and the others more about the rituals townies used, and whether any of them had any real purpose beyond increasing the amount of laundry one needed to do on account of all the spat-upon shirts.

"For these notes dutifully kept by Mr. Scridon, here, please state your full name." He settled into a formal, rhythmic tone that immediately raised my warning bells. The last time I'd heard it, it came from the man who condemned me to death.

"Anna Maria Haller." A slight tremor passed through me at the thought of giving him my surname, but it was an irrational fear. There was no way anyone here would possibly know me, nor the man I ran from, nor why.

"What was your business here on the night Reverend Father Andrei Roman died?"

I snapped back to attention. "Exploring the area. Chapels are always a good place to learn a little about the locals. You can tell a lot about the history of a place from the graveyard."

"Where were you standing when the attack happened?"

"I was hidden behind that bush for the great majority of it. There'd be evidence—"

"The boot you lost. And you saw the reverend go near the forest?"

"I saw most of it. I only missed a little as I was approaching, and then again when I struggled to get free of the thing that was h—"

"We'll get to that. Scridon, write that down. Saw most of it. You saw when the reverend launched his attack?"

"Attack? He did no such thing."

"So you didn't see it?"

"No!"

"Scridon. Didn't see when the reverend attacked."

My voice rose involuntarily. "Because he didn't do it."

"You said it yourself, you missed some pieces. You can't be sure he didn't."

"You can't be sure he did!"

"Of course. You watched most of the confrontation, then what?"

"I tried to go help, but something was holding me back. A vine or tie of some sort; but there was nothing I could see."

"Scridon. Nothing that she could see. Got it?"

Scridon seemed an expert at writing and nodding simultaneously.

"Good. Once you got free, what did the Whisper –" He whispered the word, drawing a circle in the dirt with his toes, then breaking it with a cross. That was new. "– do?"

"It retreated back into the woods."

"Make a note. Peacefully retreated."

I couldn't bear it any longer. "Why are you doing this?"

"Doing what? This is the due process of the law. I'll thank you not to interfere."

"There's nothing due or lawful about it. You're trying to make it sound like this attack was provoked and deserved. I'm not a fool. I've seen plenty of misinformation and manipulation before."

"And that gives you license to comment on something you know nothing about, arguing against the experience and opinions of people who actually live here?"

"A devil's a devil, no matter the scarf he wears."

"Scridon, don't write that down!"

He grabbed the top page of the notebook Mr. Scridon had been obediently scribbling away in and ripped it out violently along with several others. Everyone stopped to watch them flutter to the ground. The mayor's scarf slipped off in the excitement, and large yellow thumb marks were visible on the front of his neck. He took a moment to compose himself, tightened his scarf, and turned with a strained toothy smile to Mr. Scridon, who was bending to pick up the scattered pages with trembling hands.

"Leave it. We can recompose this interview from memory, can't we?" The air around him was charged with a manic heat, and I found my heart doing double time. I'd never been good at facing anger, especially that of my elders, and no part of me found him comical anymore.

"Miss Haller, I'm not pleased at all with this performance. I had hoped you'd see reason and understand the need to settle things in a peaceful manner, without agitating the rest of the citizens unduly. We could have reassured everyone there was no need to fear.... No, I see your raving insurgents have already poisoned you beyond my ability to cure. You're excused."

I wasted no time in taking that opportunity.

"One final thing," he said, "political debate is not for the faint of heart, nor for the philosophically inclined. And in our case, it's a lethal game. Remain a tourist, if you still can."

The sun rose fully as I stomped up the hill to the now-empty chapel, angry at something I couldn't name. I slunk inside for a moment's reprieve from the sun. Already, I missed the reverend's presence, and took comfort at least in a closer study of his legacy, the beautiful painted glass that would be his final sermon.

My journal was in my hand before I knew it, even though I hardly expected the mysteries of Whisperwood to be revealed to me through a handful of colored shards. But the process of questioning always settled my panicked mind, and it certainly needed settling now.

If Father Andrei used the same kind of logic that traditional church windows used, it would stand to reason that the first two figures nearest the altar were higher up in the hierarchy. That meant the shadow stag backed by a golden sun was a patron saint, as was the woman across from him. She sat in the crook of a branch, her hair green and tangled with the canopy. They were both majestic in their own way, he arrogant and resplendent, she secretive and menacing. Beneath the stag's feet, bones poked out from the dirt. I hadn't noticed those before. Beneath the roots of the green girl's tree, books were hidden.

Danger and knowledge, hand in hand. And wasn't that just how it always went?

I'd hoped to find the Dochia among the twelve paintings, but no luck. Instead, on the far end, a silver moon shone over a violet sky, and silhouetted shadows passed before it, seven, swift and fleeting, toothy and grim. The bottom of my stomach tingled at the sight. I had the feeling Father Andrei had painted his own demise.

None of the other images sparked any recognition, so I wrote down general descriptions of them along with some rough sketches and walked back down the short path to the cottage.

It pained me to see that the attack left it in far worse a state now than it had been before Perdy and I had found it, but there was little I could do. I tossed some rags down by the surprisingly still-warm embers in the hearth, and my cloak over the rags, and tried to sleep, but really spent most of that time tossing and turning to the tune of distant voices. It sounded like somewhere to the north; they were already preparing for the exploration of the Unspoken in a few hours' time.

At least the voices kept me company.

★   ★   ★

"Don't worry. It won't be as bad as you think."

I'd dreamed the words that wretched man had said over and over. It often started with his grip tight on my arm, and the clanging shut of the cellar door. Sometimes what followed was a nonsense anxiety nightmare of vivid, unconnected images. Sometimes I dreamed of his mock trial in every detail, gagged and powerless to respond. He told my family and friends I was unclean. They replied they'd long suspected it, or didn't reply at all.

This time, I shared the cellar with Father Andrei's corpse. Alec prodded and tortured the body right in front of me, but I felt the pain. I was swallowed whole by indescribable fear at how it would feel when he finally turned on me. He did, and behind him, the reverend rose to his feet, behooved and behorned, the heat from his fiery eyes burning my skin. Alec screamed in terror, crashing out the door, and I woke.

CHAPTER FIFTEEN

Blink Out

The air was abuzz with excitement, reminding me vividly of the time I'd witnessed a demonstration of the new electric currents, the way my hair stood on end and the smell of progress and curiosity.

Paul stood in the middle of a small crowd, a conductor of mysterious forces, readying his diplomatic mission to the new world. They'd set up to one side of the stone arch near the main road and bustled around happily, seeking out his counsel. It was a stark contrast to the anxious and fearful movements of the mayor's men at dawn. The one similarity was the ineffable presence of Mr. Scridon, this time sitting on a stone bench a good distance away, but still furiously scribbling in his notebook. No doubt keeping things under control for the mayor, who dared not show his face.

I'd almost slept through it. Florin had come over just as I cleared my head of a disturbing dream I couldn't quite remember. He walked me into town under the midday sun and kept both our minds busy with stories of brave adventurers and local legends, clearly almost more enamored with travel and freedom than I was. What a hard lot for a man like him in a place like that.

We stopped short of entering the crowd, not wanting to disturb Paul in his duties, but he brightened the moment he spotted us and headed our way. As he made his way through, people reached out to pat him on the shoulder or shake his hand. Ancuṭa seemed to want to do the same, but instead grabbed him by the arm and wouldn't let go. They spoke terse words that didn't quite reach us; he yanked his arm away, and she left in a huff, throwing her hands in the air and muttering.

When he reached us, he was all smiles and anticipation. "Flor! Anna. I was beginning to worry."

"It looks like everyone in town came to lend a hand. And then some."

Paul lowered his chin and frowned at Florin. "You know very well half of them are only here to see me fail."

I couldn't resist. "Ancuţa?"

"You saw that? No, she doesn't want me to fail. She just thinks I will. Her family and mine go back generations, a Warden in each of hers and a Walker in mine. They're the main reason why we haven't gone out for years, why we never attempt communication. Jumpy startlewrens, all of them. I'm done with it. I'm close to done with this whole town."

Florin crossed his arms, looking very much like a soldier's statue. "I think more people care for you than you suspect, but as you wish. What can we do?"

"I need you with me to do a once-over of the gear. I don't know enough about armor to feel confident. Anna, Eugen is right there by the arch with his Master, and he's asked for you."

Eugen waved at me as I approached. Next to him stood a tall man with a long gray braid and shockingly light beard. His beard barely hid a long-tired face, and his skin was lighter than I'd ever seen before. He kept a steady hand on Eugen's shoulder and seemed comfortable around the young man.

Eugen shook my hand; his was awkward and sweaty-palmed. "Anna! We don't have much time. Paul is pushing us like a madman. I've never seen him so spirited."

"If he's not careful, he'll get voted mayor soon."

"He'd loathe that, wouldn't he? Anna, I'd like you to meet Master Artjom. He's my teacher and one of three Praedictor Masters."

The Master carefully pulled on the tips of his leather glove and slid it off his intricately tattooed and finely scarred hand, then extended that hand to me in greeting. "Miss Anna. We have heard much about you in very little time. I'm pleased to see you're as interested in our fate as we are in yours." His voice was gentle, but his accent had a harder edge to it than I expected.

"Master Artjom, I'm pleased to meet you. I'm sorry to say I don't know anything of what you do."

"You might have to learn in quite the hurry. We predict Tides to the best of our abilities, and try to map the movements of the Unspoken."

"It moves?"

"That…" he glanced at Paul and Florin in the distance; they were laughing like schoolchildren over a slipped strap that smacked Paul in the eye, "…is a long story. I never thought the day would come when we'd have to skip all the history lessons, but it seems our services are in high demand all of a sudden."

"How can I help here?"

"You're not actually going inside, so the mapping aspect is blessedly out for now. Luckily too, since this one is miserable at what is, arguably, the truly beautiful and complex art of a Praedictor."

Eugen rolled his eyes. "I never have the patience to doodle. History and time are far more fascinating."

"For now, you're here as an alarm system, of sorts. Paul's going in the deep, ready to make a new first contact with whoever's out there. Eugen is supposed to only stay on the shore and study it. Predictors can only be drawn into the Unspoken by a highly experienced Walker, and we're woefully short on those. As for you, our unseasoned tool, we're hoping you can act as an in-between, tell us more about the shallows and keep an eye out for danger. Eugen will have plenty of time to explain on the way."

Eugen gave me his broadest grin yet as he grabbed my hand. "Anna, we're going to be the first to properly measure and map the edge of this phenomenon. The source of the Tides. And we can't do it without you."

Artjom reached into his jacket pocket and pulled out a little glass sphere encased in gold. Inside the bauble, thin clocklike hands jiggled in every direction. He shook it once, then allowed the hands to settle into a stable position.

"We have to wait seven minutes, just to be sure there's no Tide now. There was one forecast, but with a very low chance. After that, we're clear until dawn tomorrow, and you can be off."

I had a strange sensation in the pit of my stomach. It was like I was a child again, called out to answer at a lesson I hadn't listened to and wasn't prepared for. It must have shown on my face, because Eugen then said the one thing that could have made me even more nervous about it all.

"Don't worry. Nothing can go wrong."

★ ★ ★

Dangerous things are often beautiful, and I was looking at something that was clearly both.

Eugen and I stood side by side, carrying a bulky square box full of measuring equipment between us. Two large copper tubes that powered a recording device occupied most of it. A needle moved up and down on a slowly rotating wax cylinder, leaving a series of dots and scratches that were, for sure, very meaningful to the Praedictors; they spelled nothing intelligible to me, however.

My role was to be a sort of measuring tool, myself. The way I saw the edges of the Unspoken, the way they reacted to me, apparently all of it could prove pertinent because I was untrained and a stranger. Artjom called me 'raw'.

Paul smirked, licked his lips, and called me 'steak'.

He walked ahead of us, testing each tread gingerly before taking it. We were only a leisurely walk away from the crowd of onlookers – and the mayor's relentless spy – hanging back safely behind the arch, and yet it seemed like the atmosphere was that of an entirely different world.

The air was cold, colder than even the cover of lush blue-green pines could justify. Master Artjom had dressed us in thickly padded leather jackets sewn with silver string. "For protection against things both physical and unphysical," he said. That was all well and good, but none of my meetings with Whispers so far made me look forward to the prospect of needing protection from them, and the cold still seeped through and made me shiver.

Ahead of us, shimmering strands like dew-slick spiderwebs hung among the dark trees, lit up by an eerie brightness of their own. They cast lines of light across the waxy needles and reflected in so many little shards it was hard to tell what was light and what was shadow. I asked Eugen about them, but he could see nothing out of the ordinary, nor could he, apparently, feel the strange chill.

"It means we must be nearing the edge. Only a Walker like you or Paul could find the entrance, and even then, only with a lot of training. I just see a forest that feels…weird."

Artjom was right, there was a lot to be learned by sending in a trained Walker, an untrained one, and someone who was immune to the effects altogether.

"Is this the border, then?"

"Not yet. As Paul crosses over, he'll fade from our view. First from mine, the moment he leaves our world. That'll be our border. We're guessing there's a neutral zone, and then he should disappear from your view too when he's properly entered the Whispers' land. That's where we will mark the Unspoken border."

"What would happen if we kept moving forward past that point?"

"Perhaps nothing. We can't follow him properly. But we might also never return."

"Right. Keeping to our side, then."

"Don't worry. We're barely going to wade into the waters at all."

Our armor was Warded; we were staying well away from danger. Paul had parcels of offerings tied around his waist, which he was to drop off as soon as he fully entered the Whisper territory, then return and call it a successful initial diplomatic contact. I knew they had packed trinkets, hand-crafted tools, and some sort of herb-cured meat he had high hopes for. We were on an exploratory mission that, including the time it would take us to get to the border itself, shouldn't last more than an hour or two. And yet, I couldn't help but feel like we took a lot of precautions for something that they insisted would be easy.

Paul moved along slowly, testing the air ahead of him with his fingers, the grass with his toes. He disturbed shimmering strands where he passed, and sometimes seemed to push them to the side like curtains, revealing the woods behind them to be darker still.

The air was thick, almost watery, and my movements felt slow. I even heard water rushing past my ears, but it must have been my own blood echoing inside my body. Flakes of golden light floated to the ground around Paul like luminescent dandelion fluff.

Engrossed in the image, I jumped when Eugen shouted "Stop!" seemingly straight into my eardrums, and I almost dropped the box on our feet.

"He's gone, I can't see him. Can you still see him?"

"Yes." I rubbed at my right ear, hot and popping. "There's a white film over his body, like he's draped in gauze, but he's still there, touching the air."

"I knew it! There's a neutral zone. That was my theory. I'll never let them hear the end of this."

He set the box down and I barely had time to do the same to my end. Scribbling furiously, he took note of the little markings scratched into wax by the ever-accelerating needle. I briefly wondered what I was doing there and whether it was too late to turn back.

"I was right. I can't wait to show them. Anna, keep watching Paul! Don't let him out of your sight."

A useless request seeing as I was unable to look away. The more he advanced, the more his motions resembled a fervent dance. He searched left and right for pathways only he could fully comprehend, delving deeper into darkness on every step.

"Eugen? You need to hurry."

"Hmm?"

For a second, I only saw dark pine needles and shafts of light. My heart fluttered an odd staccato until Paul reappeared, stepping out from behind a shadow.

"Eugen, we need to move. Now," I said.

Something in my voice must have rung the alerts in his body. He stood up like a startled hare. "What's wrong?"

"I lost him for a moment. I'm not sure if it was a trick of the light or...I don't know. I see him now, but it's like looking across a hot spring where the steam moves all the objects behind it."

"Okay, I'm done. Let's catch up. Keep your eyes on him."

We rushed ahead, still carrying our gear between us. Paul blurred for a moment in a way that made my eyes water, but the image steadied as we drew near. It scared and fascinated me, but as the fear of the unknown increased, so did my desire to be part of it. I checked behind us, but there was nothing to see except trees and brown needle-covered ground. The town was out of sight, and we'd lost track of time. I had no idea how far away we really were.

"Don't lose him!"

"He's there. It's fine, Eugen. Breathe. We're near enough now that he's a lot clearer. How long do we think this neutral zone is, anyway?"

"Not a clue. We had no proof it existed. I'd deduced it from old secondhand stories past generations of Walkers left us."

"He's moving faster now."

"What does it look like?"

"Like there's more shadow and fog across him than there is around him, if that makes sense. He's touching the air, and every step makes him look more like the woods around him."

"That's good. Keep going."

"He blinked out for a second!"

"Do we stop?"

"No, he's there again. Slowing down now."

"Match his pace. We might be very near."

"He's there, right between those trees. Almost stopped now."

"Still searching?"

"Yes. And he's—"

I expected it fully, but still gasped when it happened. He took one step forward and just winked out of existence like he was never there. Then, a moment later, I heard rustling.

"I can still hear his footsteps, but he's gone! Does that count?"

"We're strictly forbidden from moving any farther once he's gone. Artjom would flay me alive. And Ancuţa." He shuddered. "This is it, we're marking this as their border of the Unspoken. You can have a rest now. I'll just take the notes I need and we can wait for him to return."

Eugen sat on a soft mound of needles with an "Oomph" and splayed some equipment around him. He slipped into his notes almost immediately, humming all the while. I supposed he was happy.

I took another step or two and leaned against the trunk of a tall black pine surrounded by a carpet of fresh, tiny grass shoots. It struck me, again, that there were no animals here. This forest should have been filled with birdsong. Instead, it was eerily bare and still, like the no-man's land between front lines in a war zone. I was grateful for it, though, as it allowed me to hear more of Paul's movements and perhaps track his progress a little farther.

I thought I could almost see the imprint of his boots in the grass ahead, but that might have been an illusion. I heard him take a few more steps, then stop. I wondered if calling out to him to let him know we were still here would disturb him and thought better of it. It was beyond me to even imagine what he was doing and the mental energy it took to do it. Would he even hear us at all?

Soft rustling and the clinking of metal came from his direction. That must have been him unbuckling the belts that held his parcels. I checked back on Eugen, but he was deep in his notes and his relaxed posture calmed my nerves too. Once we were done, I'd ask him whether he'd heard anything. It would be interesting to discover if even sound obeyed Walker rules.

There was a thump low on the ground. Perhaps Paul was setting down our signs of goodwill.

Suddenly, a rumble shook the very earth we stood on, lifting little clumps of dirt and pebbles from their resting places. A quiet gasp and shuffle followed, and I cried out softly, "Paul?", unsure whether I did more harm than good. Eugen looked up and half rose from his seat, but before he could rise all the way, Paul screamed. His footsteps rushed toward us, but a heavy undeniable thud chased close behind him and made me jump.

Eugen was on his feet, trapped between wanting to help Paul and not knowing what to do. I took four steps, then stopped again as strange flutters tickled the inside of my collarbone and blocked my breath. Paul blinked into view, then out again, and his face was contorted in fear and anger.

Behind him, something slithered. Only the mark of his feet in the grass told me where he was.

A growl like falling mountains rushed through the trees. His footsteps were gone. A spray of blood washed over us, drenching my clothes, my face, my lips. His parcels dropped from thin air. Then, all was quiet.

As though in a dream, I crawled to the bundles on the ground, unsure of what I wanted other than to somehow save them.

My bloody hands reached down and felt the wet squelch as they lifted the bundles.

Copper-tasting air coated my tongue. Something in my hands moved a little.

I opened a button on the side of the canvas pouch and lifted the flap.

A beating human heart.

CHAPTER SIXTEEN

Blood on the Ceiling

Eugen screamed his lungs out somewhere a universe away.

Then he rushed past me, heading for the deep woods. Cool air struck my cheek as he ran by, but I lunged forward and grabbed his elbow before he could get very far. He stopped, the tension in his body suddenly falling, and came toward me willingly, like a limp doll. We held one another for a moment. One of us trembled, one of us sobbed.

I looked down at the grassy carpet. Bloody parcels lay where I dropped them, one of them still pulsating, much less so than it did a moment ago.

He woke from his shock first. "Are we even safe?"

"I guess we would have known by now if we weren't."

"Yeah." He looked back over his shoulder at the dark woods stretching out into the unknowable world we'd just been made violently unwelcome from.

"Do you see…."

"Nothing. Nothing at all, now. Not even as much as I did before. Let's go back."

"Do we…."

He pointed at the parcels on the ground, and nausea washed over me at the thought of carrying them back to town.

"No. Why? We don't even know for sure if it's his…. I mean, they could be any…. No. I can't. Here, by the tree, is fine."

I steeled myself for the sensation of touching the blood-soaked fabric one more time and used two fingers to move the parcels under the shade of the tallest pine nearby. It would do. Nobody could ask us for anything more.

I must have been stuck there for a while, looking at them. Eugen took me by the elbow and led me away, trembling and cold. We stumbled through the woods for what seemed like a very long time. Eventually, my thoughts caught up to the rest of me, and I froze.

"Eugen, the toolbox. The notes. It's all still—"

"Leave it."

He kept on dragging us forward in an awkward shuffling dance. After a while, he was the one shuffling, and I did the dragging. We stopped to sob, then walked again. It felt like ages before we saw light, and the outline of a stone arch far away in the distance.

At first, I didn't think there was anything odd about it. We corrected our course and headed straight for it, walking a little more quickly now that the promise of safety was at hand. We were still holding hands, but no longer leaning on one another.

Eugen stared into nothing. "How are we going to tell Mara? And Perdy?"

I didn't know either. I barely knew how I would get my own heart to reconcile it. Was there more we could have done? Should have done? "We can worry about that when we get to them."

"Everyone is bound to have questions, us popping out of the woods like this."

"Where is everyone?"

We stopped dead and stared at the arch for a moment. Not a soul. The tables and some scattered tools were still visible through it, but everyone had gone.

"Would they have just left? Is that normal?"

"No. They wouldn't. They would be right there, waiting for us. Unless something happened."

"Something happened, then."

Eugen broke into a jog, and I followed. Through quick breaths, he shouted back at me, "Could this be some sort of Tide? And I got caught in it?"

I looked around us; I checked the sky. "I don't think so. There are signs. This just looks normal."

As soon as we passed through the arch, it stopped looking normal at all. Trails of blood splattered the succulent grass, footprints disappeared in every direction, and a handful of stone-cold bodies littered the crossroads. I prayed Florin and the others had gotten away in time and felt a fool for wishing. Every life was valuable, and losing Ancuţa or Mr. Scridon would be equally tragic.

Eugen's breathing became rapid, his movements frantic. I worried for him and wanted to distract him, so I gave him more questions to answer. "Can Whispers have done this? Even without a Tide?"

"They aren't supposed to be able to interact with our world this much, but they did with the reverend. Everyone said it was only because he'd invited them. I don't know anymore. We need to find the others."

"The brewery?"

He shot off again, and I trailed after him. I doubted we could be much help to anyone, but I didn't tell him that.

We found more blood in the main road, and two dead horses lying in a pool of it. A peal of thunder broke, and little drops of rain fell into the crimson puddle, causing it to tremble. In the distance, an arm reached out of a window and drew a shutter closed. There were still people, thank goodness. I hadn't realized how much that worry plagued me until I felt the relief of seeing another living soul.

The brewery doors were wide open and there was movement inside. The ground was covered in strange white feathers, but I only took the briefest notice of them before ear-piercing shrieks assaulted me from within the building.

"How did the devilled thing get to us in the first place? This is insanity!"

"Hold him still!" Mara's voice shot back, strong and brash as ever. "Hold him still, goddamn it, or he'll bleed out!"

My stomach contracted.

Another few steps took us inside, but nobody seemed to pay us any mind. It took a half second for my eyes to adjust to the darkness, but when I did, I saw Mara, covered in blood, wielding a knife while three other people held a body down onto the bar.

"Tighter! Perdy? Perdy, where's that damned water!"

Perdy came out of the back room with a steaming cauldron and almost spilled every last drop of it when she caught sight of us. "Anna! Eugen!"

"Perdy, what happened?"

Mara turned at the sound of my voice. "Oh, thank God. No time, talk later. Come help me now. You said you had some medical knowledge."

"Nursing."

"Come on, we're losing him. Eugen, come help hold him down."

Splayed out on the bar, grimacing and whining like a dog when he wasn't outright yelling, lay Florin. Perdy set the boiling water down by his head and Mara got to work right away, washing her blade and hands.

"Anna, I need you to clean up as best you can. Please."

They made room for me on the other side of the bar. As soon as I got near enough, the problem was obvious: his entire right leg was chewed up to ribbons halfway up his thigh. That was the kind of injury only a miracle would save you from.

The heaviest of the men was Rareş, the smith. He leaned with his whole weight on Flor's thigh, trying to slow the bleeding somehow. I tore off my padded jacket and took the apron I still wore beneath it, rolled it into a long cylinder, and pressed myself against the smith for stability.

"Rareş, on my mark I need you to lift his leg."

"Are you bat-shagging mad, woman? He could be dead from blood loss at any moment."

"I can help with that, just do it. Now!"

He flinched at my raised voice, and Mara looked confused and scared. The moment Rareş lifted off the injured limb, a fresh jet of blood cascaded out of his ragged gashes and dribbled off the bar to the floor. I pushed the rolled-up apron under his thigh, raised it as far up toward his crotch as I could, brought the ends together, and twisted them a couple of times before tying a knot. It slowed the bleeding, but not quite as much as I would have liked.

Glancing around us desperately, I found a wooden spoon leaning on the edge of the counter behind me and stuck the tail of it through the twist. I used it as leverage, turning the spoon around to tighten the tourniquet until the bleeding stopped completely.

Rareş whistled. "What the hell is that?"

"A turnstile. I saw someone use it on a soldier once for the same kind of injury. It's meant to stop the bleeding."

"Did he survive?"

"No, but not because of the bleeding."

Mara was ready in a moment, knife in hand. "Everyone, fair warning. The leg is coming off. If you can't stand that idea, leave now. It's hanging on by a ribbon already, but it won't be pretty. Perdy—"

"I'm staying."

"No, you—"

"I am. I'll be fine."

Everyone nodded a brief agreement to stay and help Mara do what was needed. The moment she touched the shredded thigh, Florin screamed once and then blacked all the way out, beads of sweat rolling down his forehead. For the better, poor soul.

One of the younger boys, the one holding down Flor's left shoulder, swayed dangerously. Perdy saw him right away, pulled him with uncanny strength, and shoved him to one of the nearby benches – it helped that the boy was limp and loose. She took his place and pressed down on Flor's shoulder with all her strength, even though he was no longer in any danger of thrashing.

His face was so pale I didn't think he stood a chance. Mara was quick, and doing the best she could, but even the best wasn't always enough.

"Is this the only injury?"

She was too focused to answer me, but Perdy turned to me, wide-eyed, pupils round and deeply black.

"Yes. Knocks and bruises, but nothing else as bad as this."

"We're going to have to seal the wound as soon as Mara is finished."

"How?"

I thought back for a moment to all the horrible things I'd seen in my hometown, and the things soldiers had done with red-hot knives and iron tools. Who would have thought something like that might someday save a life? If there were still any lives to save there.

I dashed through the kitchen door. The furnace was lit. We had a chance. I ran back to the small, stocky boy sitting on the bench looking dejected.

"What's your name?"

His eyes were watery, but much steadier now. "Casian."

"Casian, take my knife. Take all the knives from everyone here, go into the kitchen and set the blades into the hot coals. It's your job to watch them and turn them so that they heat up evenly. Use dishrags, don't burn yourself."

He nodded once and jumped to his feet, turning away empty-handed. The poor boy couldn't have been more than fifteen, and I didn't blame him for having a hard time.

"Casian!"

That time, he remembered to take my knife.

On the bar, whimpers turned to laborious breathing. Mara was a picture of concentration, but most of the others had given up any pretense of bravery and looked away. They shuffled about nervously, giving away their knives to Casian without any fuss. Perdy leaned on Florin's shoulder, more for support than anything else. He wasn't going to be moving anytime soon.

Mara spat sweat onto the floor. "I'm almost done. I've cut as cleanly as I can. The bone was broken neatly, there shouldn't be shards. I'm going to wash the area, but I don't know what else to do. What was that about sealing the wound?"

"It won't be fun."

She laughed. Every shade of exhaustion in the world was in the low notes of that laugh. "Tell me what you need me to do. There. Ready."

She stood stock-still for a moment, looking at the neatly severed thigh on one side, and the shreds of meat and pant and boot clumped together on the other. Wobbling, she grabbed the edge of the bar, then pushed herself to the other side of the room just in time to aggressively vomit all over the floor. Eugen was with her within moments, guiding her to a chair.

It was my turn. "Get her cold water. You guys are done for now, breathe. Rareș, how is his breathing?"

"Steady enough, considering. Do we still need to hold him down?"

"Please. I think this next bit might be worse than the one before."

"You think?"

"I'm very sorry if I gave you the impression that I do this every day."

"I can only hope you don't, girl."

"Casian, are any of the knives close to red-hot yet?"

Shuffling and scraping sounds came from the kitchen, then a high-pitched, strained voice squeaked, "Yes!"

"Bring one. Carefully."

Rareș' eyes went wide, and he leaned his head to one side when he understood what was going to happen. "You're mad, woman. I've been branded once. This is brutal."

"So have I." My voice was full of a challenge to fate. "And we're still here. It might save his life."

Taken aback, he nodded. "At least get the girl out of here."

Perdy attempted a feeble protest, but she didn't have much fight left in her. She couldn't bear not to help either, but there was plenty else to do.

"Sweetheart, I need you to do something for me. Find the cleanest cotton cloths you can get your hands on and give them a good fast boil. Then, soak them in the strongest booze you can find. We're going to need clean dressings, and lots of them."

She passed into the kitchen just as Casian came out holding the hot knife, narrowly escaping being stabbed in the gut by the boy. All we needed was another casualty.

"Anyone nearing the limit, look away. Mara, are you all right back there?"

Eugen replied in her place. "She's going to be fine, don't worry about us."

The more I hesitated, the more we were risking Florin's life, and yet

I couldn't bring myself to start. Seeing my fear, Rareş took the knife by its rag-covered handle and simply asked me, "Where?"

I showed him a large opening on the inside of his thigh that was slowly trickling blood where an important artery ended in a gaping hole. He touched it with the knife. A spasm and a shrill shout escaped Flor's unconscious body and mixed with the sizzle of his flesh.

After that first one, it was easier. Casian brought us the tools, one by one. We burned shut a few more of the worst-looking areas, little by little, with gentle taps, doing our best to keep a close eye on his breathing and heartbeat in between. By the time we were done, he was back to being a limp, unresponsive rag, and almost everyone had left the room to escape the smell of burning flesh.

We sent the other man, Lucian the tanner, to dispose of the waste. He never returned. It was just me and Rareş left, and he was leaning at ease on the counter behind him, watching me carefully apply alcohol-soaked bandages to the wound.

"Since you seem so comfortable behind the bar, pour us an ale, will you?" It was a gamble, telling a big man what to do like that.

His reaction was amused rather than aggravated, and he set to spilling beer without any complaint. "You've done some things today that not a lot of people would know how to do."

"And they are far better off for it."

"They aren't things you learn in school or out of books."

"No, they aren't."

He nodded once. We drank.

He pointed to Flor with his empty mug. "Is he going to live?"

"Your guess is as good as mine. He's survived so far, that's always a good sign."

"What else can be done for him?"

"Take him to a bed, let him rest. Stand by with tea and broth. Hope."

"And after?"

I shrugged. What the smith meant to ask was whether Flor could ever have a normal life again. I realized I didn't even know him well enough to say what 'normal' meant for him. I knew he was an aspiring fighter, and fond of battle stories. I knew he drank a little too much, frustrated by being a captive here. He loved people dearly and would do anything for them. That, at least, was good – there were a thousand ways to stand by those you loved, if he'd be willing to look for them. A thought came to mind.

"He lost his leg defending the others, didn't he?"

The broad man grunted. I asked him to lend me a finger to tie the last of the bandages tightly.

"What was it that attacked you?"

"Who even knows anymore? We used to know the five or six common Whispers. Good luck ones, trickster ones. They were mostly harmless. These nasty ones, they weren't supposed to make it in here. The Wardens know what they are, for sure, but not us common folk. They don't tell us poor shaggers a thing unless they need our money, or food, or lives."

"I can't believe it just showed up like that, with no Tide."

"The days of rules and safety are over. They were over even before the priest paid his final fare. I'll be honest with you, I wasn't even surprised when it barreled down the alley."

"Did he kill it?"

"Nah. He kept it away long enough for everyone to get out of the way. Ruffled it and injured it enough that it got mad, chomped at his leg, then ran off. It was like some sort of ungodly large eel covered in feathers – could swim through the ground without making a sound. Came to us with blood already on its mouth."

That blood must have been from the other people it met along the way; but for a moment I wondered whether it was possible that some of it was Paul's. "I'm done here. Where can we take him to rest?"

"I'll take him to one of the rooms."

I drained my ale and watched him pick Florin up with surprising gentleness. He disappeared upstairs, and I took a moment to take stock of the damage we'd done. The brewery bar room was utterly devastated. It seemed like there was more blood on the ground than could have escaped out of a single human. Bloody rags were strewn about everywhere, and toward the door more blood mixed with mud and sick and who knew what else. In a way, I was glad of it. At least the cleaning would keep everyone from dwelling too much on the ache of what had been lost.

Soon, Rareş rejoined me, and we made our way outside where our friends waited. Eugen was the first to see us come out.

"How is he?"

"Fine, for now. He's going to need to be watched constantly, though, and we're all too tired to risk it. Falling asleep in there might be the last favor we do him."

Leaning against the wall, a sobbing Perdy had her back to Mara, who vainly tried to comfort her.

Mara raised her eyes to me, doing her best to stay calm through her own tears. "We can send for some of Miss Crosman's girls. She's a harpy but she'll help. My little sister, Clara, is with them. Casian, would you…? Thank you."

Perdy was beyond all comfort. Her shoulders shook and all I could hear were her tiny sobs buried in her hands.

I wanted to ease her pain in any way I could. "He's going to be all right, sweetheart. He's a fighter."

Eugen touched my elbow gently. "It's not that, Anna. She asked about Paul. I had to tell her."

Paul. A sob nearly escaped me too. Was he really gone? Just like that?

All around us, people were beginning to leave their homes and ask after their neighbors. I realized that what had felt like days to us in the brewery was really not even an hour to everyone else. I leaned over to shut the big double doors so that passers-by wouldn't be privy to the butchery we'd just performed.

Just then, a raspy voice made its unfortunate presence known from somewhere behind me.

"Brought hell down upon our town, and came to drink to it, have you?"

The mayor stood, arms crossed, in the middle of the street, speaking at twice the volume he'd need to if he only meant for us to hear. His assistant trailed feebly behind him.

"Way to leave well enough alone. Where's that rat bastard so that I can congratulate him for his flawless leadership? Hmm?"

Eugen's fists tightened and his voice trembled. "Leave us alone. This isn't the time."

"Oh, more orders, is it? That's fair, after you've sheep-shagged five hundred years of peace and quiet."

A bundle of tight nerves, Eugen took a step toward the mayor, who was obviously oblivious to the danger he was in. Eugen's mouth was half-open, probably ready to contradict the obvious lie, but he couldn't get a word in.

"Do you expect the town to thank you idiots? Like you thought the Whispers would thank you? I suppose they didn't much care for Paul's presents. Or his presence, for that matter."

He laughed, pleased with himself. Eugen reached for his knife, but his belt was empty. All our knives were, perhaps thankfully, still inside. Before he could do anything else, I took a step between them.

As much as I could relish anything on a day like that, I relished the look of surprise on the mayor's face for the moment before my fist pushed through it and knocked him on his arse right there, on the cobblestones, in the middle of the road, in plain view.

CHAPTER SEVENTEEN

Foreign Window

A yellow door stood before me.

There wasn't anything particularly outlandish about that door, despite my expectations. It was solid, paneled wood, it was rather on the small side, it had a smooth wooden oblong knob and no knocker, and it belonged to the Wardens.

I had come straight from the brewery. We'd spent most of the day cleaning and getting organized. Mara had Perdy stay behind to be near Florin, and she arranged shifts of people to watch over both. She tasked her little sister, Clara, and her friends with ferrying messages back and forth, and the kid was so thrilled to be helping it melted my heart. It can't have been easy, being ten years old in a place like that.

The mayor, surprisingly, didn't even bother to shout at me. He just shut his mouth, shot up, and turned on his heels. I had no doubt whatever he planned next would be terrible, but I also had no room in my basket of worries for it. Rareş went home to his wife after giving me a pat on the back that almost knocked me to my knees.

The thought of going back to the house alone and waiting around to see what tragedy struck next was unbearable, so I asked for directions to the Wardens' Warren instead. I knew that Paul's death would catch up to me sooner or later, and a helpless rage nearly overcame me. The only thing that soothed me was the thought that maybe I could do something. Maybe I could better prepare and prevent any more people from getting hurt. Maybe next time, I could be useful. The Warden Ancuţa had promised me training, and I came there, to the Warren, to collect.

I stood like a cow trying to tell time, on the empty street, in front of the seemingly empty two-story house with dark windows and a dandelion-colored door. I knocked, fully expecting nobody to be home. The door opened a little, and I waited. And waited.

"Hello?" I called.

I waited another minute, torn between how awkward it was to stand there and how awkward it would be if I barged in just as they were reaching the door.

"Hello?"

Nobody answered. I considered turning around and leaving. Eventually, I caved and pushed the door open all the way, gingerly stepping inside.

"Hell—"

The moment my toes touched the doorway, I froze. It wasn't by choice, and there was no reason to – I simply couldn't move any farther. A soft bell rang somewhere in the distance, and a voice wafted down from the stairwell.

"Coming! Hold tight."

A swell of panic at not being able to move rose from my heels, and I did my best to breathe through it. My mind went straight where I wished it didn't, to being back in Alec's basement with my head underwater. It rushed in my ears and breathing caused a sharp ache right at the top of my lungs.

I focused on all the details of the lobby around me, hoping to distract myself from that ache. The black-and-gold patterned carpet, the brass lamps, the silvery strings across the white ceiling, the dark gray line of powder under my feet, the sound of footfalls approaching me.

Ancuţa condensed into my wobbly field of view and waved her hand around my face.

"Come in, friend."

She grabbed my hand and pulled me forward, and just like that, I could move again. I celebrated by almost falling to my knees.

"What the devil was that?"

"A Ward on the door. Any living thing that's a stranger here and tries to cross is transfixed until I can get a good long look at it. Now you're not a stranger anymore, come and go as you please. Come on!"

She went back up the stairs in a rush, and I followed, albeit reluctantly. My heart still raced. I didn't want to seem a coward, so I made myself take heavy, steady steps.

At the top, a large room greeted us. The entire back wall of it, facing the forest, was made of hundreds of square panels of glass all fitted together. I'd never seen so much glass in my life, and the light pouring through it was spectacular, tinted green by the pines and blue by the fog. Around the room, tables were scattered, covered in scrolls and boxes and tins of herbs and strange tools. Everything seemed hastily used and hastily left behind. The two side walls were all a mishmash of randomly sized and randomly colored bookshelves, from a fine hardwood affair that rose all the way up to the ceiling, to a small construction of bricks and planks in a triangular shape, laden with so many books it seemed it might crush the bricks at any moment. I sunk into a rich carpet the moment I stepped off the stairs and couldn't suppress a gasp.

Ancuţa laughed. "Do you like it? I insisted on the carpet myself. My feet get so cold when I'm working."

"It's beautiful."

"I took care of most of the arrangements for this place, and I'm rather proud of them."

"Ancuţa, is it magic?"

"What, the carpet?"

"No, the way you froze me at the door."

"Ha! No, it's not magic. There's no such thing. It's nature. Very obscure, almost forgotten laws of nature. Certain things have certain rules. Poppy seeds ground to dust at midnight sprinkled across a threshold won't let strangers through, and that's all they'll do. It's not magic, it's Warding."

I turned to gawp at the rest of the room. The wall facing the road was bare and only had two small, plain windows, but next to them what looked like curious telescopes loomed, peering out ominously.

Ancuţa moved from table to table, placing things back in boxes and placing boxes back on shelves, her straw-colored braids swinging with every motion.

"You've caught us at a strange time. Everyone else is out, they left in a hurry to tend to all the bodies. Everyone will blame us, so we need to stay sharp."

"Blame you?"

"For the deaths. For that damned Whisper making it in. For not defending them, as though we could. We Ward, we don't conjure lightning, this isn't some fairy tale."

"How did it get through? Did the Wards fail?"

She tugged on her dress collar and spat in her bosom.

"And what in the stars does that do?"

She gave me a solemn look. "It lightly dampens the tits, Anna."

It took two heartbeats before she burst into laughter and I joined her, an exhausted but glorious release from the pressure I'd been stockpiling. I wiped tears from the corners of my eyes.

Ancuţa shook her head. "It's supposed to ward off evil, but who knows? We just do it. As for the break-in, I don't know how that happened. Maybe the Wards were only ever a suggestion, and the Whispers decided to stop taking it. Maybe, like the mayor has been saying, someone in town found a way to invite the Whispers in."

I stood silently in the middle of the room for a moment, trying to understand her meaning. She waited for the space of one breath, then went on.

"He's been pointing at you."

I must have gaped at her like a yawning lion. She giggled at me for a moment, then rushed over and put her hand on my shoulder.

"Relax. I'm not about to pass judgment or make any big statements. I don't know whether you did or didn't. So I assume you didn't."

"But you're not sure."

"I can't be."

"I came here to ask for your help. To learn about Warding. But if you suspect me of being to blame for this attack—"

"It doesn't matter. Either you did it, in which case you clearly already have all the knowledge I could share with you. Or you didn't, in which case you'll need it. Worst-case scenario, I lose a bit of time telling you things you already know."

"There's got to be some way to prove who did it."

"There isn't. Not right now. Could have been a goat, or a child, or nobody at all. The tale I'm supposed to tell if I want money to keep funding our work and research is that Warding is a science. Nature is a constant. Everything is stable. But in truth? Nothing is that simple. I'll have time to look into it tomorrow, but not right now. Right now, the dead need tending, and you need to learn one or two things that might keep you alive for long enough to question, should it come to that."

"And it doesn't bother you to think that you might be spending time with the person responsible? What if I did it without knowing?"

She leaned her head to the right and frowned a little, but more like she was thinking to herself than frowning at me. "That'd be like accidentally knitting a sweater. And no, it doesn't bother me. The purpose of knowledge is to be shared. Whatever you did or didn't do shouldn't influence that, should it? I don't think so. Besides, I don't know you or your reasons."

"That's a very rational approach."

"Only one I've got. So, I promised you training."

She looked around, scanning the shelves, finger on her lip. I guessed it was a posture she adopted often; it suited her driven curiosity so well. Eventually, she settled on the high shelf of an improvised bookcase made out of short planks placed across the steps of two ladders. Her destination was a fair bit higher up than she could reach, and I wondered at what she'd do, but before I could consider it overly much, she was already climbing the wooden boards, precariously shaking the entire construction.

"Ancuța, be careful!"

I rushed over to push the bookshelf back up against the wall just as it leaned outward. She laughed and started tossing books down, shaking book dust all over my hair.

"Don't worry! Hah. I do this all the time. It leans a little, then stops. See? You can't have been the saboteur. You just tried to save me from death by bookshelf."

I had to dodge the next book, then she jumped down with a heavy *thunk* that would have befitted a person three times her stature. It seemed like determination was more of a factor in her speed than agility was. Before I knew it, she was repeating the process on another bookshelf, and we had a little pile of about twelve books to account for.

We scooped them up in handfuls and carried them across the room to one of the emptier tables by the glass wall. As soon as they were out of my arms, I couldn't help but be drawn to the magnificent window. I was so close that, without realizing, I'd fogged up a patch right in front of my face with my breath.

"Can I touch it?"

"The Walker Window? Sure. It's almost unbreakable."

The glass was cold and perfectly smooth, and my fingers slipped over it easily. I had planned on drawing something silly in the mist, but it quickly became an eerily accurate sketch of the thing I encountered on my first morning there, round white eyes, long ears, antlers, and all.

"Why is it called a Walker Window?"

Ancuţa thumped and slammed books behind me, sorting them into an order only she understood. "It's Warded to see the truth, just like Walkers do. Whenever there's a Tide or any strange occurrence that a normal person wouldn't really notice or understand, through this glass you can see what a Walker would. All the Whispers and such. It's a limited view, sure, but it's an important piece of forest, right by the arch."

"You didn't see…?"

"The attack? No. You were way too far in even for the telescopes to pick up. It really only serves to observe and make note of the things that come up to investigate us during Tides. And those are usually harmless."

Her footsteps shook and lifted the floorboards under my feet as she drew near me.

"Ah, I see you're familiar with the forest Vâlva." She added tufts to the tips of the ears of my fog drawing on the glass.

"Is that what it is?"

"Yeah. They're tricksters and they change shape, but the ones around here like to look like a giant variety of *Lepus cornutus*. There are a few of them and we suspect they're part of a family."

"So there are many of each kind of Whisper?"

"Some. There are many Vâlve. I don't know if they have a leader, but they seem peaceful, so they may not. Many Zmei, and they definitely have a leader. Zburătorul. Only one of him." She shuddered. "Many Samca and Iele, one queen over them."

"It'd take a lifetime to learn all of this."

"And a library." She laughed. "Maybe you should spend more time here. That's a pretty good drawing, actually. You should consider contributing to our archives. We're always looking for people to help us fill out our Whisper Compendium with images and descriptions, and good luck getting Paul to—"

Her eyes got lost in the distance for a second, then she waved her hand in front of her face as though she were brushing away cobwebs. A moment later, she was in motion again, tidying and tossing garbage into a bucket.

"Never matter. It's done now, and my chance to convince him is gone. If only I'd been subtler, more careful." Louder and more firmly, she changed the subject. "Have you seen any others?"

It didn't feel right to press. "Something the other townsfolk called Dochia."

She grimaced, showing me all of her teeth. "The Dochia. Nasty creature. Only one of her. Wait."

With great conviction she dragged one of the larger books toward her across the table and opened it, shuffling old pages to and fro. Beautiful hand-inked illustrations as well as hasty charcoal sketches peered out at me from the paper, each one more astonishing than the next. Before I could take stock, she found the right page, straightened the book out, and slapped it down with the palms of her hands.

"Aha! Here she is."

The image was almost perfect, pale against a charcoal backdrop, albeit less menacing and somewhat softer than the real thing.

"The nails and beak are a little off, but it's definitely her."

"Fascinating. I wonder what she was after. She's a kidnapper, you know. Our records over the past four hundred years show at least two dozen people put to sleep and carried away into the Unspoken, never to be heard from again."

"Is that what happened to Perdy and her parents?"

"The Samson family? No. That's not it at all. They were seen walking out into the woods with the baby, of their own volition. It wasn't even Tide time."

"Were they Walkers?"

"No. I was only a novice then, but still, it would have been on the record if they were made Walkers."

"What do you mean 'made'?"

Shafts of twilight fell on her curious face, lighting up little freckles I hadn't noticed at first. She took on a calmer, more serious air.

"I thought you knew about how Walkers come to be. I mean, I don't know what happened in your case, clearly."

"I assumed it was something we were born with. I need to learn to stop doing that."

"Being born?"

"Making assumptions!"

"Right. No, nobody's born a Walker. You end up being able to see Whispers and Walk into the Unspoken because at some point in your life, your link to this world became less solid than it is for most people."

"Less solid?" It was so obvious that the normally direct woman was suddenly using euphemisms, I wondered what she was – poorly – hiding.

She hummed, picking her words. "Less reliable. We say that Walkers are one step removed from normal people, because at some point in their past they took that one step away from life and they never came back."

"Even if I knew how to do that, I'm not sure I would."

"Well, it's not a choice. It's not something you did. It's something that happened to you."

Some of the locked drawers inside the corridors of my mind got restless, their keys slowly turning in the locks all by themselves. The rattling made my jaw clench. "You're talking about horrible events, aren't you? The sort of thing that leaves you feeling not normal for the rest of your life."

She nodded, and I could read sympathy and fear in her eyes.

I swallowed, but my throat was dry. "A while back—"

"Anna, you don't have to tell me anything. I'm not asking."

"But I want to understand."

She sat on the edge of the table, frowning at the floor. Her hands folded in her lap and I admired the beauty of her slender, nimble fingers in the orange light of dusk.

"I can respect that. Very well then, I'm listening."

CHAPTER EIGHTEEN

Relations, Revelations

"A while back, before I first started running, a man came into my life."

The story was hard to begin, but I felt almost a vicious pleasure in saying it out loud to someone. I finally had a real reason to and couldn't accuse myself of dragging it out only because I was weak and wanted pity.

"At first, it felt like we understood each other in ways nobody else could. We both wanted to escape our lots in life. He needed me. I couldn't say no. I didn't know the horrors that were inside him until it was too late. They found me quickly enough, and I tried to get out of the way."

"Tried to?"

"I was too slow to realize how dangerous he was by minutes. I walked up to his door to say I couldn't bear being around him anymore, to tell him I was afraid of him and wanted to be away from him, and I felt the steel grasp of his hand on my arm. He dragged me down. Locked me away. Judging by the look of his cellar, he'd been planning to for a long time."

Ancuța clutched the edge of the table and swallowed hard. Strangely, I felt distant and unaffected, aside from being sorry for her discomfort. As the orange sundown turned to violet-blue, so did the fire inside me cool.

"I was there for weeks. Maybe months. I heard him turn friends and family away from the door when they searched for me while I crawled helpless in the basement, gagged. I heard him tell them that I was a witch and in league with the Devil. He was relentless, exhausting. Eventually, everyone either agreed with him, or simply gave up looking. Life moves on. He tried me for witchcraft, and he was judge, jury, and executioner."

"Whatever you did, you didn't deserve any of that. Was there even any...?"

"Witchcraft? God, no. I studied science and medicine. I didn't even believe the supernatural existed, at first."

"At first? What happened then?" More quietly, she added, "You don't have to tell me anything."

Her words floated by me. I noticed them, but they didn't reach me.

"Then, this started." I sat next to her and reached for the hem of my skirt, gathering it and lifting it over my right thigh, twisting my leg so she could see the scars in the violet light.

She gasped a little.

"With every day that passed, he got wilder and scarier. Eventually, when I wouldn't give in to his demands to confess, he snapped. He burned and choked and drowned me. I came close to death so many times. After the first few, I would have welcomed it. Toward the end, I begged for it. He wouldn't let me die."

"But you escaped. Were you rescued? Is he still alive?"

"He is. Running, somewhere, I think."

She waited. Had she asked me anything else, I might have taken the opportunity to change the subject and never tell her the last part, but she sat there in the darkening room and waited patiently.

"At first, I thought I was losing my mind from the pain. Hallucinating, maybe. He'd push my head underwater, and I'd wink out into blackness. When I came back, for a few moments, there was another dark figure in the room with us. Someone who wasn't really there."

A shiver went up my spine and my arms were covered in goosebumps.

She saw, and reached her hand out to touch me, then drew back. "Someone stepped on your shadow. That's what we say when shivers...." Ancuța trailed off, leaned over, and grabbed one of the blankets draped across the back of the chair, then handed it to me. It was soft and smelled sweetly of chamomile.

I carried on before I could change my mind. "The strange figure vanished after moments, but then the next time I blacked out and came to, there it was again, more defined. It lingered longer every time."

"What did it look like?"

"Upside down, like it used the ceiling the way we do the floor. Taller than anyone I've ever seen. Half again as tall as me, and dripping darkness upward. And it had two pairs of long curved horns, like a ram. Every time, it got clearer, and I thought it was Death coming to get me. It didn't look like the Death in our legends, but who knows what Death looks like, really?"

I pulled the blanket closer around me.

"It never did anything, never spoke, but somehow I just understood – the way you do in dreams – that it wanted something. Then, I died."

She shivered and grabbed a little bundle of herbs from a nearby box. Once lit, they smelled like honey cakes.

"I hope you don't mind. It's just something I find soothing."

Somehow, it soothed me too.

"So, you died. That explains why you can Walk."

I nodded.

"Who brought you back?"

"Alec did. I don't think he ever intended for me to die. Just to comply."

I was avoiding the point again, and steeled myself to get through it. "Only then did I realize how much I really wanted to stay alive. I came to, and the figure was clearer than ever, waiting behind Alec, hand extended to me. I knew, again, the way one does in dreams, that it wanted to make a deal. Its eyes were made of fire, and I couldn't understand why Alec didn't feel the heat of them as I did."

"That sounds terrifying."

"It was, but I was far more afraid of the fact that Alec now knew how to kill me, and bring me back. The thought that he could do it over, and over, and over. I nodded my agreement to the creature, hoping whatever it gave me would be anything but that."

"What happened next?"

"It became real. Alec turned and saw it for the first time. He ran off shrieking like the Devil was after him. The ground trembled. I was in and out of consciousness. I'm not sure what happened next."

"Did your family find you?"

"They never came near the house. I wandered out after hours, on shaky legs like a drunk, riddled with infections, anemic. They gathered by the house, under my favorite tree, and watched me. When I approached, they threw stones. Even my grandmother, who raised me...."

I swallowed a sob, and Ancuța stood by me in silence. There was nothing better she could have done.

"I had to force myself back inside that house. Took his clothes. Stole his gold. Then, I walked out the village, my father shouting threats behind me." I breathed.

"That is...a lot."

I needed to change the subject. "I didn't think what I saw was real, at first. But now that I've seen Whispers, I wonder. Could it be one? Something that visits people on their deathbeds. Is there anything like that...?"

She shook her head, wide-eyed. "They're not supposed to go that far from the Unspoken. Plus, what you're describing.... That's the strangest thing I've ever heard. I'm sorry, but I just don't know."

The fact that out of all the strange things in Whisperwood, that was the strangest thing she'd heard, both stunned and comforted me. It was nice to have my pain and horror acknowledged like that.

After a while of breathing in silence, Ancuța stood. The cheerful clatter of tea-making implements was music to my ears, and a song I sorely welcomed.

★　　★　　★

We drank tea and spoke about import-exports.

We didn't particularly care about import-exports, but I needed to settle down and her expensive carpet was right there. I found out a little about how they crafted items to trade. They focused on complex handmade things like lace and tooled leather. They had to buy the hides, because there was no wild game. We spoke about how the town provided for the school, chapel, and all the Whisper-related industries, including the Wardens and Walkers.

"It's hard to be sure what it was like even as far back as one generation. We didn't keep a lot of written records of the human side until Reverend Andrei started demanding it. He said what we did here was just as important as the Whispers, even if it doesn't seem like it to us."

"He was a good man, wasn't he?"

"Not everyone loved his theories. He talked about how Whispers don't have lives, not the way we do. Not with beginnings and ends. How they're cycles that keep repeating. Lots of people used the excuse to call him crazy. Plus, he was phasing out the practice of making new Walkers and most of the town hated the idea of not having an army. Of relying solely on Paul. They thought it was a power play—"

"Hold on."

Something niggled through the layer of cold fog around my head and tickled at the back of my skull. Ancuţa must have gotten a pretty good idea of what it was, because suddenly she'd taken a few steps and put the table between us.

"Hold on. You said that before. Do you mean 'making' them on purpose? Not 'made' by circumstance, but intentionally?"

"Please stay calm."

"You said 'the practice of making'. Very clearly. You said you 'make' Walkers, like they're baskets or socks." Trembles started in my wrists and crawled up my arms, and I leaned onto the table for support.

"Anna, breathe. You don't have the whole picture."

"Tell me, Ancuţa. Tell me the whole picture."

"We need to—"

"Nearly kill people? On purpose? Is that what you do?"

I circled around the table, wanting to stand in front of her and make her look into my eyes as she told me the truth, but she kept her distance.

"You do to people what was done to me, on purpose, don't you?"

"Not...quite. Anna, I might as well tell you it gets worse."

"Worse?" My voice was shrill even to me.

I sped up, but she matched my pace and frustrated my attempts to approach her. I picked up a book, not even sure what I intended to do with it, and she ducked behind one of the pillars in the center of the room.

"Worse than the fact that you do this on purpose? Than the fact that you did this to Paul? That you almost killed him so that he could die for you?"

I moved to the pillar, book still in hand, and she peered cautiously at me from behind it.

"It's not like that. He was offered, as a child. If it hadn't been him, it would have been another."

"That's horrible!"

"It's tradition!"

"So are witch hunts!" I realized I was shouting and stopped.

She froze in an embrace with the pillar, looking at me sadly through teary eyes. I must have started crying too, at some point, because my face was wet, and my lips were salty.

Turning my back to the pillar, I leaned against it for fear I might fall from my feet at any moment. Eventually, I slid down to the floor. Behind me and to my right, she sat down with an *oof* too.

"How old?" My voice came out hoarse and defeated.

"There was always a rule that it could only be infants. Young enough that he wouldn't even remember why he is the way he is."

"I can't tell if that makes it more horrible, or less so."

"Anna, you have to understand, this is why we're here. This is more than our job. Warding and investigating and keeping the Whispers contained, Praedicting and Walking, that's our entire reason to exist. Were it not for this purpose, no town would have settled back here after the first one went missing. There would be no Whisperwood, no us. Paul would never have been born, if it weren't for the world needing us for these specific jobs."

I was tired, and the pointlessness of the argument overwhelmed me. "How do you do it?"

"Are you sure you want to know?"

"No. Who?"

"It used to be the reverend's job."

"His own father...?"

Suddenly my stomach contracted. The shock of it all overcame me, and I grabbed for a waste bucket within reach. I dry heaved a couple of times and felt dizzy, but a little better. Ancuța stroked my back, making soothing noises.

"Easy now. You're all right. Look, you're still thinking of this in terms of the outside world. I know it must be very different out there, but here, we follow the rules or we die. Sometimes, we follow the rules, *and* we die. The reverend knew that if he wanted to be our shepherd, picking Walkers was part of the job. And still, he hated the idea so much and put it off for as long as he could, but when the townsfolk surrounded his house with threats and knives, he made a choice to give his own son, rather than that of a stranger. He took the hardship on his own family. Paul was taken from him, then. He belonged to the Whispers long before they took him."

Queasy, I dropped into a nearby chair.

"The reverendess couldn't bear it and took a Silent Walk into the woods. A common cause of death, here. And still, Father Andrei believed we could all have balance and be safe. He believed we could do better. Don't judge him too harshly."

"A family ruined, and the town got their Walker. What about Perdy?"

"She was never intended to be a Walker. We don't know what happened to her when she was lost in the Unspoken, but whatever it was, it must have changed her." She paused for a beat. "Nothing is ever easy here. We're doing the best we can, and I know that can sometimes look like not enough, or the wrong thing. You know it too."

Eventually, I looked into her sad face, now lit dark blue by the end of the day, and did my best to smile.

"I suppose it's not every day that you get chased around your workplace by a crazy lady with a book for no better reason than minding your traditions, is it?"

"No, it's only every other Tuesday."

We laughed. She had her hand on my shoulder and I felt like I might survive, in spite of the horrible ache between my ribs trying to convince me otherwise. I looked at the title of the book still clutched in my left hand.

The Natural Science of Warding Against the Unknown.

I supposed it was never too late to learn.

CHAPTER NINETEEN

Salt and Silver

'Of personal Wards, few are comfortable to carry at all times. It is best to remain in the safety of a Warded structure. Should travel be necessary, travelers must be equipped, at the very least, with the following items: salt to line all resting places, bread to placate, silver to negate, and an iron knife if all else fails.'

I shut the book and reached for another, but Ancuța grabbed my hand.

"You can't expect to learn two dozen years' worth of knowledge in one night!"

"But I won't be much use unless I learn, will I?"

She gaped at me, looking for any angle of attack. She was a fierce debater. "Anna, nobody is much use against the Whispers at first!"

I was even fiercer. "Ancuța, that doesn't mean I can't do better."

"You infuriating woman. It's like you're trying to be the most quietly stubborn person that has ever entered the Warren."

"Only because you've already got loudly stubborn covered."

As soon as it was fully dark, we'd lit candles and oil lamps all across the room. Their amber light danced around and warmed our spirits. A knock on the door interrupted our banter.

"Food!" Ancuța rushed down and returned with parcels wrapped neatly in oiled paper. "I have these delivered from Miss Crosman every evening. The Wardens don't have time to cook."

I raised my eyebrow at the two hefty parcels. Clearly, the maestress didn't miss a beat and knew I'd be there.

We laid a yellowed tablecloth on the floor and sat, as if to a picnic, among the intricate dark green convolutions of the carpet. There were cheese-and-pickle sandwiches in the packets, as well as slices of carrot and radish to nibble on. I realized I hadn't eaten since the day before and dug in.

"We get few, but delicious, privileges as Wardens. We belong to the town, as do the Walkers and Praedictors, so the town takes care of our basic needs, usually by way of Miss Crosman collecting the money from the fountain on our behalf. Food, shelter, almost anything really. It does also mean that we can't overtly go against the mayor's wishes. We try to keep things peaceful. Unlike the Praedictors."

"I met one of them."

"Artjom, at the—" A gray, damp silence fell over us. Ancuţa inhaled half a sandwich in one swallow.

"What happened, Ancuţa?"

"Hmm?" She stared intently into her lap.

"With Paul."

"I only meant to warn him, but he gets – got – so defensive. Saying I never wanted to let him go inside now, after the fact, feels like cowardice. I should have tried harder to stop him."

"Do you know why he died?"

"Only in broad terms. He died because he, like many others, treated something like a guarantee even though it never is. Despite what we say to keep ourselves sane."

"What do you mean?"

"Most of the townsfolk think what we do is infallible. Or, rather, they want to believe so because it's better than nothing. You know that poppy-seed Ward at the door?" She took my shudder as affirmation. "It works just as often as it doesn't work. Sometimes, the more dangerous the intruder, the more likely it is to fail."

"Why do you even use it, then?"

"Because if we don't use it, then it'll never work, will it? Most of our Wards are like that. They will sometimes reduce the risk of death. Not always. But they're all we've got, so we shield ourselves with them as though they're as reliable as the laws by which water falls down. Here, let me show you."

She pulled on a little drawer and brought out a couple of satchels. Indelicately swiping books and documents to one side of the table, she upended a mound of salt and a heavy silver-plated chain onto the wooden boards, forming them into two lines. Then, she handed me a tuft of pale fur.

"Try blowing this across the salt."

"What is it?"

"The fur of one of those forest Vâlva, caught on a branch by the arch. Go for it."

I did, and the fur gently rolled across the salt without a problem.

"Do the same over the silver."

This time, the tuft stalled long before crossing the silver chain. I tried again, harder, just to be sure I hadn't somehow gotten it wrong. It reached the chain, then flipped over as though in a whirlwind current and fluttered right back toward me.

"Now, try both of those with this feather."

Pristine-white and shiny, the feather felt immaterial between my fingers. My first attempt shot it clear across the room, and neither silver nor salt seemed to stand in its way. On my second, it seemed to hover for too long over the salt.

"So, Vâlve can cross salt, but not silver?"

She nodded. "Salt, and almost anything else."

"And whatever creature lost the feather wouldn't be stopped by either?"

"And it might even be drawn to salt. Thankfully, that's not a predator. It's an Om Bird feather. They're good luck, and supposedly grant wishes."

"You apply scientific methods to figuring out what works and what doesn't."

"We do. Except, here's the rub – that's just a piece of fur, and just a feather. Whatever dropped that piece of fur might still be able to pass over the silver, depending on what shape it'd shifted into, or what time of night it was, or what deals you'd made with it. The point is, we know only a little. And that's sometimes worse than knowing nothing at all."

"Do you know what creature killed Paul?"

"Not really. I know he'd found this entry in an old Whisper cookbook. It talked about an offering of 'game and parsley with pepper laced, favorable to any tastes' and he wanted to use it as a peace offering. Except there's no wild game here, so he used dried jerky. I told him that even if he'd had game, 'favorable to any tastes' was a metaphor, a Warding way of saying it was quite good and might possibly work, but he swore it must mean no creature would reject it."

"But they did."

"He was a fool to go, and I to let him, and I can't tell who was the greater. Here, keep the salt, and the silver chain. They're rare and you'll need them. Return the chain if you don't need it anymore."

"You have salt crystals in the wall around town, but Whispers still get through. I understand why, now."

"The Tides reach farther than they used to each time, and the wall doesn't actually extend that far out, so for the past year or so even salt-hating Whispers have been able to just travel along it far enough to go around it. That's probably how we lost the reverend. I keep asking the mayor to extend the damned wall, but he thinks acknowledging it will just anger them more."

"Could that be what happened this morning?"

"I doubt it. It seemed like whatever it was, it came in straight through the arch. Either someone tampered with the Wards or the Whispers have some sort of advantage we don't know about. Anna, there is so much we don't know, sometimes I feel no wiser than the grandmothers who claim to read your future in tea leaves."

"But you are doing the best you can, and that's better than anyone else has done."

"I'm certainly going to try to keep you alive. That chain will help. Loop it around your waist."

"I might have something else too."

I reached into my apron pocket and took out the little ring on its own chain. Both ring and chain were silver-looking, sure, albeit dirty and dull, but I couldn't be sure they were real silver.

"I found this in Perdy's family home. I'm not entirely sure what it is—"

She snatched it from my hands and held it up to the light. "Interesting. Let's see."

On the table sat a large magnet we had used earlier to practice a Ward against a common Whisper. It had a viperlike body with metallic scales, and Ancuța had explained that a strong magnet pull could disorient its movement.

She set the ring down and passed the magnet over it – with little to no reaction. I took that as a bad sign, but she seemed pleased. Then she made a paste out of white powder and water and scrubbed vigorously at both items. I left her to it and peered out the window at the slowly lightening horizon.

"Ancuța, it's almost dawn. Wasn't Master Artjom saying we might get a Tide about now?"

"Hmm? Yes, yes. Don't worry, you won't even feel it. This whole building is Warded. Impregnable."

She wasn't paying me any real attention, and had slipped back into her 'Wards always work' routine, but by now I knew what she'd meant to say was that it would probably be fine, but maybe not. I was amazed at how well these people had learned to cope with things they couldn't control.

She cleaned the last bits of paste off the trinkets with a cotton cloth and held them up to the light again. The metal shone beautifully and threw a bright sparkle of yellow light across the room.

"Silver, all right. You're lucky. It's good quality, and a lot of it." She handed it back to me. "If you were any other townie, I'd ask you to share it with us, but a Walker's gonna need every scrap."

I joined the two silver chains together and looped them around my waist like a belt. "It must have belonged to a child. We found the skeleton in the pantry, surrounded by a salt circle, but with everything that happened, we never got a chance to properly ask anyone about it."

"Were the bones clean and white?"

"Very much so, and crumbly."

"It might date back years or decades. We've had a few missing children."

"There was something else odd about it."

"Oh?"

Her palpable interest encouraged me to tell her my suspicions. "Well, the teeth were that of an older person, and the skull itself had these regular bumps, almost like a ridge, going all the way front to back. I was wondering whether...."

"That's so interesting. You're thinking it might be the remains of a Whisper?"

"Yes! Except you said they didn't exactly die, or so the reverend thought?"

She waved her hand. "He said they were like the ever-renewing cycles of nature. They kept coming back after death. But still, their bodies die, and leave remains."

"So maybe that's what the skeleton is."

"In a salt circle? My goodness."

We were both so clearly excited by the idea. "But judging by what I've seen, that's not impossible, is it?"

"No, no, not at all. It just implies...."

"What?"

"Well, it implies it was trying to protect itself from other Whispers. Our theories suggested they were a solid unit. Like bees. Would you mind if I dropped by to take the remains? For research?"

I could tell she would have accepted a refusal, but very much wanted me to say yes.

"The door's unlocked. It's behind the back wall in the pantry."

She thanked me and paced around, muttering to herself, deep in thought. I was pleased to have made her so happy.

Walking past the window, she came to a halt. "It's Tide time."

"How do you know?"

"Look."

We stood side by side and peered into the gloom. Among the trees, not far from the arch, a long pale shape slithered, winding in and out of our vision. It neared the entrance, probing along the wall with a sneaky, sharp tongue coming out of what looked like the head of a fox.

Out of the woods a small gray shape appeared, rushing toward the arch. It looked like a very young forest Vâlva. Just as I thought it was out of reach of the lurking predator, there was a furious blur of movement. In a single muscular ripple of its body, the fox-faced serpent snatched its prey right up. The snap of its teeth closing shut was audible, and I felt it in my bones.

Ancuţa must have too, judging by her gasp. "I don't know how you ever have the courage to step outdoors, especially on Tides."

"What about actually going into the Unspoken? None of these books talks about how to do that."

Her curious amber eyes darted to me, and she looked like she couldn't understand a word I was saying. For the first time since that day at the trading post, I felt how she was able to drop coldness between herself and the people around her when she needed to. "I won't let you be the next Paul, and anyway I couldn't if I wanted to. Walking's not something I can teach. Survival, on the other hand? Maybe. Back to work."

CHAPTER TWENTY

A Time to Run

We worked through the night and eventually fell asleep strewn across a couple of armchairs.

Dreams came, hectic and disjointed; I was trapped in an underground building larger than anything human hands could build. The stairs wound in on themselves; the hallways spiraled into nonsense geometry, and the only exit I found was a waterfall into nothing. Shadowless people lurked around corners, pretending to want to help me. Something ran across the ceiling, chasing me. I steeled myself to turn back and face it, but I heard Miss Crosman.

"...leave, right now."

I woke and, disappointingly, still heard her.

"I don't care if she's engaged to the tanner's grandmother, she has to go!"

I opened my eyes to see Ancuţa and the maestress deadlocked in a heated argument that only Ancuţa tried to whisper. "We can't toss her out. With all due respect—"

"Shove that respect right up your nose. It'll only get worse if she doesn't go. I warned her again and again. The mayor did. We all did."

I shifted so that they could both see me. It was still dark, and I must only have had an hour or two of sleep. My mood stood testament. "Can we include me in this conversation?"

Crosman didn't miss a moment. "Have you got your money with you?"

"Of course, I always have—"

"Get up. Now. I'll not risk my life for you if you dawdle. Move it, you wereslug's bottom."

Ancuţa shuffled around, looking for something in a cupboard. For a second I suspected she only wanted to get out of the way, but she quickly returned with an intricately braided white charm made of the same forest Vâlva fur we'd been experimenting on.

"Shifter fur will get you through my Ward, but I don't know about the rest of them."

"I've ripped your contract up." Crosman shoved torn paper squares in my hand. She'd done a thorough job, and many of them fluttered to the floor. "Not that you did more for it than fetch one letter and get drunk with your friends. Now let's move."

"Do I get an opinion?"

"Not if you want to keep your head."

"Wh—"

"Shut up, girl. I haven't got the time. It's all gone tits up. There've been questions about what happened in the woods, and you came up as the answer. Those led to questions about the good reverend, and young Florin's leg. Again and again, they point to you. The mayor isn't saying anything, because apparently you've been a nuisance to him. Now, Pierduta's gone, and people are about ready to ask you all those questions. Some of them would like to bring pliers to the conversation. We're putting ourselves in a great deal of danger to remove the Wards and let you pass."

Perdy? Where could she have gone? Wherever it was, I needed to be alive to find her. I gathered my wits and belongings. Angry mobs were only something you ever experienced once; either you learned the lesson, or you didn't survive.

"I didn't cause any of those things."

"You know that for sure? Generations of people studying what goes on here can't say a damned thing with any certainty, and you've got answers after three days."

Ancuţa fluttered around. "There's a back door. It leads—"

The maestress raised a silencing hand. "I know exactly where it leads,

I wasn't born this spring. Hush now, and when they come knocking, you haven't seen us."

We slunk out into a navy dawn, pressed up against the low stone wall that separated the woods from town. I figured we'd cling to that wall all the way to the trading post, but she immediately reached for a makeshift wooden door that seemed stuck right in the middle between the Wardens' Warren and the home next to it. A thin pole lay across the threshold. She took it and stuck it into the gap under the door, searching for something. There was a *clack*, and it opened into a dark passageway.

"Mind your step, it goes down. Feel your way down the stairs with your toes. Quick and careful."

I was so preoccupied trying to figure out how to be quick and careful all at once that I didn't even question what we were doing until I was four steps down and the door shut behind us.

I was in a cellar. "Where are you taking me?"

"Are you daft? Out, I told you."

A dark, damp cellar. "Through a basement?" I had visions of my body hanging to dry like meat being cured.

"You don't have tunnels where you came from?" She scoffed. "You're smarter than this. Ask me what you mean, plain and simple."

A dark, damp cellar where Alec was waiting. "How do I know you're not leading me into trouble?"

"I have better things to do with my time."

I couldn't budge. "You also have better things to do than help a bothersome stranger."

"That is true, and I expect a 'thank you' whenever you please. We'll be up again in no time, on the other side of the main road. All it is is two cellars stuck together."

Goddamned cellars. I wanted to move on, but my clenched jaw and tense shoulders didn't. Moving forward at all was like dragging my feet through knee-high mud. The back of my neck tingled, and it was all I could do not to whine in terror. It took three or four steps in the dark, walking across my own blind trust that she wouldn't hurt me, but then

I saw it; there was a light ahead. A door out. My relief belied my desire to call myself trusting.

"Once we're outside again, stay as close as a shadow. Don't make a sound. Don't even think until you're out of town."

I couldn't if I'd wanted to. A heaviness in my chest took up all my concentration to decipher. Could I leave, now? Did I want to? Did I have a choice? I was being kicked out, and that thought filled me with overwhelming sadness and shame. I couldn't have fallen so hard for such a place in only a few days, but perhaps the feeling of being needed, of being able to help – that only took moments to get attached to.

Whatever it was I felt, I had to make my peace with it. I wouldn't put myself through another mock trial ever again, and that was that.

Miss Crosman pushed the doors open just a hint. Light flooded down the dusty stone steps and brought a sigh of relief to my lips. "How are we going to cross town unseen?"

"Hush." She peeked outside and gestured for me to follow.

The stairs took us up to a small alley right next to the bakery. It was quiet, but serious voices from the main road floated down the breeze. Miss Crosman dragged me by the sleeves into a doorway I hadn't even noticed her opening.

Behind her, a startled baker, elbows-deep in flour, held up a blob of dough like a shield between him and the inevitable. "Maestress. I—"

"Noticed nothing suspicious."

"The mayor—"

"Has no doubt offered a reward that isn't worth your wife learning about your secret midnight meetings with Miss Bianca from across the road."

"But I—"

"Haven't seen us and we haven't seen you. Nobody needs the trouble."

His face looked like his insides were trying to burst through his nose, but he turned back to his countertop and smacked the dough on the stone surface. As he worked, we scurried across the room and to another door.

A set of wooden stairs led up to a handful of cozy rooms. My heart was pounding from the fear and the surprisingly rapid pace the sturdy woman set. A little blond girl playing with her corn husk dolls eyed us, surprised but unworried. I waved at her as Miss Crosman rolled up a window.

"Are we jumping?"

She only shushed me and pointed outside.

There was a broad balcony that nearly touched on another balcony belonging to the building across the street, but with my meagre knowledge of the town's geography, I couldn't remember what that building was. The gap would be easy to hop across.

She shoved me at the window and I gracelessly gathered my skirts to cross over the mantle. As soon as my boots thunked on the wood, more voices from below alerted me to a small crowd.

Relaxed and easy, a woman spoke. "Maybe we'll finally have some quiet after they take her in hand."

"We can't just get rid of everyone we don't like, can we?"

Both voices seemed rather amused. I crouched and crept to the banister, grateful for the wind and general noises from the nearby street covering my trundle somewhat. Right below us, three shopping basket-laden women chattered away peacefully. One chimed in through a mouthful of apple. "Why not?"

"Yeah, why not? That's what civilized places do. I've read about it."

"Oh, you've read about it."

"I have. Sooner or later, we've got to be a civilized place too."

"What happens when you're the one people don't agree with, Marta?"

"Why would anyone not agree with me?"

Miss Crosman kicked my heels and nodded toward the other balcony. I mouthed, "Now?" and she nodded some more. I had been quite enjoying the time to catch my breath.

I awkwardly balanced on the banister and rose, wobbling, to my feet. A laden market cart passed on the main road just then, and I used the roll of the wheels to cover for my step across.

"Who would be stupid enough to hide her?"

The ladies chittered gaily below me and I had to suppress a laugh thinking of the view they'd get if they looked up my skirt that very instant. It'd mean my head too, most likely, but it was no less ridiculous for it.

Hopping across, I did my best to land quietly on the other side. Fully expecting the maestress to fumble as much as I had, or more, given her age, I turned with a grin, only to see her gingerly sit on the edge and gracefully slide both her legs across. She scooted over without so much as a rustle. Well, then. Country living clearly suited her.

"Did you hear about poor Franca's son, leg clean off?"

"That's what happens when you bring strangers in just to stir trouble. You get trouble. It's not complicated."

"What'll we do with her when we find her?"

"The mayor said she'd be put to rights and set to work for the town. That's not so bad, is it?"

"Depends on what he means by 'put to rights'. I wouldn't want to be in her shoes."

I rolled my eyes and moved toward the balcony door, but caught one more phrase before Miss Crosman shoved me inside, and it sent a wobble through my knees.

"That lost girl, though? If she ever comes back, I'll skin her myself."

Before I could pick up any more of the conversation, we were already rushing past rows of doors that opened into small and garishly painted bedrooms. A brothel? In Whisperwood? All was quiet, but downstairs, a dainty woman in green velvets smiled up at us from behind a counter.

"What'll the ladies be buying today?"

Her tone was almost mocking, but Miss Crosman slammed two silver coins on the counter and replied as earnestly as though she were haggling over fish. "Discretion. I understand there's no shortage here."

The woman pursed her lips and nodded, and out we went again through the back door. I was so turned around I hadn't expected to see thinning houses and a sliver of the road out of town in the distance, but there it was.

"Not out of the woods yet. This'll be the worst part."

It was full morning, bright and clear, and people stirred everywhere. A couple passed with a turnip-laden cart, but took no notice of us. We'd made it as far as the fish cleaner's house with relative ease when a gaggle of women rounded the corner. Miss Crosman shoved me behind a barrel with such force she knocked the air out of my lungs; a good thing too, for the smell coming out of the barrel put me in mind of a sea monster bedding in a pigsty.

A raspy voice cracked like a whip. "Carolina."

I peeked through the space left between the barrel and the wall. An ancient woman with a fine pair of brass spectacles brandished a wooden spoon at Miss Crosman. The maestress, looking almost spry in comparison, propped her arms on her hips in the most defensive posture I've ever seen her take, like a dog with raised hackles trying to make itself seem bigger.

"Elena."

"Us old hens don't go by our first names, Carolina. I've been Missus Balint longer than I haven't."

Miss Crosman shuffled and used her skirts to better cover my hiding place. "Out for a walk then, ladies?"

"You know very well who we're out for. Have you seen her?"

"I've not." Her voice was steady as the seasons.

"Would you tell us if you had?"

"I'd not. What for, so you can hang a stranger by the toes?"

"Did you no small measure of good when you first arrived." The old woman cackled, and I found my mouth hanging in surprise. She went on, merrily. "In fact, many say it's the only reason you've done as well for yourself as you have, Old Missus Balint's tough love."

Cobblestones crackled and Miss Crosman moved to the side to let the ladies pass, thoroughly hiding me between the barrel and her skirts in the process. If I didn't gag from the smell of fish, they'd never see me.

"Good day, Carolina dear. And keep your nose clean."

We stood in silence for another moment, then the maestress exhaled loudly, and off we went. She muttered under her breath the entire time, and though I caught 'not in charge anymore' and 'old bat', I figured it wiser to let her be for a while. As soon as we passed the last house, she swung us across the road and into a woodland trail that paralleled it.

"This leads right back to the trading post. It's the old trail from before they built the main street."

"Did I hear that right, you were a stranger here too?"

She hurried on, her skirts causing the leaves to rustle.

"How many of the people here are really foreigners?"

"This is Whisperwood. Everyone's a foreigner, even the ones born here. Nobody belongs. We do our best. This is where life put us."

I caught up to her, and we walked side by side for a time. "Maybe I don't have to leave either, then. Maybe I can just lie low until Perdy—"

"Don't kick at your last chance at freedom." She stopped and stared me down. "You have no idea the pain I went through, the prices I've paid to be where I am. The people I've had to hurt to stay safe. To keep them safe. You'd have to be a fool or cruel to stay if you had another choice."

"What about Perdy?"

She waved her hand. "She goes missing every now and then. Her aunts whip everyone into a froth like she's been kidnapped by wind spirits. She turns back up. Things settle down. She's a wild child, but nobody will harm her." For once, there was actual doubt in her voice.

"You're not sure."

"You can't help her, either way. If I only have one of you to worry about, I can maybe do something. Settle them down. Both of you, and the mayor's ire, and it'll be worse for everyone. Be on your way."

Up ahead, the trees thinned, and I recognized the lay of the land.

"This is as far as I'm going. Walk on out and don't look back, now."

"What about the Wards?"

"The contract you signed with me was one, broken when we broke it. The Vâlva fur charm in your pocket will let you pass through the one belonging to the Wardens, and the one set by the Praedictors won't be enough to stop you by itself, not if you don't let it. I didn't have time to ask them for help, so it'll sure hurt like all hell, but it won't be enough. Go."

She took a moment to spit in her bosom, draw a circle in the dirt, then cross it, before rushing back toward town, actually picking up her feet for a light jog. I believed her, that she truly didn't want harm to come to anyone unnecessarily, but I doubted that her and my definitions of 'necessary' were nearly the same.

I, on the other hand, dragged my feet through the leaves, doing my best impersonation of a petulant child. I walked in the right direction, at least, but couldn't stop my mind from wondering what I might have done to change the course of things. What if I'd spoken to the mayor? What if I had taken a job? The Warren needed more hands, or the brewery.

What if I found Perdy? I hadn't the slightest idea where she was, but the others might know something. Florin probably would.

I kicked a stone ahead, but the rustle that followed seemed too great. Holding my breath, I listened. There was a faint flutter from the trading post, then nothing. I peeked out from behind a tree, and my heart thumped up my throat.

Someone hung from the walnut tree.

I ran to them before I could think clearly, shouting for help. Two figures swung from one of the lower branches. The whole square was a mess and I tripped over something. Stumbling, I got a better look, and stopped.

The hanging figures were Pierduta and I.

CHAPTER TWENTY-ONE

A Time to Hide

A chill wind rushed past me as if trying to push me away from the wide open square where I stood exposed to anyone and anything that might be lurking. It hadn't a hope of removing me. I couldn't look away.

The hanging bodies were made of cloth and rags, but life-sized and detailed. They'd used black wool to make my long braid, and messy red strips of fabric for Perdy; even the eyes were painted on in the right hazel and green colors. Old dresses covered the pale, dirty canvas that looked unnervingly like skin, and brutal rips at the stomach exposed the hay and grasses they were stuffed with. Large stones tied to their ankles dragged them down, their necks craning against the rope at painful angles. Their mouths were filled with wild garlic. Their wrists were slashed and doused in animal blood.

Nothing was left undefiled. It must have been the work of a dozen practiced hands over a whole night. It was mesmerizing.

The square itself was a mess, feathers and bones everywhere, blood staining the soil. Buckets and boxes and stools lay abandoned, the wicker basket I'd tripped on still swaying. For a moment I thought I heard whispered laughter hidden behind the rustle of leaves. It didn't matter; I was leaving anyway. I was certain of it now.

Going through the woods would have been smarter, but I was out of smarts. I ran. The creaking of rope at my back mocked me. I couldn't help but turn; the figures swung gaily. Slipping in a muddy cart track, I went down to one knee, and when I rose again, my dress was caked in wet clay on that side. It was so cold. How long before they chased me? I'd never let them capture me. Never again.

The way had seemed brief when I came in with the merchant, Enache. It was unrecognizable to me now. Maybe coming at it from the opposite side transformed it into another road altogether. An angry, almost unreal one. Had that bend always been there? Had that fallen willow? Would the townspeople chase me?

I was out of breath before I was out of road and reluctantly slowed. The woods came back into sharper focus, as did the rustle of birch leaves. The ground got wetter by the minute, and dust no longer rose to linger in my hair. Instead, my footsteps stirred only the smell of petrichor.

Exhausted, my body kept me moving forward. I made no plans of what to do next; I had no idea of where to go. There were no angry shouts behind me, no footsteps. Nothing. Perhaps they weren't going to chase me.

The rush of freedom and release from pressure filled my body with tingles of nervous energy, and I rode it right out of town.

There was a knot of fear in my stomach too, but I couldn't do anything about it, so I let it be. I focused, instead, on newfound clarity. What had I been thinking, throwing myself into a small, isolated town like that? Meddling with their affairs? It had seemed like escape at the time, but it was nothing of the sort. If anything, it was like I'd actively searched for more of the same trouble I'd got myself into with Alec. Like I was looking for more ways to hurt myself. Like I always did.

There was a *pop* that I felt in the back of my jaw more than heard. I stopped in my tracks and looked around. Nothing seemed out of order, so I started moving again. The bridge out of town must have been close; the rush of the stream fussed at the edge of my hearing. I wondered why all the shaded areas suddenly seemed malignant.

Another *pop* and I stopped again, in spite of myself. Heat in my pocket drew my attention to the braided forest Vâlva fur, now singed at the end and smoking very slightly. I patted it down to put it out. So much for good luck; I must have gone through the Wardens' barrier. Maybe Miss Crosman's too. That left whatever the Praedictors had cooked up, supposed to be the worst of the lot.

Frustrated, I tried to step forward again. A rapid movement at the edges of my vision caught my attention, and I turned to the right to better see it. A spot of shadow lay there, appearing empty, but I was certain there was something in it. Perhaps the shadow itself was it. Whispers?

I pushed myself forward and set a brisk pace, hoping the speed of it would keep me from stopping, but the faster I went the harder it became to move. The faster I felt something give chase. I almost hoped it was Whispers, rather than people ready to grab me just as I was about to be free.

Twenty steps later, I slowed and stopped to the tune of another *pop*. There was nothing unusual around me but the sharpness of the landscape and depth of the color of it, and yet I struggled to move farther. It was as though my body saw a sheer cliff where my eyes only saw the road, and asking me to take another step was tantamount to asking me to walk off into thin air.

Steeling myself against my inexplicable terror, and reasoning that it was certainly only another Ward, I tried to step forward. My right thigh and knee tensed, but my foot did not move. It was absurd. I'd come that very same way into town. If there had been an invisible cliff, I'd already be dead. I squeezed my eyes shut, shook my head, and threw my whole body forward. Luckily, that time, my foot moved to catch me.

I opened my eyes to a pitch-black sky that was closer than any sky had any right to be. Massive orbs of swirling, writhing color hung on it. Stars? Where was I? They were gigantic, more than ten suns and ten moons put together, each looming over me. They overlapped, one behind the other, and clustered, and covered so much of the sky. Were they stars? Could they be? Were they falling?

There was a distant, massive roar that sounded like blood rushing through veins, but endlessly louder than mine. Pale gray dust rose as I dropped to my knees, my head spinning and my eyes unable to look away from the gods of the sky that seemed close enough to touch. I placed a hand on the ground to brace myself against the vertigo, and held my breath, looking for movement. Were the stars falling to the ground?

My heart pounded in my throat, the sound of it mingling with the roar of the stars. I picked out wiggly lines and spirals in beige and white on one celestial body, blue-green splotches on another. Even what looked like mountains and seas on a reddish-violet one. But for all of the motion hinted at on their surface, they were still. Not one of them had gotten closer in the minute I spent watching. My lungs burned, and I released my breath.

I rose to my feet shakily, keeping my head down and my eyes to the dirt. Still, that feeling that if I stepped forward again, I would surely walk off the face of the world persisted. Where would the cursed Ward put me next? After showing me the falling stars, did it intend to fling me among them?

I caught movement in white out of the corner of my eye. From between ashen tree trunks, an almost-transparent Vâlva gazed at me. It seemed so out of place, not only because it was there, but because it was so tranquil. It found me more interesting than the sky. Did it even see the same things I saw? They were supposed to be immune to most Wards.

Well, if the damned Whisper could get through it, then so could I.

I screamed and flung myself forward into the abyss, eyes shut against my fate.

Expecting a drop, I was startled when my foot encountered resistance at ground level. Everything was completely silent but for the tail end of my cracked shout. I opened one eye and saw nothing but clear road and a sunny sky above me. Even the shadows were gone. I opened the other eye and found more of the same. It was all gone, even the Whisper. Without thinking, I ran another fifty paces and stood in the middle of the bridge, clutching the splintery wooden railing and dragging at every breath.

The road into Whisperwood looked innocent as a lamb.

"Rotting bastards," I wheezed. My anger was unfocused, partly at the Praedictors for their terrifying barrier, partly at Whisperwood, mostly at the universe. "I hope you sneeze into your soup. I hope your toes develop mildew. I hope it rains frogs down your chimneys." I held on to the railing for dear life and shivered. Every stitch of clothing on me was soaked in sweat.

It was an obscenely sunny day every which way, like I'd crossed into a different climate altogether. The woods gathered around the town in the distance and, along with a little low mist, blocked everything from view. After the fact, it was so easy to see that the Praedictors' barrier was little more than a harmless parlor trick, conjured visions to scare away children. All you had to do was exert enough willpower to keep walking, and yet the bar for 'enough' was so high I almost hadn't made it.

"Sons of mangy mountain goats."

An hour must have gone by with me sitting on the planks, leaning against the banister, trying to strengthen my wobbly legs. All urgency left me now that I was free to go.

To my left, the sunny road hugged hills and valleys, eventually making its way back to Cibinium, a crossroads town full of coaches and markets from where the whole world opened. Cibinium was bright and civilized. There was a rail station and promises there'd be electric currents put to work within the next ten years. No Whispers, not the predatory, nor friendly kind.

I wanted so very desperately to go to Cibinium, but also didn't. I'd left it for a reason, and that reason was unchanged. Alec was still out there. I didn't have anyone else waiting for me. Nobody I owed anything good to. Nobody who could shield me from him, the people whose minds he'd poisoned about me, or any other Alec the world harbored.

I knew I was being unreasonable. The odds of him ever finding me were slim, and I didn't even think he was looking. Surely Whisperwood was more frightening? But knowing that I was being unreasonable in my head did nothing to prevent my stomach from turning to water at the thought of being out in the world, where at any moment anyone could say, "You're Anna Haller? Yes. I've heard about you."

Where that same anyone could decide to pick up where Alec left off, and put me underground again. In the water again. Helpless again. Well, if anyone thought I was being unreasonable, clearly we hadn't had the same experiences.

To the right, mist and mud eventually led to Whisperwood, where Perdy was lost. Where they were all, in different ways, lost. I pictured her following in her parents' footsteps, leaving and never returning. I pictured her hanging on the edge of the Unspoken, the way I'd hung in Alec's basement, wondering what came next, thinking there was nobody coming to help her.

Maybe each of us being alone on either side of the barrier was worse than being in Whisperwood together. Ultimately, I couldn't say whether it was fear, or love, that lifted me to my feet and made me start walking. Perhaps the two were equal, and hopefully a good deed still counted if you did it for only half the right reason.

Walking into Whisperwood was as easy as the day I first arrived.

CHAPTER TWENTY-TWO

Shared Burdens

I had to find the smith.

Never mind the townsfolk and their scare tactics. Never mind the mayor and his lies. Never mind Miss Crosman too. I half suspected she'd exaggerated the town's ire just to get me out of the way and to safety. Whatever the risk, running wasn't going to help anyone. Finding the people who had believed in Paul's dedication to change and knowledge might.

Rareş was the only sensible choice. I'd never make it back across town to Ancuţa. Even the brewery was a risk, but the smithy was right on the edge of town. I saw the plume from the brothel roof. I could find it.

Never mind what I'd do when I found it.

A thicket stood between me and my destination. It was all brambles and thorns, trunks and branches smothered by some strange ivy I'd never seen before. Vines were matted so thickly over the canopy as to block out the light. Barely any trees still stood under the weight of it, and almost none were alive. I passed over it, under it, and even pulled my knife out to cut sections away. So engrossed was I in making a path for myself, I jumped when a voice came from behind me.

"What in the devil's uncle's teat are you doing?"

It could have been anyone, but it was Rareş. I hardly deserved the good luck.

"Trimming your hedges. It was either this or dealing with your townsmen, and the hedges seemed less unruly."

I expected a laugh, but he only stared at me darkly. "Picked an odd time to visit." He shoved some branches aside and made a far better opening than the one I'd been working on. "C'mon."

"I need to talk to you."

"Gripe at me when we're sat with a cup of tea."

"I don't know how safe it is to go back." It was a half truth, but who knew how much he knew already? He could very well blame me for everything too.

"There's nobody at the forge. It'll only be us."

"Where's your wife?"

He didn't answer. We moved through the last of the brush silently, then had to cross through a clear-cut swathe out in the open. I shivered like a dog in midwinter, from tiredness and fear and cold all together. He put his arm around me, but it didn't do much. I wanted to slow down, but the frantic disquiet inside me wouldn't hear of it.

Within minutes, we were inside and warming our hands by his smoldering forge. The stone building wrapped around a square yard where the massive furnace smoked. Tools and weapons covered every surface, and I had to put hoes away to set my teacup down. The fine fired clay with blue swirled patterns was surely his wife's choice.

Once I was settled, I attempted an innocuous conversation starter. "So, I tried to leave town."

He huffed. "I don't blame you. It's as cursed as anything in the world."

"It's not the most cursed thing I've ever seen." I was surprised by how distant my memories of home seemed in that moment, but doubted they'd ever leave me completely.

"You haven't seen anything yet. What's the bother, then?"

"I haven't left, for one thing."

"I can see that."

"I want to help."

"You would." The tiredness in his voice curbed my enthusiasm.

"You're not well, are you?"

He started to speak but eyed me warily. "You know that if you're staying here, you're dead to the world?"

"I know how to leave, now."

"And I know how to please women, but you don't see me walking around with my hands up skirts."

I snorted through my tea and choked.

"Did you really figure out how to get through all the borders?"

"Miss Crosman tore up her contract herself, that was one."

"Aye, any trade you make binds you here. That's most of us sorted. Do you know, we put coins in the hands of babies as they come into the world, then replace them with acorns? So they've traded with us, and belong to us."

"Grim. Why wouldn't at least some parents protest?"

He grunted. "If they ever do, the community gathers round them to help them see the error of their ways." He said that phrase practically dripping scorn. "What else did you encounter?"

"The Wardens have something too. I don't know what it does, but I got through it with this." I showed him the charm.

"Shifter fur is a slippery thing, makes its way through anything. Shifters can bend rules." He seemed thoughtful.

"The last one was the worst. I don't think I can explain it."

"I've never gotten that far."

I gasped at him.

A hard and cold laugh burst out of his belly. "Like I haven't tried to leave a hundred times. Every time I get drunk. They say that last one takes you to the future of our world. Wanna hang a Praedictor out the Tower window with me and find out?"

"I want to crawl somewhere safe and sleep for a year."

"Aye." There was no mistaking it, he was more battered than the last time I'd seen him, and the last time I'd seen him, he helped cut someone's leg off. It didn't bode well.

We sipped some tea in silence. Blood came back into my fingers. "Rareş?"

"Mmm?"

I thought of starting with more harmless questions. "What were you doing out in the brambles?"

He stumbled over words for a moment, but to my surprise, eventually found them, albeit with a sort of wet gravel to his voice. "This is an awful place, Anna, and it's time someone made that clear to you. I had to find a hidden spot to bury my child."

His wife had been pregnant. I remembered Miss Crosman saying she would need help and prayers. It seemed all the prayers in the world didn't help. "I'm sorry, Rareş."

"Many newborns don't make it. We know that's how it goes. Most of us accept it. My wife doesn't."

I feared for her but didn't dare interrupt. People rarely told me the whole truth in Whisperwood, and the moment felt sacred.

"She took every potion, sang every unsong, made every Ward, destroyed her body and mind, all to keep it safe. Every Warden and hawker with a trinket to sell knows her by name. If that baby'd ever had any chance, she crushed it herself."

I couldn't help but get angry at his assessment, but there was no point to arguing with grief.

"I tried to stop her for a while, but she went behind my back and took the mushrooms, and the berries, and damnation knows what else anyway. So I've been ready for this day for a long time."

"Did she...."

"She survived."

I let out a breath of relief. "What can I do?"

"Listen. This place is dangerous. But the people in it are even more dangerous. Superstitious, hungry idiots, one dumber than the other. And what's on the other side is maybe worse. I had to bury the child as far away as possible."

"I thought the Wardens took care of that. Made sure that the Whispers didn't —" a dizziness swooped over me, "— tamper with bodies."

"Ex-bleeding-cuse me if I don't trust them much. Rotten vultures. For all I know, they do those rituals for their own purposes. They sure didn't do them for me and mine."

"I understand why you'd distrust everyone. Nobody ever tells the whole truth here."

"Nobody knows it. The reverend did, maybe. He had ideas. But now they've murdered him for it—"

"You think that was intentional?"

He took a sip of tea and gathered his thoughts for a moment. "I don't know. If the world weren't aflame, I'd suggest you spend some time finding out, but we have bigger problems."

"Aye." I didn't realize I'd copied his dialect and inflection, but he smirked and I smiled back. "And I don't know how to solve any of them."

He nodded. "The way I see it, you have two options."

"I'm not going to like either of them, am I?"

"Not unless you fell on your head quite hard."

"What are they?"

"Either you make a life for yourself in some way that doesn't fill you with self-loathing, or you give it up and take a Silent Walk you never come back from. So...." He paused.

"You make an enticing case for both sides."

"I'm truly gifted."

"I'm gonna stay. Give my best to whoever is willing to have it. Maybe find Perdy. That's the only option that makes me feel like a decent human being."

"You'll need help. You look like death turned you down."

"You flatterer."

"You'll look worse before Whisperwood's done with you. Any idea where your friend is?"

"Sure, she's under my skirt. Why don't you have a look?"

He guffawed in spite of himself, and I felt a little victory at that. All I'd wanted was to break through the tiredness and coax a little hope.

"I bet I know where we can find out. Those stuffy old Tower tamperers will know. She's gone over, for sure. They're the only ones who know anything about that place. If they don't, nobody else will."

"You really think she's out in the Unspoken?"

"Look at you, learning the local lingo. Yeah, it wouldn't be the first time. If you needed a break from everything and one way was blocked, wouldn't you go the other?" He chewed on that for a few seconds, and

I wandered into the kitchen to rinse off our cups. He followed. "Maybe I can help."

"Why would you?"

"Because I want to make things better around here too, in my own way." There was a tone of finality to his statement.

I was torn between pressing for more answers and taking what I already had. He'd been more forthcoming with me than almost anyone else, and if he knew more than he was saying, what business was it of mine? It was hard; I wanted to know everything. Feeling around secrets turned my stomach into sulfurous slugs. But it wasn't fair to him.

Instead, I asked him for a somewhat unusual favor.

CHAPTER TWENTY-THREE

Flying Crockery

"This is how you want to spend an hour?"

I didn't need him to understand. I just needed him to stand guard. "It is. Is that going to be a problem?"

Rareş shrugged and sat under the walnut tree, stuffing a small pipe with fragrant leaves. I rolled up my sleeves and threw myself into the work.

It wasn't about the house itself. It didn't belong to me, and never would. It wasn't about Perdy's family either, even though I hoped I could bring her back and she'd have a decent place to live, away from her aunts. It was mostly about regaining some semblance of control over at least one thing.

Placing the bedroom door back on was a simple matter of carrying it back inside and lifting it onto its hinges. The front door required crafty maneuvering, using nails and some rope, to replace the broken top hinge with something that would do until a proper one could be made. Rareş promised he'd take care of it himself.

I found an old iron rod that was just about the right size, and I cut holes in the wood on either side of the door. The rod fit across it on the inside and gave the place an extra layer of protection. If they hadn't already come up with security bars in Whisperwood, I could probably make a killing installing them.

Then, covered in mortar dust, I went to work sweeping and washing. The place was little enough that it took no time at all, and by the time I was finished Rareş had voluntarily gathered piles of firewood and repaired two chairs. I felt myself returning to sanity by the minute. There was only one thing I still had to do.

I took a huge bag of salt I'd found in the larder, naïvely thinking it was for de-snowing the front yard when I first saw it, and drew salt lines across all the windows and doors. I even salted the fireplace. The large living space was perfectly sealed now, at least against any common Whisper that might wish to trouble anyone.

"Are you pleased now?"

I rested the broom by the door. "Very. Thank you for bearing with me."

"Haven't met a person yet that didn't take some bearing with. Besides, you've given me time to think."

"Did it hurt?"

"There's still time. Listen, you're friends with that Prick-dictor in training, ain't you?"

"As much as anyone can be in a few days."

"Think he'd help?"

"I think any of us would do anything for Perdy."

He thought about it for a moment. "Tell you what. I'll gather supplies. You see if he's willing to talk his people into giving us a way in."

"You want to come with us? Are you serious?"

"Deathly. Do we have a deal?"

I didn't know what to say so I nodded like an excited schoolchild, in spite of it having been my secret hope all along that he'd reach exactly that conclusion. It didn't seem like he stood to gain much, aside from some answers and a distraction from his grief. Doing good by others was often what saved us from ourselves, and perhaps that was reason enough.

We packed up and I nervously followed him through field and ditch and bramble, avoiding all roads and pausing to check for townsfolk. It was nearly full dark by then, and there wasn't much movement. I wasn't even sure the townsfolk would do anything if they did see me. They'd had every opportunity to ambush me in that clearing, and chose to spend all that effort in frightening me instead, probably hoping I'd become more compliant. Terrifying as they were, the effigies were harmless. It was surprising how much perspective changed when one wasn't deathly afraid.

Rareş didn't seem concerned. "Lots of people are going to be at a funeral right about now, worried out of their minds, or hounding the mayor for answers." He walked on for a little while, then, more quietly, added, "And if not, I'd like to see them try me."

In the gloomy silence, distressed shouts came from inside the brewery. I dropped all caution and hurried ahead of Rareş, and almost smacked into Mara full-on. She looked like she'd just come in from the cold, muddy and disheveled.

"I said I was sorry!"

Eugen stood on the stairs, red-faced and loud, aiming the full force of his anger at her. "I was just about to come looking for you! You said you were going to sleep. I came to bring you blankets."

"I went to stop them." Tears streamed down her face.

I went by her side and took her frozen hand. She squeezed mine, hard, with both of hers. Selfishly, I was glad for the sign that she was pleased to see me.

Unbelievably, Eugen got louder. "That's insane! The mayor could have had you hanged, you can't just charge in—"

"I know!" She was roaring every word, inconsolable.

I didn't know what to do. "Maybe we can all take a breath—"

Eugen wasn't having any of it. "That was beyond irresponsible. I don't like what they're doing any more than you do, but you know they'll fight us every step of the way, claiming Walkers are a vital resource."

"They're not resources, you bastard. They're children!" She hurricaned past him and he tried to grab ahold of her, but she shook him off. "Let me go!"

By the time he could gather himself, she was up the stairs and out of sight, a violently slammed door behind her.

He turned to me next, pleading. Injured. "I just don't want her to get thrown into jail or worse. We can figure out a peaceful way to get the kids out of it, for sure. Negotiate—"

I put my hands up. "I've no idea what you're talking about, but I don't think I'm going to like it."

That wasn't strictly true. I had a heavy suspicion, but I wanted to hear it from him. He slithered down the stairs with a sigh and uncorked a bottle of something so strong I could smell it from across the room, slinging a shot himself before offering one to me. Only then did I notice that Rareş had gone, probably to avoid the conflict as much as to get the supplies he'd mentioned. I shamelessly took the offered drink.

Eugen downed another. "The mayor took children this morning. Not all of them, but so many. And far too old. State of emergency, my arse. Mara's sister must have been one of them."

I knew what that meant, but I was sick of everyone hedging the truth. "What did he take Clara and the others for?"

He shot me a glance and slunk back into his glass. The bastard knew I knew.

I wouldn't relent. I couldn't, despite knowing it served nobody. "What did he take them for, Eugen?"

"To make Walkers, even though we never send anyone Walking. He took them to make an army that never fights, so he could look like he's doing something without doing anything."

"He's going to take them to the brink of death, so they can come back and risk their lives even further."

"We don't own our lives." He didn't raise his voice or show any outward sign of distress, but it was as though all the blood in his body withdrew from the conversation and left him a hollow, empty husk.

I'd done that to him. Forced him to talk about something he was clearly in as much pain over as I was. Something that wasn't his choice to begin with. Suddenly, I couldn't remember why. Guilt had replaced that knowledge.

I poured myself another glass of brandy and sought my next words carefully. "Ancuţa would say that it's only horrible if you have a better option. Otherwise, it's just life."

He softened a little. "Sounds like her. She's not bad, for a Warden."

"I think Mara knows you have her best interest at heart."

"Doesn't seem like she does."

"She does. But she's allowed to be in pain, anyway. Knowing it's better to be cautious doesn't make it easy to do."

His sigh was so deep I felt the ache of it myself. "I love her. I do. And I agree with her. But we need to be calm, to plan things, to be clever. We can't afford to make enemies around every corner. That's not what living on the frontier is about. It can't be."

I expected him to blame me at any moment. With Paul dead and Perdy gone, I was the last Walker. The thought hadn't even occurred to me until just then. I was their very last. If I hadn't run away, maybe there wouldn't have been any need to make new ones yet. Surely, he realized? I flinched from the blow, but it never came. He must have thought it, but spared me the lash. He was a better person than I'd just been.

A thought crossed my mind. "When will they actually start?"

"The kids? In a few days. They have to figure out how to do the process as safely as possible, which isn't saying much. They'll stall, if the mayor is satisfied that it looks like he's helping."

"Maybe if I can find Perdy, bring her back, they won't have to. Maybe with her and myself working for the town—"

"You want to go after her? After what Paul.... I don't...." He shook his head at me, bewildered. "You can't be serious."

"But would it help?"

He stuttered. "I – I guess it might. Perdy hated the process of making Walkers as much as any of us. She spent so much time looking for other ways to teach people to Walk."

"Maybe she even knows a way. Maybe she hadn't wanted to stir things up while there was no need."

He raised his eyebrows, but didn't disagree. "It's possible."

"Would you help me?"

He glanced up the stairs, probably thinking about Mara. "How?"

"By taking me to the Tower."

It didn't take him more than a moment of consideration. "I've already made sure there's a nurse coming tonight to check on Flor. There's no reason I can't slip away."

"How is he?"

Eugen shook his head. "I don't know. I'm not ready to make any big statements either way. He has a fever, he's...." He drank, shook his head again. "I keep thinking that Paul had it better. And then I cry. I don't know."

Tingles surprised the bottom of my eyes too.

"He asks for you. I'm not sure if you should go. He's not in his right mind, understandably. Angry about what we did."

"I'll go up and talk to him. Then we can leave. Whatever he has to say, it'll be better for him if he says it."

Eugen looked at me like he wanted to stop me but didn't have the energy to even try. I knew exactly how he felt. He told me which room to look for, and I found the right door on the dusty first landing, within easy reach. Wooden boards screeched under my feet, and I dreaded their noise as though some phantom behind me had caused it. Whatever brave face I'd put on for Eugen, I only expected the worst from that encounter. But soldiering through the worst was the least we owed Florin.

The door didn't choose to go quietly either. It squealed and groaned as I pushed it. The occupant of the room was expecting me, judging by the ceramic cup that flew at my head and shattered into a cloud of powder against the wall behind me. I dodged back behind the door and dragged it almost shut.

His voice came from inside. "I'm sorry. I promised myself I wouldn't do that."

"That's fine. It's Anna, by the way."

"I know."

"Oh."

"Come in."

"You promise you won't throw anything else at me?"

"I'm out of cups. I've got some apples, but I doubt I can kill you with them."

I peered inside. He was propped up on pillows in a bed right by the window, surrounded by uneaten food and clumsily discarded blankets.

"You want to kill me?"

"No. I don't even know why I'm angry at any of you. Everything, all at once. Just don't expect me to be grateful."

I sat at the foot of his bed, doing my best not to stare at him. The sweat on his brow and incessant trembling didn't bode well.

"I expect no such thing from you."

"What am I supposed to do now?"

I saw no point in beating around the bush. "Rest, sit still, and give your body time to decide what it wants to do with you." We often comfort the dying for our own comfort, but I knew firsthand that soldiers wanted to know the truth.

He scoffed. "What do you think?"

"You're still alive. That usually helps."

"I feel like a steaming pile of vegetable peelings."

"There's nothing you can do about it but rest."

He looked out the window, uncomfortable and angry. I could only imagine all the things he did his best not to tell me.

"I'm useless now, so I need you to do something for me."

"Anything."

"It won't be easy."

"Won't it? Everything else has been so far."

He didn't even seem to notice my quip. "You won't want to do it. But you have to, you're all that's left."

"You sure know how to make a girl feel good."

His volume tripled in a flash. "Would you just shut up and listen?"

His anger was justified, I understood it fully. Still, it made me shrink back into myself in shame for trying to force a lighter mood. I picked at a bundle of grapes for something to do, giving him time to settle down and gather his thoughts. He shook in waves, and, at its strongest, it was enough to rattle the bed beneath us.

After a few breaths, he went on, visibly conserving his strength. "They told me Perdy was gone."

"I'll find her, Flor. I promise."

"I know you will. You're the only Walker left. You have to. There's no other way."

"Take it easy, I'll find her and bring her back."

"No."

"No?"

"You have to find her and kill her."

CHAPTER TWENTY-FOUR

New Heights

He thrashed about, trying to raise himself up more fully, and I was on my feet.

"Don't look at me like that!"

"You're feverish. Not making sense."

"I make plenty of sense, you just don't know it. Stop backing away and let me explain."

I hadn't realized I was moving until I bumped up against the dresser behind me. "Fine. Explain." I fully intended to let him talk and dismiss his ramblings entirely. The fact that he was perfectly lucid and clear-spoken worked heavily against me.

"I won't have time to tell you all of it. You need to go. Now. Yesterday. But here's how it is. You know her family went missing?"

"She was a baby. She came back, a long time later."

"Ten years later. They wanted to kill her on the spot."

"A child?"

"That came out of the woods claiming to be the long-lost baby of the Samson family? Of course."

"Who else could she be?"

"Anyone? Anything? What if the Whispers took a baby away and gave us one of their own, instead?"

"We have that stupid old superstition too. Changed babies. I'm surprised at you. She's one of the kindest people I've ever met."

"I thought it was stupid too. That's why I offered to guard her. I was only a handful of years older, but I was already tough as nails, been secretly training with Master Cheşa in the shadow of the Tower my whole life. I promised I'd make it my job to end her life at the first sign that she was anything other than human."

"Is that why they let her live?"

"It was the only way. I thought I was being clever and keeping them content. I got to hang out with a pretty girl. I was happy."

"You don't think so anymore?"

"Not for years. I don't know who or what Perdy is, but she's hiding something. I just couldn't get myself to do anything about it."

"You do care about her."

I sat back down on the edge of the bed by his side, hoping to calm him and soothe him somewhat. His eyes were liquid and dark, and I feared he wouldn't be able to stay up much longer. He settled into the pillows more comfortably.

"I've spent the last fifteen years of my life watching her every move. Of course I care about her. I was going to wait until I was sure she was a Whisper, then take us both out. Don't look at me like that."

It wasn't horror he saw in my eyes, but pain at what a hard life he'd been given.

"People could die because I didn't keep my word. They may already have. Because I'm too soft, and weak. You have to—"

"You might as well stop saying that. I'm not killing Perdy."

Suddenly, he was inches from my face, propped up on one arm, holding the back of my neck with the other, damp and burning. The gesture was so intimate and terrifying I couldn't breathe.

"Do you really want to be the one who didn't listen to a dying man?" He squeezed my scruff, and I couldn't tell if it was in anger or because he was struggling to hold himself up.

I swallowed hard. "I'm listening."

"Don't believe me. Go out there, find her, and see for yourself. Then, if my words make more sense to you, do what you have to do, or suffer the knowledge that you were the last chance and failed."

He collapsed back into his pillows with a wince and an exhale through clenched teeth. His trembling was the most violent I'd seen it yet, and he kept his face turned toward the window, but I didn't think it was for the sake of the view.

I picked up a heavy woolen blanket and threw it over his familiar yet incomplete form under the sheets.

"Get the hell out of here."

I didn't wait to be told twice.

★　　★　　★

Storming out of the room, I bumped into Eugen on the landing.

"Anna, what's wrong? Was it that bad?"

"Take me to the Praedictors. Now."

"Rareş's not back—"

"He knows where to find us."

He glanced upstairs, doubtful, then nodded once.

I burst out the front door with him chasing after me. Many of the doors around the brewery were marked off with a white chalk line, almost as though they were being checked off, like someone had been searching.

"Where is everyone?"

Eugen buttoned his coat behind me. "The smart ones are locked down tight. The town's all wound up and nasty, with everything that's been going on these past few days. Looking for trouble."

"And the not-smart ones?"

"Looking for people to blame, whether it makes sense or not. Come on."

He led me carefully down narrow alleys, across the main road in a rush, and off toward the mill. The few people we saw either scurried away or kept their heads down, avoiding my gaze.

"There's nothing ahead but the mill."

Eugen kept pressing forward. "Worried I got lost in the only town I've ever known? The upper floors of the mill belong to us. That's why it's jokingly called the 'Tower'. We use the rotation to power our tools and—"

Before he could say more, raised voices drifted to us from up ahead. I had planned to confront the townsfolk when I had the chance, talk to them about my desire to help and find Perdy, explain my actions. I had planned to be brave, and to trust in the support of my friends, but all of that went the way of the wind the moment I heard their angry voices. I ducked into a wheat field and Eugen followed.

We skirted around a hedgerow and he rose just enough to see the millhouse. "This is bad."

"What kind of bad?"

"Torches and pitchforks bad. It looks like the idiots are trying to storm the Tower."

"What? Why?"

He chewed his lip and didn't answer.

"You don't seem surprised."

"Everyone hates and fears the Tower. They don't understand it. The Warren has it easy, they just pound their chests and say they protect the town. What we do is complicated."

Thumps and the sound of broken wood reached us, followed by Eugen's muttered curses. "Flogging mules, they'll get themselves killed."

"How?"

"The whole place is Warded. I told you, we were expecting this to happen someday. We hoped the existence of Wards itself would put people off. The moment they start rushing up the stairs—"

A violent thump passed through my chest, and my hearing went away with it. Eugen opened his mouth, but if anything came out, it was lost to me. All that was left was a constant ringing in my ears, a sharp ache, and the wheat stalks lying flat to the ground away from the Tower. He picked me up with more strength than was strictly necessary and pushed me toward the building. My flutter of panic at the thought of facing the townsfolk returned, but not for long. Most of them were splayed on their backs, unconscious, littered around the front door of the mill. The ones nearest to it were crumpled bodies.

I tried to ask, "What's going on?" but was unable to hear my own voice, so I doubted I'd hear the answer. Instead, I followed Eugen as he circled around the millhouse through the hedges. In a place of relative safety, he stopped and sat by the wall.

He tapped my shoulder to get my attention and put his palms over his ears in a big gesture. He then turned his back to me to show me that where his fingers met at the back of his head, they were tapping away hard and steady. I tried to copy him. The roar of my fingers against my skull was almost deafening, like metal horses galloping through a tunnel, but as soon as I did it, I felt relief from the ache, and the ringing subsided.

The moment I removed my hands, he grabbed my shoulders.

"We have to save them."

I wasn't sure if he meant the Masters, the people, or both. Around the corner, more townsfolk approached. They were singularly focused on the upper levels of the mill, flinging torches and shooting arrows, but some already gathered at the front to attempt another breach.

Cries of "Stop your evil!" and "Are you hiding the girl?" rose from the crowd, but the Masters made no answer.

"Are there more Wards?"

"On the inside of the workshop door. And if they get through that, it's even worse. They could be gambling with all our lives."

He pulled at my sleeve again and directed us to the back of the building, where it nearly touched on the woods. "I used to climb up here to look at the stars."

It was easy to see why terrified townsmen wouldn't want to be anywhere near that side, where the forest watched, foreboding. The main body of the mill was only two stories high, and a thick rope of ivy made easy climbing up the first half. We had to get up the second by clambering on window ledges and a drainpipe. Then, it was a gently sloping roof all the way to the side of the Tower itself.

Eugen wasn't the quickest or the strongest, but his determination rivaled none. I imagined that, in his heart, he was racing up there to save someone who was like a father to him. He and Artjom had seemed so warm and comfortable. I wondered, were it my father up in that Tower, whether I would douse it with brandy or whiskey before setting a match to it.

I was already out of breath. "What now?"

We huddled against the Tower that rose another four or five stories above us, no visible purchase for climbing it in sight.

Eugen frowned. "They won't stop. Not now that there have been casualties. They won't relent. Once they're in the workroom...."

"What's in there, Eugen?"

He chewed his lip again, and his eyes were dewy. "Anna, I'm scared for all of them. We need to get inside."

There was no time, so on an impulse, I rose to my feet and stepped toward the front of the building, determined to do something. Anything.

"Citizens of Whisper— Oof!"

Before I knew what happened, I was pressed against the roof with Eugen holding me down.

"Stay down, you crazy lady!"

An arrow swished through the air above us.

"Get off me!" I kicked more strongly than I should have.

He didn't budge. "Not unless you promise not to do that again."

I was starting to panic. "I'll promise to kiss the Devil if you just get off me!"

He must have realized his mistake, and quickly drew back. "I just can't accept a world in which you get killed by a stray arrow. Mara will never forgive me. She's angry enough with me as is."

I huffed, but another arrow passing overhead quenched my argument. "What else can we do?"

He pointed at the mill blades, shocking white sails still against the darkened sky. "Are you afraid of heights?"

I paled.

Once, ages before, I'd seen a mill much like that one. It had been damaged in a storm and was being repaired. The men working it unfurled canvas across its wooden framed arms in a daring feat of acrobatics I'd remember on my deathbed.

"I know how these work." I tried to push confidence into my voice. If that was the plan we'd be taking, what was the point in fussing about it? "They're designed to hold the weight of a man, I've seen it. I honestly don't know if jumping on them still counts, though."

Brightly lacquered, the wooden scaffolding holding up the canvas sails seemed strong and true. It would have to be, because there was a good jump to take between the roof and the bottom sail, and once we were in the air, there was no turning back.

He pushed to the front. "I'll go first. Do you think it'll rotate when I jump on it?"

"It shouldn't. The turning mechanism must be shut, otherwise they'd be moving in this breeze. It ought to be more or less like a ladder suspended over nothing."

Eugen threw me a mad look, but wasted no more time. Surprised shouts came from below us when he lunged across the gap and latched on to the wooden framework like a magnet, cleanly and neatly. He grinned at me, then reached up and started his climb.

I lined up, ran for it, and prayed. At the very last moment my body tried to stop me from jumping, so I barely made it to the edge of the sail and clung on with arms and legs for dear life. My hands refused to let go, so I hung for a while, looking down at people looking up at me in shock.

With unreasonable heaviness, I unstuck my right arm from where it was clutching the sail and slowly shifted to the inside. I didn't look down again, and probably wouldn't have been able to if I wanted to. Above, Eugen smiled encouragement at me.

The climb was hard at first, large gaps between the beams making it difficult to pull myself up. They got shorter and shorter as we neared the axle, and before I knew it, I had Eugen pulling me onto the ridiculously steep roof.

My teeth chattered. "I don't like this."

"I don't think it's designed for entertainment."

He smiled at me again, clearly having way more fun than was sensible. Crouching, he shuffled over warm roof tiles to just above the window. The wind roared across my body. I had to crawl there on elbows and knees, too scared to stand up any higher. What an image we must have made, him perched over the window like a gargoyle and me with my bottom in the air.

"Artjom!" He called to his Master in a sort of harsh whisper, seemingly unsure of whether he wanted to be heard or not.

From below us, a similar voice responded. "Eugen? You brave fool. Get down from the roof. Without breaking your neck, please!"

"Toss me a length of rope!"

He lay flat on his stomach and stretched his arm down, moments later bringing up a coil of sturdy sailing rope. He passed it to me and pointed toward the peak of the roof where a wind vane shaped like an odd, winged snake stood.

"Can you get up there and tie this to that? Securely, as if your life depended on it."

Certainly, it wasn't what I wanted to do. What I wanted to do was go somewhere quiet, perhaps by a lake, and read a nice book. Instead, I set forth on hands and knees up the steep roof, caressing the wooden shingles like a lover and whispering sweet prayers that they wouldn't slip out from under my hands.

Up close, the greenish copper wind vane was much larger than I'd imagined, and indeed supported by a sturdy wooden shaft. Every scale on the wavy body of the creature was a different segment of metal, and the wings shot up delicately like those of a dragonfly. The same birdlike thing was represented in one of Father Andrei's stained-glass windows, a fact that I dwelled on in an attempt to procrastinate raising my hands from the shingles.

I threw the rope around the wooden beam beneath the serpent and tied it into a neat hangman's noose. It was the only truly sturdy knot I knew, but I knew it all too well.

Holding on to the long section of the rope that now dangled out over the window and into the room beneath us, I rappeled down to the edge. Eugen waved at me, but didn't wait. He was over and out of sight before I arrived even halfway down.

As soon as the ledge loomed before me, I lost my nerve. Going back down the sail didn't bear consideration, but swinging into the void that unnaturally high up left my feet cold and the sides of my legs tingling. I flattened as much as I could and crept to the edge, hoping to brace by looking over it. The drop appeared as if a portal opened to hell itself, and my head spun.

"Anna!"

Arms reached outward from the window beneath me. I didn't know whose they were, but I closed my eyes, gripped the rope for dear life, and swung out over the edge, wind blowing up my skirts for a moment.

I didn't know how to lower myself, and my shoulders started burning immediately. It only took seconds for my arms to give up and let go of the rope without any consideration for my well-being. It slid between my palms and fingers, burning my already sore hands so badly I cried out. Tears blurred my vision.

Through a watery fog, the dark opening of the window appeared before me and rushed upward. I closed my eyes, but they shot right back open when someone gripped my arm and the top of my bodice, stopping my descent and jolting my shoulder badly.

For a moment, I felt angry at the extent of damage my body kept being subjected to. The next thing I knew, I was inside the room, unceremoniously dumped onto a plank floor, and all emotion escaped me in one relieved breath.

CHAPTER TWENTY-FIVE
Beast Full of Soul

I sat on the floor for a long time, listening to my own heart pounding, the ache in my arms making me deeply ashamed of how poorly I'd handled the climb down. Dust scratched my throat, and I coughed, but nobody paid me any notice.

"You can't release it!" Eugen stood, red-faced, hands in his hair, across the room from Artjom.

The space that opened up behind him looked more like a mechanic's shop than anything I'd expected. Tools and diagrams littered every surface. The walls were lined with skulls and bones of creatures I'd never seen before. Human skulls with horns, canine skulls attached to bodies with human hands, deer-serpents, and fish-birds were the least of what hung on display.

The Master spoke calmly, his complexion whiter than a sheet, his voice low and steady. "They're not giving us a choice. If they make it inside, we're dead and they release it, anyway." He kept his hands on his hips and his eyes trained on the ceiling, where a complex mechanism slowly rotated golden stars inlaid into concentric circles of Prussian blue. His sleeves were rolled up to his elbows, showing more of the tattoos that seemed to gracefully weave together with dozens of scars running no doubt all the way up his arms.

Eugen yelled right into his face, "You can't just play with their lives like that. Dozens of people. Who knows who might get in its way? There has to be something else we can do!"

Between Eugen and Artjom, the obvious object of their argument sat stock-still. It was neither concerned nor perturbed by their flailing, and only stared at me with perfectly round, uniformly milky-white eyes. At first, I thought it was an animal. Thick, stringy white wool covered most of the body and hid the shape of it. Then, I thought it must be dead, for where the head should have been there was only a flawless black canine skull, shining like satin and ending in a long, wolfish mouth riddled with wolfish black teeth. When a silvery-pink and pointy tongue slipped out from between its jaws and licked at a long upper fang, I gave up trying to classify it entirely.

Behind Artjom, two other solemn figures waited. One, an old man, sat on a heavy chair with his hands in his lap. Profound wrinkles told a story that must have spanned nearly a century, fighting for attention with a scar running down his forehead and many others on the back of his hands. The Masters' bodies all suggested so much fighting, and all of it a long time ago. Was that what awaited the rest of us? The other man, with his back to us, alternated between studying the constellations on the ceiling and taking notes on a map open across a vast pinewood work surface.

The argument raged on, but muffled noises came through a solid wooden door and demanded attention. The door was crisscrossed with heavy iron bands and studded with iron nails at each intersection. I stood and walked toward it as quietly as possible. I kept my eyes on the creature at the center of the room the entire time, and even though it had no pupils or irises to speak of, there was the most uncanny feeling that it kept its eyes on me. I shuddered and pressed my ear against the door.

Still, all I could hear was Eugen.

"It's absurd! Any other way would be better."

I focused harder on the door. Muffled voices swam through the thick wood at me, but nothing distinct.

"Do we even have enough silver to protect all of us? Even Anna?"

Heavy footsteps thundered up the stairs, but I felt the vibration of them more than heard them. My brow furrowed and I tried to concentrate.

"What will we do when they're all dead?"

A sudden sharp *thunk* on the door had me jumping several steps back toward the middle of the room with a shriek.

Artjom finally raised his voice. "Be careful!" Suddenly, he was behind me, holding me in a bear hug. "You almost made stew of us, wiping this Ward away."

One step behind us, a line of fine silver shavings stretched out either side, eventually banking and forming a square around the motionless creature at its center. Four of those squares overlaid at odd angles formed an unusually brutish star. The beast inside it remained still, facing the window, and yet its curious white marble eyes seemed focused on us.

"What—" It felt odd to speak of the intelligent, living creature as though it were a table. "Or who is this?"

For the first time, I had the chance to be that close to a Whisper without it chasing me. For the first time, I realized how completely unlike animals they were.

"The Pricolici? Salvation, maybe." Artjom released me. "What, or who. It, or he." For a moment, he seemed to wonder himself. "A very dangerous Whisper, Anna. And may you be blessed with the time to learn all about them."

"Why is he here? Like this, without a Tide, just standing there in a Ward?" I couldn't mask the exasperation in my voice. Nothing ever made sense in Whisperwood.

"Sounds like you've spent time at the Warren. Didn't the old book nibblers tell you? Shifters have phenomenal powers. Shifters can pass through the border. Shifters—"

"Bend rules." It was the one constant I'd learned. An exhausting one, but if it was true, perhaps the curious being standing before me could be my ride into the Unspoken. An idea was forming in the back of my head, and I only hoped I'd live to have it proven foolish.

"They do. Which makes them valuable, and volatile."

"But why is he here?"

Artjom glanced at the Master with his back to us, uncertain. "Does it matter? The short version is we were persuaded we needed to do this. To learn about them, to harness their strength. I wish we hadn't."

Eugen paced. "It's not all on your shoulders. I knew what was going on too. Reverend Andrei did. So did the mayor. Hellfire, I think it was the worst-kept secret in our history."

Artjom nodded. "Which is why the people blame us for the good reverend's death and what came after."

I almost felt the puzzle pieces fall into place in my head. "When Father Andrei was pleading for his life, he swore you'd – oh, I don't remember the exact words – you'd give him back or release him. Is this the 'him' he was talking about?"

A gloom overcame Artjom, and his head drooped. "It must have been. That would explain why the Whispers are so mad. They've been expecting us to let this one go, as per his promise."

"But they killed him before he could ever deliver."

"Death is no obstacle to a Whisper. They never end. I don't think they understand that we do. They'd have expected the message delivered and the promise kept, just the same."

More noise outside was followed by a muffled shout to "Get back." The door thudded, but held fast. Part of that strength must have come from a Ward, because the hardwood and iron themselves wouldn't have been enough.

My heart raced. "What do we do?"

Eugen stepped in between us, grabbing his Master by the jerkin and holding him out at arm's length.

"I'll tell you what we don't do. We don't let this thing loose on everyone out there. We might be safe, if we're lucky, cowering behind silver baubles, but the ones storming the Tower will die. Badly. And we don't even know who's out there!"

Artjom shrugged, tugging himself from Eugen's grip, but smiled warmly at both of us. "You are a good person. I love you for it. I won't force you to do anything, but be certain you know what the options are."

I raised my hand. "Not that I get a vote, but…what are they?"

"We either let him loose and he kills the rioters before returning to his woods, or the rioters break in, kill us, wipe away his Ward by accident, and he kills the rioters before returning to his woods." Slow and light movements took Artjom across the room to where the other two figures waited. He took a seat, slouched, crossed his arms, and stared at me. "I would rather not die on principle, but I'm no dictator. You're here now, and it's your life too, so you do get a vote."

The man next to him, dressed in loose brown robes, seemed much older and even more tired. He let out a jeering, "Hmph," and looked out the window, ignoring me.

"I couldn't have said it better myself, Master Marc. Master Cheşa, what say you?"

The last man turned more fully to face us. Hard red slices crawled from his neck up over the lower part of his face, embracing his head like fleshy branches. Intricate, looping tattoos covered what I could see of his hands and neck, even across the scarred and charred areas. The pain involved in that must have been monumental. His lower lip and chin were broken and ruined, but his stark black eyes were fierce and compelling.

He sat on the edge of the table, pointed his open palm at the door, then crossed his arms and waited.

Eugen reacted first. "We can't just slaughter people to save ourselves. That's ridiculous!"

Artjom raised a finger. "Let me remind you, as one friend to another, that you're only an apprentice. You have a right to reject our opinions. You do not have a right to call them ridiculous."

A trickle of smoke crawled up from beneath the door, and the smell of it stung the back of my throat. "What are they doing?"

"Trying to burn us down, I assume. We were planning on releasing our friend when they made it to this door. Now they're here." Artjom's calm demeanor was almost irritating.

I scanned every surface, looking for any tools that might help us out, but most of them were even more unfamiliar to me than the crouching creature. His skull was obviously canine, and he must have had roughly the same mass as I. That was all I knew. That, and the unshakeable feeling that he was present, not like an animal, but like a clever soul that watched and waited and found himself amused.

Eugen flew at the window, looking for a way down, but it was clear that we'd never use that option. Even if he could save himself, neither I nor the oldest of the Masters would be able to make it down, and even if we did, the rabble waited.

A vague idea came to me. "What if we only frighten them?"

"I don't know." Eugen was foaming, furious. "Damn it, why can't they see that destroying us would do no good?"

"Wishing them to understand won't make it happen." I coughed and turned to the window behind me. "Trust me, I've done plenty of wishing. You can die wishing. We need something else."

The smoke was getting heavier and it seemed that we were surrounded by angry shouts in all directions. I leaned out the window for air, and it only confirmed my suspicions. There were people outside, on the roof of the side building, at the front of the millhouse, everywhere. I turned back into the room to find Eugen in tears, and Artjom calm and infuriatingly steadfast.

He smiled at me. "If you change your mind, all we need to do is wipe the Ward away. We have enough silver to protect ourselves."

"You said he'd return into the woods. Are you sure?"

"As sure as I can be. He wants to go very badly. The tension on his pull for home was our object of study."

"Do we have enough to leash him?"

Shrugging, he glanced around the room. "I suppose. It can't break silver, but you're optimistic if you think it won't just throw you off, or worse, drag you behind it as it eats its way back into the Unspoken, one limb at a time."

Except for the limbs, that was almost exactly what I'd hoped it would do. "All right, we'll release it."

Artjom was already halfway to the Ward, and the other Masters stirred too. "I knew you'd come around."

"With a caveat. I want to try to control it to at least some degree. I won't just let it run free."

"It won't work."

"You don't know me."

His laugh turned into a cough as the smoke thickened.

We were running out of time, and I needed them to listen to me. "When I was a nurse for the army, we had war dogs. I've seen this done a hundred times with rabid beasts twice the size of any man. It's not easy and I'll need Eugen." He wasn't the strongest of them, but I didn't trust the others not to let go.

Eugen paled.

"And if it doesn't work, we let it go, and the townsfolk die anyway. But at least we tried something. Gather all the silver."

Everyone was on their feet in moments, Cheşa helping the elderly Master to his. Marc took a gnarled cane with a silver-studded end from behind his chair and put most of his considerable weight on it.

To their great credit, they wasted no time in emptying their pockets. I did the same, and unfastened the silver chain from around my waist. We quickly donned all the bits that were too small for my purpose and made a second chain by linking several together. I used two silver rings to make sliding nooses at the end of each leash.

Cheşa and Marc spent the time dousing the door with wet blankets, but the smoke was quickly becoming overpowering in spite of their efforts. There was no time to test how well my theory would work.

Now that we had a plan, Artjom was co-operative and quick to action. "We can reach in and put these on it while it's still captive. Won't be a problem. Then we only need to wipe away the floor Ward."

"And the door Ward, can you open it?"

"If there's still one left when we're done, all it takes is a few words."

"Hopefully we can scare everyone away."

"We'll be right behind you. We can retreat to safer hiding places if it doesn't work."

I tiptoed up to the silver-white lines, stretched my arm into the star, and slipped both loops over the head of the still creature. The hairs on my forearm rose, but he didn't move, or flinch, or breathe. He was a statue, vaguely smelling of wet goat and wicked thoughts.

Without needing any prompting, Marc and Cheşa grabbed soaked blankets, standing ready to put out the fires.

Grinning wildly, I handed the end of one of the chains to Eugen. "We're going to walk out of here with him between us. When he lunges toward me, I'm trusting you to pull him back. When he moves to you, I'll do the same. Between the two of us, if we focus, we can keep him away from one another and maybe stop him from murdering anyone. We'll walk out and put these people in their places without bloodshed."

Eugen took a moment to close his gaping mouth. "You're crazy if you're asking me to hold on to thunder and trust you to do the same."

Artjom stomped up behind him and smacked him upside the head hard enough that he almost dropped the chain. "That's the only idea any of us have had." His voice was hard and smoke-dried. "And it had to come from a foreigner. We should be ashamed we didn't think of it ourselves. Shut up and do as you're told."

Eugen nodded and looped his end of the chain twice around his knuckles. I did the same with mine. The Pricolici sat arrogantly still and offensively motionless, but the floor under it vibrated with anticipation.

Artjom raised his hand in a blessing above us. "The spirits guide us, but don't oblige us." With one quick swipe of his toes, he broke the Ward. "You are unbound."

The Masters jumped back as the Pricolici shot forward with a magnificent roar I could only compare to the sound of an ancient oak tree crashing down through an unforgiving canopy. Eugen jumped too, but was quickly pulled forward and almost off his feet by the motion. Much unlike what I'd planned, the first moment was utter chaos. It almost knocked me and Eugen together before it realized we were the source of the problem and turned furiously on us.

I sidestepped to my right, trying to put the Pricolici between us, and knocked Artjom out of the way into a table full of brass measuring tools. The noise distracted the creature for a moment. Suddenly, there were too many of us in too tight a space.

"Eugen, focus! I need you, now."

He woke from his awe and pulled back to tighten the chain as much as he could. I pulled toward me, and together we held on to a killing machine we had no right controlling. He pawed the air first toward Eugen, then me. He threw his whole weight backward and forward, yanking us down. But, between the two of us, we were just about strong enough to cling on to him like determined children to a runaway sheepdog.

I kept a firm hold and looked to the door where Artjom was dousing the handle with a bundle of herbs he dipped into a cup of water. "Friend or foe, passage be clear like a babbling brook."

Before he could even stand back, the door slammed inward with a bang, and a brutish, thick man with a cudgel stood in the billowing black smoke. His face was covered by a wet cloth, but even so his shock was plain to see. Black eyebrows shot up instantly, hiding under the brim of his pork-pie cap, and he took three steps backward, forgetting the stairs and tumbling down against the curved wall in the process, taking the men behind him into the flickering haze of hellfire.

The Masters lined up by the sides of the door, wet blankets and water buckets in hand. Only chaos reigned in every direction.

"Stand back!"

184 • ALEX WOODROE

CHAPTER TWENTY-SIX

Riders and the Storm

Mayhem.

As soon as he saw the open door, our captive carnivore spared no more thought for us than a dog for the fleas on its back. Men stumbled down the stairs before us, and we were dragged through fire and smoke and corpses, knocking into each other behind the Pricolici. Luck and anger alone prevented him from turning on us.

One good look at him set people running, tumbling, screaming. Nobody wanted to be there when he passed. With a bit of fortune, they'd all run to their homes and never look back.

We crashed through the room at the bottom of the stairs, banging against what felt like every stone of every wall on our way, and burst out the main doors. I was still finding my feet when the Pricolici roared again and gave a mighty tug, knocking me and Eugen together behind him in a two-person pretzel. There were screams.

"Eugen, pull back!"

I dug my heels in and leaned back as much as I could, but it was only enough to slow the forward motion of the vicious creature. To my left, Eugen did the same, and slowed it further to almost a stop.

The crowd in front of us broke before I even got a good look at them. Most ran for dear life; only a foolhardy few took some distance and stopped again, on the edge between staying and leaving. Rareş stood his ground, and another man to his right swung a large axe and grinned.

The Pricolici made for them furiously, digging at the ground with all four black-clawed paws, but quickly realized we were holding him back. He looked at us over his shoulder, and it dawned on me that we'd forgotten all about our tactic to keep him between us. I threw myself to the ground to the right as he charged us, but he had his sights on Eugen. The Pricolici smacked into him hard enough to slam the air out of his lungs and throw him to the ground, then grabbed his leg in a rabid mouth.

I tried to raise my voice enough to cover his screams. "Don't drop the chain! Whatever you do, don't!"

The strain of the jaw pressing down on his boot caused audible creaks, but no blood ran out and I suspected Eugen screamed more in fear than pain. Was it the silver at work, or did the Pricolici have some clever plan only to frighten Eugen into letting him go?

I yanked the chain as hard as I could, snapping it taut and causing the creature to release his grip. He focused on me and lunged again, but this time Eugen was ready and pulled back. We had him between us, under some semblance of control, and I gloated, but only for a moment.

The axe-wielding brute was upon us, probably hoping to take advantage of the creature being nearly immobilized. He stepped up close enough that his overextended belly brushed a white, woolly elbow as he raised his arms above his head to strike down, and that was warning enough for the Pricolici. In one easy move, he unhinged his jaws and opened his mouth so wide that no earthly creature could have possibly matched it. At the same time, he grew in height. Something fleshy and sluglike retreated into the dark cavern of his throat, then he tilted his head sideways and grabbed the brave and brainless attacker by the belly in that unreasonable mouth. The Pricolici shook him once, a hard and sudden shake that snapped his spine with a loud crack, then dropped him limp to the ground where a halo of dust rose around his broken body.

I was in shock.

Perhaps we both were, but Eugen recovered first. "Stay away! For God's sake, stay away if you're not wearing silver! You airbrains!"

The Whisper dragged us forward again, this time stopping inches from Rareş. Everyone else had fled. Not a soul moved in sight, and the reassuring sounds of doors crashing shut and being battened came to us from the main road behind him. Nobody else would trouble the Tower for a while, at least.

"Rareş, please, get back!"

Risen to his hind feet, the Pricolici stood head and shoulders above the massive smith and sniffed down at him.

Rareş only grinned, flashing several silvery teeth I hadn't noticed before. "That's a mighty fine pet you have there." His own weapon, a silver-capped hammer, still rested by his side, leaning against his leg, but he didn't reach for it. "I've more silver in me than this whole town put together. My little treat for smithing for them all these years. I might even stand a chance at killing your dog."

A long drip of drool oozed from the creature's jaw.

"Maybe." I relaxed my grip a little and was almost surprised when nothing happened. "But we need him. And if they see you kill him, they'll just attack us again. Is that what you want?"

"Nay. I would have stopped them myself if I'd seen a way to do it without killing any. I'm even sorry for old Barry over there, utter stump that he was. But that's done now. We came here for a way into the Unspoken. Is this it?"

Both he and Eugen looked at me, and for a moment I could swear the creature itself turned with a question in its eyes.

"I had considered that possibility."

Eugen gaped at me in a shock I didn't fully believe. "Is that why you chained us to this thing? I wish you'd talked to me about it first."

"You put me in a pretty tough spot! When was I supposed to tell you I planned to ride him like a prized pony right into another world, specifically? Perdy needs us, and if you've forgotten that, I haven't."

The Pricolici reared, then with a mighty shake tried to throw us off like water from his fur. We held on and pulled the leashes apart even more tightly. Rareş took a large silver amulet from his leather apron and pressed it to the creature's chest. With another, tighter shake, the beast settled down.

"I'm sorry, Eugen." Shame at my angry outburst filled me. "I don't even know if it will work. Would you rather take him back up, instead?"

"I can't see how that's feasible now. Not now that we know they want him very badly. We'd just be inviting more attacks. But letting him drag us behind him? It's…. How did you even know?"

"I figured that if the kidnapping Dochia could take a person in, and an experienced Walker could take a person in, that meant that anyone who could cross confidently could take a person in."

"You're a lunatic."

"Will it work, though?"

"It'll work, but you're a lunatic."

"Kids. Stop arguing." Rareş stared into the perfect white eyes of the alien creature and smiled, admiration obvious on his face. "I, for one, think it's a grand plan."

The Pricolici shuddered, his matted fur releasing the illusion of ticks and hairs and fleas that disappeared like specks of light as soon as they touched the ground. He stood quietly, but I had a sense of hidden power waiting patiently, like the big coal engine of a railway car just gearing up to start moving. He twitched a pointy white ear when Artjom and Cheşa popped out of the millhouse behind us, noticing them long before we did.

"The Tower is safe, thank the spirits. For now." Artjom stepped up behind the creature and placed a silver ring-studded hand on his shoulder. He was now thoroughly surrounded. "Time to figure out what to do with our friend."

I opened my mouth, but Rareş beat me to it. "Actually, we've already decided to release it back into the wild, so to speak."

"The sensible choice."

Cheşa tapped Artjom on the shoulder and pointed at the Pricolici, then brought his thumb and index finger together in a circle and pointed at the Tower.

"Yes, we could still use him. But we won't. This was never the right choice, and we have an outstanding promise to keep. We'll take him and find a safe place to let him—"

Rareş and I both spoke out at the same time.

"I'm going with him."

Artjom looked from one to the other, slack-jawed and dumbfounded. "But why?"

Rareş cleared his throat and smiled, answering to the Pricolici rather than to the Master. "I've always wanted a look inside. That's all you need to know."

"And I need to find Perdy," I said. "That's why I came to you, to find a way in even though I'm not a proper Walker."

Artjom shook his head. "Well, you found it. Our ferocious friend here can walk you right in, easily. Whether he'll leave you alive at the end is a different matter."

"And that's another reason why I'll be there, with my hammer." Rareş gave it a thud to punctuate his argument.

Artjom nodded, impressed. "I'm tempted to join you."

Cheşa again tapped him on the shoulder and signed a large circle around us all.

"You're right, old friend. I've got some tricks up my sleeve that I can throw at protecting the Tower, since push has apparently come to shove." He turned to me. "I'm sure I don't need to tell you, of all people, how dangerous it is. If you must go, I can't stop you, but at the very least, take Cheşa and Eugen."

Eugen straightened. "What? How about we just give them the armor—"

Artjom raised a determined hand. "It's safer in numbers. Just look at our little gathering now, around a beast that could pulverize an army off guard. The armor...I think we all know how much good it did Paul."

Eugen paled, and the look he gave me was a little more tired than I'd have liked. Maybe there was even a little resentment in there, and I didn't blame him. He left Mara with an unresolved quarrel. The thought of not coming back safely to her and ending their relationship like that would be enough to justify any amount of bitterness.

Rareş stepped back and stretched his arms, nervous logs of hard-worked flesh.

"Well then. How do we do this?"

I braced myself with a deep breath. "Same way we got down here, I guess. Is everyone ready?

★   ★   ★

We walked in serene procession. Eugen and I held the Whisper between us, as before, except this time it was more than happy to walk slightly ahead of us without any struggle or hurry. The chains swung like pendulums, and every now and again he turned his head this way and that, perhaps looking for the right path. A minuscule shift to the left, and we adapted to him, trusting.

Behind, Rareş and Cheşa clung to us like shadows. Cheşa was clearly comfortable in the woods as well as in silence, but even the monolithic blacksmith made surprisingly little noise strutting behind me with his hammer on his shoulder.

We'd passed under the arch, the one my mind had irrevocably named 'the Wailing Arch' after the loss of Paul. It was, more or less, in his footsteps we followed, though the Pricolici seemed to know a straighter path. As soon as we were under the canopy I shuddered and felt fear squeezing my heart, and the sight of a pale and trembling Eugen to my right did nothing to comfort me. He probably found just as little comfort in the sight of me.

"I have a bad feeling about this, Anna."

"I know. But we have to do this."

The creature's body was so close, he no longer needed to struggle against us at all. Perhaps we were no longer struggling against him, but meekly following in what had been his plan all along. The back of my hand brushed against the thick fur of the creature as we moved, and I felt an animal warmth that I hadn't expected to feel.

For all the things I'd read in the Warren, I still didn't understand the most basic of things about the Whispers.

"Eugen. What exactly are Pricolici?"

He opened his mouth and hesitated, but Cheşa quickened his step to fall in line with him and gave the answer in signs I observed and analyzed hungrily. Eugen translated.

"It's a special sort of Whisper. When people die, other Whispers come and look for the angry bits of soul left in the body. They draw them out and make Pricolici. Whether moving or still, they are made of unfinished tasks. They alter the natural order of the world."

Cheşa wagged his finger 'no' and pointed at the ground.

"Sorry. Of our world. Of course, the Unspoken has a different sort of order and the Pricolici are part of it."

I glanced at the silent intruder, and he turned a foggy crystal eye to me. I felt no anger or disgust, rather a morbid fascination. "Curious. And how do they accomplish that?"

Cheşa kept in step with us, but this time Eugen answered. "Sometimes in small things. They cause milk to go sour, or calves to be born wrong. We barely have a dozen cows in town. They harrow all our wild animals away too. Hasn't been a bird near Whisperwood in two generations, we would have forgotten all about them if it weren't for books and stories."

"I had wondered."

"Sometimes they make people angry. Angrier than they would normally be. Sometimes, when the moon goes dark, it's because an army of Pricolici have sent their shadows to cover it."

"Their shadows?" I thought of the good reverend then, but couldn't muster any more anger at his fate, only resignation and grief.

Again, the Pricolici flashed me a pale glance, but this time I felt a curious pride coming through it.

"Most Whispers are masters of arts we can't begin to dream of. These ones have the gift of leaving their bodies behind."

"And of crossing into our world."

"We were studying the effects of having him with us. There's this constant tension from something that doesn't belong with us pulling back toward where it should be. Artjom suspected we could turn that pull into power and use it to strengthen Wards, just like you can turn the wind into a mill. And he was right. Cheşa caught this one and proved it."

"Except instead of crushing grain, you crush the people who try to leave town?"

Behind us, Cheşa snorted, but Eugen only looked down, blushing. "The barrier is for the good of everyone. It's not meant to hurt you. When Artjom arrived in Whisperwood, from wealthy and powerful cities in the north we'd never even heard of, the town only had one Ward around it. Not a very strong one either. They wanted more. Some say because the Whispers were getting wilder by the day."

"And others?"

"Because the people were. They say Artjom came to town already knowing so much about the stars and how we move through them. About what the world is made of. A genius. It didn't take long to find a use for that knowledge."

"You mean for the mayor to?"

"He ordered the extra barriers, and asked that they be impenetrable. Which is laughable. Artjom wanted his to be frightening, but harmless. We used Whisper tension to open a window into somewhere else."

"I'd hardly call it harmless."

"You've seen it, then?"

I nodded.

A little awe slipped into his voice. "That means you were, even briefly, in another reality entirely. Maybe something as foreign to us as we are to the Whispers."

We walked on in silence after that. I did my best not to obsessively check over my shoulder to make sure Rareş and Cheşa followed, but even my pride only went so far. The Master always faced forward, stoic and unflinching. He didn't have much facial expression, the lower half rigid by nature and the upper, I suspected, by choice. Only his eyes were bright and curious. Rareş tried on a smile every time I looked at him, and every time it was a little more strained.

Before long, the shadows deepened. Our steps hastened, our breaths quickened, and even the Pricolici vibrated by the back of my hand. At first, I touched his hide by mistake, then after a while out of curiosity. Now my hand was always near his flank out of sheer fascination that he would allow me that intimacy. What did he think of us?

Tricks of the light became delicate webs of rays so subtle, they were there before any of us noticed the transition. We were close to the border, and the thought of meeting whatever attacked Paul made my skin crawl. Some of the books in the Warren said that Whispers usually avoided one another, and that many were mortal enemies vying for the grace of their Whisper royalty. Kings, queens, politics, wars. They had it all.

I didn't know whether the Pricolici would help or hinder us if it came to that. I thought about asking Eugen, but he was so pale, and his knuckles on the silver chain were so white, I couldn't bring myself to.

The webs of light parted before us and seemed to peel layers off the world along with them. Each time, something changed, but I couldn't tell what other than a slight deepening of colors and an ever-increasing thickness to the air.

Eugen's whispers startled me out of my concentration. "I think we're almost there. Paul said it feels unpleasant. Brace yourselves. Grab on."

I passed my end of the leash back to Cheşa, and Eugen handed his to Rareş, giving us all a connection to our guide. We were like a stagecoach pulling four horses.

Between one web and the next, I felt it. Judging by the gasps, the others did too – a strange tug behind my navel. Where the Tides were like shock waves pushing backward through my chest, this was like being caught on a fishing hook and pulled into the water by my intestines. Uncomfortable was the least of it, but at that point the physical urge to move forward was so strong I couldn't have turned back. The forest sped by for a few seconds, flashing brightly, then covered again in shadows, over and over. It almost felt like I stood still, and it rushed by me.

A blink later we stopped, and all the discomfort vanished. Our beastly guide sat and waited while we caught our inexplicably lost breaths.

We stood in a forest, much like our own, except of a deeper emerald, and much darker. It might have been twilight or early dawn, and it must have been near freezing.

"This is it, isn't it? But it's not that different." Steam swirled out on my breath and hung in the air much longer than I'd ever seen it do so before.

Cheşa twirled his graceful fingers around, fanning them out and gathering them back again like waves, and I realized I almost understood his meaning. Not completely, but enough that I wasn't surprised when Eugen translated his words.

"This is only the shallows. It becomes more. Trust nothing, especially nothing living."

Thick, lush grass carpeted the clearing floor, but the sky was a uniform dark charcoal violet that gave away nothing. Cheşa and Rareş looked around, apparently deciding it was relatively safe by some arbitrary principles I couldn't fathom, and we rested on the ground for a moment, the Whisper still quiet and calm between us.

I closed my eyes and enjoyed the hands of the chill wind against my cheeks. Broadleaf trees rustled, and something akin to crickets or cicadas purred in the distance. A flutter of wings in the canopy was followed by a predatory squeak and the crackle of branches. Everything, everywhere, moved.

The forest was alive and we'd arrived, and all I could feel was a swirl of the exhilaration that I'd been allowed to experience it, the guilt that Paul hadn't been so lucky, and the overpowering drive to see more of what lay ahead of us, whatever that would be.

PART THREE

A WORLD, A WAY

CHAPTER TWENTY-SEVEN

Some Wishes

"We've got to kill it." Rareş was cold and matter-of-fact.

Eugen, less so. "Do you even care that this is all our fault?"

I rested my eyes by letting them focus on the violet-tinged, otherworldly dawn. Eugen seemed aged by the journey and the alien light.

A deep breath of crisp, cool air refreshed me. "We have to let him go."

Eugen glared. "Is this a bad time to tell you we're only about two-thirds sure we can get us all back? I was counting on riding the Pricolici like fleas one more time. I mean, we're not Walkers. All Praedictors have are cheap tricks meant to help in case we ever got lost while scouting around the shallows with one of you." He lifted his sleeve and showed me his arm, turning it every way.

There were stars, the smallest ones barely dotted spots of silver, the larger fully drawn in perfect angles, and all of them connected by thin black lines in dizzying patterns that spiraled up his skin and under his shirtsleeve. It was like a flesh version of the ceiling in their workshop, but with life and miraculous motion behind it.

I was in awe. "That's perfect, then."

"But it's mostly tradition and theory. None of us expected to be lost in here. Nobody ever Walked. They might not even work—"

Cheşa tapped his shoulder and gave him a reassuring nod.

"You don't know that! Wait. Do you?"

The Master rolled his eyes and nodded at me instead.

"I think we need to let our friend go either way. Can we really keep going with him, like this? Will he let us?"

In lieu of an answer, the Pricolici rose and shook hard, sending heavy strips of white fur slapping against his sides. He pawed at the ground and huffed. Even if we did want to keep him, he wouldn't come willingly.

"That's settled, then. Any special thoughts on how to cut him loose without getting eaten?"

Cheşa said nothing, but revealed a long, wicked-looking knife with a silver-tipped point and a cruel serrated edge that he'd been hiding somewhere under his dark cloak. I had no doubts he was capable of using it.

The blacksmith took his silver-capped hammer down from his shoulder, set it on the ground, spit in his palms, and gripped the handle tightly. "I have some ideas."

In the end, there was nothing complex about our plan. We found a defensible spot in the middle of a circle of pines, not far from where we entered. We had no intention of walking any farther into the Unspoken holding the unknown by the hand, so we had to take our chances. No option was completely safe.

Chesa took our satchels of rock salt, mixed the powder with a handful of silver shavings, and drew a rough circle around us. Silver against the Pricolici, salt against whatever else might take advantage of our distraction. It was a log palisade against a stone avalanche.

"Will it be enough?"

Rareş huffed. "There's no such thing as enough, is there, Praedictor?"

Cheşa stared for a hot moment, then made his reply to Eugen. Many of the signs were still alien to me, but I could guess enough to know there was a section Eugen hadn't spoken out loud. Something about the blacksmith, judging by the hammering gestures.

"The salt and the silver are a deterrent, not infallible. He can break through them with some effort, and he knows it. We can hope he wants to fly his shadow free more than he wants to kill us." Eugen continued, "But what if it just waits in front of the circle forever? Or until the rain washes it away? If it really wants to eat us—"

"We'll make ourselves damned unpalatable." I tried to put on a smile. "There's got to be something better he has to do than wait for us."

He didn't seem convinced, which was fair. Neither was I.

We stood in the circle, huddled together. The Pricolici hunched just outside our protective barrier and faced away from us, deeply interested in the horizon, pinkish hues from the brightening sky tinging his white fur. Eugen and I glanced at one another, then behind us to our armed guard standing at the ready.

Eugen went first. His hand trembled and fumbled with the loop. It caught on an arrow-sharp ear too, but with quiet dignity, the Pricolici flicked it off. The moment it fell loose, Eugen withdrew behind the others.

"Anna, quick!"

I savored a second of it being just the two of us, the otherworldly creature and me. He looked over his shoulder at me, sharp tongue lolling, unflinching.

"Anna!"

I started to lift my loop, but the Pricolici reared, impatient, and shook like a startled horse. Before I could think to let go of the silver leash, he leaped and yanked me off my feet, throwing me a good distance away from the circle and into a scraggly old trunk, chain and all. Wind knocked out of me, tears in my eyes, it was all I could do to keep breathing. He walked above me, all the while growing, nearing the size of a large bull, and placed a heavy paw on the other side of my neck, looking down at me. Observing. Judging.

Rareş's hammer glinted in the murky light behind him. The smith was well intended, but I didn't think I needed rescuing. The Pricolici could have killed me a hundred times over. He was only looking.

I tried to say so, but the creature bellowed, alerted to Rareş' presence. The sound was that of a bull too, but one amplified through some hellscape canyon; his deep, ululating roar ripped through the forest and turned back in on us tenfold, more slowly than in any earthly air, but with more weight than our earthly airways could carry. The great beast stepped mercifully away from me and turned to face Rareş, growing as though chunks of his body had been folded in and were now unfolding.

He loomed four times the smith's size, molten shadow dripping from in between the white locks of his fur. Quick as the wind, he snapped at the hand that held the hammer, fastened his mouth around it, and tossed his head from side to side. What should have torn the smith to shreds only shook him, no doubt protected by the silver he held.

When another shake flung the hammer into a cushion of thick emerald moss, the audible snap of bone made me convulse even before Rareş started screaming. Only a miracle, and possibly the rest of the silver embedded inside him, kept his arm from being ripped off at the shoulder.

Swift as a snake, Cheşa slithered up behind the creature. Swiveling again, the Pricolici jumped and stomped just as Cheşa rolled out of the way of those unforgiving claws. He rose instantly and held his knife up before him, more like a talisman than a weapon. The creature circled him, he circled back, and I could watch no longer.

I rose and ran to where Rareş lay sprawled on his belly but crawling toward where he hoped he might find his hammer.

"Leave it!" I grabbed him by the leg and heaved toward the salt and silver circle.

Eugen was still there, eyes wide as saucers and equally white.

"Help me, damn you! Help me get him in!"

It took him a second to move, but he did. Together, we dragged the massive man over twigs and stones, ignoring his complaints of broken ribs and twisted ankles, then lifted him to his feet and heaved him over the fragile barrier and into the relative safety of the circle.

Not far away, Cheşa danced around the angry Whisper. He didn't even seem like he was trying to attack at all, flitting this way and that, flirting ever closer to our safe zone. The Pricolici snapped at the air in frustration, the closing of his teeth as loud as thunderclaps.

He swiped a quick right paw that Cheşa barely rolled away from in time, then huddled down, ready to spring. The Master froze; the creature pounced. A string of greenish baneful spittle trailed behind his joyfully open mouth.

A bright silver flash shot toward the beast, nailing him straight in the face. He flinched and fumbled the landing. Cheşa bolted toward us. He'd thrown his knife and was now utterly defenseless.

I jerked forward, my body wanting to get between him and the Pricolici, but Rareş used his one remaining good arm to grab my skirts and hold me back. Eugen didn't look like he had any dreams of moving.

I shouted, "No," to nobody as the creature neared, and nobody minded me. Cheşa kept running, a moment later tumbling into us at full speed, unaware that the Pricolici had been slowing and was already turning away. It swaggered toward the woods, sluggish and probably tired of toying with us, then stretched a lazy hind leg as though it'd just warmed up by playing chase.

We'd all survived, and nobody was more shocked than I.

Rareş dropped from his elbow and smiled through ruby-red teeth. "That went well, I'd say."

He laughed out loud, then, and I couldn't tell if it was shock or hubris. The Pricolici stopped for a moment, just within our sight, and cocked an ear. For a second, I feared he had taken the laughter personally and was about to return and finish what he started. My stomach lurched.

With a tilt of the head, he listened. A moment later, a gentle cooing song drifted toward us from a distance.

Eugen gasped and a little color returned to his face. "Do you hear that? You hear it, right? It's real? Quick, close your eyes!"

I couldn't imagine something less appealing than closing my eyes on the creature still only steps away from us, but to my astonishment the others didn't seem to have that problem. Eugen, Rareş, and even Cheşa scrunched their eyes tight and tilted their heads back. In the distance, the Pricolici had firmly thrust his head downward in between his front legs.

"Anna, close your eyes, now!"

Eugen had obviously checked on me. His shouting only made me more nervous, but I didn't know what else to do.

I shut my eyes. "Why in the inferno are we doing this now?"

"It's the Om Bird! We're in luck. Listen, it's getting closer!"

"The one on the glass, and on the Tower? The one that grants wishes?"

"In Tide-times, in our world, it's hit or miss, but here! We might be in great luck. Just keep your eyes closed. The first wish you make when you clap eyes on it is the one that takes. Be careful what you think. Plan it well before looking up. Be very careful!"

As the song got louder, its rhythm became clear and hypnotic. It seemed to say 'you come and go, you come and go' over and over.

"It's almost here. Get ready."

I was so mesmerized by the ancient melody I hadn't thought of anything at all. I scrambled inside my own mind for an idea.

"Open your eyes now."

It was beautiful. He'd called it a bird, but it was nothing of the sort. Its slender, serpentine body swam through the trees on unseen currents, swooping down under the lowest branches and up over the tallest trees in a playful promenade. Carried by delicate dragonfly wings, its fluid motions never disturbed so much as a branch or leaf. It was a stream of pure white and colored light, a mirage covered in tiny satin feathers that closely imitated scales. It opened its mouth, and for a moment seemed to have fangs – but they were only soft white strands of mustache-like down hanging from its upper lip. An obvious deceiver, the Om Bird was, and no doubt about it.

It passed right above us, tracing the shape of our salt circle once, twice, three times, and as it did a single thought condensed inside me almost of its own free will. I wanted to find Perdy quickly.

"You come and go, you come and go, you come and go." Its joyous whisper full of the portents of doom surrounded us, then floated away.

A faint white trail hung in the air where the Om Bird passed, glowing slightly, and making the rest of the forest even darker by comparison. In the distance, the Pricolici slowly raised his head, cautious, almost as though he wanted nothing to do with wish-making. Tasting the air, sniffing for his bearings, he followed the pale trail with his eyes, then howled.

He faced me squarely, then rose without a sound from within himself. Heavy, the white shag that covered him dropped to the ground with a thud, and a slender shadow made of nothing shot right up into the air and on the tracks of the Om Bird. He was gone in an instant.

Darkness and solitude descended upon us.

★   ★   ★

"Your arm is a ruin, you have to go back!" My tone rose in spite of myself. I couldn't bear people bringing harm to themselves.

"I'm not going anywhere. If anyone should leave us, it's the boy. He's had so much more than he can stand, I expect him to stab us in the kidneys on the way out."

Eugen started out of his gloomy reverie at the blacksmith's accusation. "I would never—"

"I'm only kidding, son. But still, you should go if you want to."

He wanted to, it was plain as day on his face, but he looked to his Master and returned to sulking. Even if his skin-map worked, if he left, Cheşa would be unable to communicate with us easily. Some of his signs made sense to me, but not all.

Rareş found the handle of his great hammer sticking out of the moss and pulled on it one-handed. It gave a loud squelch and seemed only to burrow itself deeper into the muck beneath the green carpet. He planted his foot onto a nearby log and tried again, only succeeding in pushing the log down into the bog. Frustrated, he growled and tried to grab it with both hands, yelping at the mere touch of it. Cheşa wandered closer and patted him on the shoulder. He signed something I understood as *let me* or *I'll help*, then reached for the weapon handle.

With a mighty roar, Rareş shoved him away.

"Leave me be, you glorified fortune teller!"

Cheşa fell flat on his back, cushioned only by a dense patch of rushes and shrubs. Flabbergasted, he stared as Rareş grabbed the hammer with both hands again and grunted in pain, pulling the weapon out inch by inch, and finally winning over the hostile undergrowth.

His face red from effort and pain, he dropped his injured arm back by the side of his body and tossed his hammer over his shoulder with the other.

"Let's go."

His growl made me feel more like a hostage than a traveling companion.

Cheşa shook himself, shrugged at Eugen, and went to collect his knife from where it had bounced off the Pricolici's face.

Eugen came to me and made sure we were a good distance away from Rareş before speaking. "He doesn't seem himself. Not since the mill. He's never been a fan of anything to do with the Unspoken, but he was always kind to me. Master Cheşa has concerns too. I don't know what's going on, but I don't like it."

"Neither do I. Hang back with Cheşa, find a reason. I need to talk to Rareş."

He made loud noises about taking measurements, and clever Cheşa saw right through us. He sat on a log and pretended to study the area carefully, but as I snuck glances at him, I saw him cleaning his blade.

I walked up to Rareş. Grunting and gasping, he struggled to lash his belt around his arm and torso to hold the injured limb still. Even using his mouth for one end, it was a nigh-impossible task one-handed. I took one end without even asking, and when he started to protest, I put on my best war nurse voice.

"Hush now, be still. This needs to be done."

Surprising me again, he quieted, but still scowled at me the entire time. His arm was swollen and misshapen underneath the hasty bandages he threw around it, and I would have been hard pressed to make any promises that he'd ever be able to use it again. How he had dragged his weapon out at all was beyond me.

"You need to go back. As it stands, I'm not sure this arm—"

"I'm not going, so you might as well save your breath."

"I don't understand, but I know you won't tell me. Just tell me this, have you thought about your poor wife and how hard it will be for her to run a smithy without you?"

"My wife is dead. She took the Silent Walk this morning."

My hands froze in the middle of tightening the belt, but I forced them to carry on. "I'm so sorry."

"They kept promising and promising. Eventually, we all reach a day where one more broken promise is one too many."

I finished tightening his makeshift sling and wondered at what else I might do for that wreck of an arm. "They?"

"Them blighters. The Wardens promised protection, that the next one would be better. The priest promised we could make peace. The mayor promised we'd keep it under wraps, have it all under control, neat as can be. The Praedictors promised it wasn't getting any worse."

He looked toward where Cheșa and Eugen talked in their secret codes and spat on the ground. Eugen had his back turned, but Cheșa's eyes snapped to us and back in a fraction of a moment.

"The boy's not even bad. He doesn't know any better. Paul was tough and independent, paid no mind to nobody. This one's a lamb. Get him away from them, quick as you can. The young ones, they like you. Get them all away, if you can. That little red-headed girlie too. Drag her out by her heels if you have to."

The steely glint in his eye and sweat on his brow made me suspect a fever. But so quickly? And was it enough to justify his words?

I nodded along, unsure of what he expected me to say. "Do you think Perdy came here by choice?"

"That nonsense about her bein' one of them? Doubt it. She's just sore and tired of the town and everyone in it. Who isn't?"

Cheșa chose that moment to stalk up to us, trouble and gloom clouding his face, Eugen not far behind him. Rareș mumbled something about needing relief and slunk into the deepening shadows between the trees, but Cheșa's eyes followed him long after he was invisible to me. I suspect his ears did after that.

He tapped me gently on the elbow to get my attention and signed two directions, a question, the sky. Each time he spoke, I understood him a little better.

"I'm not sure which way to go next. Away from Whisperwood, for sure." I pointed to his hands, covered in tattoos like Eugen's. "Can those help us navigate?"

He nodded.

Eugen tapped his chin. "Anna, what did you wish for?"

"Won't telling you invalidate the wish?"

He laughed. "It's an Om Bird, not a fallen eyelash. If it chose to grant your wish, it's already done."

"Oh."

"I wished to see Mara again," he said. "Simple things work best."

"I wished to find Perdy quickly."

Cheşa clapped and Eugen smiled. "Perfect. Start walking, then. We'll know within an hour or so whether you got your wish, and maybe whether we all did. If not, we can always rethink from there."

It was the best shot we had, so I let the pull in my chest guide me. I called out to Rareş, and he fell in line next to me with surprising grace and looking somewhat more collected, his arm still tightly bound to his chest.

"Won't you tell me why you really came? Maybe I can help."

"No. All of this came from too many people offering too much help. I'll be fine, now."

He locked his jaw and walked on. I had not much choice but to do the same, but the sweat dripping into his beard in ostentatious disregard of the cold concerned me greatly.

CHAPTER TWENTY-EIGHT

Guardians of Nothing

Before long, there was a road.

We followed it for a while, ate the scant supplies we carried by a shimmering golden stream, then walked on. The bruised lilac sky had turned a deep crimson that gave almost no light. Whatever illumination it might have provided mixed with the green of the woods and turned the shapes of the trees pitch-black. There were no stars or heavenly bodies that I could see, but the forest was full of life – or, at least, motion. Things swished and whooshed, rustled and crackled. Distant birdcalls wove through the trees, and now and then a roar or squeak suggested predatory pursuits.

I had gotten used to the quiet nights of Whisperwood so quickly that every creaking branch made me jump, though if half of what I'd read in the Warren was true, I wasn't completely wrong to either. A violent green flash shot across the sky, and I wondered if it were a shooting star, and if so, of which universe?

Eugen's eyes kept darting every which way. "There's so much noise I keep expecting someone to lunge at us every few moments. It's got me on the edge of an edge."

It struck me how many times more unsettling it must have been to someone who'd never heard a normal forest before. "Don't worry. Forests move all the time, and not everything in them is bad. In fact, most things aren't."

As if in answer, faint blue lights appeared to one side of us, in between the trees, illuminating the path. Eugen only looked weary and said, "Foolsflame."

Foolsflame. I'd even taken notes on it back at the Warren, but they'd be useless in that darkness. The only thing I remembered for sure was that stepping off the path to follow them would be risky. They could lead a weary traveler off a cliff, or they could help one find their way, and there was no telling which.

I checked over my shoulder, but neither Rareş nor Cheşa seemed inclined to stray. They probably knew better than I did.

"Everything fine back there?"

Rareş rumbled. "Stellar."

"I'm going to take a quick look at those lights." Before they could protest, I raised my hands. "I'll be in talking distance, no farther. If it doesn't look like anything right away, I'll come back."

Eugen sat on the ground and Rareş leaned on his hammer. Nobody was doing well. Cheşa nodded. The blue light made his scars stand out in odd indigo relief.

The ground squelched beneath my feet as I entered the woods. They were surprisingly clear of brambles and it wasn't hard going at all; before long I was following the next light, then the next.

"I'm still here!"

"And we," Rareş responded.

Ahead of me, multiple lights danced around the same spot. It wasn't a sheer cliff, at least, whatever else it might be. The light became brighter with every step until finally, I could see my breath steaming in front of me. An odd feeling of déjà vu overcame me, so I hurried to leave it behind me.

As soon as I reached the right spot, I saw what the Foolsflame had brought me to. Their eerie, steady light shone over a small camp, battered and rotten with time, but still visible. A stone circle must have served as a firepit, and the remains of a once-sturdy lean-to hung off the side of a white pine. The branches were so low I had to crawl across a bed of needles to reach beneath it properly, and I quickly dragged out a stained and ancient-looking leather pack.

Back where the light would aid me, I sat on my haunches to check it. There was no reason not to bring it to the relative safety of the road, but I wanted to know why the Foolsflame had brought me there, first.

"Anna?" Eugen's worried voice rose through the trees.

"Right here! Only a moment, now."

I untied the leather envelope. Inside it, a short letter sat atop a bundle of blank and yellowed paper. As I started reading, the Foolsflame gathered closer, huddling around me.

Cassia,

I think I've found a way into that town across the border, but the Queen's Guard is right on my tail.

You were right, she's sent others to spy on them before. She's looking for a new king, wants to plunder more and more of them to fill our ranks. Insanity.

There's a family in town. I've heard they have an underground network, help those of us who want to get out for good. They've been taking a break on account of having an infant. They think the queen knows and don't want to risk it anymore, but they're good people. I'll tell them everything, throw myself at their mercy.

I've got a little contraband silver I can give them. Turns out, it doesn't burn at all through cloth. I've salt too, and was going to use it to protect myself like they do. Keep the Guard from getting to me. They can't hound me forever, can they?

I know you're coming this way. I hope you find this and feel reassured. There is a way out. You can leave. The queen sends her beastly spies all the time. It's not even hard. We're just stupid.

You were right.

O.

Three times I read it, then packed it away in my apron pocket. The house with the infant. Could it have been Perdy? Maybe whoever O was, they'd asked them for help and got them in trouble. Perhaps O remained in their salt circle, waiting, and faded to nothing and bones.

I pushed through branches back toward the road. If that skeleton had been a Whisper, what did that say about Perdy? Was it proof of... anything?

"Anna?"

"I'm right here." I sprung out of the bushes, steps behind the group.

"Anything?" Eugen seemed hopeful.

"Nothing that I could figure out. More lights in the distance, but I don't dare go that far. Unless you want to?"

He shook his head, and the others were already heading down the road again. I'd lied without truly knowing why, except for a feeling of dread at the thought of Perdy being connected to the note in ways I couldn't yet understand. Or worse, unconnected in any way, but blamed just the same. I'd wrestle with the decision to keep secrets for the rest of the trip, no doubt, but her safety came first, and done was done.

We walked on.

★　　★　　★

The path was easy and wide, and Eugen looked more morose by the minute. He needed a distraction, and I needed to understand what the context around that note might have been.

I smiled as warmly as I could at him. "Hey, what do the Praedictors know about the Unspoken? Are there any reports of people ever doing what we're doing?"

He perked up at that, and it seemed to me like even Rareş sped up a little to stay closer behind us.

"Yes, and no. Most of what we know comes from older generations of Walkers who actually Walked. If anyone in living memory went inside, they almost always kept it secret."

"Almost?"

"About fifty years ago, the first miller – Henric Tăbăcaru – he built the millhouse we still use today – went missing for a week and came back. He swore up and down he had gone the other way, out across the bridge, and people almost believed him. Then, after about another week, the townsfolk concluded that he was changed."

"Changed how?"

"Less human, somehow. More Whisper? Who knows?"

"What happened?"

"He was put to death. I'm not sure why, but the journal entry it's mentioned in – belonging to the reverend at the time, a terrifying man – clearly says that he was dangerous."

"After the reverend died, Mayor Eduard said something about worrying I might have been changed."

"We have no hard proof of whether a person changing into a Whisper ever happened, or what exactly it looked like when it did. We just know it's a very bad thing."

"So everyone who ever visited here either kept quiet about it or was killed? What a way to maintain the silence."

"I suppose it's called Unspoken for a reason."

From behind us, Rareş' usual boom of a voice came at a low growl. "Maybe it's called the Unspoken because we keep not speaking about it, and it thrives in the dark and the quiet like a vile infection. A creeper. Takes over everything if you don't keep it under control."

"We can't control something we hardly know anything about."

"That's always the excuse you lot use, isn't it?"

"What do you mean 'you'?"

"Never you mind."

"No, I want to—"

"Stop!" My order came out in a strangled whisper, perhaps more effective than had I yelled. Eugen froze, and the others behind us were stopped by our physical barrier.

He paled and turned to where I was looking. "What is it?"

"Do you see that? Wait. Keep looking."

We stood in the middle of what was now a wide cobblestone track, lined on both sides with ancient-looking gnarly trees. We hung motionless like dust motes in front of a sunbeam waiting, and it happened again – what had startled and stopped me in the first place.

The trees breathed.

As if on command, the two rows flanking us let out a sudden exhale of steam very much like the one drifting out of our own mouths. It came from the cracks in the trunks, from the joints of the branches, from beneath the roots; it rose and disappeared after a few moments.

Eugen gasped, and I knew he'd seen it too. Cheşa touched my shoulder, but I couldn't look away. A moment later, when it happened again, I realized I'd been holding my own breath and let it out in a billow of luminescent white haze.

Nothing moved but for the mute fume. Rareş and Cheşa had their weapons in hand, and Eugen clutched at his silver chain. He kept his eyes glued to the nearest tree, silently mouthing, counting the seconds between breaths.

I whispered, "What now? Do we have any reason to believe this is dangerous?"

Cheşa shrugged. He signed *no* to Eugen, then patted me reassuringly on the shoulder.

Bewildered, Eugen shook his head. "I've…I don't know."

Our reverent whispers barely carried within the minuscule space we all occupied, huddled against the cold and dark. Rareş's hand tapped the small of my back and gave me a gentle shove forward. The others followed, and we stayed a tight-knit group, each glaring desperately at their side of the road, daring anything to make any sudden moves.

Nothing happened for a while, except for the elasticity of our nerves slowly leaking out of our bodies, turning us into brittle driftwood versions of ourselves. That awful déjà vu sense of passing for a second time through a space I'd already been overwhelmed me, and soon I realized why. The stone trail through the tunnel of trunks was an obscure mirror image of the road leading to my temporary home in Whisperwood, down to the irrigation channel dip behind the trees.

Part of me was looking for the turnoff to Perdy's house, even though it made no sense that it would be there. The next bend came and went, and my heart leaped when it revealed a clearing and signs of former life.

Inside the clearing, a blackened and burned wreck of a large stone building shone blue in the gently pulsing wisplight. The top faded into darkness, but even so, it was an obvious ruin. A grass floor spawned creepers that crawled up bare walls and loosened crumbly stones out of the window sockets. Soot trailed down uncertain pillars, and an ivy arch hung heavy in place of a doorway. While beautiful in its own right, it was utterly dead and empty, no sign of what or who had once inhabited it.

Eugen put his hand to his lips and frowned, looking at the ancient ruin. He opened his mouth, then shut it again and shook his head. Cheşa nodded, perhaps agreeing to some Praedictor theory I couldn't fathom.

Eugen turned to him. "Master, wasn't there a map of the old Whisperwood?"

Cheşa nodded, then stretched his palm out in front of us. With his index finger, he drew shapes on it; it was easy to recognize directions. A long road intersected by another, three large buildings of note. Off to the left, many little crosses. A graveyard. He ended it all with a shrug and pointed at the building we stood by.

"It is a shame this is all there is here. We can't know."

I didn't understand. "Wasn't the original Whisperwood in the same place as the current one?"

"There's a hundred-year-old theory saying otherwise. They say the original town got physically pulled inside. Like sand shifting under water."

He headed back for the road and I looked up at what might have been a human home lost in an alien land. I jumped when Cheşa touched my shoulder.

He pointed to his ear, then to the air.

Listen.

"I can't hear anything."

Wait.

His cunning attention must have picked up something the rest of us would need another minute to notice. My grandmother always said that those who couldn't talk to people could talk to spirits, and I wondered whether any of that was true. It seemed like, if any place in the universe existed where it might be, this was it.

We walked quietly back to the road, and before long, I heard it too. It startled me, laughter ringing through the air clear as a bell was the last thing I would have expected there. Familiar laughter, at that.

As one, we all sped up, but something in our guts kept us quiet. To our left, sparkles of waterlight shone through the trees where a small lake bordered the path. The sound of merrymaking came from somewhere on the lake. We passed through the fuming tree sentinels, avoiding approaching them for no reason beyond the superstitious.

The ground sloped down gently enough that we made our way to the edge of the water without trouble. In the middle of the lake sat a small island, and it was only by a fortunate trick of light that we were able to see that far at all. I only had a moment to marvel at it, however.

There, on a ledge, feet hanging in the water, looking desolate and defeated, sat Perdy.

212 • ALEX WOODROE

CHAPTER TWENTY-NINE

Veto

We'd found her, but the finding brought me no comfort.

For one thing, Florin had been right. Perdy was far more than she appeared. An ethereal creature, seemingly made of white mist, she played around in the water and gazed wistfully into the depths as it rippled. Long horns spiraled and curved out of her red hair and I had little doubt that beneath the surface of the lake, hooves rather than feet disturbed the dreams of fish.

The other problem was that creatures very much like her surrounded her. I counted eleven others, all cavorting in the shallows, all slightly less human versions of her. Aside from the odd translucency and the horns, she was mostly Perdy; I recognized her easily. The look of utter misery on her tear-stained cheeks broke my heart. The others were far stranger, elongated faces ending in delicate snouts and black almond-shaped eyes peering from under gracefully arched white eyebrows.

The lake sparkled like blue-white starlight from their glow. When they walked out of the water and stepped onto the island, bright blue flames rose from their hoofprints. The ground was charred to a crisp, and specks of gray ash rose from it, climbing hot air currents like snowflakes in reverse.

Mesmerized, I stepped out of our shelter and into the open without thinking. Before I knew what I was doing, I was ankle-deep in the water and calling out like a cheerful child on the first day of school.

"Perdy!"

I stopped mid-wave when the horror on her face registered, bringing me violently back to awareness. She reached an arm toward me and half opened her mouth, but the others were upon her in a moment, dragging her away. She hadn't a chance.

They were a blur of white flame battling against a strong wind. One shot into the water, her reflection shimmering on the surface for a moment before rising into the sky. The curious mirror image made me blink hard, and I couldn't have sworn which the real creature was, and which the reflection. Another handful followed, and the same odd effect confused me. They plunged soundlessly into the depths, sending only mirages into the sky. In moments, they were all gone, Perdy with them, leaving nothing but bright turquoise afterimages that trailed upward and downward from where they played.

I blinked hard to clear my eyes and when I opened them again, the island was no longer visible, every little trace that anyone had ever been there wiped away into blackness. I could hardly see anything at all other than a charcoal fog and a few feet of oily water. Frightened, I turned back to my friends and found them frozen in various stages of their attempts to stop me. Rareş was nearest, the anger on his face evident. I started to say something, I'm not even sure what, when he grabbed me by the shoulders.

"You fool! You bleeding skull of an ox!"

He shook me until my teeth rattled, and I didn't know which way I was facing anymore.

Eugen's voice barely registered somewhere behind him. "Stop that!"

Rareş let go of my shoulders, swung round, and hooked him right in the face. It can't have been full strength, because Eugen staggered back but stayed on his feet. A warning shot, at most. Then, he turned on me again.

"You just cost me time I don't have."

He stormed off back among the trees, and after a moment we followed in stunned silence.

★   ★   ★

Our fire roared but lit, at most, a couple of steps around it. The dark ocher sky gave no light, and the woods around us were filled with unfamiliar noises.

Cheşa had vanished into the woods and returned with two large turtle-like creatures, armored from head to toe in interlocking steel-colored plates that reflected firelight. They struggled and tried to jab at him with the bone horn that protruded from their noses, but he held them at arm's length by the tail and they didn't stand a chance. A slice of his wicked hunting knife later, and they were meat.

I took them from his hand and placed them belly-up around the fire, letting them cook in their own shells. Cheşa emptied his pockets, which were full of an odd sort of apple. No larger than an average walnut and pale pinkish-white, they looked entirely unappetizing. He broke one open in his hands and revealed a violent blood-red and juicy pulp. The rivulets running down his hands left ruby trails.

I called Eugen over to take a look.

"I don't know, it seems dangerous. The meat can taste bad, at most, but red fruit...."

"Not all red fruit is poisonous."

"But some are lethal."

Cheşa searched among the pile of apples until he found the one he was looking for. It was battered and chewed on, covered in little nibbles where something had obviously pecked away at it.

He signed flight and poked at the apple.

Birds ate these. Many. They won't kill us.

"That's a good sign."

The turtle-things tasted muddy and bland, but were fine strong meat; the apples were every bit as sharp and sweet as their color had promised. Even Rareş ate, though he looked sicker and more feverish by the minute. After his outbreak, he never said another word beyond, "We need fire." He did the work, ate the meal, then lay with his back against the warmed-up boulder and rolled himself a cigarette of something heinously smelly one-handed.

Cheşa poked me in the ribs and nodded to him.

"Why me?" I asked.

He raised his eyebrows. I sighed.

Nearing him was like walking into a smokehouse full of spoiled eggs. He puffed and looked at me through reddish lashes, eyes sparkling behind them, the impossible fever from an infection he couldn't already have developed shining in them.

"I knew you were going to be trouble the moment I saw you handle a white-hot blade."

"Why am I trouble?" I sat by the fire, a respectable distance away.

"Because if you weren't here, I'd probably have tied the old fool to a tree, sent the young fool running home, and been done with my business by now." He puffed a circle of bluish smoke toward me, and I struggled not to gag. "Who are you?"

"What do you mean? I'm Anna. Are you well?"

"No, I'm not well. But what I meant is this – who are you to this place? A defender or an attacker?"

"What if I don't want to be either?"

"A coward's choice. Sometimes, choosing neither side is an attack to both. Coward, and a fool too, and I don't think that's you, girlie."

I didn't know how to respond to what seemed almost a compliment, but I couldn't walk away either. Cheşa was right, I had to find out what was wrong with him before he led us all into some sort of disaster.

I hoped shock would stir the pot. "Why are you dying?"

He sat there unflinching and puffed some more. "We're all dying."

"You're dying faster."

"Don't be so sure. That whole town, and you in it, don't have long."

"What makes you say that?"

"Don't you see it? Pah, you wouldn't. You don't know what it was like before you got here. It used to be hard, sure, but it made sense. There was a balance to things."

"Not anymore?"

"Not for a long time. Winter's been getting slowly harsher, Tides have been getting more erratic, more Whispers break the rules, and it happens slowly enough that most people can pretend it isn't happening. We used to have so many more animals, you know?"

"I didn't know that."

"Sure. Great healthy herds of cattle, and wild game. And healthy children."

His eyes bored dark and heavy into the fire. A rustle drew both of our attention to the right, where the edge of our firelight met with the edge of the woods, but nothing stirred further.

"There were few children left even before they were taken to make more Walkers. Now there won't be any. No sane ones, at least, to take us into the future."

On the other side of the fire, beyond the log bench, a slithery *splosh* came from the edge of the lake. We paused for a moment, staring into the darkness, but nothing appeared. Our nerves wouldn't do well under an entire night of that.

"Where do you come into that story, Rareş? Why'd you get mad at me? I met you just a handful of days ago, fit and strong and full of—"

"Anger and despair, yes, quite full of it. I'd already had enough before I lost my third child, and my wife walking off into the woods left me with little to care about. Maybe I could have taken the personal injury, but with Paul gone…he was going to do something for us, that lad. He was the one to get us in line. Sharp and tough as a steel nail. He'd have stopped the madness."

He was all that. "I'm so sorry."

"Enough of that. I'll do it my way and die trying."

"At least you admit you are here to do a specific thing, and it was never about helping me."

He smiled thinly and studied me.

I huffed, defeated. "You have your reasons, and they're not my business. At least tell me what you know about Perdy? It's clearly more than you've led me to believe."

"I know next to nothing about her fine self. I'd been so sure she was one of us. I guess you never can be sure." He shook his head and stared into the fire. "I know a little about her companions, the Iele. I suppose she's a Iala too."

"Think she's there by choice? She hardly looked pleased."

"Hardly matters. You scared them away and cost us time I don't have."

"Then let me help you."

He scoffed. "Paul said you were a helper. That's who you are, plain to see. It's just – I wonder, who will be more deserving of your help, in the end?"

"Let that be you, then. Deserve it."

He chuckled. "Do people ever get tired of you being so goddamned nice around them all the time? So goddamned nice and sweet and expecting the best in everyone. It must be exhausting for them. It must be hard for any flawed person to live up to. I couldn't bear it for long."

I almost choked on my own heart. It was unfair to hear it laid out like that, in such an inappropriate moment. The very thing Alec spat back into my face, calling it deceitful. The way I hid what a monster I actually was.

He carried on, unconcerned, but more softly. "You can't help. I came here to die, that's a fact. The only question is whether I'll be able to even the odds for our people before I go."

He leaned forward and eyed the others suspiciously. They were having their own quiet conference on the log bench, using hand signals and drawing diagrams in the dirt, comparing those to the smattering of stars that blinked into existence overhead. I was sure at least Cheşa could hear us, if not both of them, but they were smart enough to pretend not to.

"My wife, may she find her way out into the light, stumbled on many things dark and terrible in her mad search to end the curse on our line. Sometimes the tales held seeds of truth. One such tells of a powerful Whisper that sneaks into houses and curses human children who would otherwise have become too strong, so she can take them for her own. She's the queen of her kind, the thirteenth Iala."

"Thirteenth?"

"You had a glimpse of the other twelve Iele on the lake. Her handmaidens. She trusts them. They're the only way to reach her. If anyone, mortal or Whisper, tries to find their way down to her sunken throne, they drown."

We twisted to mark the progress of something fluttering through the upper branches. The quantity of motion around us was starting to unnerve even me.

"But with a Iala? Well. Even I could. This morning, when we spoke…. Was it this morning? Blast it. When we spoke, I was just starting to ask myself how I might get in here. If it wasn't for you and the hound, I'd have probably flayed myself some Prickies."

He snarled in their direction, and Cheşa nodded back. I had a feeling the Master was losing patience with the smith.

"You made a wish on the Om to find Pierduta. I made a wish to find someone who'd take me to the queen. I guess the old turkey shot two humans with one stone, eh? I never expected your little red-headed friend would be my way, but so be it. I wish I could say that changed things for me, but it don't."

"So that's why you were rabid when I accidentally scared her off. But she'll be back, surely? She has to, now that she knows we're here."

"Aye, they come back every night. I just pray it's not too late for me."

What was the fool planning to do once he got to the Queen of Whispers, exactly? I was about to ask when a strange brushing noise came from the woods, as though something exceedingly large had failed to pass through the canopy without disturbing it. Necks craned, we fixed that point, pupils wide open and searching, but the night betrayed nothing but the outline of black trees against the shallow brick-red sky.

We jumped again when a thin, raspy voice came from far below that rustle.

"Spare some food?"

Whoever it was stayed well in the darkness beyond our circle of light. Something about that voice washed waves of shivers down my shoulders and back like cold water.

Rareş and Cheşa came round the fire and stood by us, and I felt a familiar tap on my shoulder.

Don't.

Before I could ask why, the voice came again from right near the boulder. Still, I could see nothing.

"Spare some food?"

Eugen's hushed and hurried tone barely registered over the crackling of the fire. "That's twice. We have to, if he asks again. What if it's him – I know, Cheşa, but what if...."

The third time, it came from the water, without any sign that it had moved in any way from one place to another.

"Spare some food for an old fool, long of tooth and thin of wool?"

Before we could argue any further, Rareş stood with a great groan and grabbed the last of the turtle meat sitting in its upturned shell on his way up. "Show yourself and you can eat with us."

A great tumult of leaves and branches drew in from all directions, snaking through the trees and heading toward that one spot that last held the disembodied voice. A dry, gnarly looking man of indecipherable age and greenish hue stepped out into our light. His eyes were too large, and it seemed like he kept them half closed and his head half turned to compensate.

"How kind and grand, my dear young man."

"Young? Ha. I'm not young."

"That would depend on where one stands."

He twirled his fingers in front of his almost motionless face in lieu of expressions and eyed each of us in turn, lingering his viscid gaze on me a little longer. Eugen opened his mouth to speak, trembling, but Cheşa shot him a warning glance that was unmistakable. It hit me square in the chest too. Clearly, they knew what sort of danger we were dealing with, and I took my cues from them.

The old manlike thing waddled up to the food, sidestepping, grabbed it with a hooked hand, and retreated back into the shadows. He hid behind hunched shoulders and slurped away at the meat, throwing an empty shell back at us within moments. It flew between me and Eugen and we dodged, sending him into fits of raspy cackles.

"Now that you've eaten, old man, why don't you tell us what else we can do for you?"

He glared at Rareş from under weedy brows, sucking at each uncommonly long and multi-jointed finger in turn to get all the meat juices. "No, no. Your part is through. It's now what I can do for you."

"For us?"

"Just you and you alone showed kindness to my weary bones."

"I need nothing from you but peace. Be on your way."

"You want to get her. I know how."

Rareş tensed up and stepped forward toward the moldy looking thing. It hissed and drew back into the shadows, quickly continuing its speech before anyone could intercede.

"There's foul sweat upon your brow. You poisoned yourself for no reason. The queen, she won't eat human flesh, and if she did? She'd have them fresh. You're dank and dead and out of season. Nice try, goodbye!"

The words fell out of me before I could dam them. "So that was your plan, you pile-brained ox!"

Rareş shooed me with one hand. "Be quiet, girl." He took another step toward the old Whisper. "I've taken Unseemly Hemlock, that's true. There's nothing left to do now but go through with it. Leave me be."

"You won't be around for dawn."

Rareş seemed poised to send the thing to the devil again, then chewed on his lip for a moment. "And you've got a better idea?"

"Rareş, don't—"

"I said be quiet!" His voice was a roar.

The creature cackled. "I might. I might not. Might, might not. There'd be a price. A sacrifice."

"I gave you food."

"Meat only lasts a moment, much like the lives of men. What I want is eternal — shame, and regret, and pain. That's what it takes to gain the strength to live again."

The thing looked at me and I could swear its pale cerulean hair moved and wiggled in rhythm with its cadaverous fingers, still held up in front of its face. The only feature on that face noticeably alive at all were its eyes, now opened halfway, already four times what they should have been.

"A real deal, a real treat. Something fresh and juicy for these ancient teeth to eat. Her Majesty may not indulge, but I enjoy the fear, if not the meat. The remorse, in particular, is my favorite morsel."

Half-shadowed, it chuckled rusty nails and lies. Its long arms reached toward me, and even though it was much too far to touch me, I couldn't help but step back and trip over myself. Seemingly out of nowhere, Cheşa stood in front of me, arms outstretched, knife in hand.

It withdrew, sank into the gloom a little farther, and looked to Rareş again.

"My way is plain and guaranteed. Trade me one friend. Pick any. Who doesn't have too many?"

Rareş raised his eyebrows and looked at us where we huddled together.

"Don't you dare!" Eugen launched himself at Rareş, bare hands reaching for his neck, red rage all over his face.

Before he could take more than two steps, Cheşa grabbed him by the back of his shirt, twisted once, and threw him backward hard, right into the shrubs behind us. Rareş and the creature continued as if nothing more upsetting than a breeze had passed.

"How?"

"I'll make you the strongest thing that's ever been, enough power to break the queen. A day is all I need to whisper you a song. Rather than spend it dying, you'll spend it growing strong, and by the time night rolls around, you will be good and be done. And then? Well, this whole world can be yours to amend."

"Who are you, to offer me something like this?"

With a great whoosh and a bang, the thing withdrew all the way back into the woods, and its horrible slithering and rushing among the canopy resumed. All around us, the forest itself protested against the unnatural creature.

"Ask your boy. He'll name the thing that made you king." The shrill voice traveled around us at such a speed we could barely follow its position with our eyes.

Rareş turned to Eugen, who howled into the wind. "Zburătorul Zmeilor. You know his reputation, Rareş! Deceit and fear, breaking families, taking hostages, and sowing regret wherever he goes."

"Aye, the wind spirit." Rareş spoke more calmly, and I could barely hear him over the din. "But powerful as the Devil himself, and never breaks a deal."

The creature hissed. "Oldest and strongest of all the Zmei kin. If I can't give you what I said, you can wear my skin."

"If I say yes—"

I gasped and choked on dust and leafy bits. After all he'd just seen, and knowing that creature was evil, still? It was beyond belief. The wind died down to a constant, relentless low groan circling around us.

"You accept?"

"On my terms. You heal me of the poison."

"Said and done, otherwise you'd be gone. But if I've got to be this nice, I get to choose the sacrifice."

"No."

From behind the boulder, a large shape poked out halfway up the trunks. It was the head of the old creature, only massive now – the size of a small cottage, huge burning eyes like windows into hell. It snapped sharp teeth at us, barked, "Yes!" and slithered back into the woods as quickly as it came, withdrawing on what looked like a serpent's body covered in feathers, thick as a country road.

"If you won't haggle, we won't deal."

"I'll give you one veto, and that's the last I'll say. Take it now or meet your end, and I will eat your corpses anyway." The voice circled around us faster and faster. "Like I ate your foolish lad. He thought himself quite smart." A massive, upturned snout poked out from between two trunks, pointing luminescent eyes right at me. "I think you well enjoyed his heart." Then, it withdrew again.

Eugen next to me gripped my elbow tightly and, with a look of utter desperation on his face, shouted, "Paul?" but nobody answered, not even I.

"Your decision, now!"

Rareş looked to me sadly and mouthed an apology that would never have cut through the bellow of the wind. He turned back and shouted at the woods. "Deal!"

Treetops waved against the bloody sky as the massive serpent changed direction and swooped away from us. It took a long, winding arch that crashed and cracked everything in its way, not bothering to dodge between the trunks anymore, and aimed itself at us again.

At me.

The earth trembled in its wake, trees swinging away like waves behind an oar. I had no doubt that it was coming right at me, and no recourse but to turn and run, stupidly, as though I had any chance of escape.

Cheşa reached for me, Eugen tugged on my elbow, but I shook both off and ran for the edge of the clearing. Behind me, the roar got closer and closer, until I felt the vibrations of it on the back of my neck. I willed my feet not to stumble, though I could barely make sense of where I was going. What I was thinking. Then, from behind me, Rareş' massive boom of a voice rose.

"Veto!"

I felt the currents that traveled with the creature rush upward against my back, almost ripping the clothes off my body as it shot off into the air. I turned back just in time to see a serpent as long as a winter night made of cold air and dead leaves and covered in slimy green scales thunder down onto us from a great height.

It reached us in a moment and opened a scissor-filled mouth to Eugen. With more presence of mind than I'd thought him capable of, Eugen waited for the last minute before flinging himself to the side, banking on the massive creature being slower than he was. He was only partially right.

It caught him across the chest, throwing a spray of blood clear across the campsite, the boulder, and our fire. The flames went out with a hiss and plunged us into utter darkness from which only its fiery eyes glowed, glancing back at us once as it faded into the distance.

Everything went black as the inside of an oven. All I knew of the world around me was made up of heart-wrenching screams coming from Eugen, and far more disturbing and almost inhuman moans from what must have been Rareş beyond him.

CHAPTER THIRTY

Out of Control

There was no arguing with that perfect darkness.

Eugen was my first concern. He screamed not far from me, and I could maybe use that sound to find him. I doubted he had long unless I could stop the bleeding, judging by what I'd seen before the fire went out. The creature had taken a bite out of his side, maybe costing him a thigh and his flank at least. It was a miracle he was still conscious.

Beneath my hands, wet leaves slipped and confounded my efforts to stand. I half stood, half crawled in his direction, ignoring the gurgles and garbled mutterings coming from near the boulder where Rareş had been. There was only so much I could worry about at one time, and he sounded like he was breathing, at least.

Something grabbed my ankle, and I yelped and turned back as though I could have seen what it was. Before I could kick out, I felt a familiar double tap on my knee.

"Cheşa?"

The double tap again.

"We need to…I can't see you. I'm going to find Eugen."

He grabbed my arm and lifted me fully. With his fingers on the small of my back, he drew three short stripes up and down, the hand equivalent of a nod.

Yes.

"Are you injured?"

Left and right. *No.*

It wasn't much by way of discourse, but it was something. I grabbed hold of his wrist and tried to make progress, but stumbled after two steps and went down to my knees. He lifted me again, and warm frustrated tears streamed down my chilled face.

"I don't know how...."

A gentle shove propelled me forward again. This time, I took five steps or so before stumbling. My knee burned and throbbed, probably badly scraped, but I got up by myself and took more steps. My eyes were taking their time adjusting, if they ever would. By now, Eugen's screams had turned to whimpers, but it was still enough to locate him by, and we were close.

I slowed down just in time. The toes of my boot knocked into his leg and I jumped. He quaked by my ankle too, and whimpered like a lost dog.

"Eugen? Eugen, we're here. It's all right."

He whimpered again.

"Can't breathe. It hurts. Help me."

I reached down and got a handful of crumpled fabric. It was wet and warm, and as my hand lingered more warmth washed over it. I wasn't sure where to reach next, for a moment frightened to touch any exposed injury for fear of getting it dirty and causing it to become infected.

Fool. Fool and a coward too. There were matters far more pressing than infections at hand. I still couldn't bring myself to grope around and stick my fingers into his wounds, so I took off my apron and wrapped it around my right hand. I searched with my left, finally reaching up to his shoulder, and jabbed my padded right hand into where the bite in his side would be.

When I made contact, he shuddered and screamed again, then took a few quick and shallow breaths. Cheşa grabbed my hand and took it to where he'd tied more bandages around his leg. At least the leg was still there.

Eugen sputtered. "Thank...you're here."

"I'm going to take care of you."

"I thought I'd never see you again."

"It didn't get me."

"I thought I'd never get to tell you that I loved you."

Halfway through drawing breath to reassure him further, I stopped, confused.

"Ever since we were little."

He coughed. A warm spray hit me and filled my nose with the smell of iron. Cheşa shuffled by my side and squeezed my shoulder. I wiped my eyes clean and realized a little light was returning. I could almost make out my own hands.

"Eugen, it's—"

"Mara."

A niggling dread struck me. "No, no. No. This doesn't count, does it?" I turned to where Cheşa's vague shape huddled. "Does it?" I grabbed Eugen by the shoulders and put my face close to his. "It's not Mara. Look at me. I'm not Mara."

Fingers on my spine swayed their harsh horizontal flights.

No!

I brushed them off, smacking his hand harder than I'd intended, and he withdrew. Eugen convulsed next to me, choking and vomiting more warm wetness onto his own chest.

Frantic, I held his face and spoke into his ear. "I'm not Mara, you have to stay alive to see her! This doesn't count as your wish. Eugen, look at me! I'm Anna."

Again, Cheşa reached for me. I swung round and smacked at his hand even harder. That time he grabbed my wrist and pulled me up harshly, trying to drag me away. Coated in blood, my arm slipped right out of his grasp and I knelt back down by Eugen.

I held him and whispered, "Hold on, hold on," under my heavy breath like a talisman that might keep us safe. He made no more sound, but his body twitched and twisted under my hands where I tried to press my apron to his wound. He pulled away from me in small jerky motions, almost as if he wanted to avoid my hands. The fact that he had enough strength in him to react to pain gave me hope.

Cheşa pulled at me again and I struggled against him, but that time he was prepared and dragged me away a few good steps in spite of my kicking and wailing.

"He's going to die!"

His arms were busy, but I felt his head next to mine violently shaking, *No!*

In the corner of my eye, embers from the dying fire glowed a sultry orange. Either my vision was truly returning, or the fire was catching again. I wanted to go blow on them, revive them. By their light, we could tend to Eugen.

He gurgled and shuffled almost rhythmically, now, getting farther away from us.

"He's moving, Cheşa! Stop it, he's moving. He's all right."

Gripping my shoulders tightly, he turned me to look at him. My eyes were definitely adjusting, because there, inches in front of my face, I saw his. Pale and scarred, it shook *no*, eyes wide and looking over my shoulder. Frustrated, tear-washed, and more than a little scared, I whispered my anger and desolation at him.

"Why?"

He lifted his hands in front of my face, almost close enough to touch my skin, and signed hammering, then eating, then pointed.

The smith is eating. There.

I turned back to where Eugen lay and saw only vague mounds and moving shadows, but suddenly it was clear to me that the movements and slurping noises couldn't possibly have been Eugen at all.

★   ★   ★

A light breeze picked up, coaxing the embers back to fiery life by degrees. It wasn't much, but with my eyes adapted to total darkness, it afforded me enough light by which to see the unusually large thing that was working on Eugen.

Bloody fur covered most of its body, and live sinew still moved and settled under the skin. Horns were sprouting out the top of its head. It nipped and teased at the limp cadaver, and though Rareş's features were plain to see on its vicious face, I couldn't help but search the campsite with my gaze, hoping to still find him lying somewhere, horrified and as confused as I was.

Cheşa gripped at my upper arm and pulled me back into the dark. Whatever it was that used to be Rareş chewed on its meal intently, ignoring us. I tried to twist away, but we stumbled on one another and cracked some branches underfoot. Suddenly, reflective red eyes peered up at us.

A faint growl reached me. In a jerky motion, the toothy, but oddly horselike thing grabbed on to its prey and backed away, never taking its eyes off me. I backed away too, blindly, dragged by Cheşa into the undergrowth in an unknown direction. Tearing myself away from those glowing eyes seemed impossible; they glowed on the back of my eyelids long after trees and shrubs and distance hid them from me. They were burned into me, wherever I looked.

We ran for a long time. Darkness returned, but it felt safer than any campfire ever would again. I didn't know where we were, nor how much time had passed. An hour. More?

Eventually, Cheşa let me fall onto a pile of leaves and pushed me back into the hollow of a tree. I shook so hard the rough edges of the trunk dug into my back and arms painfully, and was grateful when he huddled against me. He wasn't shaking, nor did he move. All I could hear was his breathing.

It couldn't have been more than a few minutes later when I woke up with a start, every joint aching and cold. I shifted, and Cheşa tapped my knee.

"I'm fine. Cold."

He huddled closer, wrapping his cloak around me. He smelled of old linen and fresh leather.

Hours later, I woke again from a mercifully dreamless sleep. My left knee burned and ached to stretch that very moment. I couldn't stop myself from kicking out, groaning.

Cheşa jumped and stood, holding his knife. There was enough light to see by. The sky had brightened from brick red to a watery dark pink. He pointed at me.

Are you well?

"I'm so glad to be able to see you again."

I was. I craved Eugen's gentle voice, but I still relished the ability to communicate with anyone at all.

"Everything hurts. Where are we?"

He shrugged.

Sheathing his knife, for a moment he seemed ready to lie back down and fall asleep again. Instead, he shook himself off and set about gathering wood. I watched from my leafy nest, my head empty and dark. After a minute, he dropped the bundle of sticks in front of me, pretended to shiver, then mimicked the starting of a fire. He used much simpler phrases and gestures with me than he ever had with Eugen, and I was grateful.

Here. Warm up by starting this.

He handed me his flint and steel and wandered off into the woods. I didn't know how long I took to build the fire and start it, but he was right. My limbs were loose and hot by the end. When he came back, he had a skinful of fresh water and more apples.

"What now?"

Eat, drink. Rest more. Then we talk.

"We can't leave without her. I won't. Not until I learn what she wants to do. You can go if you want to."

No. We get her.

"Are you sure?"

Have to. It still wants to get to the queen. They are still the only way down.

When he signed 'it', he crooked his fingers into vicious fangs and used his arms to make large snapping jaws. The effect made me shudder, and it was almost easy to forget he was talking about my friend.

"He wouldn't hurt Perdy, would he?"

He only looked at me, ashen and grim.

★　　★　　★

We stood on a low rise, watching a pale icy blue sun go down on a salmon sky.

Resting by the fire was easier and doing so in daylight far more comfortable. We ate, we slept, we talked as best we could. I tried to ask questions that didn't require elaborate answers.

"Does anyone know for sure where they come from?"

He shrugged, then pointed at us. *Does anyone know where we come from?*

"Fair enough. Is it true that they never die?"

Yes and no. He pointed to our fire, then drew symbols in the sand. I had to ask for more explanations for some of his gestures, and he spelled some out, but I was learning his way of communicating a little more every minute. The thought I'd be almost as good as Eugen soon filled me with pride, then desolation. There was no more Eugen.

We tell stories by the fire. Over and over, he drew circles in the dirt, *it's the same story. It begins, and it ends. It dies. But then it starts again somewhere else. It changes over time, but always lives on.*

"Rareş is part of that cycle now, somehow."

He shrugged and nodded. *Probably.*

"Maybe we are too."

Another shrug and nod.

"Sometimes I wonder how I ended up here. It's like I had a dream of running away and woke up already in Whisperwood. But then I wonder, was the running a dream, or is this?"

I looked to him, and he looked back without a flinch. What I'd asked wasn't really a question at all, but I was so used to being interrupted. I expected him to have opinions. Maybe he did; either way he didn't let me know, only nodding encouragement instead.

"I saw horrible things before I came here. I even blamed myself for causing them. Life has been all about keeping things under control ever since. I've been on the move for a long time. Finding the right town in which to hide. Keeping coins in my knickers. Making friends in case I needed them. Making myself useful to them. Keeping them alive for long enough to help me. Trusting they would."

The fire crackled, and we both stared into it, but I had no fear that he was bored or thought me silly. He'd been unendingly patient and kind.

"Whisperwood made me realize how much uncontrollable chaos is truly in our lives. Things you can barely understand, let alone do anything about. And I mean back in the outside world too. We just lie to ourselves better out there than you do over here."

I thought about my village, and my family. There was only sorrow there.

"We wield family, history, and tradition to that end. I was the mayor's daughter, to be wed to the marshal's son, as per tradition. The truth is, I couldn't even keep myself and my own emotions under control for long enough to explore what lay down that path for me. But what I chose instead was catastrophic. It all went to snot in a stew every bit as quickly there as it does here."

I couldn't help but look toward the lake where Eugen lost his life.

"And there was just as much death. Only difference is they were all people on both sides."

Cheşa squeezed my shoulder and handed me an apple he'd been cooking over the fire. The warm sweetness poured some joy back into me and I was able to summon a smile.

He smiled too. I wanted to bask in the peaceful moment, but there were too many thoughts spinning in my mind for it to be still for long.

"Do you think it's true that she's going to be back tonight? Like Rareş said?"

He shrug-nodded. *Probably. He seemed sure. From his wife. She knew much. And Perdy saw you. She seemed sad.*

"And Rareş?"

He shrug-nodded again, this time with a vicious smile that made me immediately want to let the subject go.

The rest of the day passed quietly, and I doubted there would be many others like it for a while.

CHAPTER THIRTY-ONE
Bloodied and Muddied

The sun didn't take as long to cross from horizon to horizon as it would back in our world. Before we knew it, it was time to hide our tracks and find a vantage point. We settled as comfortably as we could on a high bank covered with young walnut trees and made sure we knew the way to the water, and the one away from the lake, blind. Control might have been impossible, but preparation still counted. I wondered whether Rareş was doing the same.

"Any final advice?"

Get her alone.

It sounded simple enough, but dusk came, the ethereal beings of cold flame rose from the water back to their playground island, and I still had no idea how to accomplish such a thing.

At first, only one Iala landed, her mirrored image dropping from the sky as she rose. She tested the scorched ground here and there with her rounded hoof, setting little leftover bits of grass and twigs on fire. Looking around, she hopped and skipped and finally must have deemed the place safe. The others floated up at her whistle, Perdy sad and desolate among them.

"There they are, on time."

Cheşa tapped my shoulder and pointed at Perdy.

"I saw. Do you think, if she knew we were here, she'd want to talk to us? She seems so much sadder than I've ever seen her in town."

He shrugged, then nodded. *Probably.*

"It's the only thing I can think to try. Hand me your knife."

Cleaner and much newer than mine, the silver-coated edge sparkled brilliantly in the reflected violet light of sundown. I shuffled a little closer to the shore with Cheşa on my trail.

The Iele stood knee-deep in water, white gauzy garments raised, happily stomping about chasing frogs. Only Perdy sat on the same high ledge as before, staring wistfully into the waves. Now and then she looked up, searching through the woods, maybe hoping to see us again.

I picked my moment as best I could when they were at their most distracted and aimed a reflected stripe of light at her feet. I'd hoped to get her attention, and hers alone, but it wasn't working. Between the shifting waters and burning grass, there were so many flickers about, one more was hard to spot.

I tried again, aiming halfway up her thigh. Sunlight would have made that task easy, but the nature of the light there was so fleeting, so unstable. I'd almost given the entire idea up when an errant flame from under the hooves of a Iala set fire to a dry patch of cattails, lighting up the whole clearing. Its reflection in the flat of Cheşa's knife struck Perdy right in the eyes.

She flinched and shielded herself against the brilliant flash. A quick gasp escaped her and drew the attention of all her companions. In a heartbeat, she stood and used her sudden inhale to start a song, a clever excuse to soothe her sisters. Some relaxed right away, others looked suspiciously about themselves. The knife was hidden again under Cheşa's dark cloak, and we were safely tucked behind leafy shrubs.

Picked up by many voices, the song rose in volume and bounced off the surface of the water. It had a slow but powerful rhythm, like the heartbeat of some gigantic forest creature, and made the ground vibrate beneath our feet. For a moment, I was lost in the beauty of it.

As the others carried the song forward, Perdy soundlessly slid into the water and, after a few long seconds of swiftly gliding just beneath the surface, was by my side. "Anna! I'm...."

She seemed at a loss, so I found the words for both of us. "So happy to see you. I've missed you. I've been worried."

Stunned, she stuttered, "H-happy? I think I owe you some explanations, surely?"

"Nothing owed. And anyway, we have no time."

She glanced back at her sisters, and I checked for Cheşa, who was nowhere to be seen, probably hidden in a shrub waiting for trouble.

"They won't mind that I'm gone as long as they don't catch sight of you."

"They're not who I'm worried about."

It struck me that up until that point, I'd avoided making a decision about what to do once I found her. Perhaps I was preparing for the disappointment of never finding her, or perhaps it was because I had so few options that weren't repugnant to me. What could I do? Drag her back by force? And with Rareş aiming to kill their sovereign, would I leave the others to their fate?

Perdy raised her eyebrows at me, and I took a deep breath.

"I'd love to talk to you about whether you'd be happier here, or on the other side, but Rareş is coming—"

"The smith?"

"And he's after your queen."

"We'd never—"

"We need to warn the others."

Maybe it wasn't a perfect choice, but it was one I could live with. The threat Whispers posed to Whisperwood was real, but complicated. Right before me stood twelve young women who were in imminent danger. They sang and played, carefree and not hurting anybody, their beautiful voices causing ripples across the surface of the water.

Perdy shook her head. "I don't understand. I'd half hoped, half feared you'd take me back with you. I trust you and hated running away from you, but they made me. They won't listen to you, no matter what I say."

I reached for her by instinct, not knowing for sure whether my hand would even make contact with such an immaterial being. Her hand felt solid, though, and warm to the touch, and like that of an old friend. "I know, but we have to try. It's the right thing."

Something tickled at the back of my head. I looked out over the water again, where the Iele were settling down to braid their hair and wash their gauzy dresses. Yet, somehow, the vibrations over the surface of the water kept getting stronger.

It wasn't the song. Something else was causing the ground to rumble. Something that had probably once been a smith, now come to set the world to rights according to him.

All plans out the window, I rose from our hiding place and dove into the water, waving my arms like a lunatic. Perdy grabbed the back of my dress, but it was too late. They'd seen me. I shouted, "Run! Flee!" and they listened, their blue trails chasing up into the sky. Some broke toward Perdy, arms outstretched. Others, probably more aware of the distance and danger, stopped them.

"What's going on? Anna!"

In moments, they'd all gone, and the lake became infinitely darker and far more fearsome than it had been. A flash of silver drew my eyes to where Cheşa now stood, at the ready and with a look of rage and excitement on his face that sent shivers down my already drenched and chilled spine. He stared into the woods, fixated on a point above which the treetops swayed and from where nightbirds flung themselves out with disgruntled screeches.

"Perdy, you have to go too. I'm sorry."

Her frown was held together by grim determination. "I'm not leaving you again."

I'd barely caught a glimpse of something large between the trees when shadows swooped above us, making me flinch in recognition. It could have been anything, maybe, but it wasn't. I now recognized the outlines of Pricolici as well as any newborn chick recognizes the hawk overhead.

More shadows rippled across the surrounding water, making it roil and heave. They wrapped around me and dragged me down, hands held tight behind my back. I fell with a splash and a scream, muck shooting into my throat and eyes. A desperate yelp from Perdy – she was probably as trapped as I.

My vision narrowed to a rapidly darkening stripe. The more I thrashed, the more the reality of how well secured I was sunk in. It took every inch of willpower I had just to stop and think.

If I stayed calm and kept my face above the water, I could breathe. I did, and there'd never been anything in the world as sweet-tasting as that gulp of air.

Perdy whimpered nearby, and I heaved my body toward her, uttering a prayer of thanks when it worked and I slithered forward. The Pricolici shadows didn't seem to want to drown me. My weight pressed on my elbow painfully as I shuffled across the sour, liquid mud toward her. Dry leaves crackled in my ears.

Rareş's booming voice, now even deeper and more resonant, filled the air.

"I'd love to eat you alive, Prick-dictor, but I've already got what I want tied into neat little bundles, ready to take away. We don't have to do this." A pause, followed by more booming. "Unless, as it turns out, this was your wish all along. Well, well."

I craned my neck back as far as I could, but only got a glimpse of Cheşa readying for a fight. What was beyond him was also beyond me, and I wanted to comfort Perdy more than I needed to see. I took a mouthful of rotting leaves and tasted their revolting sweetness in my nose. Perdy was only a few steps away, but the more I rushed, the more pain I inflicted on myself.

Rareş' voice rose again, in answer to I knew not what. "These woods are mine, now. I'm king here. Be very sure you want to challenge a king before you point that toothpick at one."

Focusing on his disjointed, one-way speech was impossible. It was like hearing a madman ramble to himself, and I had little doubt that he was, in fact, more than a little mad. Was there anyone in that place who wasn't? Instead, I crawled the last of the way to Perdy, on her back in the muck, and laid my head on her shoulder with my last desperate lunge.

"Hey, sweetie. Hey, are you all right?"

"They're holding me tight." Her voice was small and filled with tears. She took little gasps in between each word.

"It's fine. It will be fine. I'll get us out of here."

"He's going to kill me."

"I won't let that happen. There has to be a way out of these shadow bindings. And Cheşa will take care of Rareş."

"You don't know Cheşa, Anna."

"He's helped me and taught me every step of the way. He'll take care of us."

"They call him the Whisper Killer."

"The…." I was at a loss. Could that have been true? He'd been so, so kind to me, but there was so much I couldn't know about him. I had no immediate counterarguments.

"I stayed away from him, always. Watched from a distance. Reported back. He did things to Whispers in that Tower. Secret things. Artjom didn't know. People said he wanted to kill the strongest ones among them…us, all."

Was it 'them' or 'us', I wondered? I needed to know more, but I had no chance to ask for details. Perdy whimpered, staring over my shoulder, wide-eyed. That close, I could tell she had no earthly smell and no real weight to her body, but her pupils dilated in fear just like any regular human.

Twisting, I rested my back to Perdy and finally faced Rareş and Cheşa. They were much closer than I expected, and moving much more quickly than I thought possible. For a bare moment, there was something white and golden and massive towering over the dark-clad Praedictor, but almost immediately the two clashed and a spray of warm blood shot onto my face and in my nose. I coughed and sputtered, tasting iron all the way down the back of my throat. Tears blurred my vision and mixed with the blood to create a ridiculous pink haze filtering over the dark scene.

I choked again and shook my head, but my eyes stung and refused to open properly.

"Perdy, what's going on? I can't see."

"I don't know. I can't tell who's more injured. They'll kill me, either way. The smith, he's stronger. His horn went straight through—"

"Horn?" I choked, spitting someone's blood out of my lungs.

"He's stomping at him, pushing him back. He's so much bigger."

I blinked hard, but it didn't help. My eyes burned. I tried rubbing my left eye against my left shoulder, but it was just out of reach. "Damn it!"

"There's so much blood. Cheșa is bleeding all over Rareș' fur."

I twisted back the way I'd been, with my head on her shoulder, and rubbed my face all over her side and back. It was uncomfortable, and she protested, but her light garments were enough to clean the dirt and blood from my eyes and give me some chance to see properly.

I rocked around as fast as I could, rolling over my sore wrist this time, not caring about the pain. It was as bad as she'd said, and worse.

There was no Rareș. Not really. The only things left of him were his scraggly red beard, his bald head, and his startling musculature. All of it rippled beneath immaculate white fur now, and his eyes shone gold and red like fires. He stood tall enough for me to pass under his four long, oddly jointed legs without much struggle, and on his head a massive set of gilded horns rose like branches. I almost thought, for a moment, they looked like elk horns – but where those would be flat and rounded, these all ended in vicious sharp points, many covered in gore and dripping blood. The monstrous stag with a human face made my stomach turn.

Behind him, several Pricolici skins lay abandoned in the grass, their wearers now shadowy tendrils keeping us tied. Under Rareș' command, no less. I struggled against the shade that bound me, but while flexible, it was unbreakable.

Rareș shook, trying to free himself of Cheșa, who clung to the mane running down the back of his neck. One moment Rareș stood on his hind legs and resembled a giant version of a human being, the next he was on all fours and seemed an enormous elk. Then, when he crouched low to the ground and lunged up to shake his rider off, I realized what was odd about his joints. Though most of his appearance tried to suggest a large herbivore, really it was only a thin veneer over the body of a predator. His knees were back-jointed, like those of a feline, and his movements were no less supple and graceful. Whatever mien of herbivore he had was but a ruse.

A frustrated bellow escaped him, and the muscles on his back seemed to shudder and wriggle by a design of their own under his thick skin.

Startled and revolted, Cheşa relaxed his grip and tumbled down to one side.

Rareş stomped on him, hard. The crack of Cheşa's sternum made my vision go black for a moment. When he lifted his foreleg, however, Cheşa was there, gripping tightly again. I was petrified and couldn't even decide who I was rooting for. It should have been Cheşa, every step of the way, but nothing was certain anymore.

Rareş brought him up to chest level, preparing to trample him into the ground. Cheşa's clever little silver knife found its way between the bone and the tendon at the back of his hoof and shot out, cutting the vital tether. Rareş screamed in pain, somewhere between the roar of a waterfall and the moo of an ox. He stumbled backward, and the knife found another soft target right under his sternum. Holding on to it with both hands, Cheşa dragged downward, then collapsed to the ground like a broken doll that had finished unwinding.

Rareş fell next to him, sticky purple coils oozing out of the cut in his abdomen. For a moment, all was quiet.

CHAPTER THIRTY-TWO

Long Live the King

"They're not dead. Anna, you have to go, somehow. They're not—"

"How do you know?"

"Because that one's still got control of the Pricolici that have their shade on us. And the other one's breathing."

I heaved a heavy breath, unsure whether it was relief or frustration that washed over me.

Cheşa twitched. His shoulder jumped, then he raised his head. It took what seemed like an eternity, but eventually he sat up. He glanced at Rareş' body and threw a strange sign in his direction. I whispered as quickly as I could.

"He doesn't know Rareş's still alive. Do we warn him?"

"No."

I wanted to trust her, but staying silent went against everything I believed in. "Are you sure?"

She only stared at me fiercely. My chest was full of rocks and refusal to accept Cheşa could be as wicked as they said he was. He turned back to us. The look in his bright eyes was feral and sharp. He raised his crimson-coated knife and pointed it straight at us.

Did that mean we were next?

Then, at the sky, in what I could only assume was a greeting, or gratitude.

Slow and careful, he unclasped a small vial from his belt and popped the cork, then poured the contents over his knife. To clean it? What a strange moment to do so.

After tossing the vial over his shoulder, he searched the ground for a moment and picked up a stone. I was curious what he was doing, but not so much I wouldn't have escaped if I'd known how, but we hadn't a chance. When he smacked the stone and knife together, causing a spark that set the whole blade aflame, I was enthralled.

Fiery knife in one hand, he opened his shirt with his other, revealing the scars trailing down onto his chest. Then he placed the tip of the burning blade against his own collarbone. Holding the handle in both hands, he eased his head back and dragged the point of the knife deeply through his skin, up the neck, over one side of his chin and into his mouth. Half the length of the blade had gone in before he suddenly yanked it out again, extinguished. The blood loss would have been staggering without the fire sealing at least some of the cut shut. The gash and burn were bright red and angry, and they would eventually heal into a scar just like every single other of the hundreds of scars that rose along his neck. Was each of them a Whisper he'd ended?

"Anna, please go. Crawl away. He won't bother you."

"Don't worry, I'm right here. I'm with you."

"I don't want to be the reason you die. I can't."

She was sobbing now. It killed me that I had no comfort to offer. Even if I did, by some miracle, slip my constraints, then what? I could do nothing for her except kill Cheşa, and I doubted I had the skills for it, even if I did – maybe for only the second time in my life – have the motive.

I shouted to get his attention. "Cheşa. You're not going to hurt us, are you?"

He shook his head. *No.*

Could I trust him?

"Look at him. Whisper Killer. What can you possibly say to him?" Perdy's voice rose as much as her restricted breathing would allow, enough for Cheşa to hear. "You can kill me, but you'll never kill us all. This isn't a forest. This isn't a country. This is a world." She choked on her own saliva and the last words came out rough and wicked. "We hate you as much as you hate us."

He didn't seem to care. If anything, his expression was bemused as he caught his breath and started tying a strip of cloth around his injured leg. Behind him, something rustled.

Rivulets of moving mulch and chaff flowed and circled beneath the surface of the leaf litter, meeting and spiraling over and over, faster and faster, by some law that was clearly not gravity. Rareş started twitching.

I turned to Perdy and whispered as quietly as I could, "When they're fighting again, crawl away. Is there anything nearby?"

She thought for a second. "It's risky, but if I lead you into the lake—"

She gasped, and I followed her gaze to where Rareş was rising from the mulch only a few steps behind Cheşa, amaranthine entrails trailing from the opening in his chest, alive and animated. Concentrating on giving himself first aid, Cheşa noticed nothing until after the tendrils of muddy guts rose, wove themselves together, and wrapped around his blood-soaked neck with the speed of a garrotter in a dark alley.

He tried to grasp them and pry them loose, suffocating open-mouthed like a fish out of water, but his fingers only slipped off the living wet rope. Slowly, he rose.

Behind him, so did Rareş, his chest splayed open and his insides violently torn out. Some of his guts fell limply to the ground, then dug into the earth searching for something; others rose into the air and wove around his horns, then reached even higher for the last rays of light like real branches. The last ones were stretched out before him, squeezing the life out of Cheşa.

The moment he was in the air, the Pricolici shades around our wrists retreated, slithering slimily across my body. I had no idea why, but wasn't about to complain, and instead hissed at Perdy. "Run!"

Perdy rose and followed me without a word, but crashed into me when I stopped suddenly, face to face with the snarling, now fully clad Pricolici waiting for us.

Rareş laughed, a full-bodied bellow. Cheşa floated above the ground, suspended by the neck, his scars turning deathly blue. His knife fell out of his hand, then he stopped kicking and Rareş let him fall on top of it with a thud.

The lake was silent and still. Darkness ruled over everything again, and a damp icy haze floated low over the landscape, muffling sounds and chilling our bones. I suspected creaturelings watched the spectacle unfold from behind leaves and inside hollow trees, but if they did, they chose not to make their opinions known.

When Rareş approached us, the entire glade burst into yellow-orange light from the fire of his eyes. His animate flesh serpents slithered back toward him and nestled inside their pulsating, living vessel.

"Ladies."

I bristled at his smile. "Rareş. Let us go."

"I won't insist that you call me Your Highness, but I will insist that you don't give me orders. These woods are mine, now."

His broken torso was already mending and closing up, meaty strips of ivy reaching from both sides to pull the wound together. Either to save his strength or to appear less intimidating, he stood on all fours and his body stretched and reshaped itself so that he truly resembled a large white elk rather than anything carnivorous. Only his golden eyes and sharp, multi-pointed golden horns kept traces of his ferocity, whereas the rest of his body softened and almost begged for a pat on the flank.

Perdy stood tall, practically floating off the ground, defiant. "Was that your first act, Your Majesty? Murder?"

"Murder? I'm not the self-destructive killer he is." He paused. "Anymore."

I almost snorted. He actually did. I'd expected the new, changed smith to be any number of wild and alien things when he finally spoke to us. The one thing I hadn't counted on was him being himself. Oblivious to my surprise, he carried on.

"Never trusted the blighter, but never imagined he was a lunatic either. That was his wish, on the Om, did he tell you? To battle the king and bring him down. And he did." He gave the unconscious Master a soft kick. "For a minute. He's not dead. He'll wake up in a few hours with a hangover, ready to answer questions and discuss his future."

In spite of everything, I couldn't help but feel relief at that, and guilt at having felt relief. My voice was choked with those, and with anger, when I replied, "You killed Eugen."

He darkened and lowered his head. A sigh ripped through him. "No, the boy wouldn't have made it. But crazed and broken, I did..." he shook his mane in discomfort, "...defile his body. I never would have taken the deal if I'd known what Zburătorul would make me do. The old beast wanted a sacrifice, aye. But not just a life. If he wanted that, he'd have taken it himself. He wanted to sacrifice my humanity."

I shuddered.

"I came to as if from a dream, covered in blood and with my belly full. And I'll never forget that. And I'll never let an innocent be killed again, not if I have a choice." We stood in silence for a moment, then he whispered, "He was a good boy."

His remorse fell on deaf ears. It was his choice that'd gotten Eugen killed in the first place, and I'd remind him of that someday. But now was not the time. "Are you going to do it, then?"

"Do what?"

"Kill the queen. I'm guessing that's why you trapped Perdy here."

He stole a glance to the lake where, from what I'd gathered, Her Majesty rested. "It's more complicated now."

"You're a Whisper now."

He nodded.

"So where does that leave us? A Whisper, a human, and a..." I looked at Perdy, unsure which world she belonged to, "...person who has yet to decide. We just want peace. And you?"

Rareş smiled warmly, but sharp-toothedly. "The same."

Something cold nudged my hand, and I flinched, pulling it up. By my side, the Pricolici sniffed at my filthy clothes and looked into my eyes with his perfectly milky-white ones. He leaned into me like an oversized shepherd dog, familiar and relaxed. I had no doubt he was the one we'd ridden into the Unspoken.

It was hard to look away from him, and harder still not to clench my jaw the entire time he was next to me. He could kill me at any time and had so few reasons not to. One snap, and that would be it. The end of everything.

As if reading my thoughts, Rareş answered them. "They're my hounds now. I won't let them take any more lives either."

"Then let us go." Perdy sounded almost hopeful.

"I need your help. My goal hasn't changed, I still intend to end the feud between worlds. It just can't be by murder now. I can't."

"So what are you going to do?"

"Sometimes you sharpen an old blade, sometimes you melt it into something new. Sometimes the iron's no good but for throwing away. This new life, it lets me change flesh like I did iron. Maybe you've noticed." He grinned.

"A most enchanting skill."

"I can change things, is the point. The king's words will have weight. On this side, they've been thinking of ways to break the worlds apart ever since this shithead –" he kicked at Cheşa's body again, "– stole a pup and locked him in the Tower. So I'm going to propose we shut the borders. Completely."

Perdy considered him, curious, diffident. "True, the queen had vaguely considered how she might put an end to everything. Her latest idea was slaughtering everyone, teleporting to another world, and giving up the throne to grow turnips. It doesn't mean anything."

"Which is why I need you two beyond being my way down to see her. You're her spy. I know it would be easier if you backed my claims. Make it clear human–Whisper co-operation is over and done with. Anna could do the same. Talk about what it's like on the other side. The hardships. The tempers."

Perdy reached for my hand and wove her fingers into mine tightly. "And then?"

"Then, Anna can go as she pleases. I'd rather she was on the other side when the passage closes." When his unyielding gaze fell on me, I had to look away. "I have no quarrel with you. We shared ale and saved a life together."

"But you won't let me take Perdy back?"

"She doesn't belong there. They want you to drag her back so they can kill her."

"I never would have—"

"Of course not. But it doesn't change the fact that they would."

"They don't have to know she's not human. They don't get a say."

Perdy saw my furrowed brow and took my hands. "It's not that simple. They've been suspicious for so long, but I always had excuses. I had time to cover my tracks. After Paul and the old Zmeu clashed, they summoned me back in a hurry. I had no time. Nothing prepared. They'll know, for sure."

Tired and sore, I couldn't find my way to any counterargument. I hugged her then, and it nearly caused my legs to buckle. She was right. They'd know. They already did. I could risk my life and hers trying to bring her back into the town, but it'd only ever be a gamble at best. I wanted to take that gamble. But she had a right not to.

When we let go of each other, I could see she was shaken too. I couldn't think straight, but she was sharp as ever. "If we do this, waltz over and demand the passageway be shut, what guarantee do we have it won't hurt anyone? What guarantee the queen won't put us down?"

"None at all. All you have is my guarantee as the new king that I don't want to ever have to kill an innocent again. Hellfire, not even a guilty shagger like this prick."

Perdy squeezed my hand tight. "Anna, I think this might be best."

I had tears in my eyes that I didn't expect. "I don't know what will happen if we do this."

"Neither do I." She turned to the former smith and strengthened her tone. "So let's make a deal."

"Let's do."

"We will come speak with Her Silent Majesty and tell her anything you want us to tell her about how dangerous the situation is. We'll say whatever needs saying to get us to shut the gates, at least for now. We will help you in getting whatever you want from her, freely and voluntarily. And then we both go free."

He ruminated for a moment, gazing softly at the Pricolici now lying over my feet in abject tranquility. "As long as we convince her, I don't care what you do after. You still think you can return to them? It might be to die."

"And staying with you would mean living?"

His feral grin brought back the vivid image of sharp teeth chewing into Eugen; my stomach convulsed at the sight of his deadly fangs, and all illusions of an elk faded. "Well, now. There's no guarantee of that."

"Then let me be what I want to be after we're done. That's the deal."

I didn't think she knew what she wanted to be. She only wanted to have the choice, and that was something I could respect. I only hoped Rareş would too. Quickly, a little too quickly for my taste, he nodded.

"Then lead the way, girlie. I'll be right behind Anna."

The Pricolici rose and shook himself, ready for action. Rareş summoned him and gave him a gentle head nudge. The creature licked at his forehead with a pinkish tongue, then bounded back to me. Only then did I notice several others retreating from their still vigils behind shrubs and bushes.

The smith king stretched and tested his healed chest, then picked Cheşa's still-unconscious body up by the scruff and flung him over his back.

Perdy gave me another squeeze. "Stay close, and don't stray. It'll be strange and unpleasant. I wish I could get us both out of this safely, but there's nothing so unreliable as wishes here."

CHAPTER THIRTY-THREE

Amber Waves

I struggled at first.

For all I'd considered myself clever, I hadn't put two and two together that the Whisper Court would be beneath the lake until I was shin-deep and Perdy kept walking.

"I don't like this." I figured I'd make my stand clear, just in case the trembling was too subtle.

"Walk right behind me and you'll be fine."

Perdy's attempts to reassure me missed the mark by a fair bit. Behind me, Rareş seemed unruffled, like he fully expected the way to the queen to be ridiculous and difficult and awful all along.

"Please tell me what's going to happen. I'll feel better if I know." Sweat dribbled down the back of my neck despite the chill.

Perdy looked back at me, concerned. "Are you all right?"

"No. Tell me?"

She stared at me, her pale green irises almost luminescent, then nodded. "There's only a narrow staircase down. It moves every day, and only we know where to find it. As long as you're on the staircase, you'll be fine. You'll be able to breathe just like normal."

"And if I step off the staircase?"

"You drown." She smiled encouragement I couldn't reply to. "But I won't let that happen."

I gulped. Carefully, we circled the lake, the water lapping at our feet, silvery fishlike things scurrying away beneath the surface.

Eventually, she stopped and grabbed my hands. "Here it is. Follow me, I just want to make sure you're on it just right."

My toes hit something hard, and I stepped onto a little stone platform. Testing the edges, I found it to be barely about as wide as my shoulders. My toes quickly found the edge going toward the center of the lake, and the next step down.

Perdy hopped on it in front of me. "Rareş, are you going to make it?"

Her concern was sweet, and the smith king beamed at her. "Don't you ladies worry about me. I'm a little broad for these stairs, but I can probably shift some things into place."

Up close, the slipping of muscles beneath his fur was even more unsettling. There was a strained expression on his human face as his stag body became longer, taller, and narrower, Cheşa still lying across his back. He stretched like a loose-knit wool sweater hung out to dry, and I gulped and faced forward again. There were still some things I didn't want to look at for too long. I only had a moment to question the sadness that overcame me at the thought that Rareş was somehow gone, even though he was still right there and very much himself. Still trying to stop us from hurting each other.

Perdy nodded at me over her shoulder and started walking forward. I had to follow.

I was able to convince myself I'd be fine for as long as it took the water to reach my chest. When it did, it felt like iron bands squeezing around my lungs, and without wanting to, my body flung me back and away from it, teeth grinding and throat constricting. For a moment, everything went black. I felt nothing. It was like I'd gone away from myself completely, and only returned when we were five steps up, with Perdy holding my trembling arm and a ridiculously tall Rareş frowning down at me.

"What's the matter?"

"I've got some bad history with water."

Perdy looked doubtful. "I'm not sure you're going to make it down."

Gulping air, I threw my stubborn, "I will," at her at the same time as Rareş', "She has to."

She shook her head at both of us. "Will it help if I hold your hands? You can close your eyes."

I wanted to say no, but feared we'd never make it otherwise, so I clenched my teeth against the shame and nodded. We took our places again, and she put both her hands back for me to grab on to.

I squeezed them, shut my eyes tight, and shuddered. "Let's go."

Every step was a stumble. When the water hit my chest again, I tried to focus on what a ridiculous image the three of us would make, especially when compared to anything I'd have considered possible only a year before. I even smiled. The water kept rising, and I felt its measured crawl across my lips, nose, eyelids.

Once it rose above my head, Perdy's voice reached me, a little softened, but easily audible. "You don't have to hold your breath. It's fine."

I'd never had someone speak to me while we were both submerged, but surely that wasn't normal? My lips parted to respond, but clamped shut against the cold water. Another two steps down and the pressure in my lungs was unbearable.

"Anna, you have to breathe."

I couldn't. The pain of water in the lungs wasn't something my body would ever forget.

Another two steps.

"Open your eyes, at least!"

She seemed distressed, so I opened my eyes.

And gasped.

★   ★   ★

My legs had been heavy and slow, moving as though through water that sunny April afternoon too.

I was nearly at the edge of town, the cheerful amber sun in high contrast to the bleak scene before me. Another stone flew past my head; then another smacked painfully into my shoulder. My father, mother, a cousin. The marshall and his son I'd been meant to wed. Even my grandmother was ready to defend the town's honor from me, now certain the kindness and knowledge of plants and animals she'd passed down to me had somehow turned into poison. I was crying. I'd turned for one last look at my old home, and saw a massive, pitch-dark behorned shadow looming above them.

I started running back toward them, pushed myself to move faster, even as they flung more rocks to turn me away. It rose from behind their house, nearly blocking the sun, and I knew it was what made the air thick as water around me. I'd invited it into the village, and it wasn't ready to leave yet. It'd saved me and wanted to be paid.

Another stone drifted slowly past my left ear. I reached out, shouted, but the words didn't reach them. What I'd said was gone from my memory. Their faces, sad and angry and heartbroken, never would be.

My mother saw the shade first. She pointed at me and screamed an accusation, whatever doubts she'd had in Alec's words gone for good. And wasn't she right, by then? Wasn't I guilty of witchcraft?

The dark, devilish thing reached over our little gray stone house, where I'd first learned to make a well in the flour before adding the barm. It reached a cart-sized hand over them and covered them completely, red eyes focused and wild.

I stopped and screamed, tears slipping down into my throat. "Go away! Go away and never come back!"

It only laughed at me, a great rumble of a laugh. The gargantuan hand rose and quickly came slapping back down atop them with a clap of thunder. And just like that, it was gone, and so were they.

The final stone struck me in the chest moments after the thrower had vanished without a trace. All that was left behind them was a roiling, bubbling, oozing brown crater, and the village around it calling for my blood.

★   ★   ★

A silvery fish flew past my head, followed by another.

Water shot into the back of my throat and stung. I coughed water, breathed in more water. It moved into my body slowly, tasting faintly like dirt, and fish, and us. The stairs descended into the dark, but around us everything was lit a spectacular shade of amber. Slowly, I swiveled, my limbs feeling both lighter and heavier at the same time. Behind me, Rareş' eyes beamed honey-toned light, the source that illuminated everything around us.

The fish seemed as undisturbed as Perdy, who, now and then, smiled back at me.

"Perdy?" My own voice sounded thick and low to my ears.

"Yes?"

She nodded encouragement, and I only shook my head in disbelief. Little bubbles rose with my laughter. "We're underwater."

She smiled at that too. "We are."

★　　★　　★

The water became pitch-black quickly, and I was grateful for Rareş behind us, much as he unsettled me. After about an hour of big sluggish steps down, the staircase widened, and some of the tension left me, replaced by the tedium of the descent. It was unreal how quickly extreme circumstances became normal.

Perdy came alongside me but kept on holding my hand. I was grateful.

"You really aren't angry at me?"

I wished I could reassure her more. "How could I be? You couldn't tell anyone the truth about you for fear you'd end up hanged in the town square. Sometimes all it takes is even a whisper."

She smiled at my silly joke, which made me happy.

"Besides, I barely know anything about the circumstances."

"I don't know a lot more than you do, but I owe you whatever I do. Anything you want to know is yours to ask after."

Where could I even begin? "Were you that child who was lost in the woods?"

"I don't know. Nobody around here seems sure, or at least, they don't want to tell me. What I know with absolute certainty is that there was a family who had an infant. Some Whispers were unhappy with their lot, and looked to escape, and they used that family as a stopping point on the way out."

From behind us, Rareş hummed, appreciative. "They must have been either very foolish, or very good people. I doubt many of us would have risked our lives like that."

"At some point, the queen had had enough, and sent the Dochia to retrieve them. They tried to escape out into the world, but the barriers wouldn't let them, and they couldn't ask the town for help without admitting what they'd done."

I nodded encouragement. "This is fascinating. Didn't the barriers stop Whispers from leaving?"

"They weren't designed to, back then. Nobody thought it was a possibility."

Rareş rumbled. "So when they couldn't leave one way, they took their baby and left the other. Into the woods. I'd thought to do the same more than once."

"Must have. I don't have any memories of that, but is it because I'm someone else, or because I was too young? Some say I'm that child, turned Whisper, and that's why I can change to look human more easily than anyone else. Others say it has nothing to do with me. Everyone has ulterior motives, so I don't know who to believe."

"Ulterior motives?"

"To keep me. To send me away." She shrugged. Her life had been complicated, that much was clear.

"Perdy, what do you want?"

"I don't think it matters."

I squeezed her hand harder. "It matters to me."

"If I ever went back to town, they'd kill me. Her Majesty ordered me here, certain the townsfolk had gotten too dangerous. Nobody has time for my wishes." She shook her head. "Besides, we're almost there. We can talk later."

She took her place in front of our little procession again, and I took it as a clear sign to stop pushing. Ahead of us, the water brightened into a pale cerulean, and a forest of weeds rose from the powdery bottom of the lake. Beyond the last step, what looked like a heavy stone path led all the way into a small, sunken village. A handful of stone houses, covered in fine powder and lichen, huddled together around a little church with a steeple that shot into the darkness above us. In between them, in a simple village square, waited the queen.

★　★　★

At first, she only had eyes for Rareş.

It was hard to separate the wispy, white-clad creature before us from the stories and legends of wraiths and ghosts back home, and certainly the way she floated didn't help, but I wasn't back home. She was no ghost. Even though she looked like the moon made woman, she was a Whisper, and forgetting that could be lethal.

Around her, the other Iele hung in the water at various heights, some reclining on rooftops or hanging out windows. Other creatures gathered on the outskirts. Something large and snakelike rested half buried in the dust, and a brilliant translucent manta ray with seven tails hovered overhead.

Perdy and I waited a few steps away, demure and quiet while the queen made her introductions. I wondered how the meeting would have gone if it'd been anyone but us accompanying Rareş. I pictured Miss Crosman down there, skirts floating around her knees, chins elegantly lifted, and had to stifle a giggle.

The queen paused her speech and glared at me. I hadn't stifled well enough.

She frowned, but carried on. "...and co-operation for the future of our country. It has been long, and frankly, we need the help up there, on ground level."

Rareş bowed as gracefully as four legs allowed. "I will do my best. I've come with a proposal. It doesn't make me happy, and it won't make you happy, but it's right."

She looked at Perdy and me, and we did our best to seem harmless. "Since you've come with friends, I suspect your proposal isn't to wipe the whole town off the face of the world."

"Was that your best idea so far?"

She shrugged, her dainty shoulders startling a tiny metallic-pink fish. "There's no more stopping them, no more peace to be had. They've no control, no leadership, no restraint at all."

All those words were said while she stared directly at me, so I took it upon myself to answer. "Both sides have their faults."

She waved a dismissive hand at me. "Your people have done nothing but intrude, and stir, and take, and meddle."

Rareş scoffed. "On that, we are agreed."

"Your creatures are no innocent lambs!" I'd never raised my voice to a queen before. It was probably not a good time to start. "I'm sorry, Your Majesty, but so many of my friends are dead. I'm heartbroken. We all are."

"So am I, but they're dead of their own doing. I don't control the wild creatures of the woods any more than you do your wolves or bears, but I certainly care about them a greater measure than that. And yes, some of mine speak, but that doesn't mean they obey."

"I can control them!" Rareş sounded hopeful.

"Only the ones that let you. Not all, never. And not me." Her lip curled in a playful smile. "Never me."

"Which is why a war would be the worst possible outcome for everyone."

"What am I supposed to do? Let your humans keep poking them until they bite? Let them trap and murder them in return? It has to end."

Rareş nodded. "We are in agreement on more points than not. But it can't be with murder."

She pouted. "And why not, exactly? Clean the place up, peace and quiet for a few years. Then they'll cycle back into a new town, like they have before. And we can get the next one in hand early, before they go wild. Now that we have a king again."

Rareş stomped, but the softness of the earth and thickness of the water diminished the effect. "No. I understand things now I didn't yesterday. I understand so much more about how our lives differ. You've forgotten, if you ever knew. It isn't the same. People don't come back."

"They do, I've seen it!"

"Not like we...." He sighed. "It would take years to explain."

She smiled, and for the first time I realized it wasn't only a work partner she'd hoped to find. "Years I hope we will have."

"Before, when I was still only human, I was ready to come here and kill you to end the fight between our people."

She seemed neither surprised nor impressed. "You'd have found it hard."

"Now I'm human no longer and know both sides. The poor, broken smith that I was, and the strength of all the cycles of kings before me. I've seen nothing but death my whole human life, but never harmed so much as a rat until the day I made the choice to bring peace to everyone by sacrificing one person. And it was the hardest, and most hateful thing I've ever done, and all the water in this lake won't wash Eugen's murder off me."

My chest fluttered. I hadn't realized he felt as much pain over his decision as he did. I wanted him to, before; I wanted him to hurt over it very badly. But now that I knew he did....

"I will have that peace he paid for. Not another life lost that doesn't need to be. I'll do anything else it takes."

"Not even that one?" She pointed to Cheşa, lying unconscious where Rareş had dropped him by a half-crumbled shack.

"Not even. He can be useful to us in some way, surely? With all he knows?"

She thought for a moment. "Up top, perhaps. With the cartographers. I suppose."

Rareş took a tentative step forward. "You agree to let everyone live, then? On both sides?"

"You said you'd do anything else?"

He nodded. "I did and I'll stand by it."

With a grin, she took a flourished bow. "Then, be it as my king desires."

I was stunned by how easy it had been. No need for Perdy and myself to testify, no need for complex bargains. Surely there had to be more to it? She called one of her Iele over and whispered something in her ear. Then she fluttered to Rareş, laying a hand on his flank. He flinched.

"This next part is better discussed without company." Then, turning to me, "I'm sorry, my dear. For what it's worth, if you'd have let my Dochia bring you to me, we would have been friends by now."

Before I knew what was happening, several Iele surrounded me, grabbing my elbows and apron and skirt and hair. Several others pulled Perdy back.

She screamed. "No! Let her go!"

I thrashed, but there were so many hands that if I broke free of one, another two took its place. The water rushing around me sounded like a boiling pot. Rareş rumbled a question I didn't quite make out, and the last thing I heard before being dragged up the stairs at great velocity was the queen's soothing tone. "She won't be harmed, I promise. None of them will, if they co-operate."

CHAPTER THIRTY-FOUR

Worry the Sheep

It had started to rain, but it hardly mattered.

Big red drops fell heavily from the burnt ocher sky. They seeped under my collar and trailed down my lake-soaked shirt, making the already unpleasant business of trundling through the woods on no rest and a bellyful of berries even more hateful.

The Iele had ripped me right out of the water, flown me across a rapidly moving unfamiliar landscape to hell-knew-where, almost drying my clothes in the process, and plonked me in a blueberry shrub like I was a stray animal that needed releasing into the wild. Then, despite my protestations, they flew to the winds, scattered in every direction so I couldn't even follow them.

After grumbling and fussing for a little while, resigned to my fate, I started walking, then nearly died of fright when a Pricolici showed up out of nowhere. I froze, but he only sniffed at my feet and nudged my hand with his smooth, uncanny skull-head. I started walking, and he walked with me, shoving me a little as if to steer me. Before long, we strolled amicably. I wanted to think he was the same one I'd made friends with before, but who could be sure?

I also wanted to believe Rareş had sent him to help me.

I was utterly, hopelessly lost. My Pricolici guide strolled through the trees like he knew where we were going, but I recognized none of the landscapes. There was nobody to ask, nobody to complain to. Just me, the creature, and the rain.

"I'm calling you Charles."

He walked on, unimpressed. We stopped to rest. I didn't know if he was taking me back to the lake, or back to Whisperwood, but I suspected it could only have been the latter. They were shutting the border, weren't they? They didn't want me. I wanted to have more time with Perdy, but it didn't seem like I was going to get that choice.

I twisted, turned, and fumed a little, angry at having decisions made for me again. Angry at being helpless. Angry at losing Perdy. Eventually, I dozed off for a handful of minutes. When I awoke, Charles was checking the stars. We walked some more in silence.

Loneliness overcame me. That kind of feeling didn't often knock on the doors of nomads, but when it did, it was terrible. It wasn't a loneliness spawned from missing certain people, though certainly some in Whisperwood had lit up my love for them like a dry brush fire. Instead, it was a lifelong loneliness, an old sickness that started to grow in me the day I realized that no matter how much you cared, when the worst happened and you were utterly lost, you were always alone.

It grew a little stronger every time I had to watch people suffer alone, and every time I had to suffer alone. That didn't feel, to me, like what people were meant to do.

I stopped on a log and sobbed for a minute, my tears mixing with the soily, rich water falling over me. When I was done, exhaustion and a fierce cold gripped me, and I knew that if I didn't get up and start walking right away, I never would again. Charles nudged my hand, and I let him lift me to my feet.

Hours later, the rain stopped. Later still, trailing after my guide, shuffling one foot in front of the other, I found a path beneath me. That I could see the path at all was a sign that dawn was near; I raised my head to the view of a slash of violent violet on the horizon. It was still too early to see the blue arc of the sun rising, but the world had brightened, nonetheless. The fear that I might not make it across the border before they shut it rose in my chest. Would I even be able to cross at all?

That must have been why Rareş sent me the Pricolici. To drag me back to where I came from. I almost wanted to spit on the ground behind me, but it wasn't something I'd ever learned to do.

We stood atop a steep hill, the forest behind us and to our left. The path dipped steeply to the right where it met a grassy plain as vast as my eyes could see, and at the bottom of the hill, a giant stone face greeted it.

It must have been hewn out of a chunk of cliff that had been there for eons, for no force could possibly ever move a boulder that large save for nature herself. The bearded face was solemn. It wore a tall hat textured in swirls made to look like sheep's wool, and the strands and hairs in his beard were picked out in striking detail too. Bushy stone brows sheltered deep, sunken eyes that looked down a fiercely hewn granite nose at a solitary shepherd below – and at his flock.

The shepherd was no statue, and neither were his sheep. They stood knee-deep in ground mist that swirled and waved like foam, every single one of them covered in the blackest of black wools. Nor did I make the mistake of thinking he was human; almost identical to the statue, underneath his own wool hat and wool coat he might have appeared harmless but for the long white tail that coiled around his left leg tightly, and the perfect white eyes that gazed levelly at me.

One arm leaning on a gnarly but stout staff, he raised the other in greeting.

"Ho, there!"

I made my way down in no great hurry, wary of the shepherd and his flock, but even more so of the judgmental gaze of the monolithic statue. Charles paced calmly beside me, uncaring, and that bolstered my confidence. He'd have known if the old shepherd was trouble.

I hoped.

"Good morrow, young lady. What troubles you?"

His tail flicked out, lightning quick, and snatched at a field mouse that had been scurrying behind him in the mist. With a heartbreaking squeak, it was crushed to death. The shepherd smiled and wrapped his tail back around his leg, shrugging at me.

"They worry the sheep. I can't have worried sheep."

"Indeed, you can't." It looked like the road passed right by him, dipping around the stone figure and back into the woods that sprung up again behind the hillock, and Charles seemed to want us to go that way.

I scrambled for polite conversation as I approached. "How many sheep have you?"

"A four hundred and fifty or so. Good local stock. You're from that other place, aren't you? The one through the woods that everyone's always worried about." He shook his head. "I don't like it. Can't have worried sheep."

My shoulders bunched and I turned my side to him, looking away, making myself as small as I could by reflex. "No, that's certainly not good. I'm going back though."

"How'd you get here?"

I thought for a moment about all the unusual sights I'd seen since walking in here, and oddly, the least unusual one of them stood out most vividly. "Came by a ruined house, blackened by time and covered in vines."

"Oyah. That'll do her. You came by where the old town stood."

"Old town?"

"Yeah. Borders move a lot. We're happy to have this nice bit of pasture now, but it wasn't always here. That old town, it got shifted inside by the weather. Back in the old Weaver Queen's time, so that's...fifty cycles? Fifty-five? Wasn't nothing that nobody could do about it. Some people say we still carry blood from them folk, but I don't know."

He chewed and stared into the middle distance.

"It's this way, isn't it? The way back out?"

"Ayuh, it's not far. Back into those trees, down that path." He pointed around the monolith where the path wove. "Probably best that you do that now, young lady. This is no place for you."

"Absolutely. We can't worry the sheep."

He looked through me and I bit my slippery tongue. Before I could attempt some kind of recovery, a crack of something like thunder ripped through the atmosphere, then softened into a long, piercing hunting horn note. We all snapped to attention, eyes fixed on the horizon, myself, the shepherd, Charles, and all four hundred and fifty sheep.

"What's that?"

His voice was level, flat. It worried me more than the sheep. "Warning horn."

Another crack, another note followed. "No, hold on. Two is for retreating to the Throne, unless there's a third."

On the third crack, Charles swiftly dropped his thick, white hide right where he stood, taking his shadow form, and flung himself into the air toward the horizon. The shepherd returned to his tending.

"What's three horns?"

I suspected the answer, but my heart raced anyway when he gave it. "Three's for gathering at the border. They've all been summoned. Probably nothing good will come of it. Nothing good ever does."

"At the border?" To shut it, or....

"Terrible. My poor flock."

Above us, the sky filled with Pricolici shadows, all zipping toward where I imagined the entrance to Whisperwood would be. The forest rustled and crashed, probably brimming with whatever creatures couldn't fly. A sense of urgent dread filled me. There'd been promises that nobody would be killed, but there was so much else that could go wrong; and Rareş, in his haste, had promised "anything!" If there was one thing to be sure of with Whispers, it was that reading the fine print of any deals you made was as vital as breathing.

Whatever was going on, I had to get to town. Even if I was only a useless doorstop, I had to be there to help. To offer comfort, at least. Tend injuries, if there were any.

Desperate, I turned to the shepherd. "Can you help me? I don't know how to cross back to the other side."

"Well, that's reckless. Sending a girl across who can't even Walk alone." He rocked on the balls of his feet as he spoke. "You need two things. To be in the right place, where the border is, and to be in the right state of mind. Keep to the road, and you'll get to the place. As for the state of mind? Close your eyes and walk. The world will do, you only need to accept. Don't open your eyes, not for anything, until your hands can feel that it falls into place."

"I don't unders—"

"Yeah, you don't. Close your eyes now. I'll give you a taste of what it ought to feel like."

The last thing, the very damned last thing I wanted to do was close my eyes. The rush of creatures through the woods had ended as swiftly as it began, but there was no telling what still lurked, least of all the shepherd himself. It didn't seem like there was much else to be done, though.

I closed them and trembled.

"Now, wiggle your fingers a little. Can you feel the air? That's how you know where you are, even with your eyes closed. Do you feel that pull? Like shrugging off a heavy coat or washing off the dirt of the day, they say. The more steps you take, the harder it gets to bear, so good luck not opening your eyes. If you open your eyes, you'll be right back where you started. If you keep 'em closed, it'll feel wrong, like the world is upside down. But that's how you know you're not in the same place anymore. You Walk like that through the border, feel it with your fingers. And it all falls away."

There was an uncomfortable pull that startled me, like a tug from the core of my body into the ground. Then, the faint feeling of something rapidly whooshing past me and away, almost like it was a dream. I opened my eyes and was hardly surprised to see the same plain covered in small yellow flowers, the same sky streaked in light pink and blue, and only the giant stone face looking down at me. The shepherd, and his entire flock, had gone.

CHAPTER THIRTY-FIVE

Walk

I opened my eyes and cursed.

Finding the physical border had been easy, even without my canine friend. The path took me around the hill and shot out from between a thicket right onto the main road we'd used coming in. In daylight, it seemed downright cheerful. I was hopeful. I was confident. I was a fool.

It sounded like it should have been easy, walking forward with my eyes closed.

A frustrated laugh escaped me. It was almost impossible. The first time, my feet stopped by themselves after five steps. I shook myself, sure I was being silly and could do better. The second time, I forced myself to take eight before my eyes shot open. Certainly it could be done. I'd seen Paul go through it. I didn't know it at the time, but he must have Walked that whole stretch with his eyes closed, just like I was supposed to. I just didn't trust the world around me enough.

Maybe I was the only Walker in the world who couldn't properly Walk.

Huffing, I closed my eyes and tried again. For the first second, the undeniability of what was around me stuck to the inside of my eyelids. A tall pine on the left, a rock, six stumps in a row, a fallen branch. As soon as I started walking, it blurred into a haze and seemed to lift away from me, leaving only darkness behind. The change startled me, and I opened my eyes. Seven.

I closed my eyes and tried again. A tall pine on the left, a rock, six stumps in a row, a fallen branch. Reality shifted under my fingers. A tug in my gut pulled me forward. The terror of losing control over the world around me froze my feet. Ten. I opened my eyes and howled in frustration.

My fear was a ridiculous one, and I was ashamed of myself for it. My friends were in danger while I was flapping about, playing make-believe. Eyes open or closed, there was no control to be had over this world or any other. It had shown me that over and over again, and I simply refused to learn. The ground could open at any time under my feet whether I was looking at it or not. That was no excuse to stop moving forward.

I closed my eyes.

CHAPTER THIRTY-SIX

Wreathed in Fire and Rage

The town felt like a battle had already been fought and lost.

I passed, panting and sweaty, under a crushed arch, a pile of rubble and salt crystals reduced to powder. The low stone wall itself had been caved in in several sections, and above, a red Tide-like sky pushed crimson tentacles into a more normal, starry-black one on the distant horizon. Pricolici shadows, a writhing swirling mass of black, covered the moon almost entirely. It was obvious that the Whispers had broken down what little defense the town had against them, at last. The lack of blood and bodies was encouraging, at least.

Oh, how my standards for what I found encouraging had slipped.

I rushed into the streets, reckless and stupid, desperate to find any of my friends and lend them my hands. Surely Artjom or Ancuța would be there, defending the town?

Hasty furniture barricades made broken borders at the entrance of dead-end streets, doors were splintered open, and belongings strewn across the cobbles. A solitary child's shoe lay in the crossroads, ominously pointing toward the ever-present, ever-vigilant line of pines peeking from behind the buildings. Strands of garlic lay strewn across windows. Another tradition I hadn't even learned about yet, and might well be lost forever.

A howl resounded from somewhere in town, then several others rose to join it from different directions. My breath came hard and fast, steam forming in front of my face and falling quickly behind me in the still night air as I ran for the nearest wall. I clung to it and peeked into the mostly empty main road.

Belatedly I took my knife in my hand, though what I might do with it was beyond me. I fussed over how to hold it properly for a moment, switching between pointing it up and pointing it down, one-handed or two. None of it was going to make me a fighter. I was stalling.

The Warren's wide-opened door and books spilled out into the street suggested that would be a pointless visit. Still, no blood, and the street was clear, so I slunk over to the yellow door and peered inside. Nobody moving, just a great big mess. Someone, or something, had made it in, and someone had been dragged out, judging by the trail of scratches and upturned furniture leading down the stairs. The poppy powder across the door was pulled out into the street and scattered.

The brewery, then. Mara and Florin. They had to be there. Someone had to be somewhere.

I ran, slinking around corners and sticking to the shadows, but only found the aftermath of trouble. Torn shirts, smashed doors, abandoned packs. A rush of white passed overhead, and I recognized it as the Dochia. My blood froze, but she had no time for me, headed straight for the border, riding the wind on a flapping, fluttering coat, and carrying a small burden. One of the children.

The brewery square was right around the corner, and I slowed to take it carefully. In the absence of my clumsy clomping, great padding canine footfalls thudded behind me. Only one, I thought, but one would be one too many if they wanted to stop me, hurt me, or drag me back into the Unspoken. I pushed my legs to the point of burning and, even so, had I been a few steps farther from the little square in front of the brewery, I never would have made it.

Just as I rounded the corner, a heavy brownish bottle flew right past my left ear, so near that it disturbed the hairs on the side of my head. I didn't turn to check, but the sound of glass breaking came from behind me, then a huge roar and blast of heat hit my back. I glanced over my shoulder in time to see the Pricolici one step behind me erupt into a ball of flame and bound away whining and baying, fire tails trailing behind him. A moment of sympathy struck me, but he seemed more upset than injured.

268 • ALEX WOODROE

After a few paces, he ditched his coat and leaped into the air in shadow form, and only very little of the miracle liquid fire stuck to that. It wasn't alone, though. Another loped not far behind, and it lunged through the patch of liquid flames on the ground to reach me.

"Anna, duck!"

A familiar voice gave the order, and I ducked. Another brownish bottle struck the Pricolici on the snout and cracked into his face. The fire coated his entire head in a moment, and he shook himself like a wet dog, dribbling molten drops on my arms and dress.

Arms grabbed me from behind and dragged me across the cobbles.

Florin passed by me, wreathed in rage. For a moment I forgot that he was injured and saw the same old foolhardy Flor from before. It was obvious that he was leaning heavily to one side, though, and supporting himself on a long wooden crutch strapped around his torso and hiked under his arm. In the other, he wielded his silver-engraved sword, slicing at the beast wildly.

Harried, it turned and fled after its brother, wailing and dripping fire. My own skin burned, but Mara was there almost immediately with a wet cloth to soothe the ache.

"Where have you been? We've been worried sick. And what the devil are you doing here now, of all times? I thought you'd left for some sunny seaside town."

Tears choked me. "It was so hard to get back. I came to help."

"The Whispers made it here before you did. They're taking people. I don't know what for." She saw the dejected look on my face and hugged me. "It's not your fault, you can't race against the wind."

"I saw them. Spoke to them. I thought they were shutting the border, but then this happened. Have you seen—" I found myself at a loss as to how to explain either Perdy or Rareş.

Florin caught the dangling question. "It's been just us versus a horde of hounds for hours now. None killed on either side, strangely, but many dragged away."

"How do you feel?"

He smiled a thin smile and looked a hundred years old. "I feel terrible, but I'm still alive. Mara even said that the infection might be pulling back. I'm tired, but they've all been helping."

"They?"

"There's a full house in there."

He nodded to the stout brewery. The windows were mostly shuttered, but pale faces still peered from behind drawn curtains on the upper floors here and there. The door opened suddenly, and Miss Crosman fluttered out.

"Burn cream here, and more firebrew. I've the girls filling them as fast as they can, but we're almost out. Well, spitblood. Look who it is." She hiked an eyebrow at me. "Trouble."

Mara took the crate of bottles from her arms. "It's slowing down. We might make it."

"Don't you celebrate before it's done, girl!"

Miss Crosman shoved burn cream into my hands and immediately spat in her bosom. The familiar gesture made me smile.

I struggled to open the lid, but admired Mara's bottles more. "What is that stuff? It burned like nothing I've seen."

"I've been playing with it for a long time in the distillery. Quicklime, salt, a few other things. Ancuţa's been teaching me. It doesn't really do a lot of damage, just scares 'em off, but it's a start, isn't it?"

She sounded so hopeful my heart rose to meet her. "It's a wonderful start. Is Ancuţa here?"

Mara shook her head. "At the chapel, Warding the heck out of that bell. Most of the kids are being kept safe there."

Miss Crosman had pulled clean bandages out of her apron pocket and neatly pushed Florin back until he sat on the edge of the fountain with an, "Oof." Mara shook her head and took the little vial of burn cream from my hands, opening it easily and applying it with her fingers on my forearms. It was cold and smelled of fresh pine. From his uncomfortable perch, Florin scowled over at me.

"How did you fare?"

The dreaded question I wanted to avoid, and shout about, at the same time. "It's complicated."

"Did you find her?"

Mara perked up and tilted her head at me.

"Well, did you?"

I hated being cryptic, and inside me a raging hellfire burned to tell him off for ever sending me to harm Perdy in the first place, but now wasn't the time. "I found her. She's well. She hopes she can come back, but there's no guarantee."

Florin gave me a strange look of grief and relief, but the pain of his injury being cleaned wiped it quickly away. The maestress probably did that on purpose, tutting us for being gossips. "There's no time for any of that now. More of these things could come at any time."

Mara drew close and near-whispered, "Has Eugen come back with you? I need to apologize. When he left, I wasn't myself. I have to make sure he didn't take it too personally."

I was so tired of delivering bad news to people, for a moment, I almost considered not saying anything. It wouldn't have been right. "Mara, Eugen is gone. I'm sorry."

She swallowed hard and her face tensed up instantly. Her next inhale came in waves.

I couldn't offer her much comfort. "He loved you. He wanted you to know. You were the last thing on his mind."

She didn't seem to hear me. Her hands kept working, but her gaze was vacant. She breathed heavily and mumbled. All I caught was, "Have had enough." As soon as she was done with me, she rushed back inside the brewery. I felt a sudden wave of relief. She was going inside, where there were people and friends and arms to catch her. I hadn't realized how terrified I'd been that after this final straw, she'd choose a Silent Walk instead. The world in which that happened briefly touched on ours, and I shuddered.

Florin stood, but his chances of catching up to her were next to none. The maestress shoved him back down so hard he nearly toppled into the fountain.

"Let the poor girl be. She's at the end of her rope. I'll send Greta down to help you with the bottles in case any more of these critters arrive, but it looks like we might be through it on this side."

"I don't like leaving her alone," he protested.

"I don't like a great number of things, starting with the first stake of the first building your great-grandparents ever laid here. But here we are."

"What can I do to help?" I didn't know what use I could be.

Miss Crosman didn't question my offer for a moment. "Most of the creatures are gone from here. The chapel was the other place we set as a gathering point. There are strong Wards there, defending the children." Her face showed far more concern than her words suggested. She paused and spat into her bosom. "The mayor is there too." That didn't sound like she counted it as a positive. "Go take some firebrew and burn salve, in case they're still fighting. Don't get eaten."

She thrust the box in my hands and rushed back into the building. On the doorstep, she turned to me with shaded eyes.

"I don't know if, at this point, you owe more to us or we to you. Only the dead know."

Florin rose and wobbled toward me, his eyes intent on opening me up and revealing my secrets. "I don't know either, but maybe now isn't the time to find out. I'm coming with you. You need the protection, and I –" he paused, looking toward the forest, "– I have questions to ask. And maybe amends to make if they can still be made."

We hurried as best we could toward the chapel, he loping, almost wolflike, and I dragging my feet, tired of body and soul.

★   ★   ★

While we walked, I told Florin what had happened with an almost sadistic joy at detailing every look, move, and word of Perdy's. Tired of secrets and half truths, I scanned his face with every revelation. Grim determination when he learned she truly had been a Whisper spy, warm longing when I revealed that she was still entirely herself, and hope when she bargained for her freedom.

Finally, a veil of forlorn exhaustion settled over everything. "I sent you to kill her."

His matter-of-fact tone didn't leave me room to guess whether that was an accusation, or an apology. I stayed silent and gave him time to decide.

"We never learned much about them, you know? Hard to get to, mostly lethal. All I ever knew since I was a kid is that if she's a Whisper, she has to die. It didn't matter what the person was like, how kind or sweet or graceful. It was as if she had an illness that had no cure and would eventually use our trust to spread that illness. Involuntarily. Unconsciously, maybe. Maybe she wasn't even evil. But she had to die."

We had to stop for a moment to let him catch his breath. Walking on one leg and a crutch took its toll. In the distance, the chapel bell rang slowly but steadily, a sign of hope that gave us leave to take some time.

"I don't think I even really believed all of it. But when I lost my leg, I was so angry." His jaw clenched. "I still am. I'm so angry that my whole life is changed, forever. I'm so angry that now, I have to deal with this on top of everything. The thought that she might have something to do with it makes me want to throw up."

"But she didn't."

"But maybe she could have prevented it. It's never simple, is it?"

That didn't take much thinking to answer. "Nothing ever is."

"Maybe the right choice would have been to just learn more about her. Maybe running her out of town would have been enough. If I'd taken any of those choices, would they have blamed my fondness for her for whatever catastrophe came next? I would."

"Guilt isn't where good decisions grow."

"Yet that's all I've got. A whole lot of guilt on behalf of this entire flogging town that we didn't learn more when there was still time. That all we did was swing swords like children, and I the child chief."

We walked in silence for a minute. The mood was sour, and I wanted to lift it somehow. "All of this aside, tell me one thing. When you heard she was alive and well, what did you feel? Beneath your head chatter, and all the guilt and worry."

A brief smile flicked across his face. "Relief so great it winded me and set my hands shaking."

It was reassuring to know that, at his core, there was a good and caring heart. I could only hope over time, he'd learn to speak and act from that place, rather than the fear and guilt that hounded him.

CHAPTER THIRTY-SEVEN

Getting a Point Across

The chapel still stood, but that was the only good news.

A massive pack of Pricolici had gathered there, final stragglers streaming in from across town. Cheers and whoops came from deep within various streets, survivors glad to still be standing, oblivious to the fact that the final battle had yet to be fought. Several Iele led the assembly, and I immediately checked for Perdy among them. I was sad and relieved she wasn't there. Picturing her leading a kidnapping was nigh unthinkable, and I had to believe, whatever her role in this was, if any, she was coerced.

The Iele riled up the hounds and hurled insults at the chapel. The frantic pacing of paw and foot in front of the building had worn field and path and grass alike, almost digging a trench. The Pricolici barked and brayed and flung themselves at the doors, but every time they tried the bell rang again and they were shot back with violent force. It seemed a pointless dance, but they snarled and paced and refused to surrender. They looked obsessively to the horizon, marking the victory of clean black starry sky over the ever-withdrawing red tendrils.

There was no way we could reach the front doors, but I suspected the little hidden back door Father Roman had slipped out of on his last day on earth would still be clear. Only problem was, sneaking around wasn't something Florin could do, not around the hill, through grasses and shrubs. He argued with me for a while, but eventually saw the sense in waiting nearby. We'd agreed that I'd run to him for help if anything chased me.

There was enough reddish-gray light by which to navigate, but even so, it was too dark to see every rock or dip that twisted my ankles. I had my knife out at first, but then the risk of stabbing myself in the eye grew such that I put it through my belt for safekeeping.

Before long, I found myself looking at a stripe of light coming from the back door of the chapel. It was open. Briefly, it flashed open wide, something shaded passed through it, then just as quickly it shut back to a sliver.

A familiar shape stood halfway down the hill, short and plump and agitated. He gestured and directed a steady stream of children walking out of the chapel, down the slope and off into the distance. I only realized it was Mr. Scridon, the mayor's helper, when his nervous, wiry voice reached me. He spoke softly, and I had to be nearly atop him before hearing it at all.

"One by one, in a row. That's the ticket, there you go. Don't be frightened, you'll be fine. We can make it out in time."

He giggled and made wide gestures with his arms that I'm certain nobody needed.

"Mr. Scridon, what are you doing?"

He jumped a little, as though he hadn't noticed my approach at all.

"Oh my, I'm not sure. I'm not sure at all. I have to get them out."

"Why?"

"It's Mr. Mayor."

He stopped, clearly expecting me to be satisfied with that answer, and went on directing the last of the children.

"What about him?"

"He-he's —" he stuttered, "— at an impasse. With the Warren girl. Oh dear. I won't speak ill of him."

"Ancuţa? Has something happened to her?"

"Won't. But maybe you can help."

"Are the children going to be safe?"

"If we go now, maybe. They're distracted. A roundabout way back to town. If only I knew where to go. I needed to get them out before.... Oh, Poor Mr. Mayor."

"Where is he?"

He looked balefully up at the steeple, then back to me. I wished to help them so badly, but I feared the worst inside the chapel, so I gave him instructions to make for the brewery and told him where he might come across Florin on his path. He nodded, then put his hands on the shoulders of the last child in line and walked off, choo-chooing like a train car under his breath. The exhausted child wanted none of it.

★   ★   ★

I walked into the candlelit chapel hall and dropped the supplies I'd brought on the nearest pew. Stark, beautiful paintings on the glass looked down at me. I finally understood so much more of them. The green fields covered in black sheep, the dark wood lit up by blue fires, the violet sunset over a dark ruin – things Father Roman knew of because the Whispers spoke to him. Imperfect, yes, as though painted from descriptions rather than experience, but evocative in the way only a truly great listener could manage. Things I had seen for myself, and now regretted never having had the opportunity to show the reverend.

Oddly, the sound of the bell wasn't nearly as harsh on the inside as it was outside. A trick of acoustics, perhaps, but one that I greatly appreciated.

"Mayor Eduard?"

I craned my neck to see up the spiral staircase that led to the belfry, and mad eyes peered down at me. Bloodshot and shifty, they seemed to be tuned into a world of their own.

"Young lady, I'm warning you, come no closer!"

The mayor stood halfway up the stairs, half suspended over the railing, a red-faced and rabid Ancuţa holding him at bay with the end of a rusty but sharp crucifix as long as her wingspan, the pointy end probably designed for sinking into dirt. She saw me and yelped, but before I could ask her anything she rushed up the stairs, the mayor right after her.

Younger and sprier, she leaped onto the bell rope before he'd made it halfway to her, rang the bell once one-handed, then jumped back down, waving the cross and hollering bloody murder.

I didn't know where to begin. "What the devil is going on?"

"Anna! Help me, I can't keep doing this much longer."

The mayor reached for her, clearly upset. "Then stop and let them take you like the baleful witch you are."

I twitched at that word but chose to put my issues aside and not escalate the situation.

Ancuţa had no such qualms. "Begone, you useless ram's nipple of a man!"

The staircase rang under my feet and I nearly tripped on my way up. One turn below the mayor, I stopped and caught my breath, unsure of how to help. Ancuţa held him at bay well enough, but he didn't seem like he wanted to relent.

"Mayor Eduard? Why don't you tell me what the matter is?"

"The matter?" His grin was maniacal, his hair on ends. "We had a deal, that's what the matter is. It was all going to be fine. We'd resolved everything with diplomacy like civilized people. We spoke to their king. And then this witch!"

That word rankled again, and I could stomach him less and less by the moment.

"Their king lied!" Ancuţa said. Her cheeks shone like red apples.

"He did no such thing!" The mayor poked the air in her direction. "We'd made a deal. They can't go back on a deal."

As long as they were talking, maybe there was still a chance I could pacify them. "What was the deal, Lord Eduard?"

"They were only going to take what they needed. The Praedictors, the Wardens, and a handful of children. And that would be that, over, forever! Borders shut. Nobody else lost ever again. A peaceful, civilized town. Everything under control. And she ruined it."

As if on cue, Ancuţa gave another tug of the rope. The mayor tried to make a lunge for her, but I grabbed his pant leg on instinct.

As soon as she had him in check again, she shouted down to me. "*He* lied, Anna. Not Rareş; the mayor. I saw them through the Walker window, making a deal. But then he turned back to the town and lied!

He'd told the town everyone was safe. He was going to let them be taken in their sleep. I had to tell them!"

Of course, she had to. I probably would have done the same, even knowing the chaos it'd cause. There was nothing right about tricking helpless people who put their lives in your hands.

Mayor Eduard didn't seem to think the same. "So instead, you rang the warning bell and let chaos decide who stays and goes? It could have been a peaceful transition! You just wanted to save your own skin!"

"I did not! You oafish toad, I don't care about my skin!"

"Then stop ringing!"

"Not until the children are well away from you monsters!"

With a scream, the mayor grabbed the end of Ancuța's holy spear, tugging her down the ladder. She let go of the end and reached for the bell rope again with just enough time to ring it while he fumbled with the unwieldy object. I climbed as close as I could behind him and grabbed him by the elbows, determined to restrain him somehow, but the chances of bringing us both hurtling down the stairs were too great. He slipped from my grasp.

"Please, stop!" My voice broke. I wasn't sure what we'd do even if the mayor backed off; but I was sure we needed more time to figure it out.

Before I knew it, he was on the top landing by Ancuța, and with one wild shove sent her careening over the edge. She grabbed on to the railing with both arms and a leg, holding on for dear life, but the bell had now been silent for too long. Something clawed at the door, dug at the threshold.

He only stood there, arms on his hips, looking somber. "I could push you off, you know. But I won't. Now, they'll take you and the others and be off, as agreed. It's not too late to honor the deal and get rid of more than one problem all at once. Hear that growling? That's the end of problems."

I panicked and reached for him again, positioning myself on the side of the landing, backed against the wall so he couldn't push me off. I didn't want to hurt anyone, but the last notes of the bell had all but faded and Ancuța's grip was slipping. The door cracked and, looking over my shoulder, I saw a black skull poke through the splintered opening and eye us.

The mayor flung himself at me, incoherent and screaming. Before I knew what I was doing, warm liquid poured over my hand.

I opened my eyes. There was a crash behind me, and the door collapsed completely, throwing bright reddish light into the room.

The mayor was transfixed, staring off into the distance behind me. My knife, embedded in his side, pointed up to the sky. When push came to shove, my hand didn't need time to decide which way to hold it – it was simply there.

Before I could stop him, he slipped out of my grasp and onto the ground, the weapon still in my hand. It shone like a ruby and looked nothing like my knife at all.

I stumbled the two steps to where Ancuța hung, stretched over her, and grabbed the back of her belt, heaving up. The moment she'd set foot safely on the landing, I reached for the bell rope, only to find it gone.

A slimy black shadow held it high above us, coils upon coils far beyond our reach. There was nothing I could do, no way I could reach it. I thought of the firebrew – but I'd left it below, out of the way. The mayor gurgled on his side, and I hurried to him instead. My apron was already gone trying to save Eugen, so I ripped a huge chunk of my underskirt and hoped it'd fare better. The knife wound was in the lateral lower quarter of the abdomen, and he stood a good chance of surviving it. Maybe my hands had known that too.

I shoved the balled-up fabric over the injury ungracefully, then tied my belt around him and the makeshift dressing.

Beneath us, a silent congregation of hounds looked up in glimmering, satin-black menace. And behind them, in russet relief, the shattered door framed a majestic white stag with sharp golden horns adorned in ivy and flowers, gazing up at me.

★   ★   ★

Rareş, the Smith King, the Stag King, the King of Whispers, waited outside the door. His hounds withdrew, a few waiting by his side in the yard but most of them taking to the sky.

"Anna." His voice boomed through the building. "Fine."

I didn't understand what he'd just decided, but obviously he'd just decided something.

"Fine. This is better. Come, both of you. Come out. I need your help."

My shoulders ached, and my hands shook, and my eyes were heavy. All of me wanted to be anywhere else, any time else than in the moment, sitting on the floor next to a bleeding man I'd stabbed. I imagined a sunny day, chatting in the chapel with Father Roman; we looked at colored glass and spoke about the beauty and majesty of nature.

Before a second's time, Ancuţa grabbed my elbow. "Are you all right?"

I nodded.

"Thank you."

My head felt heavy and confused. "What for?"

"Believing me."

Every bone in my body ached. Getting up, setting myself in motion again, bruised and burned and battered as I was, was a nightmare. Without Ancuţa, I might never have made it. I shuffled like a dead thing out the door with barely enough energy to pick up my own feet.

Rareş didn't wait for us. As soon as we were out the door, he turned and made for town at a brisk pace, Pricolici hounds at his side. It didn't seem like we had a whole lot of options, so we followed. After a minute, Florin popped out from between the willow trees and fell into step with us, somber and guarded.

He leaned in and whispered, "Kids made it to Crosman. What do we do?"

I shrugged.

"Do we attack him?"

I shrugged again, then changed my mind. "I guess now is one of those times when learning more before acting is probably the right call."

He grunted and nodded but didn't take his eyes off the back of the Stag King's head for a moment. I was surprised the white fur on his graceful neck didn't burst into flame. I asked Florin to send someone to the chapel to tend to the mayor the moment he could and left him behind. Hoping the Pricolici wouldn't rip me to shreds, I jogged to Rareş. They didn't, and instead Charles broke off from among them and came by our side. I felt like I was able to tell him apart now.

We walked for a few paces, but I couldn't hold my tongue. "Kidnapping? Really?"

Rareş sighed. "You know very well I had no choice. I'd promised her anything. This was the price for ending things without bloodshed. It was either this, or a broken deal and murder."

"Children?"

"I negotiated down from every child and every craftsman to just the Unspoken Crafts, and ten children. That was it, she wouldn't take a hair less. Even that cost me some promises I didn't want to make."

"Like what?"

He harrumphed. "None of your business."

I rolled my eyes. Behind us, Ancuţa and Florin studied the wolfish creatures all around us warily.

"I'm doing my best." Rareş shook his horns. "But the deal was made, and then the town reneged."

"They didn't even know about the deal. Ancuţa warned them."

"She's one we were meant to take, so excuse me if I find it a mite convenient."

"She'd never—"

"It doesn't matter. It's all gone tits up either way. Through all of this mess we've managed to get one Praedictor—"

"Artjom?"

"Not even. The old one who can barely move. We also got two of four Wardens, and one child. The queen is a heartbeat away from drowning this entire town under a lake, and I need your help to stop her."

"How?"

"You'll see."

The moment we reached the main road, it was clear a stalemate was in place. Beyond a hasty barricade of all the tables and chairs in the guesthouse, as well as several bed frames and assorted herb talismans, people milled, treating injuries and bringing comfort to each other. Several stood at the ready, bottles of firebrew and silver-pointed weapons in hand. I suspected more than one of the improvised spears were only dipped in paint, perhaps in an attempt to look more menacing.

On the near side were the last of the Whispers, stalwart but involuntarily flicking their eyes to the tree line where only thin squiggles of red remained. Perdy was with them at the back, just as dejected as Florin now seemed. Clearly terrified and subdued, she stared at the ground and spoke to nobody, but when she looked up to us, I could see the love and despair on her beautiful face. She started to lunge to me, but something she must have seen on Florin's face behind me made her freeze in her tracks.

Rareş, now in his finest unthreatening elk form, sauntered up to the barrier, sleek and soft and wonderful. Seeing him like that, it almost made sense to call him 'Majesty' and swear fealty. Anyone who hadn't seen him eat might have thought of him as a benevolent god of the woods.

I couldn't.

He turned back to me and harrumphed, making sure all eyes on both sides were on him, then loudly proclaimed, "I need you to mediate."

CHAPTER THIRTY-EIGHT

Egress

Rareş nodded, satisfied.

I was not. "Mediate?"

"We don't have a lot of time. I need you to mediate."

"I'm surprised you think I'd do anything for you after you stormed into town and kidnapped a bunch of people, but all right, let's hear it."

He shook his head and hoofed at the ground in what I guessed was irritation. Clearly, human–Whisper relations would mean learning a whole new set of physical cues. "The Unspoken is not self-sufficient. It never has been and never will be. It needs people in so many more ways than I can explain."

"To kill and turn into Whispers?"

"That's only the least, and most unfortunate, need among them."

I huffed.

"The woods are filled with people. The cities beyond. The world. There are so many crafts Whispers can't learn, like working iron or wood. So many skills. So much exploration. Worlds beyond worlds. And yes, sometimes, people turn into Whispers. By choice."

I raised my eyebrows.

"No, it hasn't always been by choice. But it will be from now on. My decisions, and all the things I've gone through. They're in the king's cycle now. Forever."

I didn't pretend to understand, but as long as we were talking about sparing lives, I was willing to listen. "What now? The town's decided they won't give you any more people."

"And I still need to get them to the other side, or risk losing many lives."

"Can't you refuse her requests?"

His laugh was half bark. "After all this, don't you believe that if I could, I would?"

I did. "I think we're all tired and ready for this to end. What can we do?"

He hoofed the ground again, then gazed toward the rubble of the Wailing Arch in the distance. Outlined against the dark woods behind her, a sleek and almost transparent woman shone, a crown of lake weeds on her delicate head. Her legs were so dainty they seemed to vanish into nothing at times, and her shift was the shiniest, purest white. Her Majesty oversaw everything from a safe distance, surrounded by her Iele.

"The process to shut the border is already begun. The Crones are singing the unsongs as we speak, and it won't be long. Once it's done, it's done for a very long time. It'll take a cycle before another border can be opened, and it might not even be in this place. Even with all my good intentions, the Unspoken needs people in the meantime, and she's adamant. Before the closing's done, there will either be compromise or bloodshed."

"What do you expect me to do?"

"Talk to them and help them see sense. We only want nine more young ones, and the specialists. The border closes when the sun's fully risen. So, let's not dawdle."

Ancuţa, Florin, and I walked past the barricade. The guards eyed us suspiciously, but made no protest, and I recognized and greeted Lucian, the tanner, among them.

Miss Crosman and her girls scampered about distributing cups of something hot to everyone present, and when Greta, the maid, offered me one, I took it with glee. The warmth from it seeped through my palms and into my bones, and I only held it for a while with my eyes closed, enjoying that feeling and the sweet smell of fragrant herbs. When I finally tried it, the fresh sour taste of lemongrass and leeks hit my tongue first, followed by spicy mint. A restorative herb soup, no doubt, and one

I was most grateful for. I scarfed the first two cupfuls down and only on the third properly opened my eyes to see everyone staring right at me.

Miss Crosman wasted no time. "Won't."

"They—"

"I know what they want. Won't, and we're ready to fight them. And they better give back the ones they've already taken."

I rubbed my eyes and temples, tired of being constantly spoken over, wondering what else I could have expected. Behind her, people stirred. It seemed like most of the town was there, bravely facing whatever came, tired of cowering behind closed doors. Artjom waved to me from a far row, and I was glad to see him, but angry at what a hand his guild had played in bringing this all to pass. There was never anything simple in caring for people.

"All I can do is tell you what I know. They mean no harm but need people to fill their ranks. They want ten children, and the specialists—"

"I know what they want, and I know that fool of a mayor promised it to them. Your little friend told me all about it before you got here."

Perdy had spoken to her? And survived? That certainly explained the forlorn look.

The maestress put her hands on her hips. "Just because the mayor was wrong doesn't make what they're doing now right."

Many of the people behind her nodded, but not all. Weary eyes rose from the dirt to the tune of "But what about the orphans?" and "I'll go if they've got better beds than we do." Some even chuckled. There was never any chaos great enough that human beings could not become accustomed to it.

The maestress rounded on them. "Hush, you all. Nobody's going anywhere! We'll have no more. We're angry and have been hounded and harried and will have no more."

Behind her, Florin was flush against the barrier, looking over it to where Perdy stood. She waved a tentative little finger-wave at him. The whole universe and I stood in rapt anticipation for the breaths it took for him to make up his mind, then sighed in relief when he waved back. At least those two still had some hope.

"Miss Crosman, would you say it's wrong to force people into doing what they don't want to do?" I cocked my head and feigned innocence.

She crossed her arms and scowled. "Was I unclear? I said so. We won't hand them over."

"The Whispers won't leave without a fight, and you'll only lose more lives. Guaranteed."

"We're not giving them anyone."

"What if we call for volunteers, instead?"

A murmur rushed through the crowd. The maestress raised her hands, asking for silence, and considered me for a moment.

"What if there aren't any? And they certainly won't be children!"

"I don't know whether there will be or not, nor who. I don't even know if the Whispers would agree. But if they did, would you?"

She pressed her lips together and shook her head. "Seeing as you only just got my agreement that keeping people against their will is wrong, I haven't a choice, have I? Rather than think you're clever and can entrap me, try being straightforward next time. I'm not a fool and want loss of life no more than you do."

I smiled but reddened down to my toes. I had thought I was clever and should have known better. Wasting no time, for there was none to spare, I rushed through the barricade to where Rareş waited, grim. "Well?"

"A compromise. You said you needed numbers."

"I did."

"And you said you'd treat them well."

"I will."

"What if I convinced them to allow for volunteers?"

"How many?"

"I don't know. That's part of the deal. Everyone here gets to make a free choice. Everyone has to respect that choice. Could be half the town."

From the shadow of the woods, the queen let out a sharp whistle. Rareş sent her a look that was a few drops of murder in a spoonful of sugar. "There's no time." He thought for a second, then nodded. "I'll make it work, somehow. I'll convince Her Majesty. You make it work on the other side."

"We have a deal, then? Freedom of choice for everyone? Including the ones already taken?"

"If I say we do, and it ends up going to hell because one side or the other loses their grip, we're both responsible. Hand in...." He looked down at himself and chuckled. "Equally."

He was right. "We are. But I couldn't live with not trying. So do we have a deal?"

"We do."

★ ★ ★

I spoke to them as best I could.

It took a lot of strength to step up on a crate and tell them the truth. I told them what it was like, what little I'd seen of it. I told them what Rareş said about there being worlds beyond worlds to explore, but that we couldn't know anything for sure, not even if they would be safe. Finally, I told them what I believed, in my heart, to be true. That Rareş was trying his best and was being honest about his intentions. It proved my point further when the ones he'd already taken were flown back safely and dropped right on our doorstep, Master Marc among them.

As soon as I'd finished, arguments broke. Young sons wanted to leave; mothers wanted to keep them. Husbands wanted to sacrifice themselves. Sisters wanted to be free and explore. For a while, it seemed like chaos. Then, over the course of half an hour, it settled.

Some went to protect their families. They knew having enough volunteers would keep the Whispers from complaining that not enough of them were children. They were reluctant but determined. Fierce. I admired them more than the ones who sought adventure, because they were afraid, but did it anyway.

All in all, two dozen people got ready and passed through the barricade as the others waved and spat in their bosoms, terrified looks on their faces. It was a blow, but not a surprise to see Ancuţa among the migrants.

She hugged me one-armed, holding a massive backpack full of books with the other. "I'll miss you, stubborn lady."

"Are you sure this is what you want?"

"Are you kidding? The chance to study my life's work from within?" She whistled. "Besides, the moment that border shuts, the entire Warren library becomes a collection of fiction. My job becomes obsolete. This makes sense for me."

"Then, I hope you take the Unspoken by storm."

"By the way, you were right about your skeleton. Whisper, for certain. I never got the chance to find out what kind, but maybe there's more information on the other side. They're resting, buried on their side of the arch, now."

"Thank you." The personal connection I felt with the mysterious O was inexplicable, but there, and I was truly grateful to know their remains were at peace.

Not knowing what else to say, I held her close for a long moment.

Artjom was waiting when we finally let go of each other. I was less saddened, but even more surprised to see he'd packed.

"You too?"

He smiled and shrugged. "I have so much blame in what happened. I knew all along that keeping a Pricolici wasn't right, otherwise we wouldn't have had to hide it. But I didn't want to let Cheşa down, and I wanted to learn more about the creature, and I let love and knowledge cloud my kindness. So here I am. Doing the right thing, this time."

"You'll find Cheşa there."

He drew a sharp breath. "I hadn't dared hope he was still alive, and the relief might knock me flat." He paused for a moment, obviously considering his next words. "I'm sorry for everything that happened out here, and for whatever happened in there. I don't think I have a right to say whether any of us are bad people, but at the very least, he's not worse than the rest of us. I promise."

"I've seen him be incredibly cruel, and incredibly kind. I don't know, either, but I know you all come from a time and place I can't even begin to understand, so maybe it's best I embrace not knowing. Try to keep him from doing any harm, though? To himself, as well."

"Maybe I can find a way to calm whatever pains him now that I'm no longer lying to myself about him being in pain."

There were some pains that couldn't be eased from the outside, and I knew firsthand that trying made things worse, but it wasn't my place to judge his path. All I had was hope.

We said our goodbyes, and he joined the others. Even Master Marc was among them, ready to head back into the fray from which we'd returned him. I hadn't guessed nearly how tough those people really were.

Ancuța led the way through the still-distrustful guards, and the other volunteers followed her. Some gathered to say goodbye and wish them well, but not all were as gracious. Many of the bystanders muttered about betrayal and lies and how it'd all be back to the same old tomorrow. Miss Crosman fluttered among them, distributing reminders about 'even more death' and 'battles that can't be won', reminders she herself for sure found distasteful.

"Traitors!" A muted growl rose from the crowd.

One of the men leaving town heard and shot it right back. "Maybe if you weren't a relentless arse to everyone around you, Plaeter, people wouldn't be in such a hurry to leave."

From behind the first row of onlookers, Plaeter let out an incoherent grunt and bent over, fumbling with something by the barricade. I assumed he felt the sting of the put-down and pretended to tie his shoe, and I turned my attention back to the volunteers saying their goodbyes, but a moment later Plaeter's voice rose again.

"This is how we deal with beastly scum!"

The woman nearest him screamed as he drew his arm back to launch a thick brown firebrew bottle over the crowd and into the mass of Whispers on the other side of the barricade. At Perdy. In a flash, I envisioned all of the work we'd done and sacrifices we'd made go up in flames. There was no way I'd have made it to him in time, but my body moved me anyway. I took two steps, and the bottle was already in the air.

A flash of silver from behind the reckless reprobate connected with the bottle midair. Florin, still stationed where he could keep an eye on Perdy, swung his sword like a bat, swatting the bottle down toward the ground and away from its course. It shattered against an oak bench right under his feet, a spray of liquid fire bursting everywhere. The crowd parted instantly, but not enough so to prevent several of them from catching alight, Flor included. The barricade itself was ablaze in moments.

I made it to him at the same time as Ancuța, and we swatted him out with our bare hands, burns be damned. Perdy was suddenly by my side, comforting him, whispering reassurance. Miss Crosman appeared with burn salve and started tending the injured while the others tried to put the heaping piles of furniture out. It was an obviously futile effort, and they drew back from the roaring blaze almost immediately.

A gallop from beyond drew my attention. At the mouth of the barricade, surrounded by fire but unflinching, Rareș huffed and fretted. "If this is some trick, it'll be the last—"

I stepped forward, almost tripping over Perdy, who had the same idea. We ended up in a tangle, holding on to each other. I spoke first. "An accident!"

He growled under his breath.

"The deal remains unchanged. Nobody was harmed."

He looked back over his shoulder, but the smoke clouded everything. Pacing, he spoke without looking at me. "For everyone's sake, we need to go now. No more waiting around for accidents."

I checked that everyone was being tended to, then asked Perdy to come with me and followed him out to the crossroads. The queen and her handmaidens were already gone, and most Pricolici soon followed. One neat row of tranquil hounds waited, and Charles, after nudging my hand with his head one more time, joined them. With a wave of his horn, Rareș gestured to the volunteers. "Mount and let's be off!"

Almost all balked, but Ancuța had her skirts hiked up and her leg across Charles's rump before Rareș even finished speaking. Seeing her comfortably perched and waving down at them, the others took heart.

I smiled at her, and at her ride, and wished her well in her new role as citizen of the Unspoken. I wished them all well.

Then, they were gone. Only Rareș and Perdy remained beside me.

I took a deep breath. "Well. This has been an unmitigated disaster."

Rareş chuckled, a smith among friends again. "Could have gone worse too. She was right ready to eat you all alive. Who'd have guessed. The upper class of the Whispers are just as self-centered and near-sighted as ours."

"And now you're among them."

He smiled, but it was tired and cold. "I'll shake things up yet. There's a use even for rusted iron. It's time we left now, though. No more than a quarter hour before it's all gone for good. Farewell."

I nodded. He sauntered off, stopping after a few steps to look back at Perdy and me. It almost made me burst into laughter, watching the dots slowly connect, written plainly across his face.

"You can't be serious. They just lobbed a firebomb at you."

Perdy shrugged. "Freedom of choice for everyone, you said. Deal's a deal. I'm staying right here."

We held hands as he disappeared into the trees, grumbling and flicking his tail.

CHAPTER THIRTY-NINE

Nomad

The remaining townsfolk were scattering before my eyes, eager to get about their business in the new dawn. To my surprise, Miss Crosman led the small group heading out into the world.

"What will you do?" I shook her hand.

"Salt the ground and move on from this awful place. Do the same if you're smart. There's got to be better lives women like us can have."

Fewer than twenty people joined her in her desire, but sometimes twenty people was all it took to start something great. Heck, sometimes all it took was two.

Salt the ground and move on. Maybe someday, I wouldn't have to.

Perdy got twisted looks from nearly everyone she passed, but everyone was far too busy making decisions about their future to worry her. She went straight to Flor and sat on the ground in front of his eyes, so that there was no way he could avoid looking at her. I didn't know what she said, but his frown deepened, then loosened. Later, I heard him crack a laugh, and it was as sweet as honey. By my side, Mara watched them as well.

She placed a gentle hand on my shoulder. "Anna, thank you."

"What for?" All I'd done was bring her horrible news. I wanted to be able to do so much more for her, but there was so little that could make up for what she'd been through.

"For saving me, in a way. I think in my head, I was ready to give up living. One of the things keeping me sane right now is the thought that you came here with nothing and nobody, and must have lost so much in the process. And yet you kept going, and found us, and meant so much to us after only a few days. Did so much. It makes me feel like maybe

I'll be able to still have meaning too. Still be there for Clara. Still do good things."

"You already mean everything to everyone who knows you."

She wiped at her already reddened eyes.

"What will you do?" I asked. "Stay, go?"

"I'm staying. For my sister and for the community." She drew a breath that was half a sob. "And for Eugen. He's here too."

I stood by her in silence as she settled, holding her hand.

After a few moments, she nodded to herself. "I'll be all right. The brewery still needs to run. We can have a little industry, set up a proper little town. I'll take over Miss Crosman's duties. Keep my hands and head busy."

I nodded back. Sometimes, moving forward involved a lot of actual moving. I had every faith she'd change the shape of the town before long. I hugged her and wished her well before heading back to Perdy's house to gather what little I'd left there.

Dawn broke. It was by far the maddest sky I'd seen in Whisperwood yet, light blue to the east rising into pinks and greens, still pitch-black and starry above, and tinged by a final, dwindling line of blood-red at the north toward the Unspoken. Just like that sky, inside I was made of chaos, a leaf in the wind again.

I gathered my belongings as best I could, greeted those few townsfolk who would bear me, and bought or traded a few useful things. I filled my pack with food and water, a waterproof skin and blankets, cooking tools. All needful things for someone on the road.

The main street was a tumbled mess, but somehow peaceful. I wanted to walk down the cobbles one more time. Empty and scarred, most of the buildings stood testament to how many had left, but many others were already being set to rights. The dark and empty guesthouse was the hardest to look at, heavy with the intensity of its former master.

"Anna!"

Perdy ran to me, Florin hobbling along behind her. They carried packs and supplies too, him carrying a far heavier load than she did. She looked almost human now, only a faint trace of horns still telling the story of her unusual biology. She'd made her choice, then. Quietly and without fuss, her whole identity decided by one desire she'd finally accepted. I beamed at her.

"We're leaving too."

"Together, then?" I hadn't expected her to want to stay in town, but half wished he'd convince her. Whatever their decision, I'd be pleased for it. There was too little joy in the world not to rejoice in the happiness of others.

Florin caught up with us. "Together. We both have a lot of explaining to do, and a lot to make up for."

"Flor, n—"

"But also a lot to be grateful for. If this infection clears—"

Perdy and I spoke in unison. "It will!"

He laughed, and it was so very nice to hear. "When it clears, we might be able to see the world a little. I'm a passable fighting instructor, if not a fighter any longer, and Perdy's a gifted healer. We can always find something to do. More importantly, maybe we can learn about what it's like out there."

"And each other."

I hoped against hope they would, gave them every blessing I knew how to give, and held Perdy until I couldn't hold her any longer.

"Are you sure you wouldn't walk with us awhile?" Her cheeks were damp. "Or even stay with us? I've so many things I want to tell you about. Everything. No more secrets."

"I'm sure. I still have to say my goodbyes, and you have even more important things to say than that. This isn't the last of you and me, Perdy. I promise. You'll get to tell me all those things."

"Then let's meet again soon at the house. I saw you've put it in order. It's your home too now. Anytime you want it."

I laughed. "I suppose we'll both have to remember we have roots now."

She squeezed me one more time before turning away and falling into a slow, measured step alongside Flor. I watched them for a while.

There was nobody left to greet, but there was one more thing I had to do. Weaving through the mess of burned-down rubble and abandoned belongings, I found my way to the fountain at the heart of Whisperwood. It seemed like it couldn't possibly only have been a handful of days ago that I arrived and tossed a copper coin into that very fountain for luck.

Had it worked, I wondered? Was what had happened luck?

I rifled through my satchel and gathered together the handful of gold coins that had been weighing on me ever since I ran away, my stolen safety net that I could never bring myself to use. The measure of imaginary control I thought I had over the world. One after the other, I dropped them into the fountain, savoring each heavy, wet *plonk*.

"Good riddance, Alec."

Plonk.

"Good riddance, guilt."

Plonk.

"Good riddance, gold."

Plonk.

"Go down like the day and drown evil away."

Plonk.

"Go down like the sun until evil is gone."

A flurry of *clinks* and *plonks* drowned out the final line of my improvised unsong. After the last of them faded, I yanked on the collar of my shirt and spat in my bosom for good measure.

"There."

I had no doubt Mara would put them to good use for the town's benefit, and I smirked picturing the look on her face when she found them. A million stones lighter, I floated down the main road one last time. With every moment that passed, the sky drained of all alien colors and returned to a resplendent deep blue that you could almost swim in. At the crossroads, I turned to all four directions and took it in. The air pulled almost unnoticeably toward the forest, and I fancied it a side effect of the Whispers withdrawing their influence from the world. It caused my fingers to lift and caress it like a warm current under the ocean.

"Well, I guess this is goodbye."

I said those words, then started one final Walk into the Unspoken.

FLAME TREE PRESS
FICTION WITHOUT FRONTIERS
Award-Winning Authors & Original Voices

Flame Tree Press is the trade fiction imprint of Flame Tree Publishing, focusing on excellent writing in horror and the supernatural, crime and mystery, science fiction and fantasy. Our aim is to explore beyond the boundaries of the everyday, with tales from both award-winning authors and original voices.

•

You may also enjoy:
Thirteen Days by Sunset Beach by Ramsey Campbell
Think Yourself Lucky by Ramsey Campbell
The Hungry Moon by Ramsey Campbell
The Influence by Ramsey Campbell
The Wise Friend by Ramsey Campbell
The Haunting of Henderson Close by Catherine Cavendish
The Garden of Bewitchment by Catherine Cavendish
The House by the Cemetery by John Everson
The Devil's Equinox by John Everson
Hellrider by JG Faherty
The Toy Thief by D.W. Gillespie
One By One by D.W. Gillespie
Black Wings by Megan Hart
The Playing Card Killer by Russell James
The Sorrows by Jonathan Janz
Will Haunt You by Brian Kirk
We Are Monsters by Brian Kirk
Hearthstone Cottage by Frazer Lee
Those Who Came Before by J.H. Moncrieff
Stoker's Wilde by Steven Hopstaken & Melissa Prusi
Creature by Hunter Shea
Ghost Mine by Hunter Shea
Slash by Hunter Shea
The Mouth of the Dark by Tim Waggoner
They Kill by Tim Waggoner
The Forever House by Tim Waggoner
Your Turn to Suffer by Tim Waggoner
We Will Rise by Tim Waggoner
Hunter Called Night by Tim Waggoner

•

Join our mailing list for free short stories, new release details, news about our authors and special promotions:

flametreepress.com